Cindi Myers is the author of mor[...]
When she's not plotting new roma[...]
skiing, gardening, cooking, crafting and daydreaming. A
lover of small-town life, she lives with her husband and
two spoiled dogs in the Colorado mountains.

USA Today bestselling author **Barb Han** lives in north
Texas with her very own hero-worthy husband, three
beautiful children, a spunky golden retriever/standard
poodle mix and too many books in her to-read pile. In her
downtime, she plays video games and spends much of her
time on or around a basketball court. She loves interacting
with readers and is grateful for their support. You can
reach her at barbhan.com

Discover more at millsandboon.co.uk

LET'S TALK

Romance

For exclusive extracts, competitions and special offers, find us online:

- MillsandBoon
- @MillsandBoon
- @MillsandBoonUK
- @MillsandBoonUK

Get in touch on 01413 063 232

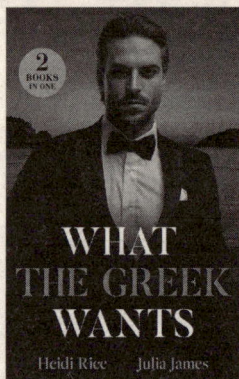

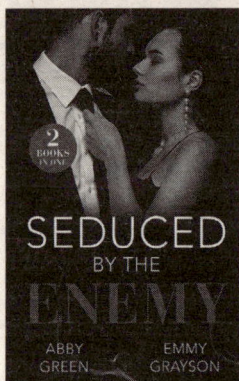

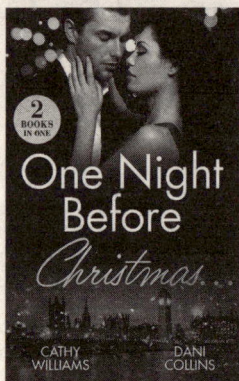

PEAK SUSPICION

CINDI MYERS

TWIN THREATS IN AUSTIN

BARB HAN

MILLS & BOON

First Published in Great Britain 2025
by Mills & Boon, an imprint of HarperCollins*Publishers* Ltd
1 London Bridge Street, London, SE1 9GF

www.harpercollins.co.uk

HarperCollins*Publishers*
Macken House, 39/40 Mayor Street Upper,
Dublin 1, D01 C9W8, Ireland

Peak Suspicion © 2025 Cynthia Myers
Twin Threats in Austin © 2025 Barb Han

ISBN: 978-0-263-39734-5

1125

PEAK SUSPICION

CINDI MYERS

For teachers.
You have one of the most important jobs in the world.

Chapter One

DON'T THINK YOU CAN BREAK THE LAW AND
GO UNPUNISHED.

The bold black letters, all caps in blocky print, stood out
against the half sheet of white paper. Miranda "Mira" Veronica looked over at her friend and fellow teacher, Shayla
Green. "Someone left this on your car?" Mira asked.

"Yeah." Shayla tucked a strand of dark brown hair behind
one ear and the line etched between her perfectly plucked
eyebrows deepened. "Who would do something so creepy?"

Even though she was pretty sure they were alone, Mira
glanced around the staff parking lot. At this time of day—
almost five o'clock—the staff lot was more than half-empty.
She and Shayla were parked side by side at the back of the
lot, farthest from the school building. Mira had walked out
to her car a few minutes ago, only to find her friend hunched
over this piece of paper, practically trembling. "What are
they talking about?" Mira asked. "How did you break the
law?"

"Did you read the whole note?" Shayla nodded to the
piece of paper.

Mira glanced at the note again. In smaller print beneath

the accusation of wrongdoing were the typed words: *Just because your pets are cute doesn't mean they're legal.*

"I adopted a fourth cat," Shayla said.

Not the awful crime Mira had anticipated. "Is that illegal?"

"There's supposed to be a cap of four pets in the city limits." Shayla sighed. "I have a dog, too, so that makes five animals. But honestly, she's not hurting anyone. All the cats are indoor cats. Most people never even see them, and it's not as if they make any noise, either. And the shelter is so full this time of year I couldn't resist giving another one a home." She bit her lower lip, close to tears.

"No one's going to send you to jail for having an extra cat." Mira folded the note and passed it back to Shayla. "This is just someone being a bully. If one of your students put this on your car, we need to find out who they are and see that they get counseling. This is no way to treat people."

"I can't believe it would be one of my students." Shayla folded the note again. And then again, until it was a square the size of a postage stamp. "I've got a good batch of kids this year. And I haven't told anyone about the new kitten."

"Maybe one of your neighbors found out? Or one of the shelter employees said something?"

Shayla stared down at the folded square of paper in her palm. "I don't understand why someone would be so mean."

Mira patted her friend's shoulder. "I don't understand, either," she said. "If I knew who did this, I'd give them a piece of my mind." She looked around the parking lot again. "I don't think the security cameras reach this far out."

"I never even thought of that," Shayla said. "I always park here because it's easy to get in and out. And I figure walking a few more steps a day couldn't hurt."

"Do you remember who was parked near you?" Mira asked. "We could find out if they saw anyone near your car."

"Mitch Anders's SUV was a couple of spaces over." She indicated a now-empty spot. At Mira's questioning look she added. "He's the technology teacher and athletic coach. You probably haven't met him yet."

There were so many people Mira hadn't met yet. She'd only arrived in Eagle Mountain three weeks ago to start a new job teaching Spanish to middle and high school students in the small district.

"I'll ask him tomorrow if he saw anyone who might have left this." Shayla closed her hand around the folded note and shoved it in her pocket. "I just hope whoever wrote this isn't telling other people about poor little Muffin."

"Try not to let it upset you," Mira said. She checked the time on her phone. "I have to go now, but we'll talk tomorrow."

Shayla forced a weak smile. "Thanks."

Mira had been in a good mood until her encounter with Shayla. The move from her native Santa Fe had been a big step for her, but it was working out better than she had dared hope. She enjoyed her students, and her fellow teachers and administration had been friendly and welcoming. Eagle Mountain itself was beautiful. She had even qualified for a rent-controlled apartment in a complex set aside for teachers and other essential employees. No place was perfect, of course, but it was disturbing to realize that even here, there were mean people determined to make others as miserable as they were.

She wasn't going to let them upset her. She had too much to look forward to, including this evening's meeting. After she left the school, she followed the directions she had been given to the headquarters for Eagle Mountain Search and

Rescue. American and Colorado flags snapped smartly in the breeze next to a large garage-like building. Mountains, their red-and-gray peaks not yet capped by snow, towered against a turquoise sky in the distance. Mira parked her car in a slot near the door labeled Visitor and followed a concrete walkway to the entrance.

The door opened into a large, concrete-floored room occupied by more than two dozen people. Several heads turned as she entered and a tall blonde moved to greet her. "I'm so glad you could make it." Sheri Stevens, another teacher at the high school, took Mira's hand and led her farther into the room. "Grab something to eat and drink and say hello. We're all friendly here. We'll get started in a few minutes and I'll officially introduce you."

"Thanks." Mira dropped the backpack she carried onto a folding chair near the front of the room and headed for a table spread with sub sandwiches and drinks. People smiled and moved over to make space for her. They were mostly young people, though a few were old enough to have graying hair. She spotted some familiar faces, but no one she could put a name to yet. This was one reason she had accepted Sheri's invitation to volunteer to help—she wanted to meet more people in what she hoped would be her new home.

She was pondering the selection of sandwiches when a man approached. He had straight dark brown hair, long on the top and short on the sides, and striking green eyes—the color of moss. "Hey there," he said. "Are you a new volunteer?"

"Not exactly." She selected a turkey sandwich and arranged it on her plate next to some pepper strips.

"Oh, mysterious." He grinned, flashing white, straight teeth. Handsome. Charming. And very sure of himself. She had met his type before. "I'm Carter Ames."

"Mira Veronica."

"So you're not a new volunteer. Did you just drop in for the free food?" His tone was teasing. He had a distracting dimple at the right side of his mouth. And the attitude of a practiced flirt. That was okay. She could play this game, too.

"Well, I am a teacher," she said. "We can't afford to turn down a free meal." She popped a pepper strip into her mouth and chewed.

"Are you here with someone else?" He looked around them.

She was about to confess her real reason for being here when a woman's voice rose above the other conversation around them. "I can't believe someone would do this!"

She and Carter glanced over at a cluster of volunteers around a couple. A woman with curly auburn hair was visibly upset, the dark-haired man beside her watching with a worried expression. She waved a sheet of paper. "If this is someone's idea of a joke they have a mean sense of humor," she said.

"Uh-oh." Carter set aside his cup. He started toward the couple and Mira followed. "What's up with Deni and Ryan?" he asked another man on the edge of the crowd. Mira did a double take. The man Carter spoke to looked enough like Carter to be his twin.

The man must have read Mira's confusion. "I'm Dalton Ames," he said. "You can think of me as the better-looking twin."

"You wish." Carter punched Dalton's shoulder.

"We're not doing anything wrong." The man beside the woman—Ryan?—put his arm around her. "Whoever wrote this can't do anything to us."

"Apparently, someone sent Ryan and Deni a letter complaining about the work they're doing on the house they bought near Owl Lake," Dalton said, keeping his voice low.

"What does the letter say, exactly?" a man with a thick mop of blond hair asked.

Deni handed over the note. "Read it out loud, Caleb," Ryan said.

"'Don't think you can break the law and go unpunished,'" Caleb read.

Mira gasped, and fumbled to keep from dropping her plate of food.

"What is it?" Carter reached out to rescue the tipping plate.

She held up a hand and leaned forward to hear the rest as Caleb continued reading. "'The mess in your front yard violates half a dozen ordinances. You have a legal requirement to clean up your property or there will be consequences.'" Caleb looked up. "Those last four word are in bold italics."

"Have any of your neighbors complained?" a young woman with dark hair almost to her waist asked.

"No," Ryan said. "They've all been great. They know we're remodeling."

"They're glad we're fixing up the place," Deni said. "No one has lived there in two years, and the renters who were there before that really trashed it." She shook her head. "And it's not that bad. There's some materials stacked up—neatly. And a construction dumpster. Not exactly an eyesore."

"Another teacher at school got a note like that," Mira said.

Everyone turned to look at her and she suddenly felt too warm. "Who are you?" someone asked.

"I'm Mira Veronica," she said. "I'm the new Spanish teacher at Eagle Mountain schools."

"I invited Mira here tonight." Sheri moved in beside her. "You say someone else got a note like the one Deni and Ryan received? Who was it?"

"I'd rather not say," Mira said. What if someone else

got upset over Shayla's fourth cat? "But her note was similar to this one. Someone left it on her car this afternoon. It started the same way, with that line about lawbreakers not going unpunished."

"Is she remodeling her house?" Ryan asked.

"No. This note was complaining about her having too many pets."

"How many pets does she have?" Caleb asked.

"Four cats. And a dog," Mira said. "I guess that's one over the limit."

"I don't think anyone enforces that ordinance unless someone complains, or the animals are neglected." A woman with short dark hair reached down to pat the black poodle by her side. The dog wore a blue vest—apparently it was a member of search and rescue also.

"Sounds like someone has too much time on their hands and is trying to stir up trouble." An older man with graying hair and goatee spoke. "Probably best to ignore them."

"We will." Ryan took the note from Caleb and ripped it in half. "That's what I think of this message."

"Let's get the meeting started." A lanky man at the front of the room addressed them. Gradually, everyone fell silent and moved to various seats around the room. Mira returned to the chair where she had left her pack.

"For those who don't know me, I'm Danny Irwin, captain of Eagle Mountain SAR," he said, with a nod to Mira. "We've got a few announcements to cover, then tonight's training session will begin." He turned to Sheri. "Why don't you start by introducing our guest?"

Sheri moved to take Danny's place and motioned for Mira to join her. "I want to welcome Mira Veronica," she said. "Some of you probably already know she's the new Spanish teacher at Eagle Mountain schools and she's agreed to offer a special course in Spanish for first responders. Mira, please tell us about the course."

Mira smiled. She was more comfortable here, in the role of instructor, than she was interacting one-on-one with strangers. "Thanks, Sheri. And thank you all for welcoming me tonight. As Sheri said, I teach Spanish to high school and middle school students. But for several years I also taught Spanish for first responders in Santa Fe, my hometown. Now that I'm in Eagle Mountain, I want to offer the same course here. It's designed to teach you not only basic conversational Spanish, but the specialized law enforcement and medical terms you may need to interact with people you meet in the course of your job."

A hand shot up and she nodded to a man on the right side of the room. "So the class isn't just for search and rescue?" he asked.

"That's correct. I hope to have students who are paramedics, fire department volunteers as well as local law enforcement."

"Can't let those guys get one up on us," someone said.

"The class also qualifies as a continuing education credit," Mira said. "If that applies to search and rescue. We'll meet twice a week for six weeks, at the meeting room at city hall." She named the tuition fee. "That includes all the course material."

"We have a grant that will cover half of that fee for anyone who enrolls and completes the course," Sheri added.

"I have some flyers with the details and my contact information if you have questions," Mira said. "There's also a link to the sign-up page online. Does anyone have a question they'd like to ask right now?"

Carter Ames raised his hand.

"Yes?"

"Are you single?"

Laughter rose around the room.

"Don't mind him," a young woman with curly dark hair said. "He flunked out of charm school."

"And they kicked him out of obedience school," Dalton said.

"But I'm still Mom's favorite," Carter said, beaming.

Mira shook her head. She had pegged Carter from the first—a flirt who counted on charm to get him through every situation. He was going to be disappointed to learn she was immune to such tactics.

"Are there any questions about the Spanish classes?" Sheri asked.

There were none, so Sheri thanked Mira for coming, and she collected her backpack and headed for the door while Danny began a discussion of protocols for treating suspected drug overdoses.

The sun was just sinking behind the mountains above town as she drove home. She was never going to get tired of this view. The meeting had improved her mood. She loved teaching kids, but it was good to interact with people closer to her own age. She had enjoyed teaching the course in Santa Fe. It was a great way to meet people, and a source of extra income.

She hoped some of the people she had met tonight would attend her class. Maybe the young woman who had teased Carter. There was definitely a family resemblance there, so maybe a sister? The two of them could compare notes—Mira had four older brothers. They could be as exasperating as they were lovable. And they were scattered from California to Boston. She didn't see them all enough. Next summer she'd have to try to visit. Family was too important not to make the effort.

She parked in her assigned space and climbed the steps to her second-floor apartment. A few feet from the door, she froze. The breeze fluttered a piece of paper stuck to her door. Probably some notice about maintenance or something. She removed the tack holding the paper in place and unfolded it.

DON'T THINK YOU CAN BREAK THE LAW AND GO UNPUNISHED. *David is gone but not forgotten and I know you are the one to blame.*

Chapter Two

"'Don't think you can break the law and go unpunished.' Hah!" Sergeant Gage Walker glared at the half sheet of notepaper in his hand, then continued reading. "'Your dog was running loose in the town park, in flagrant violation of the leash ordinance. Don't think because you're the sheriff's brother you're above the law.'"

Gage transferred his glare to the man seated across from him—his brother, Sheriff Travis Walker. The two shared the same dark hair and eyes, though Gage was taller, with broader shoulders. "Major was not running loose. He saw Casey at the playground and was so excited he pulled the leash out of Maya's hand. He ran straight to Casey and Maya caught up to him right away."

"Now that you've confessed, I'll have to write you a ticket." Only the twitch at the corner of Travis's unsmiling mouth gave away that he was teasing.

Gage laid the note on Travis's desk. "If this is someone's idea of a joke, I don't appreciate it. Casey was in tears, thinking Major would have to go to dog jail or something."

"I hope you told her we don't have a dog jail." Travis leaned forward and reread the note. "We've had several calls from people who have received similar notes in the last few days. There are probably more we don't know about. People don't want to report their rule-breaking to us."

"Are all the letters like this?" Gage asked. "Petty stuff that could even be a matter of misinterpretation?"

"Let's see." Travis consulted a notepad on his uncluttered desk. "A woman's trash cans left out over twenty-four hours after trash collection."

"That's not against the law," Gage said.

"No, but apparently it violates her home owner's association rules. Another letter was sent to a man who, the note claims, routinely speeds on Fern Valley Road."

"Everyone speeds on Fern Valley Road," Gage said. "Something about that long, straight stretch of road is irresistible to some people, no matter how many tickets we write."

Travis nodded. "Larry Yarborough was pretty upset about receiving a note that accused him of stealing from his employer. He swears it isn't true. His boss confirmed Larry had permission to take some leftover construction material to build a playhouse for his kids."

"We need to find out who's sending these notes and have a talk with them about minding their own business," Gage said. "They could be charged with harassment."

"It would be difficult to prove a person was responsible unless they confessed." Travis pushed the note aside. "We have bigger things to focus on. Someone tried to abduct an eleven-year-old boy yesterday evening, about eight o'clock. Shane took the call. The boy's okay, but pretty shaken up." He passed over the report.

Gage scanned Deputy Shane Ellis's summary. "Not a lot of details to go on," he said. "White SUV, slender person of medium height dressed all in black jumped out and tried to grab the kid." He looked up. "The boy isn't even sure if it was a man or a woman. They were wearing a hood and didn't say anything, and fled when the boy fought back. Do we think he's telling the truth? A kid might say something like this to get attention."

"There were signs of a struggle where he said the attempt took place," Travis said. "And Shane found a man who reported seeing a white car speeding one street over. The timing matches up. The boy has bruises on his arm with definite finger marks where someone grabbed him."

Gage passed the report back over. "I'm glad the kid is okay. What was he doing out alone at that time of night?"

"He was walking home from a friend's house at the end of the block. Before that, he and his friend were shooting hoops in the friend's driveway. They both say they didn't see anything suspicious."

"This is the kind of thing that gives parents nightmares." Gage thought of his oldest daughter, Casey. At nine, she was used to roaming the neighborhood with her friends. Even with his experience in law enforcement, he had been lulled into thinking their small town was safe. "Do we have anything else to go on?"

"We're putting out a plea to the public on social media, warning parents to keep their kids close and asking for any information on the car or about anyone acting suspiciously," Travis said. "I sent Jamie out to talk to every house in the boy's neighborhood. We're hoping someone will have seen something, or caught footage of the vehicle on their door cam."

An Eagle Mountain native, Deputy Jamie Douglas probably already knew most of the people she would talk to. Most wouldn't hesitate to share any information they had with the affable young woman.

"There are a lot of white SUVs out there," Gage said. He

took out his phone. "I'm going to send a heads-up to Maya. Casey doesn't usually walk home alone but I don't want today to be the exception."

"I sent a bulletin to all the schools this morning," Travis said. He picked up Gage's note. "I'll add this to our files, in case we find out any more about our mystery harasser."

"Our letter writer would do better to pay attention to a real lawbreaker like this than concerning themselves with imaginary crimes," Gage said.

"ARE YOU OKAY, MIRA?" Shayla put her hand on Mira's shoulder as she passed her in the teacher's lounge. "You look like you don't feel well."

So much for thinking concealer could hide the effects of a sleepless night. "I'm okay," Mira lied. "Just a little tired. How about you? Any more anonymous notes?" She managed to ask the question without her voice shaking.

"No. I went home and walked the dog, then played with the cats. Whoever wrote that nasty gram is a pitiful loser, as far as I'm concerned."

Mira wished she could dismiss her own note as easily. The door to the teachers' lounge opened and she stepped aside to allow a man to enter. "Hello, Mitch," Shayla said. Mira didn't miss the lilt in Shayla's voice as she addressed their fellow teacher, or the heightened flush of color beneath her dark brown skin. Shayla turned to Mira. "Have you met Mira Veronica? She's the new Spanish teacher. Mira, this is Mitch Anders."

"It's nice to meet you, Mira." Mitch nodded at her. He was in his early thirties, with sandy hair, only a couple of inches taller than Mira's five foot eight inches, with a lean build. Nice-looking, in a very clean-cut way. Shayla smoothed her hair and beamed at him. Maybe there was more than one reason she had parked near Mitch's truck.

"It's nice to meet you, too," Mira said.

"Mitch, did you see anyone near my car when you left yesterday afternoon?" Shayla asked. "I was parked a couple of spots down from you."

He considered the question for a few seconds. "No. I don't remember seeing anyone. That part of the parking lot is usually pretty deserted. Why? Did someone do something to your car?"

"No." She waved off the question. "It's nothing."

"Did you two hear about the message the sheriff's department sent over this morning?" he asked.

"What message?" Mira's heart pounded. Had someone called the sheriff and accused her of having something to do with David Ketchum's disappearance?

"Someone tried to snatch a kid last night," Mitch said. "I guess the boy got away, but the sheriff wants everyone to be on the lookout for anyone acting suspicious around the kids."

"That's horrible," Shayla said. "Who was the boy?"

"I don't know," Mitch said. "And apparently, he wasn't able to give much of a description of the person who tried to grab him. The bulletin from the sheriff's office mentions a white car, but that's about it."

"Lots of people drive white cars," Shayla said. "Mira has a white car. So does Principal Martin. So do you."

"I think it's one of the most common car colors," Mitch said. "So that's not going to help the cops much."

"I hope they find whoever it was before some child gets hurt," Shayla said.

The bell rang, signaling classes would begin in ten minutes. "We'd better go," Shayla said.

"You ladies have a good day," Mitch said.

Mira followed Shayla out of the teachers' lounge and made her way to her classroom. She nodded to students and fellow teachers who greeted her, even as her mind raced with her memories of David Ketchum's disappearance three years ago. The nine-year-old boy had been snatched off the street and found dead several days later. The crime had dominated news headlines in Santa Fe for weeks, but the killer had never been found. That someone would think Mira had anything to do with such a horrible thing shook her badly. The news that someone had tried to abduct a child here in Eagle Mountain was too eerie a coincidence. The two incidents had no connection, surely, but it unsettled her.

Once in her classroom, she booted up her laptop and pulled up a search engine. Her first period was open. She was supposed to use it for meetings with students who needed extra help, or working on the day's lessons, but she had no appointments today. Instead, she searched for information about David Ketchum.

Mira had been a second-year teacher at the time. David had been one of her youngest students, in a Spanish-language class for elementary school students. Mira traveled from the high school two days a week to play language games with third and fourth graders. The emphasis was on conversational Spanish and she tried to make the classes fun. David was a charming boy with beautiful brown eyes and a sweet disposition.

He disappeared two weeks before school let out for the summer. The news that he had vanished on his way home from school shook everyone. Mira had joined her fellow teachers in searching for him. As she scanned online accounts of those days she was startled to come upon a photo of herself, standing with other teachers in a field just outside of town. The caption said they were a group preparing to search for the missing student.

Three days after he disappeared, David's body was found in a shallow grave on public land a mile from town. He had been strangled. Mira felt sick all over again as she read the news accounts. David's murderer had never been found, though the police questioned hundreds of people. As far as she could tell, there had never even been a suspect.

So why had someone suddenly decided that *she* was to blame?

She was still reading through the news stories when students began arriving for her second-period class. Hastily, she shut down the laptop and focused on the day's lesson. By the time class ended, she was feeling calmer. By the end of the day, she had decided to chalk the letter up as someone's idea of a sick joke. She would ignore them, they would see they couldn't get a rise out of her, and eventually she would forget this had ever happened.

She maintained this positive attitude until she unlocked her car door and stared at a folded sheet of paper lying on the front seat. She had left the front windows rolled down a scant half inch to keep the interior of the car from getting so hot and someone must have slipped the note through the gap. She picked it up and sat, staring at the blank side of the paper, afraid to unfold it and read the message. She told herself she was being silly, and opened the note.

You can try to ignore what you did, but I won't. David's ghost cries out for justice.

She glanced around. Someone—Mitch Anders—was walking toward her. She looked down the row of cars. There was Mitch's SUV, three vehicles down from hers.

She couldn't let him see her like this. With shaking hands, she fastened her seat belt, then started the car and pulled out of her spot. Mitch lifted a hand in greeting as she passed and she forced a smile to her lips. *Nothing to see here. Everything's fine.*

She didn't drive home. She was too terrified she would find another note there. Instead, she turned onto the highway out of town—the road that led up into the mountains. The soaring peaks, rushing waterfalls and crystalline sky never failed to lift her spirits.

Except today she had a tough time focusing on the scenery. Her mind kept replaying the messages in those notes, alongside the details of David's disappearance and death. How could anyone believe she had anything to do with that horrible crime? And why focus on her now, almost three years later? None of it made sense.

Her heart raced, and with it, her car. She didn't realize she was driving too fast until she skidded around a curve. Heart in her throat, she stomped on the brake, but that only made things worse. Her car slid, then fishtailed. She wrestled with the steering wheel, trying to bring the vehicle under control, but found herself helpless as the car careened off the road. The world tilted and she swallowed a scream as the car rolled onto its side, the seat belt choking her.

Chapter Three

Carter accelerated up the steep slope leading to the top of Dixon Pass. For once he wasn't leading a tour group into the mountains. He'd borrowed a Jeep from the rental pool at Alpine Jeep Tours and Rentals, the family business, and headed out for a solo trail run. There was plenty of daylight left. He wasn't interested in anything too extreme, just a chance to stretch his legs and get some fresh air.

A white Toyota SUV with a solitary driver was just ahead of him on the otherwise deserted road. The car's tires squealed as it took a curve a little too fast. Carter wasn't known for being an especially cautious driver, but working search and rescue had given him a healthy respect for these mountain roads. Probably the most common type of call he had responded to in his short time with Eagle Mountain SAR was traffic accidents.

He lost sight of the Toyota on a series of S curves as it surged ahead, and shifted his attention to watching for the turnoff to the trail he wanted to check out. Another half mile or so to go, he estimated. The directions to the trailhead said to take the first left after an old mine tram. He slowed for a particularly sharp curve and hit the brakes even harder at the sight of fresh skid marks on the roadway, leading over the edge. He craned his neck, trying to see if someone had gone over the side, but the angle was too steep. He slowed further, then pulled onto a narrow shoulder, shut off the engine and switched on his emergency flashers.

He hurried to stand on the edge of the road and peer down below. The drop wasn't straight down from here, but a series of rock ledges. The white Toyota was on its side on the first ledge, about ten feet down, wedged against a stout pinion pine. He cupped his hands to his mouth. "Hello! Can you hear me?"

He listened, but the only sounds were the pinging of the Jeep's engine cooling, and the gravel beneath his feet as he shifted his stance. He pulled out his phone, saw that he had a signal, and punched in 911.

"Rayford County Emergency Services. What is your emergency?"

"I'm here on Dixon Pass and a car just went over the side. It's wedged on a ledge about ten feet down. I can see someone in there, but they're not moving or responding to my shouts."

"What is your name and location?"

He did his best to describe his position, gave his name, then added, "I'm a volunteer with Eagle Mountain Search and Rescue. I'm going to try to get down to the vehicle."

"Assistance will be there soon," the operator assured him. "Please wait where you are."

"Right." He hung up, then studied the scene. The slope down to the SUV wasn't that steep, and there were plenty of small shrubs and outcroppings to serve as handholds. He returned to his car and donned his Eagle Mountain SAR high-vis vest, slipped on a pack filled with first aid supplies and emergency equipment, and started down.

It only took a few minutes to reach the ledge. He approached the Toyota slowly, wary of causing it to shift, or even fall farther. But the vehicle was wedged tight. Even when he was close enough to touch it, it didn't move an inch. He looked up toward the driver's door. "Hello!" he called. "Are you okay?"

"Help me!" The voice—a woman's—was clear but filled with fear.

"Hang on," he called. "I'll be right there."

He boosted himself over the tire and lay across the driver's-side door and looked in. All the windows of the vehicle were shattered, sheets of green glass fragments like beaded curtains hanging from the frame. He carefully pulled away this debris and looked in at the Toyota's driver. She had been thrown sideways, held up by the shoulder harness and lap belt, the deflating airbags settling around her like rising dough. As he leaned in, she turned her head to look at him and he was shocked to recognize the bloodied face. "Mira!"

She stared, clearly trying to place him. "It's Carter Ames," he said. "We met at the search and rescue training session last night."

"I remember." She licked her bloodied lip. "What are you doing here?"

"I was driving behind you. I saw the skid marks where you went off the road. What happened?"

She tried to raise her hand, but the seat belt and her awkward position prevented her from lifting it more than a few inches. "I was distracted. Didn't realize I was going so fast. Lost control."

She closed her eyes.

"Stay with me, Mira." He brushed broken glass from her shoulder. "Does it hurt anywhere? Do you think anything is broken?"

"My neck is sore."

"You got thrown around in the fall, I imagine. What about

your head? Did you hit it? You're bleeding a little." A line of blood as thick as a pencil trailed down one side of her face.

"I don't think I hit my head. Maybe the glass…"

"Can you move your feet?"

"Yes. Can you get me out of here? It's really uncomfortable."

"Let's wait until help gets here. We want to make sure we don't do any damage trying to move you."

"Will they be here soon?"

"They will be." Depending on how far away the first responders were, it could take as little as fifteen minutes up to a full hour to reach an accident victim. But he wasn't going to tell her that. His job now was to keep her calm. "What distracted you?" he asked. "Did an animal run out in front of you? Or did you see something that took your attention from the road?"

"I was upset about the note."

"The note?"

"I got a note from whoever is writing everyone letters."

"No kidding? I'm almost jealous. Seems like everyone is getting those things. A friend of mine got one complaining about the way he speeds down this one road in his neighborhood. Like going a few miles over the speed limit is a capital offense. What horrible crime did yours accuse you of?"

Silence. He wondered if she had lost consciousness. "Mira? Are you still with me?"

"Yes."

"So what did the note say?"

"Oh. It accused me of jaywalking."

"Jaywalking?"

"Yeah. They said I was setting a bad example for my students."

He laughed. "I'm sorry. It's just so ridiculous." But she

wasn't laughing with him. He sobered. "Sorry. I didn't mean to make light of your situation. Obviously, something like that is really upsetting. Is that why you were driving so recklessly?"

"I was not driving recklessly!"

He was glad she couldn't see the smile he quickly hid. Maybe she wasn't too badly injured if she was angry with him. "I was driving behind you and you were going pretty fast."

The sound of sirens rose in the distance. "Hey, I think help is on the way. I'm going to move away for just a minute so I can talk to them. But I'll be right back. I promise."

The siren stopped almost directly overhead. Caleb moved away from the car and looked up. "Hey!" he shouted. "We're down here!"

Deputy Jamie Douglas looked down at him. "What's the situation?" she asked.

"Single female driver. Mira Veronica. She's banged up—says her neck hurts—and has some cuts from broken glass. She doesn't report any other injuries. The car is stable—it's wedged tight against this tree."

Jamie glanced up the highway. "The ambulance is just pulling up behind me," she said. "Search and rescue should be here soon. What happened?"

"I think she took the curve a little too fast and lost control. Easy enough to do on this road."

Jamie said nothing, but disappeared from view. Moments later Search and Rescue Captain Danny Irwin appeared and Carter repeated the story for him. "Sit tight," Danny said. "We'll get some people and equipment down to get her out."

Carter returned to the car. "We'll have you out in a few minutes and the paramedics will check you over," he said. "Is there someone you want us to notify?"

"No," she said. "And don't tell anyone what I said about those notes. I mean, the note. Please."

"Okay, but why not? You should tell the sheriff. You're being harassed."

"No. Please!" She clutched at the seat belt and shifted, until he was afraid she would injure herself further.

"It's okay." He tried to soothe her. "I won't say anything, I promise. Just hang on another few seconds."

He turned to see Danny, Ryan, Harper Vernon and his own sister, Bethany, descending to the ledge. He stepped back to allow Danny, a nurse, to climb up and assess Mira's condition. While Danny was talking to Mira, Carter helped assemble the litter and unpack the hydraulic extraction tool—more commonly known as the Jaws of Life. "If we cut away the pillar between the two side windows it makes it easier to load her onto the litter and bring her out without risking further injury," Ryan explained.

Danny rejoined them. "Bethany, you're the smallest," he said. "It will be easier for you to climb into the car with Mira and brace her neck and back. Keep her calm and shielded while we cut away the pillar, then we'll get her on the litter and bring her out."

"What can I do?" Carter asked.

"You already did a good job keeping her calm," Danny said. "You can help get the litter up to the road."

Bethany eased her way into the car. Conversation ceased shortly thereafter as the extractor screamed through the metal car body. Minutes later, Mira was free of the car, strapped into the litter. "My pack," she said, and tried to sit back up.

"I'll get it," Carter said. He returned to the car and spotted the black day pack half under the front passenger seat. He leaned in and, with a grunt, managed to pull it free. He returned to the litter. "I'll carry it up for you," he said. "You lie back and enjoy the ride."

He knew from training that the experience of being carried up a steep slope wasn't exactly relaxing, but his fellow volunteers did everything they could to make the journey as safe and comfortable as possible. They talked to Mira all the way up, reassuring her she was in good hands. He followed with Mira's pack and his own.

Once they reached the waiting ambulance, Paramedic Hannah Gwynn assessed Mira and allowed her to sit up. She cleaned the minor cuts on Mira's face and applied a couple of Steri-Strips. "You should consider going to the hospital and having your neck x-rayed," Hannah advised.

"I'm feeling much better now that I'm sitting up," Mira said. "I'd like to go home."

Carter, who had been standing nearby, moved in. "I can take you home," he said.

"What about my car?" Mira looked toward the drop-off.

"You'll have to arrange for a wrecker to retrieve your car," Jamie said. "I'll give you some information, and you'll need to contact your insurance company."

"Okay, thanks."

Jamie returned to her cruiser and Mira shifted her gaze to Carter. "If you could take me home, that would be nice."

"Of course."

Jamie returned and handed Mira a sheet of paper. "Here's everything you need to know about dealing with your car. I wrote my number at the bottom. Call me if you have any questions."

"Thanks." Mira stared at the paper, too numb to absorb whatever was written there.

"Let me help you up." Carter offered his hand. She hesitated, then took it. Her hand was cold, and felt fragile in his grasp. She trembled, and he wondered if this was merely the aftershock of what she had been through, or if she was still afraid.

MIRA EASED HERSELF into the passenger seat of Carter's Jeep. "I'm going to be sore tomorrow," she said.

"Soak in a hot bath with some Epsom salts when you get home," Carter advised.

Was this the same guy who had been flirting so hard with her yesterday? He was all serious concern today. "Did you learn that in search and rescue?" she asked.

"Nah. High school wrestling."

An image flashed into her mind of a younger Carter in a wrestling singlet. With his earnest green eyes and dazzling smile he had probably had half the girls in school in love with him. "Where was high school?" she asked.

"Vermont. A little town called Waterbury. How about you?"

"Santa Fe. I was born and raised there. Eagle Mountain is only the second place I've ever lived." Did that make her sound unsophisticated? Naive, even?

"I've never been to Santa Fe. But I hear it's pretty."

"It is. It's in the mountains. Like this, only different."

She fell silent, gaze focused out the window. The realization that she had come close to never seeing this beauty again was beginning to sink in.

Carter cleared his throat. "About that note you received. Or was it more than one? You said something about 'notes,' plural."

So he had picked up that slip of the tongue. "There were two notes, actually." She shifted toward him. He was probably wondering why a note about jaywalking would upset her so much. "One was left on my front door and another in my car. It's just so creepy. Whoever wrote them knows where I live and what my car looks like. They knew where I parked at school." She wrapped her arms around herself, determined not to give in to fear.

He nodded. "That's freaky. But those things aren't hard to find out in a town this size. They could have followed you home one afternoon, or to work one morning. Have you seen anyone suspicious?"

She shook her head. "No."

"Any men giving you a hard time? Someone you turned down for a date?"

Other than you? she thought. But that wasn't really fair. He may have come on a little strong initially, but he hadn't been creepy or rude. "Nothing like that," she said. "I mean, I've only been here three weeks."

"And no one's asked you out? Guys around here are usually faster than that."

The mock outrage that accompanied this assertion surprised a laugh from her. This was the confident flirt she was used to. "Am I supposed to be flattered?"

"I'm just surprised." He turned onto the street leading to her apartment. "So would you go out with me?"

Guess she should have seen that coming. "Now's not a good time."

She braced herself for the pushback. The cajoling. Maybe even scolding. Instead, he said, "That's cool. Maybe you'll change your mind and if you don't, no pressure." He flashed a grin. "I just wanted to make sure you knew I was interested."

She wanted to frown at him. To let him know she wasn't falling for his charm. But she didn't have it in her. It would be like being angry at a puppy. A really cute, buff puppy, but just as harmless, surely. And she couldn't forget how kind he had been in the aftermath of her accident.

He parked and unfastened his seat belt. "You don't have to go in with me," she said.

"At least let me walk you to the door." At her hesitation, he added. "In case there are any more notes."

Maybe it would be a good idea not to be alone if that happened. "Okay."

He followed her up the steps to her front door. She froze a few feet away. A piece of paper—pink this time—flapped in the breeze, tacked in the middle of the door.

Carter moved past her to read the notice. "Looks like the exterminator came by," he said.

She choked back a sob. He returned to her side and put an arm around her. "Hey, it's okay. Let's go inside and I'll get you some water."

She let him take her keys and unlock the door while she tried to pull herself together. "It must be the aftershock from the accident," she said. "I guess I was more shook up than I thought."

"Anyone would be." He returned her keys, then moved to the kitchen, found a glass and half filled it with water from the tap, and returned to her side. "Sit over here and sip this," he said. "I'll stay until you're feeling better."

She sat on the sofa and he took the chair across from her and watched her carefully. Everything about him radiated concern, not threat. "I'm sorry," she said, though she wasn't sure what she was apologizing for.

"It's okay," he said.

"Thanks for bringing me home," she said. "And for listening."

"Is there anything else I can do to help?" he asked. "You don't have a car now. Do you need a ride anywhere?"

"I can walk to school from here. I'll talk to my insurance

you've done anything in your life to warrant someone hurting you like this."

He didn't wait for an answer, but left. She clutched the note and stared after him, the soft click of the door as it closed behind him filling the sudden silence. Only when she was sure he was gone did she begin to cry.

She wanted to believe Carter Ames was a nice guy. But she would have said the same about everyone she had met in the last three weeks. People had welcomed her to town and been eager to include her—from her colleagues at the school to the volunteers she had met at the search and rescue meeting.

But one of those people wasn't nice at all. One of them had accused her of the worst crime of all, and every motive she could imagine for that made her more afraid.

Chapter Four

The following Monday evening, Mira double-checked her computer and Wi-Fi connections for the fourth time and rearranged the stack of handouts on the corner of the table at the front of the meeting room. She resisted the urge to check her face in the mirror again. She had done her best to cover the minor cuts and bruises from her accident with a thick layer of makeup. If she kept the lesson material interesting enough, maybe her students—the ones who didn't already know about her wreck—wouldn't notice.

Her stomach fluttered with a mixture of nerves and excitement. She had taught this course enough times that she was confident in her ability to engage her students, but there was always an initial uncertainty.

At the sound of voices approaching, she turned to greet her first pupils. Carter Ames pushed open the door and grinned. "Are we the first?" he asked.

His twin, Dalton, pushed past him. "You might as well get the dunce cap ready for this guy," he said, patting Carter's shoulder. "I'm the one in the family who always got straight A's in school."

"Hello, Mira." Bethany stepped forward. "You're looking much better than the last time I saw you. How are you feeling?"

"Pretty good," Mira said. "Thank you again for all your help." Her gaze shifted to the fourth man—taller, with close-cropped, darker hair, but the same family resemblance.

He stepped forward and offered his hand. "Deputy Aaron Ames, with the Rayford County Sheriff's Department."

"I'm glad you could join us, Deputy Ames." She took in the four siblings. "Any other family members I should expect?"

"We're the whole crew," Carter said.

"Do you have brothers or sisters?" Bethany asked.

"I have four brothers," Mira said.

"And I thought three were bad," Bethany said.

"I could tell you stories," Mira said. Having four brothers had been overwhelming at times, but now that they were all scattered around the country, she missed them.

Other students arrived and began filling the room. "All right everyone. Let's get started," Mira called.

She moved to the front of the room and waited while everyone settled behind the long tables that filled the conference room. "*Bienvenida*," she said. "Welcome. *Mi nombre es* Mira Veronica. My name is Mira Veronica. Let's start by going around the room and introducing yourselves. Let us know what organization you're with and if you've had any previous Spanish classes."

As each student introduced themselves, she matched the names with the registration forms she had received. She had a couple of paramedics, two more sheriff's deputies, three firefighters, and four more search and rescue volunteers. A good group. About half of them had taken a Spanish class or several in school, but none of them admitted to being fluent.

"My goal isn't fluency," Mira said when the introductions were done. "That wouldn't be practical in a six-week course. But by the time we complete our time together you should be able to communicate necessary information to people you may encounter in your work. You should be able to get your message across and understand the basics until a qualified interpreter comes on the scene."

"You might end up being the closest interpreter," a good-looking brown-haired man with smile lines around his eyes who had introduced himself as Sergeant Gage Walker said. "The sheriff's department used to call on the previous high school Spanish teacher from time to time."

"Oh." Mira told herself she shouldn't have been surprised. Eagle Mountain was a small town and though she took it for granted there were plenty of Spanish speakers in the area, this wasn't Santa Fe. "Of course I'd be happy to help. Though if you do well in my class, you probably won't need me."

"We'll always need you."

She didn't have to look over to know that Carter had said this, to the laughter of his fellow students. When she did look at him, he sat up straight and picked up his pen. "Ready for the first lesson, teacher." He smirked. Was he taunting her because he knew her secret? Or at least some of it? No one else had said anything to her, so she didn't think he had told anyone about the note she had received and its reference to David.

She turned away, ignoring him. "We'll start with the basic information you'll need from people you encounter." She passed out a vocabulary sheet and they spent the next forty-five minutes practicing quizzing each other on their names, addresses, ages, occupations and physical conditions. They learned to ask *What is the trouble?* and *Where do you hurt?*, *How can I help you?* and *Who can we call to help you?*

By the end of the two-hour class, Mira had identified the

students who had an aptitude for language, and those who would have to work harder. "Your homework is to keep practicing using those phrases," she said. "Get together with each other and try out different scenarios. You might copy the phrases you think you'll need to use most and put them where they'll be handy in an emergency. I'll see you all again on Wednesday."

Several of the students lingered to talk with her after class, including Carter and his siblings. "How are you doing?" Carter asked, his expression serious, gaze probing enough to make her feel uncomfortable.

"I'm fine," she said. "Nothing exciting going on at all." He could make of that what he would.

"That's good," he said.

Could a conversation be any more banal? It couldn't be over fast enough for her.

"Says the man who lives for excitement." Bethany nudged him. "Don't let him fool you, Mira. Carter is the real daredevil in the family."

"She's just trying to make me look bad," Carter said.

"Ha!" Dalton said. "The way you drive I'm surprised you haven't heard from whoever is sending scolding notes to people all over town."

"Eldon's girlfriend, May Delgado, got a letter yesterday," Bethany said. "It said she was violating her lease agreement because Eldon is practically living with her." She shuddered. "That's just creepy, the way this guy is spying over everyone."

Carter didn't say anything. He wasn't even looking at her.

"What makes you think it's a guy?" Dalton asked. "It could be a woman."

Mira turned to Aaron Ames. "What does the sheriff's department think about all these letters?" she asked.

"They're annoying," he said. "But so far no one's gotten into real trouble, and the letter writer hasn't carried through on any of their implied threats." He shrugged. "We're collecting the letters people report to us, but we don't have any leads on who might be writing them."

"What about the boy who was almost abducted?" Carter asked. "Do they have any idea who tried to grab him?"

Why had Carter asked that question? Had he figured out who David was? How Mira was connected to him?

"I couldn't tell you if we did," Aaron said.

"You don't have to tell me who your suspect is," Carter said. "Just yes, or no, do you know who tried to grab the boy?"

"No," Aaron admitted. "But whoever they were, they haven't made a second attempt. That we know of." He glanced behind Mira, to the clock on the wall. "It's almost time for my shift to start. Thanks for the class. It's going to be very useful."

"We'd better go, too," Bethany said. "Thanks, Mira."

She said good-night, then returned to the front of the room to gather her papers.

The door to the room opened and Carter moved back in, leaving the door open behind him. "I came back to talk to you alone for a minute," he said.

"I really don't have time," she said. She tried to pack up her things faster, but when she grabbed for a stack of handouts they slipped from her hand and cascaded to the floor.

She knelt to gather the scattered papers and Carter met her at floor level. He scooped up a handful and handed them to her. "You don't have to be afraid of me," he said. "I know I've been a jerk, but I never meant to add to your distress. I have a habit of not thinking before I shoot off my mouth."

He rubbed the back of his neck. "That remark at the start of class—about needing you—that was out of line."

"It was."

He nodded. "And so was my reading the note you were sent. But I've already apologized for that. What I came back tonight to say is that whatever is going on, your secret is safe with me. But if you ever do want to talk to someone about it, or you need help, I'm here for you."

"Because you want to go out with me."

"No!" He stood, and she rose also. He shoved both hands in his pockets. "I mean yes, I'd like to go out with you. But that's not why I offered to help. Whether you believe it or not, I think of you as a friend. And I help my friends." His expression was defiant, chin jutting, eyes fierce, but with a hint of pleading that threatened to melt at least some of the ice around her heart.

This was the Carter who had comforted her when she had been suspended so uncomfortably in her wrecked car. The man who volunteered his time to save the lives of strangers. "Thanks," she said. "That means a lot."

He took out his phone. "Let me give you my number. If you need help, call me. I don't live far away. What's your number?"

She hesitated. "I promise I won't call and harass you," he said. "I'm not *that* full of myself."

The way he said the words—all injured pride—had her biting back a smile. "All right." She gave him her number and a moment later her phone pinged with a text. "If you get any more nasty grams, or see anyone hanging around who makes you uncomfortable, call me," he said. "It doesn't matter when it is. Now, I'd better go." He turned to leave.

"Carter?"

He stopped and looked back.

"Thanks," she said.

He dipped his head, almost bashful, then turned and left.

She leaned back, a little weak at the knees. His offer to help—to look after her—had touched her. He had sounded so sincere. But could she trust that wasn't just an act to reel her in? She took a deep breath, steadying herself. She didn't have to figure Carter out all at once. The best approach was to move cautiously. Wait and see.

But she had never been the patient sort. That had gotten her into so much trouble before.

Poison-Pen Letters Plague Local Residents
By Tammy Patterson, Examiner Staff

A rash of anonymous letters have appeared in local residents' mailboxes, on car windshields, or tacked to front doors. The letters accuse the recipients of such petty crimes as littering, and violating homeowners' association covenants. According to recipients, the information in the letters is either wrong, or has blown a minor incident out of proportion. "It's nosy, invasive and just plain mean," says Meadow Wilcox, who received a letter complaining that she left her trash cans at the curb overnight. "Yes, technically, I'm supposed to bring the empty cans into the garage right after trash pickup. But I was away at a work conference. No one was harmed by my leaving them out an extra few hours."

Even local law enforcement hasn't been immune from the letter writer's wrath. Sergeant Gage Walker received a note scolding his wife for violating local leash laws when their pet dog pulled the leash out of her hand and ran a short distance at the local park. "We're not letting our dog run loose," Sergeant Walker said. *"That someone took the trouble to write a letter reprimanding me for something like this sounds like a deliberate attempt to annoy people."*

"Frankly, it's scary that someone is paying that much attention to all these little things," said Deni Traynor. She and her partner, Ryan Welch, received a letter accusing them of violating an ordinance against excessive debris in their yard. The pair are remodeling a home. "We have construction materials, neatly stacked, and a construction dumpster," Traynor said. "And we have a permit for all of it. It's ridiculous."

According to Sheriff Travis Walker, the few true crimes cited in the letters he has seen, such as an accusation of speeding, are unenforceable on the basis of a letter. "I can't write a ticket for speeding if I or one of my deputies doesn't catch the driver in the act," Sheriff Walker said.

When asked what penalties the letter writer might face if apprehended, Sheriff Walker said he would probably talk to the person first and ask them to stop their letter-writing campaign. If they persisted, however, the scribe could be charged with harassment. "The sheriff's department is collecting letters, if anyone would like to add theirs to our file. We're comparing the messages and ask that anyone keep an eye out for someone delivering the letters. Or, if you have a friend or family member you suspect is behind the letters, let us know. The letter writer should be concerned about their own safety. People are pretty upset about this and someone might try to exact their own justice. I would caution people not to take matters into their own hands, but the best thing for everyone would be for the letter writer to turn to a healthier outlet for their frustrations."

Volunteers were called to search and rescue headquarters Thursday shortly after noon to assist in the search for an elderly woman who had wandered away from her home a few hours earlier. "Her name is Helen Wakefield. She's eighty-two years old, white hair, about five feet five inches tall, 120 pounds." Danny read off the particulars the sheriff's department had forwarded. "She was recently diagnosed with dementia, but has never done anything like this before. She lives with her daughter and son-in-law, who reported her missing about half an hour ago. They thought she was taking a nap but found her missing when the daughter went to check on her because she didn't show up for lunch. She could have been gone as long as a couple of hours."

"Could she have tried to go back to the home she used to live in?" Carter asked. "Or to see a friend or relative? Before my grandmother died, she would talk about going to see her sister, who had been dead ten years by then."

"There's no mention of anything like that in the information we have," Danny said. "Sheriff's deputies and family members are searching the streets in their neighborhood. We've been asked to focus on a ravine behind the house that leads down to Timber Creek."

"I hope she didn't end up down there," Ryan said. "That's pretty rough country."

"That's why they called us," Danny said.

They split into groups to search the area they had been assigned, and piled into vehicles to make their way to the missing woman's neighborhood. Carter ended up in a Jeep driven by Tony Meisner, with Ryan, Deni and Grace. "Deni, I saw you were quoted in the article in the paper today about those anonymous letters," Tony said as he pulled the Jeep in line behind Carrie Andrews's SUV.

"Tammy didn't print the whole quote," Ryan said.

"That's because I was so angry about that letter everything I had to say wasn't fit for a family newspaper," Deni said. "I just hope the publicity puts a stop to whoever is behind this."

"They haven't stopped yet," Tony said. "I got a letter today."

Carter, Deni and Ryan, all leaned forward from the back seat. "What did your letter say?" Deni asked.

Tony's knuckles whitened as he gripped the steering wheel. "The letter accused me of climbing illegally on the via ferrata while it was closed. It threatened to report me to the owner and said as a member of the climbing community I should be ashamed of myself."

"Who does this person think they are?" Deni said. "Talking to all of us like we're three years old."

"I wasn't climbing illegally," Tony said. "I'm helping Ian Seabrook design a new climbing route. I had his permission to be up there after he closed for the day."

"Ian told me about that," Carter said. Ian Seabrook was engaged to Bethany and though he and Carter hadn't hit it off initially, Ian had turned out to be a pretty good guy.

"The sheriff said he had a file of letters people all over town have received," Deni said. "But I bet there are a lot of people who haven't said anything to anyone because they really did break some minor rule. Or because the letter writer reveals something they'd rather keep private."

Carter thought of Mira. Whoever David was, the mention of him in the notes she had received had really upset her—so much so that she didn't want anyone to know about them. "Has anyone received more than one letter?" he asked.

"I haven't heard anything like that," Deni said. "Why? Do you know someone who got more than one?"

He shook his head. "I was just wondering." Why had

Mira been singled out? He wished she would trust him enough to confide in him. Maybe he could help her. It was his own fault she was so wary of him. He'd worked so hard to try to impress her he'd looked like a jerk. Dalton was right—he'd never been smart about a lot of things—certainly not women.

They reached the unpaved street in the shadow of the mountains where Helen Wakefield and her family lived. The sheriff's SUV was parked in front of the house. Danny spoke with Sheriff Walker briefly, then directed the SAR volunteers to begin their search.

Carter was assigned to a section of the ravine near the creek, along with Deni and Tony. The three of them moved diagonally up the slope, pausing every thirty seconds or so to call for Helen. Occasionally the echo of other searchers drifted to them. Dry twigs and last fall's brown leaves crunched beneath their feet.

Tony stopped just ahead of Carter and held up his hand. Carter froze. "What is it?" he whispered.

"I heard something up there." Tony pointed up the slope. "I thought I saw something move in that oak brush."

Carter leaned forward and stared at the area Tony had indicated. The branches of the oaks rustled. "Helen!" Tony called. "Helen, is that you?"

Something burst from the brush, sending Carter and the others stumbling back. The mule deer buck stood for a moment, staring at them, then shook its head, a branch caught in its antlers drifting to the ground, and bounded off, away from them.

The radio mounted on Tony's chest chirped and he keyed the receiver. "Everyone stand down," Sheriff Walker said. "Mrs. Wakefield is home safe."

They trudged back to their vehicles. The return hike

seemed longer and more grueling, and no one spoke much. Sheriff Walker waited at their vehicles. "Thanks for coming out," he said.

"Is Mrs. Wakefield okay?" Deni asked.

The sheriff nodded. "A neighbor came home from work and found her asleep on a chaise on his front porch. He woke her up and brought her home to her family."

"I like a happy ending," Deni said as Tony drove them back to headquarters.

As they pulled into the parking lot of search and rescue headquarters, their phones pinged. "It's another callout," Deni said.

The others groaned. Like Carter, they were ready to go home, eat and relax. "Looks like it's going to be one of those days." Tony pulled out his phone. "What is it this time?"

"It's another missing person," Deni said. She looked up, frowning. "A little kid."

Carter read the message on his phone screen and a chill shot through him. "Possible abduction," he said. Someone had tried to kidnap a child. This time, had they succeeded?

Chapter Five

Mira was packing up to go home from school Thursday afternoon when Shayla slipped into the classroom and shut the door behind her. "I was hoping you were still here," she said. "Do you have a minute to talk?"

"Of course."

Shayla collapsed into a student desk on the front row. She wore a denim skirt and a red knit top, the color vibrant against her dark skin. But her face was pinched. "Is something wrong?" Mira asked.

"What do you think of Mitch?" Shayla asked.

Mira blinked. She hadn't really thought much about the coach. "I don't really know him," she said.

"But you think he's a nice guy, right?"

"Uh, sure." She studied her friend more closely. "Is someone saying Mitch isn't a nice guy?"

Shayla shook her head, then nibbled her thumbnail. "It's just, you know. He's a coach. Some people might mistake him for a dumb jock."

"But you don't think he's a dumb jock, do you?"

"No." Shayla sat up straighter. "He's really smart, but he's not the type to show off, you know? I mean, he didn't go to an Ivy League school or anything, but he's incredibly well-read and he knows a lot about a lot of different things. He's the technology teacher, too."

Mira suppressed a smile. "It sounds like you've spent a lot of time talking to him."

"I have. He's so easy to talk to. Yesterday we stood in the parking lot for over an hour after school let out, talking about, well, everything."

"Has he asked you out?" Mira asked.

Shayla flushed. "I think he wants to, but every time it feels like he's getting close, I change the subject."

"Why would you do that? You like him, don't you?"

"I do, but…" Her voice trailed away.

"But what?" Mira asked.

Shayla groaned. "My family. They're kind of snobs. They aren't impressed unless someone has a string of degrees after their name. And he's white. They would never say anything, but I know that would bother them, too. But it doesn't matter to me. I don't think it matters to him, either."

"Why don't you go out with him and see where things go from there?" Mira asked. "You might find out he has horrible table manners or something like that that turns you off."

"I doubt that." Shayla's smile was dreamy. "We sat together at lunch once and I didn't notice anything off-putting about his table manners. And he's so kind and patient. Did you know he takes care of his elderly father? I mean, he supports his dad and they live together. Mitch said his dad made some bad decisions when he was younger so that he needs Mitch's help now. But Mitch never talks like he resents it or anything. That says so much about his character, don't you think?"

"It does," Mira said. "So the next time you think he's about to ask you out, let him. And say yes."

Her smile faded. "I've probably already scared him off."

"Then you ask him out," Mira said.

Shayla laughed. "Maybe I will."

A knock on the door made them both start. "Come in," Mira called.

Mitch Anders opened the door. "There you are," he said to Shayla. "I've been looking for you."

Shayla smoothed a hand over her hair. "What can I do for you, Mitch?" she asked.

He glanced at Mira. "I just heard a boy has been kidnapped."

"What?" Mira stared, trying to organize her frantic thoughts. "Who was kidnapped?"

"Bryce Atkinson. Molly Atkinson's youngest boy."

"Oh my gosh!" Shayla gripped the edge of the desk with both hands. "His sister, Ariana, is a sophomore."

The image of the slight strawberry blonde flashed in Mira's mind. "Ariana Atkinson is in my Spanish I class," she said. "How old is Bryce?"

"I don't know," Mitch said. "My dad called with the news, but he didn't have a lot of details. He said the sheriff has called search and rescue to help look for him."

"How did your dad know about this?" Mira asked.

"He has a police scanner he listens to all the time." Mitch grimaced. "He can tell you everything going on in this town."

"Bryce is eleven, I think," Shayla said. "But he looks younger. He's small for his age. A sweet kid. I can't believe this is happening."

"What else did your dad tell you?" Mira asked Mitch.

"Dad said the boy was walking home from school, like he does every day, with his friend Max Eckert. Max went into the coffee shop to buy a snack. Bryce waited outside and somebody must have grabbed him. Pamela Jenkins was coming out of the bank two blocks down and she saw a white SUV stop. She heard a yelp, and the car sped off. When Max came out of the coffee shop, Bryce was nowhere to be seen."

"Your dad heard all of that on the police scanner?" Mira asked.

Mitch shook his head. "Not exactly. But our neighbor is one of the 911 dispatchers, so he walked over and talked to her. She called a friend, who it turned out had talked to Pamela, and she passed on the details to my dad."

How much had the story changed during this game of telephone? Mira wondered.

"I just checked the local Facebook page and it's on there, too." Shayla looked up from her phone.

Mira's stomach churned. This was worse than when David had disappeared. Back then, when they first heard the boy was missing, everyone assumed he had stopped to play and lost track of time. Or maybe he'd even run away. They didn't have the experience to believe he'd been abducted and murdered.

"His poor family," Shayla said.

"You say search and rescue is looking for him?" Mira asked.

"Yes." Shayla studied her phone again. "Someone else posted about seeing a boy running away from the highway up by Galloway Basin. The description of the boy sounded like Bryce, so I guess the sheriff sent search and rescue up there to check it out."

"I should go check on my dad," Mitch said. "He sounded pretty shook up when he called. I just thought you'd want to know about the missing boy."

Shayla stood. "I should go, too," she said. "I'll walk with you to the parking lot." She glanced at Mira. "If you'll be okay?"

"I'll be fine. Go." Mira waved her away.

Alone, she stared at her half-empty backpack and the stack of student tests she needed to take home and grade. But the news of another child victim had left her stuck to her chair. What had she been doing when the announcement came that David was missing? She couldn't remember. The next day she had gone with some other teachers to volunteer to help search for him. The next day—or maybe the next?—she had attended a candlelight vigil organized by the family's church. The child's disappearance—and the discovery that he had been murdered—had been a tragedy that brought strangers together. At first everyone was focused on taking care of the family and monitoring the news and social media feeds for any updates about the murderer.

But after a while, when the crime remained unsolved, people returned to their regular lives. David wasn't forgotten, exactly, but memory of the tragedy faded.

Someone here in Eagle Mountain remembered it, though. And had decided to connect Mira with it. Nothing about that made sense to her.

She picked up her phone and thought about texting Carter. To say what? *Be careful? Good luck?*

Instead, she slid the phone into her pack, along with the papers that needed grading. She found her keys and headed to the rental car—a small red sedan—that her auto insurance company had provided while they determined whether they would pay for her Toyota to be repaired or declare it totaled. When David had disappeared, she had gathered with friends and family. With Shayla busy with Mitch, she was keenly aware of how alone she was. How much of that was circumstance, and how much her own fault for always keeping people—men—at arm's length?

"WE'RE LOOKING FOR Bryce Atkinson, age eleven," Danny told the assembled volunteers. "Four feet three inches tall, eighty pounds. Blond hair, blue eyes. He's wearing a blue Eagle Mountain Raptors T-shirt, blue jeans and white-and-gray tennis shoes. He may have a blue backpack."

"How do we know this report of a boy running from a car in this area is even accurate?" Dalton asked.

"We don't," Danny said. "But we have to assume that a boy might be out there who needs our help until we learn otherwise."

Sheriff Travis Walker came to stand beside Danny and the volunteers fell silent. "I've spoken with Bryce's father," the sheriff said. "He tells me Bryce hiked up here with the family last summer. Bryce is in Scouts and likes the outdoors. His dad thinks he would look for a trail and head down, toward town. But if he's afraid of a pursuer, he would hide, so be sure to search any caves and rock crevices that might be big enough to conceal a child."

"Do you think the kidnapper is up here, too?" a woman farther back in the crowd asked.

"The only other car in the parking area when we arrived—a bright blue Jeep—belonged to a couple of hikers," the sheriff said. "They didn't see anything or meet up with anyone else on the trail. If the kidnapper was here, I think they're gone now."

They divided into groups of three and set out to sweep the section of the map they were assigned. They moved slowly, a few feet apart, striving to look under every shrub and behind every large rock and in every hole, and over every ledge. In addition to Bryce himself, they searched for any sign he had been here—small footprints, torn pieces of clothing, or any kind of distress signal he might have fashioned.

Carter tried to put himself in Bryce's shoes. If a person he didn't know grabbed him and forced him into a car, what would he do? Had the kidnapper tied up the boy? Or knocked him out? Then what?

"Why would someone bring a kid all the way up here?" he asked fellow volunteer Vince Shepherd.

"Maybe the kidnapper knew he had to get out of town quickly, but thought they might meet up with too many cops or nosy people if they took the highway to Junction," Vince said. A tall, muscular man with dark hair, Vince had a reputation for being quiet, but dependable. "There's a lot less traffic up here in the high country. Not too many tourists this time of year. Maybe he stopped to restrain the kid better or threaten him or worse, and the boy saw his chance and got away."

"I hope he did," Harper Vernon said. "And I hope he hurt his kidnapper when he did."

They continued the search, alternately calling Bryce's name, and identifying themselves as search and rescue. Carter climbed up a steep jumble of car-sized boulders and stood at the top, surveying the landscape below. At first he saw only stillness—gray and red rocks, dark green trees, and the occasional flash of paler green or green-yellow from aspens on the verge of changing to the gold of fall.

Something flashed blue in the corner of his eye. Was that a bird? There wasn't a breeze, but that tree limb had definitely moved. He looked over his shoulders and saw Vince and Harper searching below. He checked to his left again. Whatever was down there was moving away from him. Was it because they were afraid?

The blue flashed again, farther away this time. Definitely not a bird. If that was Bryce, he was fast moving out of sight.

Carter scrambled down and began heading in the direction of his last sighting. No more methodical searching—he was almost running, stumbling over loose rock and flailing to maintain balance as he slid on the heavy duff of dried piñon needles. When he caught a glimpse of blue again, he stopped and cupped his hands to his mouth. "Eagle Mountain Search and Rescue!" he shouted. "We're looking for Bryce Atkinson."

Whatever was ahead of him was crashing through the underbrush, making so much noise Carter wondered if they could even hear him. He took a deep breath and charged forward again, batting aside branches and ducking under larger limbs.

He came to a low stand of mountain willow, the thin branches repeatedly snagging at his pants, when he caught the flash of blue out of the corner of his left eye once more. He froze, and pretended to focus on freeing himself from the willow, but watched the blue. It wasn't moving, and as he watched he thought he could make out the shape of a person, crouched in the underbrush, scarcely six feet away.

Carter straightened. He still didn't look at the boy, but said, in a conversational tone, "My name is Carter Ames. I'm with Eagle Mountain Search and Rescue. Bryce, if you're ready to go home to your mom and dad, I promise I'll take you to them."

He waited, holding his breath. Then twigs snapped and leaves rustled. A boy, dressed only in a blue T-shirt and white underwear, rose up out of the willows. He stared at Carter's blue-and-yellow search and rescue vest, then began to push his way through the willows toward him, a pained look on his face.

Carter tried not to show his alarm at the blood trickling down the boy's legs. But Bryce noticed him staring. The boy looked down at his legs, which were lacerated with a thousand shallow scratches from the willow branches. "He took my pants and shoes," he said. "He told me it was so I wouldn't run away. But first chance I got, I did run."

Carter crouched to get a closer look. The boy wore dirty and tattered white crew socks. "Your feet must be pretty sore, running over all these rocks," he said.

Bryce made a face. Carter thought he was trying hard not to cry. One of his eyes was swelling shut. Had the kidnapper done that to him? A surge of fierce protectiveness brought a lump to Carter's throat. He swallowed hard, and fought to keep his voice even. "You're a brave kid," he said. "Are you ready to go home?"

Bryce pressed his lips together tightly and his throat convulsed. He nodded.

Carter took a bottle of water from his pack and offered it to Bryce. "You ran a long way," he said. "Drink this."

The kid drained the bottle and handed it back to Carter. "Would you like some more?" Carter asked. "Or something to eat? I've got some protein bars."

"No thanks. Let's just go."

Carter stowed the empty water bottle and considered the boy. "Since you're hurt, I'd better carry you," he said. "Is that okay?"

Bryce nodded.

Carter shifted his pack around to his chest and crouched. "Can you climb onto my back?"

Bryce did so, his legs locked around Carter's waist, arms over his shoulders, hands clasping the side of the pack. Carter rose slowly. He staggered back a little, then got used to the extra weight and balanced. "You doing okay back there?" he asked.

"Yeah."

They set out, moving slowly as much because of the rough terrain as the awkward load Carter carried. He followed the sounds of other searchers calling for Bryce. He had a lot of questions he wanted to ask the boy, starting with did he know who did this to him. But other people, with more authority than Carter, would be asking those questions. People with more knowledge about how to get the answers they needed without further traumatizing the boy.

"How did people know to look for me up here?" Bryce asked.

"A woman in town saw you waiting outside the coffee shop. Then she heard a yelp, a car screeching away, and you were gone. Your friend came out of the coffee shop and told her you had just been there. Then someone else saw the news online that you were missing and reported seeing a boy who looked like you running from a white car up here."

"I guess I'm pretty lucky someone saw me," he said. "I thought I was going to have to spend the night up here, with no pants or shoes."

"What would you have done if that had happened?" Carter was genuinely curious.

"I was going to try to find a cave and see if I could make a fire, the way we learned in Scouts."

"You can do that? Make a fire without matches? I'm impressed."

"Don't be," Bryce said. "The book showed us how to do it by rubbing sticks together or striking a spark on a rock, but none of us were able to actually do it. Still, I was going to try. It was either that, or be cold."

Carter boosted the boy up higher on his back. "I have some sweats in my pack, if you want to put them on," he said. "They're miles too big for you, but you'd be warmer."

"Maybe that would be good," Bryce said. "I don't really want to meet a lot of people like this."

They stopped and the boy got down. Carter opened his

pack and found the sweatshirt and pants. He had to fold thick cuffs on the pant legs and pull the drawstring tight in order to keep them from falling off of the boy, but the kid cheered up. "That feels better," he said. "Thanks. I'd like to walk now."

"Sure."

They set out walking, slowly, and Carter wished he had shoes for the boy. Bryce picked his way among the stones and gravel, wincing every now and then, but never complaining. In another few hundred yards, they met up with Ryan and Danny. Bryce hung back, but Carter put a hand on his shoulder. "Those are more search and rescue people," he said. "Come on. I'll introduce you."

The two men stopped and waited for Carter and Bryce to approach. "Bryce, this is Captain Danny Irwin, with Eagle Mountain Search and Rescue, and another volunteer, Ryan Welch."

"We're really glad to see you, Bryce," Ryan said.

"We sure are." Danny crouched and looked the boy in the eye. "How are you feeling?"

"My legs and feet are all cut and bruised," Bryce said. "The guy who grabbed me took my pants and shoes."

"Did you get a good look at him?" Ryan asked.

Danny scowled at Ryan and shook his head.

But Bryce seemed unperturbed by the question. "He was wearing a ski mask and gloves," the boy said. "I couldn't tell much about him, except I'm pretty sure it was a man. Not too tall, but strong. And he whispered, like he was trying to disguise his voice."

Danny patted Bryce's shoulder. "The sheriff will want to hear all about it."

The boy took a step back. "The sheriff?"

"You're not in trouble," Danny said. "Come on. Your parents are waiting for you."

The quartet made their way down the trail toward the parking area. Other volunteers fell in behind them, forming a parade down the mountain. By the time they arrived at the trail head a number of locals as well as officers from area law enforcement agencies and the press had gathered.

"Bryce!" The woman's voice rang out over the conversations of the crowd.

Bryce looked up and seconds later a woman rushed forward and scooped him to her. A worried-looking man followed. "Son, are you okay?" he asked, his voice breaking.

Carter left the family reunion and joined the other volunteers who were packing gear, ready to head back to SAR headquarters. Ryan caught up with him. "How did you find him?" he asked.

"I saw movement and a flash of blue in the distance," Carter said. "I headed toward him, then stopped when I got close and pretended I was looking somewhere else. But I said, kind of loud, that I was with search and rescue and looking for Bryce Atkinson. I told him I was there to take him to his parents. He came crawling out of a willow thicket, his legs all bruised and bleeding. The guy that grabbed him took his pants and shoes to keep him from running away."

"Brave kid, to run anyway," Ryan said.

"That's what I told him."

Ryan slapped his back. "Good job. We don't get happy endings on searches like this often enough."

Carter accepted congratulations from others as they heard the news, but he downplayed his role. Anyone else would have done the same, if they had been the one to spot the boy first.

By the time they reached SAR headquarters, the news had spread. People from all over town had gathered, anxious to hear details about what had happened. Carter tried to slip away before anyone could spot him and start firing questions. He was glad Bryce was safe, but he didn't want to be singled out for being the one to find the boy. Everyone there was giving of their free time to look for a missing kid. They all deserved credit.

"Carter!"

He looked around at the sound of his name and saw Mira jogging across the parking lot toward him. "I heard what happened," she said. "Are you okay?"

"Sure. I'm fine."

"Somebody said you were the one who found him. Bryce."

"We were all searching in the same area. Someone would have found him soon. I was just in the right place." Did that sound too humble-brag? "I'm glad he's okay," he added.

He braced himself for the next questions. She would want to know details. What had happened to the kid? But none of that was really his story to tell.

She put a hand on his shoulder. Last night, at Spanish class, she had treated him like any other student. But this felt different. His heart beat hard at the contact. When she looked up at him, he found himself focusing on her lips. So soft. Beguiling. Not a word he could remember using before.

"Do you have to be somewhere else right now?" she asked.

"No." His parents were probably looking for him, not to mention Bethany and Dalton, but he wasn't a lost kid they had to keep track of. "I'm free."

"Could you come back to my place?"

His heart beat even faster at this. He didn't want to jump to conclusions, but was she, well, propositioning him? Surely not, but…

"I want to talk to you," she said. "I want to tell you about David."

Chapter Six

By the time Carter's Jeep pulled in behind her at her apartment complex, Mira was second-guessing her decision to invite him over. She should have suggested they go to a coffee shop, or a bar—someplace less intimate. But would she really have been able to tell him her story if there had been a chance of other people overhearing? He had been here before, of course, the day of her accident. He hadn't done anything to make her uncomfortable then.

He followed her up the stairs to the second floor and waited while she unlocked the door. She could feel his gaze on her, studying her, but he didn't say anything. She led the way into the apartment and locked the door behind them. When she finally faced him, she was struck by how weary he looked, fine lines she hadn't noticed before at the corners of his eyes, his shoulders a little slumped. "How long were you out searching for Bryce?" she asked.

"A couple of hours." He rolled his shoulders and grimaced. "Before that, we had a call to look for a missing elderly woman. Her relatives found her at a house down the street and we had just gotten back to headquarters when the call went out about Bryce. I worked all day before that so…long day."

"Can I get you anything?" she asked. "Have you eaten dinner?"

"No." He glanced toward the kitchen. "I don't want to put you out."

"I can make you a sandwich."

"That sounds great." The genuine gratitude in his smile touched her more than any flirtatious smirk could have.

"Sit down and rest," she said. "I'll be right back."

Instead of sitting down, though, he followed her into the kitchen. "Do you want something to drink?" She opened the refrigerator and surveyed the contents. "I've got flavored seltzer and, uh, cranberry juice? Or water."

"The seltzer is good."

She handed him the can, took one for herself and pulled out the sandwich makings. He sat at the breakfast bar and watched her work. "I was surprised to see you at headquarters this evening," he said.

"My friend Shayla texted me that Bryce had been found and a lot of people were going to search and rescue headquarters to find out what happened. I decided to go and see if you were there." She opened a container of salad and layered lettuce on the turkey and cheese sandwiches.

"Because you wanted to tell me something?"

She gave him points for not bringing up the subject before now. "Let's eat first," she said.

She took a bag of potato chips from the cupboard and handed it to him, then set a sandwich down in front of him. She settled onto the other barstool with her sandwich.

His sandwich disappeared with alarming speed. She was too nervous to do more than pick at hers. She ended up cutting it in half and passing half over to him. "Go ahead and eat it," she said. "I'm not that hungry."

"Thanks," he said when that, too, had vanished. "I was

hungrier than I thought." He looked at her expectantly, and she knew she had put this off as long as possible. She pushed the remains of her sandwich away and stood. "I want to show you the notes I received," she said. "Both of them."

She went into her bedroom and retrieved the notes from her dresser drawer, then laid them on the bar in front of him. "You saw one of them already," she said. "But the other one was first."

He scanned both the notes, then looked up at her. "So, who is David?" he asked.

She settled onto the second barstool and shifted to face him. "David Ketchum was a student at the elementary school in Santa Fe where I taught Spanish two days a week," she said. "He disappeared three years ago, a couple of weeks before the end of the school year. A few days later, his body was discovered on public land not far from town. Police have never found his murderer."

A single line formed on his forehead, and he looked older. "And the letter writer is accusing you of having something to do with this—the murder of a little boy?"

"I didn't have anything to do with it. I hardly knew David."

"Were you ever a suspect?" he asked.

"No! I wasn't even questioned. I don't know why this creep thinks I had any connection at all."

Carter scowled at the two notes. "Maybe they heard you were from Santa Fe. They remembered the crime—it must have been all over the news back then—and decided that was enough of a connection to accuse you." He tapped a note with one finger. "None of the things this person has written about to other people are real crimes. They obviously get off on annoying people."

"Then you believe me?"

He jerked his attention back to her. "Of course I believe you."

"Thanks." She slumped on the stool, wrung-out—from her worry over Bryce, her accident, the notes—everything. "I'm sorry I lied at first and told you the letter was about jaywalking."

"Hey, in your shoes I probably would have done the same thing. Though maybe I'd have come up with something more exciting than jaywalking." There was that grin again, teasing her out of her bad mood. Or trying, anyway. She would give him props for that.

"What would you have said?" she asked.

"I don't know. Maybe I'd been accused of telling criminally bad jokes."

"I've never heard you tell any kind of joke."

"I'm a Jeep tour guide. It's part of the whole schtick to tell bad jokes. It's a hit with the kids in the group and that makes their parents happy. How do you get a squirrel to like you?"

"I don't know."

"Act like a nut."

She groaned. "See?" he said. "It works every time." His eyes met hers and she fought the sensation of being off-balance. As if she might float to the ceiling or slide off her stool. "Um, what do you think about the notes?" she asked. Anything to keep him from looking at her like that—as if he wanted to see past the surface, to uncover all her secrets.

Carter studied the notes again. "Nothing really stands out about this. They're both typed—or rather, printed. Plain white paper. No envelopes?"

"No. Just the folded paper. The first one was tacked to the front door. You can still see the hole from the tack at the top there. The other one was pushed through a gap I left in my car window. It lay on the driver's seat when I left class the day of my accident."

At mention of the accident, he looked at her again. "How are you feeling?"

She shrugged. "A little sore. And determined to drive more carefully. My insurance is paying for a rental while they decide what to do with my Toyota."

He nodded and returned to his study of the notes. "The message is pretty melodramatic, isn't it?" he asked. "If not for the seriousness of the accusation, it would be almost funny."

"There's nothing funny about it," she said. She hugged her arms more tightly around her.

"The timing of these notes is interesting," he said.

"What do you mean?"

"It sounds like you got them about the time someone tried to snatch that other boy—last week. The kid who got away. Maybe that's why you received the note. The letter writer heard about the attempted abduction and was reminded of the case in Santa Fe and decided to single you out."

"The first note came before the abduction attempt." She reached for the can of seltzer and drank some more, focused on keeping her hand from shaking. "It's such a creepy coincidence. And now this has happened to Bryce. I can't help thinking he could have ended up like David."

He swiveled to face her, their knees almost touching. "I know you said you don't want to go to the sheriff, but why not?" he asked. "Maybe this letter writer is harmless, but what if they aren't?"

"But what if the sheriff believes the accusations?" she asked.

"You didn't do anything wrong."

"No. But innocent people get accused of crimes all the

time." She shook her head. "I remember what it was like when David disappeared. People made all sorts of unfounded accusations. At one point the police there questioned his own father for something like nine hours. I don't want that kind of attention. And maybe attention is what this person is after. I think if I ignore them, they'll give up and move on to something else."

"Maybe."

"I haven't had any new notes," she said. "Maybe whoever this is has already moved on to someone else."

"Maybe," he said again. He sounded so doubtful. Had she made a mistake, confiding in him? "Please don't tell anyone about this," she said.

"I promised I wouldn't," he said. She heard no irritation in his voice, only conviction.

"Thank you," she said.

She slid off her stool. "I just wanted you to know the truth. It feels better, telling someone."

He stood also. "If anything else happens—more notes or anything that upsets you, call me," he said. "You have my number."

He seemed genuine. "Why do you care so much? You hardly know me." Was this a ploy to get her to go out with him?

His expression remained serious. "I told you, we're friends now. You shouldn't have to deal with everything all by yourself."

He was either the smoothest operator she had ever met— or he was sincere. His words brought a lump to her throat, so that she could only nod. She followed him to the door and locked up after she closed it behind him, then sank onto the sofa, overwhelmed by the events of the past few hours.

She ought to feel relieved. She had told Carter about

David, but she hadn't told him everything. The thing she didn't want anyone to know. Especially the sheriff.

WHEN CARTER REPORTED to Alpine Jeep Rentals the next morning, he braced himself for his parents and sister—maybe even Dalton—to make a fuss about him being a hero for finding Bryce Atkinson. He'd gone out of his way to avoid attention at search and rescue headquarters the evening before, but if his family wanted to make a big deal out of it, that was okay.

"You have a family from Cincinnati booked to go up to Raptor Ridge at ten," his mother said as soon as he stepped into the small office off Eagle's Mountain's main street.

"Right." Carter collected a set of Jeep keys from the board and scanned the clipboard with the paperwork for a family named Packard—mom, dad, grandparents and two kids.

"Skip the overlook at Galloway Basin and stop up the road at the turnoff to Anderson Falls instead," Mom continued.

"Why?" Carter asked. The parking area at Galloway Basin had restrooms and a good view of the surrounding mountains—a good place to let the customers stretch their legs and take pictures.

"I talked to your brother this morning and he tells me the sheriff's investigators will be working up there. We don't want to upset our guests."

Aaron would have filled his mother in on all the details of yesterday's excitement. "I guess they're looking for evidence in the kidnapping case," Carter said.

"Guess so." Mom was focused on the computer once more.

"I guess Aaron told you what happened yesterday," he said.

"Uh-huh." She looked up. "Did you know he's training to

be part of the SWAT team? As much as I worry about him putting himself in danger, your father and I are so proud."

"That's great," Carter said. "Good for him."

The door burst open behind him and Bethany rushed in. "Sorry I'm late," she said. "I had a hard time getting to sleep after all the excitement yesterday and I didn't hear my alarm this morning."

"You don't work here anymore," Carter said. After her engagement to Ian Seabrook, Bethany had left the family business to work for Ian's climbing business.

"I'm filling in while Kaitlynn is at her sister's wedding in Oklahoma." Bethany shoved her purse into the bottom drawer of the desk and sank into a chair beside their mother. She frowned at Carter. "I told you. You just don't listen."

"Speaking of weddings, did you look at the photos of flower arrangements for the reception that I sent you?" Mom asked.

"I did and they look great, Mom. Ian likes them, too."

"It's going to be a beautiful wedding," Mom said. "And you are going to be a beautiful bride."

"Aww, Mom." Bethany hugged her.

The door opened again and Dalton came in. "Dalton!" their mother said. "Tell me what you did to the scheduling program. I tried to enter all the information for the Taveres family reunion bookings for next month and the computer won't let me."

"You don't have to do that." Dalton pushed past Carter and moved in between him, Mom and Bethany. "I revised the software so that once you have a customer's details entered once, you just hit this button here and it automatically fills in the info on subsequent reservations."

"You are a genius!" Mom declared, and leaned over and

kissed him on the cheek. "What would we do without you? And don't answer that. I don't even want to know."

"I'll get the Jeep ready for the Packards," Carter said, though he doubted anyone heard him.

He checked the Jeep's fluids, the air in the tires and that the first aid kit was fully stocked, then loaded a cooler with bottles of water. He laid folded blankets on the seats—in the high country it could get cool in the open Jeep. As he worked, he tried to shrug off his disappointment that his mom hadn't even said anything about Bryce Atkinson. Maybe Bethany or Dalton had told her he didn't want anyone making a big deal out of his role in the rescue. That was probably it. His mother was respecting his feelings.

Except Mom wasn't really like that. She always did and said exactly what she wanted when it came to family. She had embarrassed each of her four children at various times in their lives. When Carter was sixteen, she had informed his prom date that Carter didn't know how to tie a tie and that Bethany had picked out the date's flowers "since Carter has no taste in these things." At his high school graduation she had said—loudly—that he was the one child she feared wouldn't graduate since "he was a beautiful child but not blessed when it came to brains."

Maybe all parents of multiple children were like that—assigning each sibling a role in the family. Aaron, the oldest, was the responsible, serious one. The hero risking his life as a law enforcement officer. Bethany, the only girl, was sweet, if impulsive. She was finally getting her life on track by marrying a handsome—and rich—man. Dalton was the family brain, the baby who Carter suspected was his mother's favorite.

Which left Carter to the role of charming rogue. Good-looking and not-too-bright, always ready for a laugh.

Except there was more to him than that. He might not be a genius, but he was intelligent enough. He hadn't done well in school because he'd been bored. People liked him, sure, but did they all think he was so shallow?

He was on his way back into the office when the fire alarm at the station two streets over sounded. The wail echoed off the peaks around town. Dalton came out of the office. "What's the alarm for?" he asked, almost shouting to be heard over the piercing sound.

Carter shook his head. The siren continued for a full minute, then died away. Bethany rushed out of the office. "Mom called Aaron and he said the siren sounded because there's an emergency at the school."

"Which school?" Carter asked.

"The high school."

Mira's school. Was she all right?

"Aaron wouldn't say what's going on," Bethany said. "Mom's mad because he hung up on her."

Carter took out his phone. "Aaron will hang up on you, too," Bethany said.

He wasn't calling his brother. Instead, he punched in Mira's number. The call went straight to voicemail. She probably kept her phone off while she was teaching. He tried to come up with something to say that wouldn't sound too pushy, but words failed him.

The door to the office opened and his mother emerged. "I found out what's going on at the school," she said.

"What is it?" Carter asked.

"There's a bomb threat. Can you believe it?"

"Probably some kid who wanted to get out of a math test," Dalton said.

"What if it's real?"

Everyone stared at Carter. He shoved the Jeep keys at

Dalton. "You take the tour this morning," he said. "I have to get to the school."

He didn't wait for them to protest, or to tell him he had no business interfering. He had to make sure Mira was all right.

Chapter Seven

Mira stood with Shayla and half a dozen other teachers on the sidewalk across the street from the school. Administrators had given up trying to get the students to wait outside in orderly groups, especially after word of the bomb threat spread and their parents began arriving. They had dismissed classes for the day an hour ago. Most of the students had dispersed, leaving the staff to linger in the parking lot while a team called in from a neighboring county searched the building with dogs and electronics designed to detect explosives.

Shayla hugged her arms across her chest. "How much longer is this going to take?" she asked. "I wish I had thought to grab my purse and my keys."

"Someone said they're searching all the classrooms, offices and lockers," Mira said. "I guess that takes a while."

"If this turns out to be a prank, I hope they find who's responsible and make him do detention for a year," Shayla said.

"It must be a prank," Mira said. "Why would anyone want to blow up the school?"

"Why does anyone do anything awful?" Shayla asked. "Why did someone try to kidnap Bryce Atkinson?"

"Have you heard anything more about that?" Mira asked. "Have they found the kidnapper?"

"I have no idea," Shayla said.

"I thought maybe Mitch's dad had heard something on his police scanner."

"If he has, I haven't heard."

Something in her voice made Mira look at her more closely. "Is something wrong? You sound upset."

Shayla shook her head, eyes downcast. "It's nothing."

Mira nudged her. "You sure you don't want to talk?"

"It's so silly." She uncrossed her arms and shook her hands, as if trying to dry them. "I feel like I'm thirteen again."

Mira laughed. "That sounds like every relationship I've ever been in."

"I tried to work up the courage to ask Mitch out yesterday, but I couldn't do it," Shayla said. "And as I was stumbling over my words, he looked at me so oddly. He probably thinks I'm losing my mind."

"He was probably just distracted," Mira said. "He was worried about his father."

Shayla nodded, though she didn't look convinced.

"Mira!"

They turned to see Carter making his way through the crowd. He stopped in front of them, out of breath.

"What are you doing here?" Mira looked around. "Did someone call search and rescue?"

"It's just me," he said. "I heard there was a bomb threat at the school. I wanted to make sure you were okay."

The flutter in her chest at these words made her a little lightheaded. Her cheeks heated and she had to shift her gaze away from his face, so full of concern. For her. Over Carter's shoulder, Shayla stared at her, eyes wide, eyebrows raised. "Um, Shayla Green, this is Carter Ames." She managed the introduction with a calmness she didn't really feel.

"Nice to meet you, Carter," Shayla said. "That's so sweet of you to worry about Mira's safety."

He looked around at the crowd of teachers and administrators. "What's going on?" he asked. "Was there really a bomb?"

"There are people and dogs inside, searching," Mira said. "We haven't heard that they found anything yet."

"We're all waiting around until they allow us back inside to retrieve our belongings," Shayla said. She shifted from foot to foot. "Standing on this concrete is definitely getting old."

"Attention!" A muted rumble of a hundred shuffled feet rippled through the crowd as everyone turned toward the speaker at the front of the school. "The building has been cleared," a deep male voice intoned. "You may return to collect your belongings."

"Finally!"

"About time."

"Did they find anything?"

The crowd—and their crisscrossing conversations—surged toward the building. Mira moved in that direction, too, Carter at her side. They were at the bottom of the steps when the principal, Peter Martin, intercepted her. "Mira, can you come with me, please?" he asked.

As he spoke, Sheriff Walker and a man in a dark suit moved closer. "What is it?" Mira asked. "Is something wrong?"

"We need to ask you some questions," the dark-suited man said.

She felt faint again, but not in the heady, happy way she

had felt with Carter. Then his hand was on her arm, warm and steadying. "I'll come with you," she said.

"Who are you?" the man asked.

"I'm Carter Ames. Mira's friend. Who are you?"

"Detective Jameson Porter, Colorado Bureau of Investigation. We need to speak to Ms. Veronica alone."

"Am I under arrest?" she asked, panic rising.

Porter—a thin-faced man with piercing brown eyes—studied her a long moment before answering. "Not at this time."

"Then I'm not going anywhere alone with you," she said.

"Carter can come with her," the sheriff said.

Porter looked as if he wanted to argue, but pressed his lips together, turned and headed toward the school.

Mira and Carter followed, the sheriff and Principal Martin behind them. Carter still held her arm, his presence steadying her.

They passed a crowd of fellow teachers exiting the building and entered the principal's office. Principal Martin closed the door, shutting out the murmur of conversation in the halls. "Sit down, Mira." He indicated the two chairs in front of his desk. Mira sat in one, and Carter sat beside her. He had released his hold on her, but sat close enough that their legs were almost touching.

Detective Porter sat behind the desk. The sheriff stood against the wall behind him. Principal Martin leaned on a credenza to Mira's left. Porter reached beneath the desk and took out a paper bag. From the bag, he pulled a pair of boy's jeans. "Do you recognize these?" he asked.

Mira stared at the jeans. They were definitely a child's, with scuffed knees and one frayed hem. "No. Do they belong to one of the students?"

"They were found in the bottom desk drawer in your

classroom," Porter said. "Do you still say you don't recognize them?"

"No. How did they get into my desk? Did a student put them there?" But why would someone do that?

"They belong to Bryce Atkinson," Porter said. "He was wearing them yesterday when someone grabbed him off the street, shoved him into a car, restrained him, and removed the jeans and his shoes. Now would you like to tell us how they came to be in your possession."

"If they were in her drawer, they weren't in her possession," Carter said. "Anyone could have put those there. The classroom wasn't locked, was it?"

"No," Mira said, before Porter could speak. "My class isn't locked. And I don't know how those pants ended up in that drawer. I don't even know Bryce. He's not in any of my classes. As far as I know, he doesn't even go to this school."

"I'm the person who found Bryce," Carter said. "After he escaped from his kidnappers, I was part of the search and rescue volunteers looking for him up above Galloway Basin. He told me he was pretty sure the person who grabbed him was a man."

"He didn't get a good look at his kidnapper," Porter said. "They wore a mask and gloves." He looked at Mira. "You're what, about five-seven?"

"Five-eight," she said.

"To a panicked boy, you could look taller."

"I didn't have anything to do with Bryce's kidnapping," she said.

"Where were you yesterday afternoon between three and four thirty?" Sheriff Walker asked.

"I was here at the school," she said. "In my classroom."

"Classes are over at three o'clock," Principal Martin said.

"I was working on lesson plans," she said.

"Did anyone else see you there at that time?" Porter asked.

"Yes. A student—Camila Sepulveda—came to talk to me about an extra-credit project she's working on. Then Shayla Green came and we talked for a few minutes. Then Coach Anders came and told us about Bryce being kidnapped."

Porter showed little change of expression. "Have you seen anyone near your classroom who shouldn't be there?" he asked.

"No."

"Does this have anything to do with the bomb threat?" Carter asked.

Porter said nothing.

"Was there a bomb?" Mira asked. "Did you find anything besides these jeans?"

"There was no bomb," the sheriff said.

"Maybe someone called in the threat so that you would have to search the school and find these pants," Carter said. "Someone who wanted to implicate Mira."

"Why would someone want to implicate Mira?" Porter asked.

Carter turned to her. "I think you should tell them about the letters," he said.

She wanted to protest. The letters were an annoyance. They weren't serious. But this—Bryce's jeans in her desk—was serious. What if she had been alone in her classroom during that time? Would she be on her way to jail now?

"What letters?" Porter asked.

"Someone has been sending anonymous notes to people around town," she said. "I've received two of them."

Porter looked back at Travis. "What kind of notes?"

"They accuse people of petty crimes," Travis said. "Or nonexistent crimes. Everything from unleashed dogs to failing to bring in their trash cans from the curb." He looked at Mira. "You said you received two notes?"

"Yes. One was left on the front seat of my car here at school. The second was tacked to the front door of my apartment a couple of days later."

"What do these notes say?" Porter asked.

She sighed. "It's a long story."

"We have time," Porter said.

MIRA TOLD THE lawmen and the principal the same story she had related to Carter, about David Ketchum's disappearance and death, and the anonymous letter writer's implication that she was somehow involved in the crime. "I had nothing to do with David or his death," she said. "Like everyone else, I thought he had run away or gotten lost. I was shocked when his body was found. I was never a suspect. I was never even questioned by law enforcement."

"If they had questioned you, what would you have told them?" Porter asked.

"He was one student in my twice-weekly elementary school classes," she said. "A friendly, bright boy with a nice smile. I didn't know much about him or his family. What happened to him was horrible but I have no idea who was responsible."

"Why would someone write notes to you about it?" Porter asked.

"I don't know," she said. "I've lain awake nights trying to figure that out."

"Whoever is writing these notes obviously likes to harass people," Carter said. "I thought maybe they found out Mira was from Santa Fe, remembered the crime and decided to connect her with it. Not because she did anything wrong, but because they knew it would be unsettling and, well, mean."

"But now someone is trying to connect me with another child's kidnapping," she said.

"Who is upset with you?" Porter asked. "A parent whose child you flunked, a former student you gave a bad grade, or a neighbor you argued with over a parking spot?"

She shook her head. "Nothing like that. I've only been in Eagle Mountain less than a month."

"Why did you leave Santa Fe?" Porter asked.

"I'd lived there all my life. I wanted a change. And this was a good opportunity. Eagle Mountain is beautiful."

Carter sensed her nervousness, so that he felt jumpy himself. He wanted to protest they should stop hassling her, now. Couldn't they see she hadn't done anything wrong?

"Is there anyone in Eagle Mountain who you knew in Santa Fe?" Travis asked.

"No one," she said. "And everyone I've met here has been really nice." She didn't look at Carter, but he hoped she was thinking of him when she said this.

"Have you seen these notes?" Porter asked Carter.

"I have," Carter said. "They look just like the other notes I've seen that other people in town have received. Printed on a half sheet of plain white paper. A short message, unsigned. They don't accuse Mira of anything specific, just a connection with David—no last name, just David."

"We'll need to see the notes," Porter said.

"You can come to my apartment and get them," she said. "Or I can bring them to the sheriff tomorrow."

"Bring them to the sheriff's department as soon as you can," Travis said.

"Can I go now?" Mira asked. She looked utterly drained.

"You can go," Porter said. "We'll be in touch if we have more questions."

Carter stood and offered his hand to help her up. She

didn't take it, but when she was standing, she leaned toward him slightly. They exited the office together. She waited until they were out of the building before she spoke. "Thanks for coming in there with me," she said.

"You're not angry I told them about the letters?"

"No. I should have told them before, I guess. It's just..."

"You hoped if you ignored the letter writer, the harassment would stop," he said.

"Yes." She gripped his arm. "Do you think the same person sent those letters and put those pants in my desk drawer?"

"If it was the same person, that means they kidnapped Bryce," Carter said. "It's the only way they would have those jeans."

"Then does that mean they killed David Ketchum, too?"

"Not necessarily," he said. "Maybe they just heard about David's case and wanted to commit a similar crime. They thought throwing suspicion on you would make it easier for them to get away with it."

She stopped and closed her eyes, face pale. "Thank God Bryce escaped. But what if they try again?"

"Everyone is on guard now," Carter said. "We have to hope the cops can stop him. Obviously, the state is also involved now."

They continued walking to her car. She looked around the almost empty parking lot. "How did you get here?" she asked.

"I walked." Ran, really, but she didn't need to know that.

"I can give you a ride to wherever you need to be."

"That would be great. I should probably get back to the office." Though he didn't look forward to the lecture his mother would likely give him for running out on a tour.

As Mira pulled into the parking space nearest the entrance to Alpine Jeep Rental, Bethany emerged. She hurried to meet Carter as he exited Mira's rental car. "Where did you disappear to?" she asked. "Dalton had to take your ten o'clock tour and Mom is furious. Oh, hello, Mira." She looked from Carter to Mira and back again, clearly curious.

Carter leaned back into the car to address Mira. "Thanks for the ride," he said. "Are you going to be okay?"

"I'm better now," she said. "Thanks. For everything." She shifted the car into reverse. "I'll see you Monday night."

"Monday night?" Had they made a date he'd forgotten?

"At class."

Right. Class. She smiled and he felt the full force of the look. She made him feel more like a real hero than any praise anyone else could have heaped on him.

Chapter Eight

Mira explained her absence from school during her off-period Monday by saying she had an appointment for a checkup. No one wanted to hear details of her visit to her gynecologist, but news that she had a meeting with the sheriff would cause talk for days. She had called the sheriff's department Saturday morning to arrange to give the accusing notes to him, and learned he was away until Monday. She had decided to wait. She wasn't comfortable handing the notes over to just anyone, but trusted the sheriff to keep them confidential.

She was surprised that no one had commented on her closed-door session with Sheriff Walker and the CBI agent Friday afternoon, but it seems that in the rush to collect their belongings and leave school after the bomb threat, no one had noticed. Principal Martin had apparently said nothing, either. For that, she was grateful.

"I brought some letters the sheriff wanted to see," she told the woman at the reception desk at the sheriff's department.

"Mira Veronica?" The woman sized up Mira from behind red-framed bifocals. "Sheriff Walker has been expecting you."

The woman rose and ushered Mira through a locked door

and down a short hallway to a door marked Sheriff Walker and knocked. "Come in," Travis Walker said.

The woman opened the door. "Ms. Veronica is here." She glanced at Mira with an unreadable expression—not exactly hostile, but not friendly, either—then left.

"Come in, Mira," Travis said. He looked up from behind an almost spotless desk, empty except for a laptop, a neat stack of file folders and a photograph of a smiling woman with twin toddlers.

"I have the letters you wanted to see," she said, as she perched on the edge of the chair across from him.

He took the sheets she offered and spread them on his desk in front of him. "Do they look like others people have received?" she asked.

"They appear similar." His gaze met hers, his expression stern. "After speaking with you Friday, I did some research on David Ketchum's case."

"Is there any new information?" she asked. "Do they know who killed him?"

"No. When we spoke to you Friday, you failed to mention you were connected with George Suarez."

For a split second, she couldn't breathe. Her heart beat as hard as if she had run a race, but she couldn't move. "I... I'm not connected with George," she stammered. "He... he's a terrible person."

"You were living with him when David Ketchum disappeared."

"Yes. But that was before...before I knew what he was really like." She stared at her hands, knotted in her lap, unable to look the sheriff in the eye anymore. Shame—the emotion she always associated with George—swamped her, along with all the old questions to which there were no answers. How could she have been so blind? How could she have not seen what he was really like?

"When was the last time you spoke to Mr. Suarez?" Travis asked.

"The day he was arrested." She would never forget watching the police officers handcuff her lover and lead him away, while another group of officers carted away their computers and a safe, which she later learned were full of horrible recordings of child pornography. Thinking about it sickened her. "I didn't know he was doing those awful things," she protested. "I never would have been with him if I had. I did everything I could to help the police with their investigation." She had surrendered her own phone and computer and allowed investigators to comb through all her personal belongings. The experience had been a nightmare she might not have survived if not for the support of family and friends who rallied around and believed her innocence. Her ignorance.

"After his arrest, Suarez was questioned about David Ketchum's murder. But he had an alibi."

She nodded, but couldn't speak around the knot in her throat.

"You were his alibi," Travis said.

She tried to clear her throat. "I told the truth," she said. "Not because I wanted to protect George. I didn't. He deserved every punishment for what he did. But I told the truth. He couldn't have killed David because he was with me."

"Did you leave Santa Fe because of George Suarez?" Travis asked.

"Partly." She forced herself to lift her head and meet his gaze. She shouldn't act like a guilty person. She hadn't done anything wrong. Except falling for a pedophile who contributed to the exploitation of innocent children. "I had family and friends who stood by me after George was arrested. The school district kept me in my job. I could have stayed in Santa Fe. But people would always remember what happened. And there were parents who I knew didn't trust me with their children. I thought it would be better to start over. Then I received these letters…" She gestured toward the notes laid out on Travis's desk and blinked back burning tears.

"Have you heard from George Suarez at all since his arrest?" Travis asked. "Has he tried to contact you?"

"Right after he was taken into custody he called a few times and left messages protesting his innocence and asking for my help." She shook her head. "I saw the videos the police seized. I mean, I saw the titles and the pictures on some of the covers. I saw a few files they showed me on his computer. Those weren't things an innocent man would own." And she remembered signs she had previously ignored that all wasn't right—how he would lock himself in his home office, sometimes for hours late at night. He didn't even like her going into his office and his computer was protected with multiple layers of passwords. She had even joked to a friend that maybe George worked for the CIA, he was so security-conscious.

She had been so naive, truly blinded by love. Or what she thought was love.

"Do you think George Suarez could have sent these notes?" Travis asked.

"No! He's in prison."

Travis shook his head. "He was paroled in April. At this time, no one knows where he is. I'm wondering if he came to Eagle Mountain."

"Isn't he supposed to be supervised?" she asked, alarmed.

"Like, register as a sex offender and check in with a parole officer?"

"He's supposed to do those things, but he hasn't. Have you seen anyone in town who might be him?"

"No." The idea appalled her. She didn't want George Suarez anywhere near her.

The sheriff said nothing. Did he think she was lying? "If I thought George had anything to do with these notes or Bryce's kidnapping or David's murder, I would tell you," she said.

"Are you afraid of George Suarez?" Travis asked. "Did he ever threaten you?"

Was she physically afraid of George? "No," she admitted. "He was never violent or threatening." He had been a very gentle man. A kind and considerate boyfriend. Thoughtful and quiet, with good manners. Which had made the extent of his crimes that much more shocking. "I don't think George is a violent person," she said. "For all his…perversions… I don't think he would kill someone. But I never thought he would be attracted to children that way, either." She had been closer to George than she had ever been to anyone and to discover she hadn't known his true self at all had made her doubt everything.

Travis folded the letters and slipped them into a folder. "We'll keep these with the other letters people have turned in," he said. "Let us know if you receive any others."

"Did you find out who called in that bomb threat?" she asked.

"No. We looked at security camera footage at the school and we didn't see anyone acting suspiciously before the call came in. No visitors we couldn't identify."

She stood, anxious to be out of there. "I have to get back to school," she said.

He rose also. "Thank you for coming in."

He walked with her to the lobby, and watched as she left the building. The sheriff had a good reputation as a by-the-book lawman and a family man. He hadn't accused her of a crime or said anything to make her think he didn't believe her. She knew she hadn't done anything wrong.

Then why did she feel so guilty?

"Thanks, Carter. That was a terrific tour." The big man from Texas—six feet seven inches tall, not including the cowboy hat—pressed a twenty-dollar bill into Carter's hand and grinned. "We all had a great time."

"Thanks." Carter slipped the tip into his pocket. "Come back anytime."

"Hey, Carter!" The man's oldest son, a freckle-faced ten-year-old, held up a hand and Carter gave him a high five.

"You were a great copilot, buddy," Carter said.

The boy grinned, revealing braces threaded with purple rubber bands.

A middle-aged blonde approached and offered another twenty. "Thank you for the great tour," she said. "We promise to give you a good review online."

"Thanks, I appreciate it," he said. Good reviews were good for business, Mom and Dalton said.

Everyone made their way to their cars. He collected empty water bottles and refolded blankets, then drove the Jeep around to the back. It would be washed, checked and refueled before the next trip. His father was in front of the garage, bent over the engine compartment of one of their older vehicles. As Carter approached, he straightened and lowered the hood. "I think I've figured out the problem," Dad said. "I just need to order the part."

"That's great, Dad." Carter wished he had his dad's mechanical aptitude. He could change oil and do basic stuff, but the workings of engines were a mystery to him.

He returned the Jeep's keys to the pegboard in the office. Dalton and Bethany were both huddled over the computer. "What's up?" Carter asked.

"Dalton's showing me this new module he developed for the reservation system," she said. "It identifies people who left positive reviews for past tours and sends them an offer for a 10 percent discount on a new tour. It's already generating repeat business."

"I showed it to Ian and he's talking about switching the via ferrata over to using this system," Dalton said. The climbing route was Eagle Mountain's newest tourist attraction. "He's going to help me pitch it to other tourism businesses in the area as a comprehensive reservation and marketing package. It could really take off."

"You'll be a tech billionaire before you know it," Carter said.

The door opened and the UPS driver entered. "Got a package for you, Bethany," he said, and handed over a flat cardboard box.

"Thanks, Gary." She accepted the package. "It's my veil." She picked up a pair of scissors and by the time the door closed on the driver, she had the package open. She folded back layers of tissue paper and lifted out a silver tiara of sculpted leaves and flowers, from which cascaded a cloud of filmy gauze. "It's so beautiful!" she exclaimed, her eyes shiny.

Carter was surprised to feel a little choked up himself. What had been an abstract concept that didn't really affect him—his sister's wedding—now felt very real. "You'll be beautiful in it," he managed to say, his voice breaking only slightly.

She startled him by throwing her arms around him and hugging him tightly. He patted her back. "I can't believe my little sister is getting married," he said.

She struggled out of his arm. "I'm older than you."

"But you're so much shorter." He patted the top of her head.

She packed the veil carefully away in its shroud of tissue. "So what's going on with you and Mira Veronica?" she asked.

"Something's going on with Carter and Mira?" Dalton looked up from the computer.

He shoved his hands in the pockets of his jeans. "We're friends."

"More than friends, judging by the way you raced out of here when we heard about the bomb threat at the school," Dalton said.

"She's made it pretty clear she's only interested in friendship." He was trying to respect that, though it wasn't easy.

"You finally found a woman you couldn't charm?" Dalton winced. "That must be a blow to your ego."

"My ego can take it." He didn't want to charm Mira. Or seduce her. Well, he might want to seduce her, but not in a "let's just have fun and not get serious" way. Mira meant something to him, though he couldn't put the feelings into words. She was smart and funny and beautiful and…and someone had hurt her. He felt that hurt and wished he could make things right.

"Have you been practicing your Spanish for tonight's class?" Bethany asked.

"*Sí, señorita.*" Carter grinned. That was what people expected of him—jokes and clowning. It worked with the tourists and most of the time it worked with his family, too.

He had been trying to show Mira a different side, but he

wasn't sure he was succeeding. Maybe there really wasn't much more to him than a dazzling smile and corny jokes. That had felt like enough before, but not for a woman like her.

AT MONDAY NIGHT'S Spanish class, Mira was pleased to note that only one student had dropped out after the first week. She took this as a good indication that people found the course useful and even enjoyable. And almost as important to her, it meant her portion of the fee would be almost enough for the down payment on a new car she was going to need, now that her insurance company had decided her Toyota was totaled.

Carter was one of the last to arrive. She was embarrassed that she had been watching for him. Embarrassed because she didn't want anyone to see how interested she was in him. And she didn't *want* to be interested in him. She didn't want to get involved with anyone. Not right now.

"Hey, Mira." He slid into a chair at the front of the class. The same one he had occupied before. Right where there was no way she could avoid seeing him. "How are you doing?"

"I'm fine," she said. A lie. She had been a wreck since being questioned by the sheriff, afraid that other people in town would hear about her connection to a convicted pedophile. The association was horrible for anyone, but especially for someone who worked with children every day. And to be accused of being connected to the kidnapping of not one, but two boys on top of that—she might have to leave town if that came out.

Carter was still watching her. Did he see the dark circles beneath her eyes that she had tried to cover with makeup? Or the tension that never left her shoulders these days? She avoided his gaze and addressed the class. "*Hola,*" she said. "*Buenos tardes. Cómo están todos?*"

"*Bueno,*" they answered, or "*Estoy bien.*"

"*Excellente!*" This last from Carter. Of course. He grinned at her and she fought back a smile.

She continued with the lesson. This evening, they were focusing on communicating instructions to people in an emergency. They practiced how to say things like "Please calm down."

"Are you hurt?"

"Where are you hurt?"

"Wait here."

"Help is on the way."

"Keep your hands where I can see them" and "Pay attention."

"What do I do if I ask someone where they're hurt and they reply with a barrage of words I can't understand?" one of the search and rescue volunteers, Caleb, asked.

"You can ask them to speak more slowly," she said. "*Hable lento, por favor.* Or you could ask them to show you what hurts. So *¿Dónde le duele?*—where does it hurt?—with *muéstrame*—show me. *Muéstrame dónde le duele.*"

"*Muéstrame dónde le duele,*" the class dutifully repeated.

They broke into groups to practice scenarios, using worksheets she handed out. "Why couldn't we just use a translation program on our phones?" one of the firefighters asked.

"You could," she said. "Those apps can be very useful. But what if you're in an area with no cell coverage? Or what if you need to act quickly? If you find someone in a burning building do you really have time to dig out your phone and use it? Wouldn't it be better to know how to tell someone to come with you? *Ven conmigo!*"

"I guess so." He looked down at the worksheet. "I'm not sure I'll remember any of this in an emergency."

"Keep practicing. That will help, I promise."

For the duration of the class, at least, Mira didn't think about Bryce or David or the unfounded accusations against her. The two hours raced by. Everyone seemed surprised when she announced their time was up.

Carter lingered after everyone else had left. Mira pretended not to see him and busied herself gathering papers. "I was wondering if you'd like to go out for a drink," he said. "Or ice cream?"

"Thanks," she said. "But I need to get home."

"Are you okay?" he asked. "You look tired."

"I haven't been sleeping well."

"Did you give those notes to the sheriff?"

"Yes."

"What did he say?"

She stiffened. Had he heard something? "Nothing much."

"Did he think they looked like the other notes?"

"Yes. He said they were similar."

"I asked my brother if they had any suspects in Bryce's kidnapping. He wouldn't say, but I got the impression they haven't come up with anything."

She nodded. The silence between them stretched and she gave up pretending to organize her papers and simply stared at the desk, waiting for him to leave. Something mechanical kicked on and made a distant low hum. With every breath Mira inhaled, she took in the scent of Carter's shaving cream or soap—clean and woodsy. Masculine.

He leaned closer, his voice gentle. "Have I done something to upset you?" he asked.

She shook her head. "No."

"You just…you won't even look at me."

The real anguish in his voice startled her. The last thing she wanted to do was hurt this man. Carter had been a real friend to her. "You haven't done anything," she said. "You've been wonderful. It's just… I'm dealing with a lot right now."

"You don't have to go through whatever it is alone."

But she did. How could she trust anyone else to understand? "I'll be fine. Right now I just need time." Though it wasn't as if more days or months or even years were going to change the past.

His phone buzzed. He pulled it from his pocket and looked at the screen. "It's search and rescue," he said. "I have to go."

"Be careful," she said.

"I always am." He shrugged. "I know I come across as not taking things seriously sometimes. But mostly, that's just an act. I'm a lot more serious than most people think." He tucked the phone away. "See you later."

When he was gone, she sat at the desk and thought about what he had said. It was true—when they first met she had dismissed him as a flirt who was used to women falling at his feet. Someone who relied on charm to coast through life. But when he responded to her accident on Dixon Pass, she had seen a different side of him. Was everyone like this— with a facade that made them seem one way, and a reality that was completely different? If that was so, how was she supposed to form an accurate impression of anyone?

Chapter Nine

"It's Helen Wakefield again," Danny told the search and rescue volunteers who answered the summons. "She told the daughter she lives with that she was going to her room to watch TV, but when her son-in-law looked in on her two hours later, the room was empty. The TV was on, the sound turned up, but Helen was nowhere in the house. The back door was unlocked and he is sure he locked it right after supper. They believe Helen went outside and wandered off. She's done it before and they usually find her a short distance away, but this time they searched everywhere they could think of with no sign of her, so they called 911."

"I guess they checked the neighbors' house, where they found her last time they called us?" Tony asked.

"They did," Danny said. "No one has seen her. The sheriff's department is doing a house-to-house search in the neighborhood. They need us to concentrate on the undeveloped areas—vacant lots, mountain slopes and ravines."

They had searched the same areas before, only this time it was after dark, in an area with little residual illumination from streetlamps or even house lights. The neighborhood they were in had been built according to dark sky principles, which meant light was confined to a very narrow space. This made for great stargazing, but difficulties maneuvering rocky, uneven terrain.

As Carter joined Vince and Bethany in searching their assigned area, he thought of the hundred ways there were to get hurt out here, from tripping over a tree root to tumbling down a ravine, to being attacked by a mountain lion. Someone who loved Helen Wakefield was probably thinking of all of that right now, too, and depending on this group of strangers to save her.

"Do you remember Grandma Russo?" Bethany asked as he followed her up a set of half-buried logs someone had long ago set as steps up a slope behind the Wakefield house. At every step twigs or dried pine cones crunched under their feet. He tried not to think about falling and to search on either side for Helen. They might pass right by her without seeing her in this darkness.

Carter had a vague memory of a tiny, white-haired woman confined to a bed in a nursing home. "Not really," he said.

"She babysat us a few times before she had to go in the care home," Bethany said. "You and Dalton were still tiny. Just crawling. I thought she was so funny because she'd give us ice cream for lunch or put your diapers on backward. And she'd call us by the wrong names. I was always Diane and Aaron was Don."

"Diane is Mom's name," he said.

"Right. And Don is her older brother, Uncle Don. Grandma thought that's who we were. Not too long after that she had to go into memory care. It was so sad."

"Let's hope we don't have a sad ending for this family," Vince said. "Or not any sadder than it already is."

At the top of the slope they were on a high ridge. They stopped and looked back the way they had come. Carter could make out the roof of the house where Helen lived. He cupped his hands around his mouth. "Helen!" he shouted. "Helen, are you okay?"

They walked east along the ridge, alternately calling and sweeping the beams of powerful flashlights across the landscape, looking for a flash of Helen's white hair or the pink sweat suit her daughter had told them she was wearing. They could hear other groups of searchers around them doing the same.

The ridge began to climb higher, merging with an even steeper slope. At the base of this slope they met with half a dozen other searchers. "We've found her," Tony said. "She's standing on a rock at the edge of a ravine. When we tried to get closer, she started throwing rocks at us."

"She hit me." Ryan wiped at a muddy smudge on his cheek. "For a woman that age, she's got a pretty good aim."

"We had to back off way over here before she calmed down," Carrie said.

"What do we do now?" Bethany asked.

"We're waiting for her daughter and son-in-law to see if they can talk her down," Tony said.

Crunching leaves and snapping twigs announced the arrival of the family members, bent practically doubled as they scrambled up the slope, flanked by two sheriff's deputies. "Where is she?" Helen's daughter asked. She was a fifty-something woman with long dark hair streaked with gray and a round face.

"She's on a ledge above a ravine," Tony said.

"Let's move a little closer so you can talk to her," Deputy Jake Gwynn suggested. Jake was also a SAR volunteer.

He and Shane escorted the couple to within a few yards of Helen, who stood leaning back against the rocks. A flashlight beam held by one of the deputies illuminated the new arrivals. Helen turned to face them. "What are you doing here?" she asked.

"Mom, please come down and come to bed," the woman called.

"Go home and mind your own business." This was followed by a rock, which whizzed close by the daughter's right ear.

"Mom, stop that nonsense!" the son-in-law shouted.

Her response was another rock. This one hit the son-in-law in the chest.

"Mom!" the daughter shrieked.

Helen laughed, an eerie, hoarse sound. She held up both arms and executed what Carter thought must be a victory dance, but stumbled and slid perilously close to the edge. "Be careful!" someone shouted—perhaps one of the other volunteers, or one of the neighbors who had gathered below to witness the scene.

"Look what you made me do!" Helen shouted. "Are you trying to kill me? Go away!"

"Mom, come down from there!" the daughter tried again. "You're going to get hurt."

"I was fine until you showed up."

Jake moved in and said something to the daughter. Her husband put his arm around her and the two, along with Jake and Shane, made their way back down the slope. "Let's give her a chance to calm down," Jake told Tony when they were even with him.

"It's past her bedtime," the daughter said. "If we leave her in peace, maybe she'll lie down and go to sleep and you can slip up there and grab her."

"I don't like the sound of that," Tony said. "She might startle or wake up suddenly and fall. It would be better if we could talk her into coming down on her own."

"She won't come to me," the daughter said. "She's too angry."

"What is she angry about?" Jake asked.

"I told her I wanted to visit a new senior living facility in Junction. I told her they were having an open house and I had heard it was very nice. I was hoping that would start a conversation, or that Mom would even like the place enough to consider moving there. But she read it as we want to put her away in a home tomorrow. She's got it into her head that I'm going to take her up there and leave her and she's not having it." She sighed. "I remind myself that she's just speaking out of fear, but it's hard sometimes, when she says mean things to me."

She started to cry and her husband put his arm around her. "Come on," he said. "Let's get where she can't see us and let her calm down." He led her away.

Tony was on the radio with Danny. He ended the transmission and turned to the volunteers. "We need to get most of the volunteers down and out of sight," he said. "We'll keep a couple of people up here to watch her, maybe try to have another conversation in a bit."

Carter approached Tony. "Could I try talking to her?" he asked.

Tony didn't answer right away. "You really think she'd listen to you?"

"I have an idea. I won't get too close to her, I promise. And if she gets upset or throws rocks, I'll retreat right away."

Tony looked over his shoulder at Helen, who was still on the ledge, a slim silhouette that appeared to be watching them. "Let me check with Danny and the sheriff," he said, and moved a few feet away to make the call.

Carter moved into the shadow of a boulder, his eyes still on Helen. He tried to put himself in her shoes—confused, afraid of being forced from her home. Terrified of losing herself.

Tony returned. "You can give it a try. But don't try to approach her. See if you can get her to come to you."

He nodded. "Somebody put a light on me so she can see me," he said.

Someone switched on a portable spotlight that illuminated a somewhat flat stretch of ground halfway up the slope, about the size of an apartment patio. Hands in his pockets, Carter strolled into this light. He had performed in some drama class productions in high school. This felt somewhat the same, like being on a stage, the lights making it impossible to see the audience. But so much more depended this time on him making a good performance.

He studied the ground and kicked at a rock, pretending to look for something.

"Who are you?" Helen called after a few seconds.

"I'm Carter."

"What do you want?"

"I'm looking for something."

"What are you looking for?"

"I think I dropped some money out here."

"That was careless of you."

"Yeah. I'm like that sometimes." He leaned down and pretended to pick something off the ground.

"What did you find?" she asked.

"A quarter. Do you want to see?" He held up a quarter he had palmed from his pocket.

"Don't come any closer," she shouted. "You can't trick me."

"I wouldn't dream of it." He crouched and continued to study the ground.

"How much money did you lose?" Helen asked.

"Around fifteen dollars." He tried for a sum that might be enticing, but not too large. "Lots of change and some loose bills."

"You shouldn't be so careless," she said.

"I know. My mother tells me the same thing all the time." True. He reached forward and pretended to pick up something. "I found a dollar bill." He hoped the combination of dim light and aging eyesight would keep her from seeing he had lied.

She moved to the edge of the ledge and leaned over for a look. He rose. "Be careful," he said. "It's a long way down if you fall."

She looked alarmed and stepped back.

"Do you want to help me look?" he asked. "I'll give you part of the money."

"How much?"

"How about whatever you find, up to five dollars."

"If it's lying on the ground, you can't prove the money is yours," she said. "Finders keepers."

"Then you might as well come look for it and not let someone else claim it," he said.

In answer, she moved carefully off the ledge. She stepped onto a faintly discernable trail and walked toward him, watching the ground and moving carefully. When she was still six feet away, she stopped. "You don't try anything," she said.

"I won't," he promised. He returned to his pretend survey of the ground, while watching her out of the corner of his eye. She was bent over, hands on her knees, staring intently at the leaf litter.

"I need a flashlight," she said. "Can't see anything in this dim light."

"I have one you can use." He reached into a side pocket

of his pack and felt for the flashlight. She started forward, hand outstretched.

Then she was falling, landing sprawled in the leaf litter. Heart racing, he rushed to meet her. "Helen, are you all right?" he asked.

"I tripped." She tried to push herself up, but didn't have the strength.

"Lie still," Carter said, one hand resting lightly on her shoulder. "I have some people with me who can help." He looked back toward his fellow team members and raised an arm to motion them forward.

Five minutes later Helen, unharmed except for a skinned knee, was reunited with her family. "A person can't even go for a walk without everyone making a fuss," she groused.

"Mom, you scared us," her daughter scolded. "Please don't do that again."

"As if you never scared me," Helen said. "That time you rode the Simpsons' mare bareback and tried to jump that fence. Broke your arm in two places."

The daughter looked puzzled. "I never did anything like that."

"You always were a terrible liar, Frances. And I got in trouble, too, because I was supposed to be watching you when you ran off to the horse."

The daughter glanced up at her husband. "She's talking about her sister, Frances. She's been gone twenty years now."

They led Helen away and the searchers made their way back toward their vehicles. Danny caught up with Carter. "That was smart, pretending to look for money and inviting her to help," he said. "How did you come up with that?"

He shrugged. "I knew I needed to distract her and get her away from that ledge. I thought I'd give it a try."

"You talked Bryce Atkinson into coming out of hiding, too," Danny said. "You have a real knack for it."

"Maybe you need to become a cop like your brother and go into hostage negotiations," Vince said.

"Or become a politician." Dalton punched his twin's shoulder. "Who knew your gift of gab could be so useful?"

Carter laughed along with the rest of them but inside he was still unsteady. Helen could have fallen off that ledge when she stood to see what he was doing. And when she did fall while standing near him, he had been sure she would snap a bone or hit her head on a rock. Maybe his words had helped, but he had also potentially put her in more danger. And now everyone was laughing as if what he had done were a joke. A clever trick. All he had done was talk. Something most people learned to do as toddlers. It wasn't a skill like treating wounds, scaling cliffs, solving crimes or writing computer programs. Talking was an ordinary, sometimes even annoying, thing. Just like him.

THE WEEK PASSED QUICKLY. When no new notes showed up and no one else wanted to talk to her about Bryce or David, Mira began to relax a little. She taught the Spanish class on Wednesday and spoke briefly with Carter, but he didn't ask her out again. She was annoyed at herself for being so disappointed that a guy who was a self-confessed flirt wasn't flirting with her.

By Friday, almost one week since Bryce's abduction and escape, there were no new developments and everyone's interest appeared to have moved on to other things. "You're going to be at the barbecue tomorrow, right?" Shayla stopped Mira in the school's main hallway after lunch. While they talked, students flowed around them, their voices an excited hum, like bees around a hive on a sunny day.

"Barbecue?" Mira blinked, trying to remember.

"The school boosters annual fundraiser?"

"Isn't that, like, for the public? Parents and townspeople?"

"Teachers are expected to be there." Shayla made a face. "I have to be there. My mother is the booster president this year. So please tell me you'll come. I need the moral support."

Mira had no plans for Saturday. And it would probably look good for the newest teacher to show up and mingle. "Okay. I'll come."

Shayla brightened. She moved in closer and lowered her voice. "I'm going to introduce Mitch to my parents," she said. "Not as my boyfriend, or anything, just… I want to see what they think of him."

"Have you two been on a date yet?" Mira asked.

"We shared a concession stand burger after the junior varsity track meet last night." She beamed as if she was talking about a lobster dinner at a fancy restaurant.

"Hot date," Mira said, amused.

"I'm not sure he even saw it as a date, but it's a start." She shifted her book bag to her other shoulder. "I'm going to suggest we skip out early on the barbecue and catch a movie or something."

"After he meets your parents?"

"I figure we'll both want to get away after that, so why not escape together?"

"Then I'm happy to help you," Mira said. They began walking again, toward their respective classrooms. "If you need me to distract your mom and dad while you make your getaway, I promise to spill my tea or drop a plate of food or some other distraction."

"Thanks." She nudged Mira. "So tell me about Carter."

Mira kept her expression neutral. "What about him?"

"He's really good-looking. How did you two meet?"

"He's with search and rescue. He's taking the Spanish for First Responders class I'm teaching."

"Uh-huh. And why haven't I heard about him before now? You've never mentioned him."

"We're not dating," Mira said. "He's just a friend."

"A friend who ran across town to make sure you were okay when he heard about the bomb threat."

"It wasn't across town. It was only a few blocks. I'm sure he was just curious."

"The way he looked at you wasn't curiosity, it was concern." Shayla elbowed her again. "You should ask him out."

Mira shook her head.

"Why not? You told me that's what I should do."

"I'm not interested in getting involved with anyone," Mira said.

Shayla's expression sobered. "Nothing wrong with that. But you should tell Carter that. Just in case he's getting the wrong message."

"I've told him. We agreed to be just friends."

"Does that ever really work?"

"Men and women can be friends," Mira said.

"Sure they can," Shayla agreed. "If both of them are on the same page about their feelings. But I think Carter might be more into you than you realize."

And I might be more into him than I'm ready to admit. They reached the door of Mira's classroom. "I'll see you at the barbecue tomorrow," she said. She could stand back and cheer on Shayla and Mitch's romance without worrying about one of her own.

Mira entered her classroom. A couple of students were already there, standing just inside the door and staring at the whiteboard behind her desk.

"Ms. Veronica, it was like that when we came in," one of the students, Douglas Graham, said. An earnest kid with brownish-red hair, his skin was so pale right now his freckles stood out like sprinkled cinnamon.

Mira followed his gaze to the foot-high letters scrawled in red marker on the board and gasped. *Kid killer*, the message read, marker smeared below it like dripping blood.

Chapter Ten

"No one is supposed to enter the building without a pass," Principal Martin's voice shook as he spoke to Deputy Ryker Vernon. "To enter any door but the main one requires an electronic key card that is only issued to staff. The front entrance has a camera and a metal detector everyone must pass through. Visitors then have to check in with the front office and receive a pass. That goes for parents, spouses or local dignitaries. No exceptions."

"No one asked me to check in at the office when I arrived," Ryker said.

The principal glared at him. "This is not the time for sarcasm, Deputy."

"I wasn't being sarcastic. I'm assuming someone dressed like a law enforcement officer could enter unchallenged."

"No one reported seeing a law enforcement officer in the halls today," Principal Martin said. "And we have a camera on that door. You can check it."

"Do any of the other doors have cameras?"

"The back door to the gym and the outside door to the cafeteria."

"How many unmonitored doors are there?"

"Half a dozen? But they all require the electronic key card."

"Has anyone reported their card missing?" Ryker asked.

"Not that I know of, but I'll check."

"Please do." Ryker turned to Mira. She had been seated at her desk, her back to the damning message, stunned. Her two students had been sent to the office to wait for their parents to arrive. After that, they would be questioned, but they had already said the classroom had been empty when they arrived, and they hadn't seen anyone out of place in the halls.

"Do you know of anyone who could have written this message?" he asked. "A student or another teacher?"

"No." She glanced at Principal Martin. "No one else knows about the anonymous letters I received, or Bryce's pants being found in my desk."

"Someone could have leaked that information," Ryker said.

"I suppose." She looked at the principal. He certainly knew about the pants.

"I haven't said a word to anyone," he said. He eyed the whiteboard. "We need to clean this up. We canceled the fourth period Spanish I class but we need this room for the rest of the day."

"It would be better to move to another classroom until we can get this processed," Ryker said. "And we'll need the footage from all the door cameras. We should talk to the students, too, and try to determine if any of them saw anyone suspicious around this classroom while Ms. Veronica was at lunch."

"We have almost a hundred students enrolled," he said.

"We'll need to talk to all of them."

"You're going to disrupt classes for a prank like this?" Principal Martin looked alarmed.

"Maybe the principal could make an announcement, asking if anyone saw someone near here at lunch, to report to the school office," Mira said.

Ryker considered this, then nodded. "We'll try that. It would be better to talk to each student individually, but I'm not sure we have the staffing for that."

She stood, feeling stronger. "I can use the robotics lab for the rest of my classes," she said. "Mr. Connors doesn't have classes on Fridays. I'll put a sign on the door to direct students there." She looked to Ryker. "If that would be okay."

"That would be fine," he said. "We'll try to be as unobtrusive as possible."

"Thank you. I appreciate that." The principal turned to Mira. "In the future, you should lock your classroom door when you leave, in order to prevent more incidents like this."

She wanted to point out that she wasn't the one who scrawled a threatening message on her whiteboard, but merely pressed her lips together and nodded.

Somehow, she made it through her final two classes of the day, dodging students' questions by telling them the sheriff's department had asked her not to discuss the situation. This was probably only going to inflame the gossip more, but she was too emotionally drained to come up with a better answer.

At the end of the day, Ryker stopped her in the hallway. "You can have your classroom back," he said. "We went ahead and wiped the board so students wouldn't see it."

"Thanks. Did you get any information from the security cameras?"

He shook his head. "We didn't find anyone sneaking in or acting oddly. A couple of students came forward to say they saw a couple of kids in this area during lunch, but they turned out to be German Club students putting up posters about a fundraiser they're having. Someone said they saw

Coach Anders here, but he was looking for his father, who was supposed to meet him here. Apparently, his dad had a physical therapy appointment at the clinic down the street and he walked down to ride home with his son. He's done that before. We saw him on the camera—he entered by the front door. His walker set off the metal detector but someone helped him around it and he obtained a pass from the office."

She couldn't see how Mitch or his dad had had anything to do with this. Maybe it really was a student who had heard about the accusations against her and decided to stir up trouble. "Thank you for your response," she said.

"Let us know if anything else happens," Ryker said.

"I will." Though she prayed nothing would happen. She didn't know how much more of this harassment she could take.

All she needed was to relax, she decided. She'd go home, grill some chicken for dinner, have a glass of wine and a bubble bath. Curl up with a good book. Maybe paint her nails. A little pampering would give her a better perspective.

She was walking in the door of her apartment when her phone rang. A picture of her mother's smiling face appeared on the screen. "Hello, Mama," she said.

"How are you doing, *hija*?" her mother asked.

"I'm good," she lied. She was not going to tell her mom about her anonymous harasser. She wouldn't put it past her mother to send her father and at least one brother to Eagle Mountain with a moving van to bring her back to Santa Fe. "How are you?"

"I'm doing okay. Missing my girl."

"I miss you, too, Mama." As much as she valued her independence, it would have been nice to have her mother here to coddle and reassure her. She hoped she was never too old for that kind of comforting.

"I wanted to tell you about the cutest little house that just went up for sale on the next street over from ours," Mama said. "It's that little rosy pink stucco with the courtyard and the sunburst design on the front wall? Do you remember?"

"I don't, but I didn't travel down that street very often."

"They just listed it today. The woman who owned it passed away and her daughter wants to get rid of it quickly, so it's listed at a very good price. I'll email you the listing information so you can take a look."

"I'm not interested in a house in Santa Fe, Mom."

"Even if you don't move into it now, it would be such a good investment," her mother said. "And my friend Carmen Peralta tells me Our Lady of Sorrows School is going to need a new Spanish teacher next semester. Sister Theresa who has taught there for years is finally retiring."

"Mom, I don't know that I'd like teaching at a private school." She had flashbacks of the stern-faced nuns who had ruled her parochial school. "I like my job here. I like Eagle Mountain."

"We just miss you, *querida*."

"I know, Mama. I miss you, too. You should plan to visit soon. I'd love to show you around."

"You know how hard it is for your father to get away from work. You should come here instead. At least come look at this darling house and talk to Carmen. She says it's a very good job."

"I'm sure someone else will love the house and the job. And I appreciate you thinking of me, but I'm happy here." Despite all that had happened, this was true. She liked her new job, her apartment and the friends she was making. Maybe one friend in particular, she thought, as the image of Carter filled her mind. She was still wary of getting too attached to anyone, but he was proving very hard to resist.

She refocused her attention on her mother. "It was good talking to you, Mama," she said. "I need to go now. I love you."

The called ended, Mira poured a glass of wine and began preparing the chicken. Returning to Santa Fe was tempting, if only because it would probably end the harassment she'd experienced here. But leaving Eagle Mountain would feel like running away. Like giving up and letting her persecutor win. She was far too stubborn to do that.

WHEN CARTER REPORTED for work Saturday morning, his mother handed him an envelope. "This was taped to the front door when I got in this morning," she said.

The white legal envelope had no information on it other than Carter's name, neatly typed, centered on the front. He tore it open and took out a folded sheet of paper. Goose bumps rose on his arms when he saw the typed words on the sheet. DON'T THINK YOU CAN BREAK THE LAW AND GO UNPUNISHED.

"What is it?" Mom asked.

"It's one of those anonymous notes people have been receiving around town," he said.

"The ones the paper wrote about?" Mom moved in to look over his shoulder. She had to stand on tiptoe. He lowered the paper to make it easier for her to see. *Tour Jeeps aren't exempt from no parking rules*, the note read. *Yet I've seen you parked on the shoulder up near Anderson Falls multiple times with your load of tourists. Stop it now or you'll be reported.*

His mother looked at him. "Are you parking illegally near Anderson Falls?"

"I've idled there a few times to let people take a picture," he said. "I'm not parking and I'm not blocking traffic. We're never there more than a couple of minutes. I've even seen sheriff's cruisers up there and the deputies have never said anything to me."

Mom shook her head. "Someone has too much time on their hands. Throw that away and get busy. We've got three tours this morning and four this afternoon."

"Four? Who's doing the extra afternoon tour?" He and Dalton and an older man named Clayton were the regular tour drivers.

"Your father is going to take them up."

"Dad?" His father was a good mechanic, but not the most garrulous person in the world. "He knows he has to talk to people, doesn't he?"

"Your father can talk plenty when he needs to."

"You should send Bethany with him." He looked around. "Where is she, anyway?"

"Ian needed her at the via ferrata. They've got a big group coming in. I can handle the front desk by myself."

He folded the note, replaced it in the envelope and tucked it in his pocket. "What are you going to do with that?" his mother asked.

"I'll give it to the sheriff to add to his collection."

"I would think the sheriff would have better things to focus on than a bunch of petty letters sent by a busybody."

"Sure. He could come narrate the afternoon tour," Carter said.

His mother sent him a look that told him she had no time for his foolishness. "Get to work," she said, and left the room.

THE EAGLE MOUNTAIN school boosters' annual barbecue was held in the gymnasium, from noon until three o'clock, with grills set up in the back parking lot and tables loaded with potato salad, cole slaw, two kinds of beans and a variety of other sides set up in front of the home bleachers. Volunteers dished up bowls of homemade ice cream beneath the basketball net at the north end of the gym while cheerleaders mingled with the crowd and sold raffle tickets for items donated by businesses in the community.

Mira, in a red-and-blue sundress—the Eagle Mountain Raptors colors—cradled a plastic cup of sweating lemonade and watched as Shayla, in a blue sheath that showed off her curves, smiled up at Mitch Anders. Mitch, in a red Raptors polo and black track pants, nodded at something she was saying, his freshly shaven jaw sharp as a chiseled statue.

Mira's attention shifted to the ice cream servers. Shayla's mother was dishing up chocolate cones to a trio of elementary school–age girls. If she had seen her daughter with Mitch, she wasn't paying any attention now.

Mira studied the rest of the room. She recognized many of the people here—parents, other teachers and business owners who had contributed to the raffle.

The sheriff was here, too, with his wife, who Mira had learned was an elementary school teacher. They each carried a child on their hip—boy and girl twins who looked to be about two. The sheriff wore his khaki uniform, neatly pressed as ever.

No one had asked her about the message left on her classroom whiteboard. Either word hadn't spread, or people were more interested in other things. Either way, Mira was happy to not have to talk about it. She hadn't even told Shayla, and her friend was clearly too interested in other things at the moment.

Shayla and Mitch moved toward her. "Mira, I want you to meet my mom," Shayla said. She looked up at Mitch. "Come with us and you can meet her, too."

As they approached, Shayla's mom looked up and beamed. She was a little shorter and a little heavier than her daughter, but had the same smooth brown skin and smattering of freckles across her cheeks. Her natural hair was cut close, and she wore large gold hoops and a cream-colored jumpsuit. "Mom, I have some friends I'd like you to meet," Shayla said. She touched Mira's shoulder. "This is Mira Veronica. And this is Mitch Anders." She didn't touch Mitch, but her smile broadened slightly as she grinned at him. "Mira and Mitch, this is my mom, Andrea Green."

"It's a pleasure to meet you." Mrs. Green wiped her fingers on a towel and shook hands.

"Thank you for working so hard to help put this together, Mrs. Green," Mitch said. "I know it's a big help to the school."

"Oh, it's a labor of love," she said. "Are you both teachers?"

"They are," Shayla said. "Wonderful teachers. We're lucky to have them on staff."

Mrs. Green turned to Mira. "What do you teach?"

"Spanish," Mira said.

"Oh, *hablo español un peux. Una lengua mas bonita.*"

"*Si,*" Mira said, holding back her amusement. "It is a beautiful language." *And so was French, which Mrs. Green apparently spoke* un peu.

Mrs. Green turned to Mitch. "And what about you, Mr. Anders?"

"I coach track and basketball, and teach technology."

Mrs. Green looked him up and down. "I should have guessed."

Shayla frowned, but said nothing. A couple walked up and asked for ice cream. "We'll let you get back to work, Mom," she said.

"It was nice meeting you," Mitch said, and Mira echoed the sentiment. Shayla led them away.

"Your mom seems very nice," Mitch said.

"I don't know what she meant, saying she should have known you're a coach."

"Probably by the way I'm dressed." He patted her shoulder. "I wasn't offended."

She looked up at him. "I was wondering if you'd like to go to a movie with me this afternoon," she said. "We could leave the barbecue a little early and catch a showing in Junction."

"I'd like that," he said.

They were staring into each other's eyes, oblivious to everyone around them, when Mira slipped away.

She was halfway across the room when two khaki-clad deputies entered the room. One of them was Carter's brother Aaron. She waved to him, but he didn't acknowledge the greeting, his expression grim. He and his fellow deputy scanned the crowd until they spotted the sheriff and made their way to him. He handed off his baby girl to his wife and moved a short distance away to confer with them. Then the three of them moved toward the silent auction table.

They passed up the items available for bids and stopped in front of Shayla and Mitch. Seconds later, Mira stared, horrified, as they placed handcuffs on Mitch and led him away.

Mira pushed through the crowd, the hum of conversation rising around her. When she reached Shayla, her friend was holding back tears, her face ashy as those around her peppered her with questions. "Come with me," Mira said, and took her hand and led her away, into the hall. Mira tried doors until she found one that was unlocked and they entered what turned out to be a science lab. Mira shut and locked the door behind them.

"Over here," she said, and led Shayla to a lab bench in the far corner of the room, out of sight of anyone who might look through the narrow window in the door. "What happened?" she asked. "Why did they arrest Mitch?"

Shayla began to cry. Mira held her hand and waited as her friend fought for control. "They said…" Shayla began, then swallowed and tried again. "They said they were taking him into custody…in connection with Bryce Atkinson's kidnapping!"

Chapter Eleven

Carter was washing the Jeeps, shirt off and barefoot in shorts, humming to himself as he scrubbed and rinsed. He was thinking about the two tours he had led that day. In the morning, he had hosted a pair of couples who were traveling Colorado together. The husbands had been friends in high school and the couples had known each other for forty years and traveled all over the world. Yet they had still been thrilled to see the mountains and waterfalls around Eagle Mountain, laughing at all of Carter's corny jokes and teasing the younger couple who were also on the tour.

In the afternoon, one family on the tour had been from Mexico. Carter had tried out some of the Spanish he was learning, then explained he was taking a course for first responders. This led to dozens of questions about his work with search and rescue, as well as more Spanish lessons as the family's two teenagers offered the Spanish words for everything they encountered on the tour.

All in all, it had been a good day. Interesting people, good weather, no breakdowns and good tips.

"Carter?"

He turned and was startled to see Mira standing a short distance away. She didn't look at all happy. In fact, he thought she might be close to tears. He dropped the water hose and hurried to her. "What's wrong?" he asked.

"Sheriff's deputies arrested Mitch Anders this afternoon," she said. "One of them was your brother Aaron. They said he had something to do with Bryce's kidnapping."

"Who is Mitch Anders?"

"He's a coach at the school. And he's the man my friend Shayla is interested in. She was with him when he was arrested and she's terribly upset."

"And they think he's the kidnapper?"

"He couldn't be," Mira said. "He was at the school that afternoon. I talked to him."

"If he was there when someone was grabbing Bryce, he can't be the kidnapper," Carter agreed.

"He came to tell me and Shayla about the kidnapping," she said. "He had heard the news from his father, who lives with him. So that was after the kidnapping. And after Bryce escaped, because he mentioned search and rescue had been called out. But I'm sure he was at school before that. He has sports to coach." She shook her head. "I don't know what to think. He seems like such a nice guy but I've been wrong before."

"Come sit down," Carter said. He paused to turn the water off at the faucet, then led her to a bench in the shade next to the garage. "Tell me what happened."

She told him about the barbecue, about Shayla introducing her and Mitch to her mother, and then the deputies—including Aaron—arriving and arresting Mitch. "Shayla had just arranged to go to the movies this afternoon with him," she said. "They handcuffed him and led him away. She is devastated."

"I remember Shayla. I met her the day of the bomb threat."

"That's right, you did. Can you call your brother and find out what kind of evidence they have against Mitch?"

He shook his head. "Aaron won't tell me. I don't think he legally can."

She slumped over, chin in hand, elbows on her knees. "I feel so bad for Shayla."

"Maybe if we go to the sheriff's department, we can find out something there," he said.

"They're not going to let us in just because we're nosy," she said.

"But we'll have a reason to be there," he said. "You can tell the sheriff about talking to Mitch at the school that afternoon. And I got a note today from the anonymous busybody."

She sat up straight and stared at him. "When? Where? What did it say?"

"It was taped to the front door. My mom found it when she opened up this morning. I've got it here." He stood and retrieved his shirt from the gatepost where he had draped it and fished the folded envelope from the pocket. He handed the letter to her, then slipped on the shirt, but didn't button it.

She examined the envelope, then took out the letter and read it. "Are you illegally parking?" she asked.

"I'm not really parking, just stopping there a few minutes so people can take pictures."

She returned the letter to him. "It's like the ones other people have received—nagging them about something they really have done. Mine is the only one accusing me—or at least insinuating—that I've done something wrong when I didn't do anything at all."

"I still want to show the sheriff this note. He can add it to his collection. If he gets enough notes to compare, maybe he'll find something that will help identify the writer."

He hadn't expected her to be cheered by his news, exactly, but she looked even more dismayed. "What is it?" he asked. "You don't want to talk to the sheriff?"

"It's not that. I got another message yesterday. Not a note, but someone sneaked into my classroom while I was at lunch and wrote 'kid killer' in red marker on my whiteboard."

He sat beside her once more. "Why didn't you tell me?"

"I didn't tell anyone—except the deputy who came and took a report, and the principal. I just… I want this all to go away. I don't want to have to deal with it."

He rubbed her back. "It's awful," he said. "I'm sorry. We don't have to go to the sheriff. We can do something to get your mind off of this. Go for a hike. Or I could give you a personal Jeep tour."

A smile flickered across her lips, but quickly faded. She straightened her shoulders. "Let's go to the sheriff. Maybe we'll find out something that will help Mitch or Shayla."

He began buttoning up the shirt. "Let me put on some shoes and we can head over there."

He was aware of her watching as he did up the shirt buttons. Too bad she wasn't the one undoing them. His gaze flickered over the hint of cleavage at the neck of her sundress. It had buttons down the front, too. He'd enjoy unfastening them. One at a time. Slowly revealing her beautiful body.

Get it together, he scolded himself. Now wasn't the time. She was seriously upset about her friend and he needed to focus on helping her.

Fortunately, Aaron wasn't in sight when they arrived at the station. Carter knew his brother would see past any story Carter concocted and send him on his way. Inside, they found office manager Adelaide Kinkaid, a feisty sixty-something who had no patience for fools, but a soft spot for handsome young men. Or so Carter had heard. "Good afternoon, Adelaide." He offered his most charming smile. "You're looking lovely this afternoon."

She gave him a sour look. "Your brother is busy processing a new arrest," she said. Her gaze flickered to Mira. "Is there something I can help you with?"

"We need to see the sheriff," Carter said.

"The sheriff is busy, too."

"I need to show him this." Carter held up the envelope. "Another poison pen letter. He'll want it for his files."

"You can give the letter to me and I'll make sure he gets it." She held out her hand.

"Mira needs to talk to him, too," Carter said.

"Why do you need to see him?" Adelaide asked Mira.

"I have evidence. It's related to Mitch Anders. I know he was arrested this afternoon in connection with Bryce's kidnapping."

"Just a moment." Adelaide stood and disappeared through a door behind her.

"You said the magic word," Carter said. "*Evidence*."

"It may not help us find out what they've got on Mitch."

Adelaide reappeared. "The sheriff can give you a few minutes."

Travis looked up from his desk when they entered his office. "Adelaide said you want to tell me something about Mitch Anders?"

"Yes. The afternoon Bryce was kidnapped, Mitch is the one who told me and Shayla Green about the kidnapping. He came into my classroom and told us Bryce had been taken."

"What time was this?" Travis picked up a pad and pen and began making notes.

"Just after four thirty. I know because I had planned to

leave school at four and Shayla interrupted me, so I stayed a little later."

"What time was Bryce taken?" Carter asked.

Travis ignored him. "Did Mitch say how he had learned about the kidnapping?"

"He said his dad had told him. His dad listens to the police scanner and had learned about the crime there." She frowned. "I'm trying to remember exactly what he said. Something about one of their neighbors being a 911 dispatcher. He—the dad—talked to her and she told him Bryce's name and that someone had seen a kid they thought was him up at the Galloway Basin parking area, and that search and rescue had been called out."

Carter was scrolling through his phone. "The call for search and rescue came at 4:05," he said.

Travis nodded. "Did you see Mitch before he came to your classroom?" he asked.

"He was monitoring the pickup line out front when school let out at three," she said.

"Thank you for sharing this information," Travis said. "We'll get back to you if we have more questions."

"I have something for you, too," Carter said. He handed over the envelope. "Someone stuck that to the door of the tour office this morning. My mom found it when she opened up."

Travis scanned the letter. "Do you have any idea who sent it?" he asked.

"None," Carter said.

"I'll add it to the file."

"Why do you think Mitch had anything to do with Bryce's kidnapping?" Mira asked.

"I can't share that at this time." He stood. "Now, you need to go."

Carter followed her out of the sheriff's office, through the lobby and onto the sidewalk. "I need to check on Shayla," Mira said.

"Do you want me to come with you?" he asked.

"No thanks."

He started to turn away, hiding his disappointment. She put out her hand and touched his arm. "Thank you," she said. "For all your help. And for being patient with me."

"Patient?"

"I like you. But it's hard for me to trust people. I have my reasons." She leaned in, the citrus and vanilla scent of her momentarily stunning him. She kissed him, the softest brush of her lips against his cheek.

Then she was gone, walking away, leaving him in a fog of desire and hope.

Chapter Twelve

Saturday evening, Shayla let Mira into her small rental home on the other side of town from Mira's apartment. A small white dog barked at her from the sofa and two cats wound around her feet as she greeted her friend. Shayla rubbed at the streaks of mascara beneath her bloodshot eyes. "I'm sorry I'm such a mess," she said. "I can't stop crying."

"Don't apologize," Mira said. "You have every reason to be upset."

She followed Shayla to the sofa, where two more cats had settled in beside the dog. Shayla sank down next to them, while Mira took the adjacent armchair. A black cat—one that had greeted her at the door—immediately joined her. "I can't believe Mitch had anything to do with this," Shayla said.

Mira stroked the cat, who began to purr, and tried to think of something comforting to say. She had been in Shayla's shoes, not believing a man she loved had been capable of such evil. In her case, police had shown her undeniable evidence of his guilt. And even George hadn't denied his guilt. He had only asked her to understand that he couldn't help himself and he had never really hurt anyone—a rationalization that had sickened her further.

But what proof did they have of Mitch's guilt? "Carter and I went to the sheriff's office," she said.

Shayla looked more alert. "Did you find out anything? Did you see Mitch? Is he okay?"

"We didn't see Mitch and the sheriff wouldn't tell us anything about the case. But I told him about seeing Mitch here at school during pickup at the end of the day, and again about an hour and a half later when he came to tell the two of us about Bryce's kidnapping."

"I don't see how he could have snatched Bryce, driven him up to Galloway Basin and gotten back to school in that time, do you?" Shayla asked.

Mira thought it might just be possible, though it didn't seem probable. "The sheriff will interview other people at the school," she said. "I'm sure someone will have seen him. Wouldn't he have track practice after school?"

"Not on Thursday," Shayla said. "That's the day junior varsity competes, but they had a bye week, so he was free that afternoon." She hugged a pillow to her stomach. "My mom called."

"She was probably worried about you. What did she say?"

"That she hoped I would stay far away from a man like Mitch."

"Oh, Shayla."

"I told her I knew he was innocent and she had no right to judge him." She rocked back and forth. "But what if I'm wrong? What if he really did do it?" She burst into sobs.

Mira moved over to the sofa, displacing one of the cats, and rubbed Shayla's back, knowing there was no comfort she could offer but her presence. And maybe the benefit of her own experience. "What are you doing tomorrow?" she asked.

"I don't know. Probably what I'm doing right now. Sitting at home. Crying."

"Come hiking with me. You'll feel better if you do something active, outdoors." After George's arrest, she had walked miles and miles in the mountains around Santa Fe. It was the only thing that kept her from completely falling apart.

"I don't know," Shayla said. "I'd be terrible company."

"No you won't. And it will make you feel better. I promise."

"All right. I'll come with you. Where do you want to go?"

"I'll think of a good trail by tomorrow. Be ready about ten?"

"Sounds good." She wiped her eyes, then squeezed Mira's hand. "Thanks. You're a good friend."

"So are you." She would do her best to distract Shayla from her worst thoughts. And if those thoughts turned out to be true, she would give her a shoulder to lean on. She was someone who had been through a similar situation and come out the other side, wounded, but still standing.

SATURDAY NIGHT, CARTER STOPPED himself three times from calling Mira. If she wanted to hear from him, she would contact him. She had asked him to be patient, so he had to do that—no matter how impatient the idea made him.

Dalton looked up from his computer. "What's wrong with you?" he asked. "You're like a hyperactive puppy that can't sit still for two seconds. You're making me nervous."

"I'm just restless." He stopped to look over Dalton's shoulder at his computer screen. But the strings of numbers there made no sense to him.

"Then go for a run. Or to the bar. Just get out of here."

"Good idea." He grabbed his keys and headed out the

door. Not for a run, but to Mo's Pub. The server at the door greeted him. "You're with search and rescue, right?" she asked. "Those guys are at the big table in the back."

"Is this a meeting no one told me about?" he asked as he approached the table. Ryan, Vince, Eldon, and Tony, their girlfriends, and several climbers Carter recognized but didn't know well were crowded around the table, with pitchers of beer and platters of pizza between them.

"Carter! Come join us." Vince scooted over to make room and Carter pulled a chair from another table. "You know Tammy." Vince introduced the curly-haired blonde with him. "She writes for the paper."

"Hi, Tammy," Carter said. Several other people introduced themselves. Someone handed him a beer and someone else passed over a platter of pizza. He helped himself. "So what's going on?" he asked.

"We just all ended up here," Ryan said.

"Some of us were climbing over in Caspar Canyon and came here because we were hungry and thirsty," Eldon said. "The others just showed up, like you."

"Everyone ends up at Mo's sooner or later," Tony said.

"Hey, anybody know what's up with Mitch Anders?" one of the climbers at the other end of the table asked. "I heard he was arrested."

"Mitch?" Ryan's girlfriend, Deni, asked. "What for?"

"Apparently, they think he's the guy who tried to kidnap that kid. The one we searched for and found up above Galloway Basin," Tony said.

"No way," the climber said. "Mitch?"

"I heard he has an alibi," Carter said. "He was at school that afternoon. I know a couple of people who saw him."

"Who?" Ryan asked.

"Mira Veronica and another teacher. She said Mitch was at school all afternoon."

"Then why arrest him?" Tony asked. "They must have some evidence."

"I don't know," Carter admitted.

"Your brother is a cop, isn't he?" Vince asked. "What does he say?"

"Aaron doesn't talk about stuff like that." He took a bite of pizza, an excuse to stop talking.

"Mitch always struck me as a good guy," Ryan said. "It just goes to show you never really know about people. They must have had some good evidence to arrest him."

"Maybe the kid identified him," Eldon's girlfriend, May, said.

"Maybe they got DNA or something," someone else suggested.

"Hey, I ran into some guy today who was telling me that he took up climbing because he had this DNA profile done that said he would be good at it," one of the climbers said. "I think he got taken because the guy was seriously awful."

The conversation turned to climbing and Carter excused himself to go to the bathroom. On his way back to the table, he passed the bar. Raised voices stopped him and he turned to see the bartender, a blonde named Cherise, arguing with a customer. Carter moved closer. "I can't pour you another one, Ed," she said. "You've already had too many. You need to go home. Let me call you a ride."

"I want another drink!" the older man shouted. He was about five foot seven, thin and bent, with scraggly long gray hair and stubble, a red-and-black-plaid flannel shirt open over a gray T-shirt and baggy jeans.

"You need help, Cherise?" Carter asked.

"I'm just trying to find Ed here a ride home," she said. "He's in no shape to get behind the wheel."

"I don't want to go home!" Ed bellowed. "I want another drink."

"Who is he?" Carter asked.

Cherise turned away from Ed and lowered her voice. "He's Mitch Anders's father. You heard what happened with Mitch."

"Yeah."

"It's awful. I get that Ed is upset, but he's had way too much to drink. I'm afraid he's going to pass out and fall and hurt himself. He can hardly get around as it is. I can't believe he drove over here."

"Let me see if I can talk to him," Carter said.

The barstools on either side of Ed were vacant. Carter slid onto one of them. "Hey, Ed," he said. "I'm Carter."

"Will you buy me a drink?" Ed asked.

"How about a Coke?" Carter asked. "Or a cup of coffee."

"I don't want any coffee!" He slammed a fist on the bar, making his empty pint glass jump.

"Guess you had a rough day," Carter said.

"My son was arrested," Ed said. "They had no right. He's innocent."

"I want to hear about your son," Carter said. He took out his keys. "Let me take you home."

Ed looked at him with watery blue eyes. "Do you know Mitch?"

"Sure," Carter lied. "He's a coach at the high school. A great guy." He stood. "Come on. I'll take you home and you can tell me more about Mitch."

Ed hesitated, and Carter braced for another argument, but then the older man dragged over a metal walker Carter hadn't noticed. Ed struggled to his feet, then pushing the walker in front of him, started for the door.

Carter hurried to open it for him, then led the way to his Jeep. The old man refused any help getting into the vehicle and despite his bent frame and shuffling gait had a muscular upper body. "That's my car over there," he said, pointing to a faded red Jeep.

"It will be safe here overnight," Carter said. "I'll play chauffeur for now. What's your address?"

"Five twenty-eight Moose Way." Ed closed his eyes and leaned back in the seat. Before they were even out of the parking lot, he was snoring. He woke with a jerk when Carter pulled into the driveway and shut off the engine. "What? Where are we?"

"We're at your house." Carter got out of the Jeep and walked around to open the passenger door. Ed shook off his hand, slid to the ground, grabbed the walker and hurried up the walk to the front door. Carter hastened to catch up with him.

Ed shoved open the door and left it open behind him as he shuffled into the living room.

The house was small and dark—dark wood floors and paneled walls, heavy drapes over the windows. Ed switched on a lamp on a table by the sofa and flopped down onto the cushions. "There's beer in the refrigerator," he said. "Get us both one."

Carter wasn't sure the old man should be drinking, but he fetched two cans of a cheap domestic beer from the refrigerator and handed one to the old man. He opened his can but didn't drink it.

Ed drained half his can in one long slug, then looked at Carter from beneath bushy eyebrows. "Mitch is a good son," he said, his words only slightly slurred. "Don't tell anybody, but me and Mitch's mom never married. Not because I didn't ask her, mind you. But I wasn't good enough for her family. They didn't want me around and pretty soon she didn't, either. I wasn't in his life much but I tried to make up for it later. When I needed a place to live he took me in. He's a good son. He doesn't deserve this."

Carter tried to think of something to say, but Ed drained the rest of his beer, not seeming to expect an answer. Carter looked around the room, which was decorated in southwestern art—paintings of desert scenes in pastel colors.

Ed slammed his empty beer can down on the coffee table. "Mitch's mother was an artist. That's all her work. He keeps it up there because of her."

"Nice," Carter said. His gaze shifted to a framed photo on the table beside them, a color image of a man and a boy standing together on a dock with fishing poles and a large fish. "That's me and Mitch," Ed said. "He was eight."

The man in the photo had the build of a rodeo bull rider—stocky and muscular, and slightly bowlegged. He squinted at the camera from beneath a shock of thick brown hair, one hand on the shoulder of the grinning boy.

"That was a great day," Ed said. "I didn't see him again for almost twenty years." There was no regret in his words. He sounded almost detached.

"Why didn't you see him?" Carter asked.

"Things happen. Time gets away from you."

Carter looked at the photo again. Was Ed the one who had kept it all these years, or Mitch? When Mitch looked at his father now, did he see the man he had been that day, or the one who had been absent twenty years?

He turned to look at Ed again, but the old man's chin was down on his chest and he was snoring.

Moving carefully, Carter stood and crept to the door. He

left the can of beer on a table by the entrance and hurried to his Jeep and drove away.

He debated going back to the bar, but decided to go home. His mind was too full of his encounter with Ed. Ed was lucky to have a son like Mitch, but was Mitch lucky to have a father like Ed? Carter hadn't seen the man at his best, but he doubted a sober Ed would be a big improvement. He had admitted he had neglected his son, and turned to him only when he had nowhere else to go. Had that lack of a father in his life led Mitch to commit the crime of which he was accused?

Or were his friends right and Mitch was blameless?

Smarter people than Carter would try to figure that out. All he knew for sure was that he was glad he had been born into the family he had. For all he sometimes felt smothered or overlooked by his parents and siblings, they had always been there for him, and never asked much of him. Did that make him weaker than someone like Mitch? Or stronger in ways he hadn't yet figured out?

Chapter Thirteen

When Mira arrived the next morning, Shayla was waiting in front of her house, dressed in jeans and a button-down shirt, her hair pulled back and wrapped in a scarf. Her eyes were a little puffy, but she offered a wan smile and a travel mug of coffee as she slid into the passenger seat of Mira's car. "You still have the rental," she said.

"Yes. I'm waiting on the insurance check, then I'll have to get something new. Or something different, at least. I can't afford new."

"The sheriff took Mitch's SUV." She looked away and sipped her coffee.

"I thought we'd try the Gold Lake Trail," Mira said, determined to turn the conversation away from Mitch and his troubles. "The scenery up there is spectacular and the weather today is perfect."

Shayla said nothing. Mira made a few other attempts at conversation as they drove, remarking on a new house being built, and asking Shayla what trails she had hiked in the area. But her friend answered in monosyllables. By the time they arrived at the trailhead, Mira was beginning to think this had been a bad idea. Shayla didn't want to be distracted or cheered up. Maybe Mira was making things worse.

Two other cars were parked at the trailhead—a camper van and a red pickup. Mira pulled her daypack from the back seat and settled a sun hat on her head while Shayla stood beside the car, finishing her coffee. "Are you ready?" Mira asked. She half expected Shayla to say she had changed her mind.

"Sure," Shayla said, and set her coffee mug inside the car. "Let's go."

The first section of the trail was steep, and they were both breathing hard within ten minutes. Shayla kept up and made no complaint. Mira focused on the scenery, admiring the sunlight on the slopes and trying to clear her mind.

"Let's stop a minute," Shayla said after the first half hour.

They halted and Mira offered Shayla a water bottle. She drank, and when she returned the bottle, offered a smile and an apology. "I'm sorry I'm such a grump. This really was a good idea. I needed to get out of the house."

"I hope it helps," Mira said.

"I'm a worrier," Shayla said. "It's just the way I am. I'm worried about Mitch, and I'm worried about his dad, too. From what Mitch has said, he does pretty much everything for Ed. He does all the shopping and cooking, and takes him places."

"His dad doesn't drive?" Mira asked.

"He does, some. He has an old Jeep he drives around town. But he uses a walker. I'm not really sure what's wrong with him, but he apparently can't do a lot of things."

"How old is he?" Mira thought of her own father, still very active. She couldn't remember the last time he had even had a cold.

"I'm not sure. Early sixties? But I gather he led a hard life. I think he may have been homeless when Mitch took him in. Which is amazing when you think that Ed wasn't a part of his life growing up. Mitch told me his mom and dad were never married and he only saw Ed a few times when he was a kid. Which goes to show what a sweet, generous guy Mitch is, to take care of the dad who never took care of him."

"Maybe tomorrow you can find out more," Mira said. "Maybe Mitch will be able to get out on bail."

Shayla nodded, lips pressed tightly together. She breathed in deeply and looked around them. "Did you do much hiking in Santa Fe?" she asked.

"Oh sure." She stowed her water bottle and they set out again. Mira talked about the landscape around Santa Fe, and growing up in a large, close-knit family. "Do you miss it?" Shayla asked.

"I miss my family sometimes, but it was good for me to get away. To try new things."

"Were your parents upset when you decided to move here?"

"They were sad to see me go, but I was the last to leave home. My brothers are scattered all over the country. Though I know they'd like it if I moved back. And maybe one day I will, but for now, I'm happy to be here."

"I'm glad you're here," Shayla said. "Thanks again for getting me out here this morning."

The trail flattened out, making talking easier, and they exchanged stories of their childhoods, talked about places they had visited on vacation, and places they hoped to see one day. The sadness didn't leave Shayla's eyes, but she seemed less burdened than she had when they had set out.

The trail ended at an overlook, where they admired the view and shared a bag of trail mix, then began to retrace their steps to the parking area. "Let's drive over to Paradise and have lunch," Shayla said. "There's a cute little tearoom there I haven't visited in years."

"That's a great idea," Mira said. "I haven't driven over there yet, but I've been wanting to see it."

"It's a really cute little town. Very Victorian. And they have some great shops. We'll have to check them out."

Engrossed in conversation, they didn't see the dark figure emerge from beside the trail until it collided with Mira. Shayla's screams mingled with Mira's cry of pain as she was slammed to the ground and blinding pain shot through her. Her vision blurred and she was sure she would be sick, then another wave of pain washed over her as her attacker began to pummel her. She stared up at a black ski mask, unable to make out any features past the narrow slits for eyes, nose and mouth. The man—she was sure it was a man—pummeled her with gloved fists, but remained absolutely silent.

"Stop it! Get off of her!" Shayla shouted.

Her attacker grunted and shied away as a rock hit him in the shoulder. Shayla picked up another, larger rock and held it over her head. The man abandoned Mira and launched himself at her. Mira tried to get up, but a wave of dizziness pinned her to the ground. She tasted blood and every part of her ached. She tried to call for help, but only managed a low moan.

Then everything was silent. Mira thought she must have lost consciousness, because the next thing she remembered was someone shaking her. She opened her eyes and looked into Shayla's frightened face. "Hang on," Shayla said. "Help is coming."

"That man," Mira said, unable to say more.

"He ran away. I called 911. Help is coming. All we have to do is hang on."

CARTER HAD THE day off Sunday. He slept in, then spent the morning doing laundry in their landlady's garage. Dalton was working, so he had the apartment to himself, but was unmotivated to do much of anything. He wanted to call Mira, and thought he would eventually give in to the urge to do so, though he was holding off as long as possible, not wanting to look too needy.

He was taking the last load of clothes out of the dryer when his phone sounded with an alert for search and rescue. Injured hiker, Gold Lake Trail.

He left the laundry, grabbed his pack and keys, and headed for SAR headquarters, the familiar adrenaline rush humming through him. He wondered what they would find on the trail. It could be anything from a sprained ankle to a head injury from a fall. Whatever it was, the team would figure out what to do to help someone, and maybe even save a life.

He was surprised to see Sergeant Gage Walker standing with Danny to address the gathered volunteers. "Two women were attacked by an unknown man on the Gold Lake Trail about eleven thirty this morning," Gage said. "One of them sustained the brunt of the attack. Her companion reports she's bleeding from a head wound and may have a broken arm."

"Where is the attacker?" Harper Vernon asked.

"He fled the scene. He was described as wearing all black. He ran away down the trail, toward the parking area. We have deputies searching for him and questioning other hikers."

"Our job is to take care of the injured woman," Danny said. "Let's load up. Two litters, oxygen, cold and hot packs, first aid supplies."

They had the vehicles loaded and were on their way to

Gold Lake in under ten minutes. As they regrouped at the trail head, Aaron approached. "Jake and I are going with you," he told Carter.

"Do you think the attacker will come back?" Carrie Andrews paused, her arms full of blankets.

"Probably not, but we don't want to take chances," Aaron said. "And we need to talk to the two women and find out what they know about this guy."

Danny assigned volunteers to head up the trail, while others waited in the parking area in case backup was needed. Carter was in the first group. He carried half of one of the litters and a medical pack, Vince behind him with the other half of the litter. Aaron was at the front of the line, with Danny, Jake bringing up the rear.

The first portion of the hike was through an open meadow bathed in golden light, a cloudless blue sky providing a backdrop for red rock peaks. It was hard to imagine a brutal attack in such a peaceful setting.

The trail began to flatten out when a woman ran down the path toward them. Carter stared. "Shayla?" he asked.

She stopped talking to Danny and Aaron and glanced at Carter. Then her face crumpled. "Oh, Carter!" she moaned. "It's Mira. Mira is hurt."

He wasn't clear on what happened next. Someone must have taken the litter and pack from him. Someone else— Aaron?—took hold of his arm, whether to steady him or keep him from rushing to Mira he couldn't tell. But he was standing over her, watching as Danny and the others assessed her injuries.

She was lying on her back in the middle of the trail, blood trickling from a cut on her forehead, her arm cradled against her body, knees drawn up to her chest as she moaned. "She's going to be okay," Aaron spoke in his ear. "She has a broken arm. Maybe a concussion. She's going to be okay."

Carter nodded, and wet his dry lips. "You can let go of me now," he said. "I'm not going to freak out."

Aaron released his hold, but remained close. Danny fitted Mira's arm with an inflatable splint, which required first straightening the arm. Mira cried out and Carter bit the inside of his mouth until he tasted blood, but he never looked away. He didn't think she had seen him yet, surrounded as she was by the people tending to her. Carrie cleaned her head wound and Harper held her uninjured hand and talked softly to her. They gave her oxygen and wrapped her warmly against shock, and placed an ice pack on her swelling eye. Then they gently transferred her to the litter for the trip down the mountain.

"There's somebody here who wants to talk to you," Danny said, and motioned for Carter to come forward.

He forced a smile, though he had little confidence it was convincing. "Hey," he said, and rested one hand lightly over the tips of her fingers. They had placed an IV in the back of the hand and he was afraid of disturbing it. "Hey," he said.

"Hey." Her voice was a whisper. She tried a smile, but it turned into a grimace.

"How are you doing?" he asked.

"Better now."

Aaron moved in on her other side. "What can you tell us about the person who attacked you?" he asked.

"Not much." Her words were distorted, her lip swollen and still dotted with blood. "He was dressed all in black—gloves and a ski mask, too."

"Was he a big guy? Tall? Heavy?"

"No. He was about my height. Not much taller than me. And not heavy, but strong. He hit me really hard."

"Did he say anything?"

"Nothing. He didn't make a sound until Shayla hit him with a rock. Then he grunted." She turned her head. "Shayla! Is she all right?"

"She's fine. She's with another deputy."

"Is she hurt?"

"Only a few bruises. She said the guy seemed to be mainly after you."

"I don't know why," Mira said. She closed her eyes. "I can't believe this even happened."

Aaron stepped back. "You can take her now," he said. "We can talk to her more later."

Carter moved out of the way, too, and fell in step beside his brother. "What happens now?" he asked.

"I'll follow the ambulance to the hospital in Junction. After she's treated I'll interview her again and see if she remembers any more details."

"Maybe another hiker saw the guy running away, or remembers his car in the parking lot," Carter said.

"Maybe."

The ambulance was waiting and Mira was loaded in right away. Shayla climbed in after her. Carter didn't get a chance to speak to Mira again. When Aaron arrived at his patrol vehicle, Carter was there. "I'm coming with you," he said, his hand on the passenger door.

Aaron said nothing, but slid into the driver's seat and waited until Carter was buckled in. They followed the ambulance down the mountain, though it soon outpaced them.

"No lights and siren?" Carter asked.

"I won't be able to talk to her again until the doctors are done," he said. "Might as well give them some time."

All Carter wanted was for her to be all right, out of pain and healing.

"So are you two dating?" Aaron asked.

"Not exactly."

"What do you mean 'not exactly'?"

"We're friends. I want more and she says she's not ready."

"And you're okay with that?"

"I don't have a choice."

"So you think she's worth waiting for."

"Something like that." He slid down farther in the seat. "I hope I'm not making a mistake."

"Someone sure seems to have it in for her," Aaron said. "Maybe it's just as well you're not too involved with her. It sounds like she's made some enemies."

"Is this supposed to make me feel better?"

"Her description of her attacker sounds like the same guy who grabbed Bryce Atkinson," Aaron said. "I have to wonder if there's a connection."

"If it is the same guy, that lets Mitch Anders off the hook," Carter said.

"It's not public knowledge yet, but they're releasing Mitch Anders this afternoon. At least half a dozen people saw him at the school at the time Bryce was being kidnapped."

"Why did they arrest him in the first place?"

"Someone's door cam caught the vehicle driven by the kidnapper," Aaron said. "Same make, model and color as Anders's. Only the first three letters of the license plate were visible, but those matched Anders's also. He fit the description Bryce gave, too. That added up to probable cause."

"Could someone else have driven his car?" Carter asked. "His dad lives with him."

"His dad can hardly walk," Aaron said. "I can't see him manhandling a fighting kid."

At the hospital, they waited while Mira's arm was set. "She has a concussion and we're keeping her overnight for observation," the doctor told them. "You can talk to her, but keep it brief."

What was it about hospital beds that made people look so small and vulnerable? Carter thought as he followed Aaron into the dimly lit room with its soundtrack of beeping machinery. Mira seemed to float on a sea of green sheets, her dark hair spread out on the pillow around her, her face almost as pale as the bandage across her forehead. But her eyes were open, and she smiled at him. "So I didn't dream you were here," she said.

"I'm here." He took her hand and she squeezed it tightly, hanging on.

"How are you feeling?" Aaron asked.

"A little floaty," she said. "They gave me something for the pain. The doctor says I have a mild concussion. And a broken arm." She lifted the cast, swathed in pale blue wrapping.

"What do you remember now about the person who attacked you?" Aaron asked.

"He was strong. And fast. Not too tall. Dressed all in black." One of the monitors began beeping faster. "He wanted to hurt me. I thought he was going to kill me."

A nurse came into the room and checked the monitor. She laid a hand on Mira's shoulder. "How is your pain?" she asked.

"Not too bad." Mira forced a smile. "Getting better."

The nurse looked at Aaron and Carter. "Don't upset her," she said, and left, the soles of her shoes squeaking on the tile floor.

"How is Shayla?" Mira asked.

"She's fine," Aaron said. "She only has a few bruises. Her parents picked her up a few minutes ago."

"Mitch is being released this afternoon," Carter said. He ignored the scowl Aaron sent him.

Mira's smile was genuine now. "I'm so glad." She looked to Aaron, the tense look returned. "Do you have any idea who attacked us? Or why?"

"Not yet. Do you remember anything else about him? His eye color? Any particular odor? What he sounded like?"

"I couldn't see his eyes. He didn't smell like anything in particular, and he never spoke."

"We're still looking for hikers who might have seen the man in the parking area or on the trail," Aaron said. He glanced at Carter. "I'm going to get some coffee and I'll check back with you in a minute. We'll need to head back."

"Thanks."

"That was nice of him to give us some time alone," Mira said.

He leaned over and kissed her forehead, just to the right of the bandage. "I was so afraid when I saw you lying there on the trail."

"I know. But I was glad to see you."

"I hate that I have to leave soon, but you probably need your rest. I'll come back tomorrow to take you home."

"I'd like that."

He started to pull his hand away, but she held on. "I've been thinking about how much time I've wasted."

"What do you mean?"

"I was with a man before who turned out to be completely different than I thought. It made me doubt my judgment. I was afraid to be with anyone again. But you keep proving you're dependable."

His heart sank. "That's me. Dependable. Steady. Not at all exciting."

"I don't want exciting. I just want you." She pulled his face down to hers and kissed him. On the lips. Hers were swollen and tasted a little of antiseptic, but he didn't care. She wanted him, and that was all that mattered.

"Humph."

He drew back to find the nurse standing at the end of the bed, scowling at them. "I'd better go," he said.

"I'll see you tomorrow," Mira said, and closed her eyes.

He walked out of the room, though it felt a little like floating. Aaron was waiting in the hallway, a paper cup of coffee in one hand. "All good?" he asked.

"All great."

Chapter Fourteen

From: Miranda.Veronica@emisd.net
To: cman@mtntel.com and 14 others
Subject: Spanish for First Responders

Tonight's class has NOT been canceled. I expect to see you all there. Estar listo para trabajar.
Mira

Mira taught the class the next evening seated in a chair at the front of the room, her arm in a sling. "Tonight, we're going to take advantage of my recent experience and practice all the questions deputies, search and rescue, and paramedics might have needed to ask if I had spoken only Spanish."

"You don't think that's too traumatic?" Deni asked.

"No," Mira said. "I was pretty out of it at the time, so I think this will help. I'm counting on some of you who were there to remember what you asked. We'll skip the part where I'm lying on the ground, though." She held up a whiteboard marker. "I'll need a volunteer to write down, in English, all the questions you come up with, then we'll work on translating them into Spanish."

Bethany took the marker. "Dalton, why don't you start?" Mira asked.

They covered search and rescue first, then she called on Aaron for the law enforcement perspective. Hearing the questions about her attacker once more did not, as she had hoped, elicit any new information. Earlier in the day, the sheriff had told her they had no new leads on the black-clad man. He had managed to avoid being seen by any other hikers or passersby.

They finished up with questions for the paramedics about her injuries. She called on different students to try their hands at translation and Bethany recorded the correct results under each question. Then they practiced repeating the phrases until it was time for class to end.

"How are you doing?" Carter asked as he helped her pack her things to leave. She wasn't able to drive yet, so he had brought her to class and would take her home. He had been a huge help, but things still felt tentative between them. She sensed he was holding back, afraid to push her for too much. She needed to find a way to let him know she wasn't so fragile, despite the cast and stitches.

"I'm fine," she said. Only a slight headache, but that was starting to fade. "Everyone else did all the work tonight."

He picked up her book bag. "Are you ready?"

"I am."

On the steps of the building he paused, shoulders tensed. He had never said so, but she knew he was looking for another dark figure who might emerge from the shadows to attack her. After a few seconds' pause, he touched her uninjured arm. "I think it's okay," he said, and escorted her to his Jeep.

He went through the same routine at her apartment, looking carefully before they emerged from the vehicle and staying alert all the way to her door. Inside, he checked all the rooms and double-checked the locks. When he was done, he said, "You're probably tired. I should go home."

"Don't leave yet." She moved in closer, and slid one hand to the back of his neck. He took the cue and kissed her, very gently. "I won't break," she murmured, and pressed against him.

"I don't want to hurt you," he said.

"You won't."

He kissed her again, like he meant it this time. The sensation buzzed through her. "That's better than any painkiller," she said when their lips parted.

"I can do better," he said, and proved it by pulling her closer, grasping her waist with both hands, leaving no doubt of his arousal.

If only this cast wasn't between them. She shifted, trying to make room for it. "Sorry," he said. "I'm crushing you."

"Come over here," she said, and led him to the sofa. She pushed him down, then sat in his lap. "How's this?" she asked.

He slid one hand beneath her shirt. "Nice," he said, and kissed her again.

She began to undo the buttons of his shirt, running her fingers over the taut muscles of his abdomen. His breath caught and a thrill rippled through her. His eyes met hers and the heat of his gaze burned through her. This was what she wanted. What she needed.

She was working her way around to straddle him when the strains of banda trumpets sounded. She groaned and pressed her forehead to his. "Is that your phone?" he asked.

"I'll ignore it." She pulled the phone from her pocket and glanced at the screen. "It's my mom."

"If she's like mine, she'll keep calling," he said.

"You're right." She swiped up to accept the call and slid off his lap. "Hi, Mom."

"I'm calling to see if you got the email I sent," her mother said.

"I haven't checked my email this afternoon," she said.

"Well, you need to read it. I sent you a whole list of cute houses for sale here. And more information about the job at Our Lady of Sorrows."

She was aware of Carter rebuttoning his shirt as her mother rattled on about the job and the houses. "Mom, I'm really happy here in Eagle Mountain," she said. Other than a dangerous stalker, life here was almost perfect.

"You could be happy here. One day when you have a daughter of your own, you'll understand how hard it is to lose her."

"You haven't lost me, Mom."

"You will always be my baby, and I worry about you."

"I'm fine. Really."

"I had a dream last night that you were hurt. I almost called you then."

A shiver ran up her spine. "I'm fine," she repeated.

"I just needed to make sure. *Te amo, hija.*"

"I love you, too, Mama."

She ended the call. "You didn't tell her about the attack," Carter said.

"No. I didn't want to frighten her."

"Are you sure you're okay here by yourself?"

Her mother wasn't the only worrier. "I'm fine," she said.

"I could stay here."

She smiled. "If you did that, neither one of us would get any sleep."

"True." He bent to kiss her again, but pulled away quickly. "Call me if you need anything. Anytime."

She nodded. "I will."

She followed him to the door and locked it behind him, then sank onto the sofa once more, too weary to move. The attack had taken more out of her than she wanted to admit. She wouldn't let Carter see that. Not because she didn't trust him, but a woman was entitled to a little pride.

THURSDAY'S MEETING AT SAR headquarters began with an announcement. "Joel Chessman let us know today that he's restructuring his charitable giving and not to expect a check this year," Carrie, who served as the group's treasurer, said. "That's ten thousand dollars we were counting on for our budget."

"Whoa," Caleb said. "Did he say why he's leaving us out this year?"

"The letter says he wants to focus on helping different causes," Carrie said.

"Who is Joel Chessman?" Carter asked.

"He owns a big consulting firm or something," Tony said. "He's given a big gift to us the last three years. That's more than generous."

"I'll draft a nice thank-you letter and tell him to keep us in mind in the future," Carrie said. "In the meantime, we need to come up with some ideas to fill the funding gap."

"We could hold another dinner-dance," Sheri said.

"The last one was a ton of work and only raised a few thousand," Eldon said.

"Nothing we do is going to net ten thousand dollars at once," Sheri said.

"We could look for more grants," Deni said.

"That's a good idea," Carrie said. "But those can take months or years to come through. We got word today that the boiler in this building might not make it through the winter, so we need to set money aside for a replacement."

"We'd like to put in an electric heat pump," Tony said. "And we've talked about adding more solar panels."

"All that is going to take more than T-shirt sales and raffles," Danny said.

"I think we should talk to Mr. Chessman," Carter said. "Impress on him how valuable his contribution is."

"Are you volunteering to talk to him?" Sheri asked.

"That's a good idea," Ryan said before Carter could answer. "You seem to be good at persuading people."

"I'm not going to impress a billionaire," Carter said. "I'm still a rookie. I think a veteran should go."

"I'm captain, so I guess I should go," Danny said. "But Carter needs to go with me. He can do most of the talking."

"I don't think—" Carter began, but was drowned out by the voices of the other volunteers, in support of the plan.

"You might as well try it," Ryan said. "He's already decided not to donate. If you can't change his mind, we're no worse off. And you might succeed."

Carter nodded. He wasn't a climbing expert. He didn't have medical training. He wasn't particularly strong or technically proficient or possessing any of the other skills that stood out to him as valuable to the organization. But he could talk. "I'll try," he said. Sometimes his words made a difference. Maybe this would be one of those times.

Chapter Fifteen

Local Man Confesses to Writing Harassing Letters
By Tammy Patterson, Examiner Staff

Edward Anders, 61, has confessed to being the author of a rash of anonymous letters sent to various residents of Eagle Mountain over the past few weeks. The letters accused people of various petty crimes and code violations, many of which proved to be unfounded.

Anders was apprehended after a doorbell camera captured him tacking a letter to the front door of the home of Martin and Tina Robinson. Anders's letter accused the Robinsons of putting trash in their recycling bins.

Anders, the father of high school coach Mitch Anders, defended his actions, telling sheriff's deputies that he wanted to show people that everyone breaks the law, but most of them go unpunished. Anders has been released on his own recognizance, pending a sentencing hearing.

The following Friday morning Ed Anders's arrest made front-page news in the weekly edition of the *Eagle Mountain Examiner*. Mira, who was largely recovered from her concussion, sought out Shayla at school. She was collating worksheets in her classroom. "How is Mitch?" Mira asked. "Is he very upset about his dad?"

"He's concerned, of course." Shayla arranged the second sheets of the handout on top of the first sheets, face down. "And feeling guilty that he didn't realize what his dad was up to. He's made an appointment for Ed to see a specialist. We think there must be some dementia going on. Why else would he do such a thing?"

"I'm sorry he's having to go through this," Mira said. "I'm sure he's glad to have you to lean on."

"I hope I'm helping."

"Have you met his dad?" Mira asked.

"A couple of times. He wasn't very friendly, but Mitch said that's just his dad's personality. He's very gruff, and I guess he's in a lot of pain. He has terrible arthritis and can hardly walk. I worry about him driving his old Jeep around town, but Mitch says he never goes far."

"I suppose the judge will take all of that into consideration when he sentences him," Mira said.

"I hope so. Mitch did say his dad had some trouble with the law when he was younger. He didn't elaborate and I didn't want to pry."

"The paper didn't mention that."

Shayla began stapling the stacks of worksheets together. "I get the impression it was a long time ago. Anyway, as horrible as this is, it's brought Mitch and me closer together. We're seeing a lot of each other."

Mira handed her the next set of papers. "What do your parents think?"

"They're not happy. But they're trying to be subtle. My mom is trying to fix me up with the nephew of a friend. She keeps sending me pictures of him and talking about how successful and handsome he is and how interested he is in meeting me." She wrinkled her nose. "So what if he's all those things? Mitch is the man I'm attracted to. You can't fight fate."

Mira didn't know if she believed in fate. She was attracted to Carter, but she blamed hormones more than destiny. Nothing wrong with hormones. It was a relief, after all this time, to know that that part of her was still alive. But she wasn't going to pretend there was some supernatural force bringing the two of them together. It was enough for her that he was a good man who treated her—and everyone around him—well. He made her laugh and sigh and the fact that he had a gorgeous body didn't hurt, either.

The ordeal with George had vanquished all the stars from her eyes. She hoped she saw more clearly now.

JOEL CHESSMAN AGREED to meet with Carter and Danny at his home in a picturesque canyon above Eagle Mountain on Saturday afternoon. As they wound up a paved drive to park near the front door, Carter stared at the house constructed of massive blocks of stone that seemed to emerge from the mountainside. Joel—he said to call him Joel—greeted them at the front door. A thin, graceful man with blond hair shot through with silver and a Vandyke goatee, he answered the door dressed in jeans and a loose linen shirt, barefoot, and led them into a home office with a wall of glass that offered a view of the snowcapped San Juan Mountains and colorful canyon walls.

"We wanted to thank you for your support of Eagle Mountain Search and Rescue for the past several years," Danny began.

Joel settled onto a leather sofa across from the club chairs he had directed them to. "A good friend of mine was saved by search and rescue when he fell while climbing in California," he said. "I realized how important the work was. I read an article in the paper about how the local organization was struggling to raise money for equipment and I wanted to help."

"You've been a big help," Danny said. "We received your letter that you had decided to contribute to other causes and wanted to find out if we had done something to offend you."

"Not at all. I think you're a fine organization. I've just decided to shift my focus to other causes. To spread the wealth, so to speak."

"What kind of work do you do?" Carter asked.

"I'm a project management consultant. I mainly handle big infrastructure projects."

Carter nodded, trying to look as if he had any idea what this man was talking about. "Maybe you can help us in another way," he said. "With advice instead of money."

Joel looked interested. "What kind of advice do you need?"

Carter leaned forward, carefully choosing his words. "We offer our services to people for free," he said. "And everyone involved with Eagle Mountain Search and Rescue is a volunteer. But like any other business, our expenses increase every year—from the cost of electricity for our headquarters and gas for our vehicles to the price of medical supplies, climbing equipment and training. We receive a small amount from the county and a little from the state. We sell T-shirts and bumper stickers and hold various fundraisers but we don't really have a way to generate money beyond asking for donations."

"You need an endowment that will generate funds every year," Joel said.

"That would be ideal," Danny said. "But where would we get the endowment?"

"You're asking the wrong question," Joel said. "The better question is what would you do with the endowment if you get it?"

"That's why we need someone like you," Carter said.

"You need more than one someone. You need investment advisers. Preferably a firm that specializes in nonprofits."

"Do you know someone?" Danny asked.

"I might. And I probably know some people who would be interested in investing in your organization. I'd be willing to make another contribution, too. Get enough big donors and you could set a challenge and ask for matching funds. You raise half the money you need through smaller donors and the larger donors contribute the rest."

"That sounds ideal," Danny said. "But can we really get together the funds to make that happen?"

"It won't happen overnight," Joel said. "But eventually, you wouldn't have to depend so heavily on donations. If you go about this in the right way, you can build a fund whose earning could support everyday operations for years to come."

"That sounds like a great plan," Carter said. "We'd appreciate your help—both your expertise and any funds you could contribute."

"What changed your mind about contributing?" Danny asked.

"I was sure you were coming to see me today with your hand out, asking for more money," he said. "I wasn't offended by that. I'm used to it. But you surprised me. You didn't ask for money, you asked for advice. You valued my expertise as much as my cash. That got my interest. If you're willing to meet with me again, I think I can help you set up a plan to put you on a better financial footing and ensure a more stable future."

"Yes," Danny said. "We're really eager to learn what you and any advisers you can recommend have to say."

Joel stood. "I'm excited about this, too. Thanks for coming today."

"Thanks for seeing us."

"You did great," Danny said when he and Carter were back in his car.

"All I did was ask a question."

Danny grinned. "You seem to have a knack for asking the right questions."

TRISHA ISBELL KEPT a close eye on her children. She made sure they wore bike helmets and never let them go to the park unless they were with her or another parent. Since the local kidnapping attempts she had scarcely let them out of her sight. No more riding their bicycles around their quiet cul-de-sac. They played inside or in the backyard.

But a break in the septic line had rendered the backyard off-limits while repairs were being made. And the lure of a sunny Monday afternoon had seven-year-old Noah and his five-year-old sister, Riley, begging to go outside and play in the front yard. Anna finally relented. She took her lawn chair out with her, parked it in the shade of a pine tree and watched as the children chased each other in a game of tag. She smiled as Noah deliberately slowed his steps to allow Riley to catch up with him. "Tag, you're it!" she shouted gleefully.

From somewhere in the house she heard her phone ringing. She must have left it on the counter again. She should let it ring out, but she was expecting a call from their insurance company about a bill she had protested. She glanced at the children. Noah was pursuing Riley now, making roaring noises and pretending to be some kind of animal. A lion? Or maybe a bear?

She had to get the phone. With a last glance at the children, she hurried inside. There was the phone, on the kitchen counter. "Hello?" she answered, hoping she didn't sound too out of breath.

"Mrs. Isbell, I'm calling about the bill you questioned."

"Yes, thank you for returning my call." She hurried to her desk, and pulled the bill from a pile of papers there.

She was making notes in the margins of the bill and listening to a convoluted explanation from the woman on the other end of the line when the screech of tires on the road outside distracted her. Then a child screamed. Not just any child. *Her* child.

She dropped the phone and raced outside, banging her knee painfully on the porch railing as she hurtled down the steps toward the curb, where Noah struggled with a black-clad figure at the open driver's door of a white SUV. Riley stood beside them, wailing. Never slowing down, Anna grabbed the nearest weapon she could find—a scooter one of the children had left in the driveway. Raising it over her head she brought it down on the man's head.

He swore, and shoved the scooter back toward her, toppling her over. But she managed to wrap one arm around Noah and drag him with her. "Riley!" she shouted. "Run to the house!"

For once, Riley didn't hesitate, but raced across the lawn and through the front door Trisha had left open. The man jumped back into the car and sped away.

Trisha lay back on the grass, both arms wrapped around Noah. "Shhh," she said, rocking him back and forth. "You're safe now. Mama's got you."

They lay there several minutes. Riley joined them, both children clinging to her, all three of them crying. Trisha could feel a knot rising on her forehead where the scooter had hit her. Slowly, she sat up and, the children still clinging to her, made her way inside. She found her phone and picked it up. The woman from the insurance company was still talking, apparently oblivious to Trisha's absence.

"I'll have to call you back," Trisha said, and ended the call. She dialed 911. "A man just tried to kidnap my son," she told the operator who answered.

Tuesday afternoon, Travis Walker studied the man across from him in the modest living room. Mitch Anders was a stocky, clean-cut man in his early thirties with blond hair and blue eyes. He looked nervous, but most people would under the circumstances, being questioned by law enforcement again so soon after his release from jail.

"Someone tried to snatch a little boy from the yard in front of his house yesterday afternoon," Travis said. "The car the man was driving matches the description of your car."

"There are a lot of white SUVs in this county," Mitch said.

"Where were you yesterday afternoon between four thirty and six thirty?" Travis asked.

"I was at my girlfriend's house."

"Who is your girlfriend?"

"Shayla Green."

"Address?"

"Twelve-fourteen Wild Rose."

Two blocks from the Isbell house. "Was your car there?"

"No. Shayla picked me up this morning and she drove to her house."

"Was your father at home?"

"Probably. He doesn't go many places."

"Where is your dad now?"

"He's in his room. Taking a nap."

"Could he have driven your car?"

"Dad has an old red Jeep he drives. He doesn't like my SUV. He says it's too hard for him to get in and out of. You've seen him, Sheriff. He can hardly walk. How could he snatch a kid?"

"Is there anyone else who would drive your car?" Travis asked.

"No. Why would they?"

"We talked to your neighbor. She's sure your car wasn't in your driveway that afternoon."

"It was."

Travis glanced out the window. He could see the white Toyota from here. "Can we take a look at the car?"

"I guess."

Travis and his brother, Gage, followed Mitch out to the car. It shone in the afternoon sun, and smelled like wax. Gage opened the passenger door and looked inside. "It's been cleaned recently," he said. "It's spotless."

Mitch frowned. "It wasn't like that this morning."

"Are you sure?"

"I'm sure." He walked around to the driver's side and opened the door, stuck his head in and sniffed.

"Maybe your dad took it to be washed," Travis suggested. "As a surprise for you."

Mitch stepped back from the car. "My dad isn't really like that. And I told you, he doesn't drive this vehicle. He prefers his Jeep."

"What's that in the back seat?" Gage asked.

Mitch looked inside. "I don't see anything."

"On the floorboard." Gage slipped on gloves, then reached in and picked up something black from the back floorboard. "It's a sweatshirt," he said. "There's a pair of pants and a mask and gloves in there, too."

"This matches the description of the clothing the boy's mother told us the suspect was wearing," Travis said.

Mitch took another step back, all color drained from his face. "I don't know how those got in there."

Travis stepped forward. "Put your hands behind your back, Mr. Anders," he said. "You have the right to remain silent…"

FRANTIC POUNDING SENT Mira running to the front door of her apartment Tuesday afternoon. She checked the security peephole and saw Shayla waiting there, wringing her hands. She hurried to open the door. Shayla collapsed against her. Mira embraced her with one arm, the cast on her other arm cradled between them. "Shayla, what's wrong?" she asked.

"Mitch has been arrested again. I told them he couldn't have done it, but they didn't believe me."

"What?" Mira shut the door and led Shayla into the living room. "Tell me again. I didn't understand what you said."

"They've arrested Mitch. For the kidnappings. Someone tried to take another little boy this afternoon and the mother described Mitch's SUV. Only Mitch wasn't in the car. He was with me. I told the sheriff's deputies that, but they wouldn't believe me. They found the clothing the kidnapper wore in the back seat of the car. And the car had been washed, as if someone was trying to hide evidence."

"They think Mitch washed the car, but left the clothing the kidnapper wore in the back seat? That doesn't make sense."

"Nothing about this makes sense," Shayla wailed. "Mitch

called me from the station to ask me to look in on his dad, so I went over there and the old man wouldn't even let me in. He told me to go away and slammed the door in my face."

"Shayla, I'm so sorry. Sit down and let me get you some water." Mira retrieved a glass of water from the kitchen and hurried to rejoin her friend. "What happened with the boy, do you know?" she asked.

"Apparently his mother fought off the kidnapper."

"What kind of clothes did they find?"

"Black sweatpants and shirt, a black ski mask and gloves."

"That's the same thing the man who attacked us on the trail was wearing," Mira said.

"I know that wasn't Mitch," Shayla said. "He would never hurt me. And he wouldn't hurt you, either."

Mira tried to think back. Had the man who had rushed at her been Mitch Anders? Everything had happened so fast. And she didn't know Mitch well. How could she be sure?

"Shayla, do you think there's any possibility Mitch did have something to do with these abductions?" she asked.

Shayla jumped up, her face flushed. "How can you say that? Of course he didn't. Didn't you hear me? I was with him this afternoon!"

"What did the sheriff say when you told them that?"

"They said the boy's house was only two blocks from mine. That Mitch could have left while I was in the shower."

"Could he have done that?" Mira asked.

"He didn't! Why don't you believe me?"

She wanted to believe her friend. But she had wanted to believe George, too. "The most wonderful seeming people in the world can do terrible things," Mira said. "I dated a man in Santa Fe. Everyone loved him. I loved him. And then he was arrested for possessing child pornography. He had a big collection I knew nothing about. He was part of a whole network of collectors. Pedophiles. And I never saw that side of him."

Shayla was sobbing, her face contorted by angry tears. "I can't believe you'd think something like that about Mitch," she said.

"I don't think it. I don't want to think it. I'm just saying you need to consider the possibility. To protect yourself."

"Love isn't about protecting yourself," Shayla said. "It's about wanting to protect the other person." She turned and ran from the apartment.

"Shayla, please!" Mira ran after her, but Shayla was already hurtling down the steps and running to her car. Mira sagged against the doorframe, sick to her stomach. What had she done? And what had Mitch done?

Chapter Sixteen

Message from: Carter Ames
Got some news to share. Can I stop by?

Yes!

Carter was startled when Mira opened the door to her apartment and embraced him. "I'm so glad to see you," she said, her face buried against his shoulder.

He pulled back enough to look at her. "Have you been crying?" he asked, though it was clear she had, her eyes puffy and red.

"Did you hear? They arrested Mitch Anders this afternoon."

"Again?" He let her lead him into her living room. "What happened?"

She told him about the latest attempted kidnapping, Mitch's car being identified, and the clothes the kidnapper had been wearing being found in his car. "Shayla told the sheriff's deputies that Mitch was with her when the boy was grabbed, but the kid's house was only two blocks from hers. She admitted she took a shower. Mitch could have sneaked out while she was in the shower."

"That seems pretty risky," Carter said. "And why would he leave the clothes in the back of his car?"

"I don't understand any of it," she said. "All I know is that Shayla is furious with me now because I asked if she thought Mitch might really be guilty?"

"You think he's guilty?" he asked.

"I don't know!" She put one hand to the side of her head, the other, in its cast, hugged to her chest. Tears filled her eyes again.

He gathered her close, mindful of her broken arm. "I'm sorry about Shayla," he said. "And about Mitch, too. What happened with the boy?"

"His mother apparently went after the kidnapper and chased him off. As far as I know, the boy is okay."

"This guy has struck out three times. Maybe he'll give up now."

"I don't know if people with those kind of compulsions can give up," she said. She pulled away from him and combed her fingers through her hair. "Your text said you had some news. Was it about Mitch?"

"No. I didn't know anything about that."

"Come sit down and tell me."

They sat side by side on the sofa. "My news isn't that exciting," he said. "I just wanted to share it with someone."

She smiled. "I'm glad you chose me."

He told her about the visit with Joel Chessman and his promise to donate more money to search and rescue and help them develop more reliable funding. "That's wonderful," she said.

"I was just happy to be able to do something to help the organization," he said. "So many of the volunteers have high level skills and training. They tell us that everyone is important, even if all we do is help carry supplies. But it's nice to be able to contribute more."

"You don't give yourself enough credit," she said. "Your talent is communicating with people. I remember how you were able to calm me down after my car accident. That's an important skill, too."

"I guess so. Though I never thought of talking as a skill. Almost everyone can do it."

"Lots of people can use words," she said. "Not everyone can make them really mean something."

She kissed him. He wanted to keep kissing her, and maybe pick up where they had left off last time they were together. But he sensed a tension in her. A holding back. He looked into her eyes. "What's wrong?" he asked.

She looked away.

"Are you still upset about Shayla?"

"Yes. I don't think she'll ever forgive me. Especially if Mitch turns out to be really innocent."

"You were worried about her safety if he's guilty, though."

"Yes." She met his gaze then. "I learned the hard way that people aren't always what they seem. Even people you love."

He said nothing. Waiting.

"I lived with a guy in Santa Fe," she said. "His name was George. He seemed like such a sweet, gentle man. The kind of person everyone likes. Then one day the police came and arrested him. Turns out he was part of a secret club of men who traded child pornography. He had dozens of DVDs and files on his computer. He must have spent hours watching that stuff. It made me sick to my stomach."

"Oh, Mira." He pulled her close. "I'm sorry you had to go through that."

"I thought I was in love with him," she said. "And I didn't even know him."

"No wonder you didn't want to trust me," he said. "I may have my faults, but I promise, I'm not into anything like that." The very idea repelled him.

"I believe you," she said. "But when Shayla was telling

me about Mitch, it brought everything back. I didn't want her to have to go through what I did. And now she hates me."

"I'm sorry," he said. "Maybe one day you can make her understand."

"It helps having you here," she said. "You're not only a good talker, you're a good listener."

"I've spent a lot of years getting by on a glib attitude," he said. He stroked her shoulder. "I know how to be charming and I'll admit I've used that a lot of times to get what I want from people. I'm a flirt and I like to joke around, but that doesn't mean I'm shallow."

"I don't think you're shallow," she said.

"The truth is, I come across a lot of the time as confident and cocky, but it's all an act." He swallowed, wanting to let her see this side of him, but afraid of what she would think of him. "I'm lost inside, a lot of time," he said. "I worry about what people think of me. Everyone else seems to have their act so together. Aaron is a cop. A good one. Dalton is a computer genius who's probably going to make billions from his software. Bethany is sweet and kind and everyone's friend. And she's smart and brave and pretty much every other good adjective you can come up with. The best anyone can come up with for me is 'he's charming' or 'he has the gift of gab.'"

She turned to look him in the eye. "I believe you're a good person. You volunteer with search and rescue. That's a big commitment. And there's a lot to be said for being good with words. You proved that today. After all, I teach language. I'm all about words."

"I love you," he said. Scary words. But not hard to say to her.

"Oh, Carter." She kissed him again, a deep, open-mouthed kiss that made any more words unnecessary.

CARTER'S CONFESSION HAD stolen Mira's breath. She couldn't speak with such confidence yet, but she thought soon she would be able to. In the meantime, she would show him her feelings. They kissed until they were dizzy, then she pulled away and reached for her phone. "What are you doing?" he asked.

"I'm turning this thing off," she said. "No more interruptions." She tossed the phone aside and cupped his face in her hand. "And now I'm going to make love to you until we both can't see straight."

He reached for his own phone, switched it off and tossed it next to hers. Then he slid both hands beneath her T-shirt and began tugging it off. "That's the best idea I've heard all day. All year."

After carefully maneuvering around her cast, the shirt joined the phones at the end of the sofa. Then he pressed his face to her cleavage and began running his tongue along the edge of her bra. A tickling, electric sensation teased through her. His tongue slipped beneath the lace edge of the bra cup, brushing her nipple. She gasped, and jolted against him. "Do you like that?" he asked. He moved his mouth to the fabric over her nipple and exhaled a hot breath. "How about that?"

She should have known he wouldn't be a silent lover. As he removed her clothing and explored her body he kept up a stream of sexy murmurs, announcing his pleasure at what he found, or asking what she enjoyed, or tantalizing her with descriptions of what he intended to do. The conversation was every bit as erotic as the physical foreplay, which he excelled at also, caressing, stroking and teasing with just the right pressure, until she was gasping and writhing against him, wondering how much more she could stand.

But she didn't let him have all the fun. She was quick to divest him of his shirt. "That day you were washing the Jeeps," she said as she licked her way down his chest. "I was so distracted, trying not to stare at you." She paused to circle his nipple with her tongue. "I was jealous of every drop of water."

He made a growling noise low in his throat, then stood and pulled her to her feet. "Why don't we go somewhere more comfortable?"

Laughing, she led him to the bedroom. "As much as I want to take you to bed, I'd like to do another lap around the house," he said. "Just to watch you walking naked in front of me."

In the bedroom doorway she turned and cupped her palm to his crotch. His erection strained against the fly of his jeans. She stroked one finger along the ridge and he let out another growl, sending a thrill down her spine.

She took her time lowering the zipper, then took him in her hand, jelly-legged with wanting, but refusing to rush. When his eyes met hers, they were heavy with lust. He bent his head and kissed her hard, and she arched against him.

They fell back on the bed, then tore at the last of their clothes. She started to straddle him, but he stopped her. "Just a minute," he said, his breathing ragged.

She thought he wanted to catch his breath, but instead he retrieved his jeans from the floor and pulled something from his pocket. She laughed when she recognized the condom packet. "You were pretty confident," she said.

"I've been carrying these around for weeks," he said.

"These? Plural?"

"You said something about 'until we couldn't see straight,' didn't you?"

She fell back, laughing, but the laughter died as she watched him roll on the condom. Then he moved over her. "You're so beautiful," he said. "I want to know every part of you."

She closed her eyes and lost herself to sensation. She had

spent so much time thinking and analyzing, it was freeing to just feel. She focused on the way he smelled—like pine soap and washed cotton and male musk. His fingers were calloused and dragged against her skin, sending shivers up her spine. Then his mouth closed around her, warm and silken. He tasted of citrus and salt, and she told herself she would never forget that combination.

And then they slid together, shifting and rocking, slow, then fast, friction and flow, tension building. She gripped his shoulder and arched her back and he thrust up to meet her. Her climax shuddered through her, and he held her tightly until her body relaxed. Then he thrust again, moving more deliberately, winding up the tension, until she came a second time, just as he found his release.

They lay together for a long moment, still connected, unspeaking. Then he slid from beneath her, got up and disposed of the condom. When he returned to bed, she cuddled against him. "I learned something about you just now," she said.

"What's that?" His eyes were closed, his breathing slowing.

"Talking isn't the only thing you're good at."

WEDNESDAY MORNING CARTER was still at Mira's apartment when her phone rang, the blare of Banda horns jolting him awake. "When did you turn that back on?" he asked, one arm draped over his eyes to shield them from the dawn light that streamed through her bedroom window.

"Right before we went to sleep," she said. "Remember. You turned yours on, too."

"Obviously, I was distracted by you." He reached for her, but she swatted him away. She finally found the phone beneath their discarded clothes. "Hello?" she answered.

"Mira, this is Sheriff Walker."

She sat on the edge of the bed and wrapped the blanket around her. As if the sheriff might see her through the phone. "Hello, Sheriff." She looked over her shoulder and met Carter's eyes. He sat up, expression alert.

"Have you received any more messages?" he asked. "Any letters or other threats?"

"No," she said. "I thought Ed Anders was sending those letters."

"Ed confessed to sending letters to many people in town, but he denies responsibility for yours. We feel the tone of the ones sent to you is different—and given the message on your classroom whiteboard and the attack on you on Gold Lake Trail, we think your harasser is someone else."

In the back of her mind, she had suspected this, but having the sheriff confirm it unsettled her. She could no longer tell herself she had nothing to worry about now that Ed had admitted guilt.

"The reference to David Ketchum's murder makes us believe whoever wrote to you has a connection to Santa Fe and your past," Travis continued. "We've learned that Mitch Anders was born in Santa Fe. Do you remember running into him while you were living there?"

"No! Hasn't he lived in Eagle Mountain for years?"

"He has, but he could have gone back to visit family."

"I'm sure I never saw Mitch before I came here," she said. "And he's never said or done anything to make me suspicious of him."

"Some people are very good at hiding their true intentions."

She knew that too well. "Please let me know if you learn anything else," she said.

"I will. In the meantime, be careful, and alert us to anything suspicious, even if it seems insignificant."

She ended the call and rested the phone in her lap. Carter

scooted closer. "I heard most of that," he said. "Now they think Mitch is the one who targeted you?"

"Why would he do that?" She shook her head. "I can't think of any connection between us."

He rubbed her shoulder. "I don't like knowing that someone is still out there who tried to harm you."

"If Mitch is responsible, he's in custody," she said. "And I'll be careful, I promise. I'm only going to go to school and my night class and to see you."

"It wouldn't be a bad idea for me to stay here when I can," he said.

She turned toward him, letting the blanket slide down. "That wouldn't be a bad idea at all," she said, and pushed him back on the bed. "I have a little time before I have to leave for work." She knew one way to shove her fears aside. At least for a little while.

WEDNESDAY WAS OFTEN the slowest day at the tour company. Carter and Dalton spent the morning detailing Jeeps and making small repairs. But Carter's mind wasn't on his work. Instead, he was worrying about Mira. She should be safe enough at school, but then again, someone had sneaked into her classroom and left that sinister message. He would feel better if he knew for sure the sheriff had found the person responsible.

"Dude, that's the third time you've checked the air in that tire," Dalton said. "Is something wrong with the gauge?"

"Nothing wrong with the gauge." He rose. "I'm just distracted."

"Too much sex will do that," Dalton said.

Carter sent him a sour look. "I'm worried whoever hurt Mira is still out there," he said.

"Guess the sheriff's office has been too busy with the

child kidnapping attempts to track down Mira's attacker," Dalton said.

"They're still working the case," Carter said. "The sheriff called her this morning. But they don't have much to go on."

"She doesn't have any idea who it might be?" Dalton asked.

"She says not, but I wonder about her ex."

Dalton leaned across the hood of the Jeep. "Trouble there?"

"He ended up in prison. She says he was a mild-mannered guy before that, but maybe prison changed him. He might have spent his time inside resenting her for dumping him."

"If he's still locked up, she shouldn't have anything to worry about," Dalton said.

"He's been paroled. Then he disappeared."

"I could try to track him down."

"I'm sure the cops have already tried that," Carter said.

"But they don't have a hacker like me." Dalton grinned. "And even if they have looked and found out stuff about this guy, they're probably not telling you everything. And you want to know everything, right?"

"Yeah, I do."

"Then leave it to me." He straightened. "I'll need the guy's name and anything else you know about him."

"His name is George Suarez and he was arrested in Santa Fe a couple of years ago."

"What did he do?"

"You can't tell anyone," Carter said. "It would really upset Mira."

"I would never do anything to upset Mira."

He explained about George's involvement in child pornography. Dalton made a face. "Doesn't sound like they kept him in prison nearly long enough. I'll see what I can find out."

Chapter Seventeen

Mira tried to apologize to Shayla at school on Wednesday, but her former friend refused to speak to her. She turned her back whenever Mira approached, and left the room while she was still talking. Mira swallowed back tears and stopped trying to make amends. She was happier than she had ever been with Carter, but the loss of her friend meant she had no one to share her happiness with.

At least the Spanish class for first responders was going well. The students had moved on to more complex medical and legal terms. Wednesday evening, they were deep in a discussion of how to explain the use of a defibrillator when phones starting going off all over the classroom.

"We've got a callout," Carter said. "A teen in distress."

The mood of the room shifted as if someone had flipped a switch. The air practically crackled with adrenaline. Mira felt the anxiety herself. "Good luck," she said, as people began to exit. "Be careful."

Carter stopped to kiss her cheek. "I'll call you later," he said.

Within seconds, she was the only one left. She began gathering papers and straightening chairs. She thought of the first responders, heading out in the dark to search for someone's child. This must be a parent's worst nightmare.

And she thought of the child, and said a prayer that they would be found safe.

It put her own problems in perspective, and reminded her that if she was ever in trouble again, there were people who would respond to help.

THE SCENE ABOVE Dixon Pass was tense, spotlights illuminating the figure of the fifteen-year-old boy near the center span of the bridge over the canyon, the road closed to traffic, rescuers arrayed on either side of the bridge, fearful of approaching too close. "He's threatened to jump," Deputy Declan Owen said. "He says he wants to die. A photographer was trying to get a shot of the moon reflected in the water below the bridge and spotted the boy and called it in."

"Do we know who he is?" Danny asked.

"We don't," Deputy Owen said. "He said his parents kicked him out of the house and he doesn't have anywhere to go."

Carter winced, thinking of his own close family. He couldn't imagine anything he could have done that would have made his parents ask him to leave home. Not at fifteen.

"We're trying to get a professional on scene," the deputy continued. "Meanwhile, we need to be ready to move in quickly."

"We can stage rescue climbers above and below the bridge," Danny said. "And a water rescue crew in case he goes into the water."

Carter looked over the side of the bridge to the water splashing over shallow rocks below. If the kid jumped into that, the odds were high the water rescue would turn into a body recovery.

"What's the ETA on the professional?" Danny asked.

Owen shook his head. "We've made some calls but we

haven't found anyone yet. They'll probably have to come from Junction, or farther."

"We may not have that kind of time," Danny said. "Let Carter talk to him."

Carter took a step back. "What if I say the wrong thing? I'm no professional."

"You have good instincts," Danny said. He looked at Declan. "He does. I'm seen him in action. He talked a woman with dementia off a ledge."

"She wasn't threatening to kill herself," Carter said.

"Don't try to talk him out of taking his own life," Declan said. "Just keep him talking until we get someone else to help."

"I can try," Carter said. His chest hurt, thinking about the possibility that he might mess up.

"Take this." Danny handed him a radio. "That way we can communicate with each other."

The walk to the middle was a long way in the darkness. He followed the white line on the edge of the roadway, his boots crunching on loose gravel. A brisk wind swept down the canyon, cutting through his SAR windbreaker. He wondered if the kid on the span below had a jacket.

He stopped at the edge of the spotlight, at what he judged to be the middle of the bridge. Leaning over, he could see the curve of the supporting structure. The boy stood with his back against the concrete, one hand up to shield his eyes from the glare of the spotlight. Carter keyed the radio. "Cut the light," he said. "You're blinding him."

A few seconds later, the light blinked, then went out. Carter leaned over to look again. The boy was only a thicker shadow in the darkness now. "My name's Carter," he said.

"Are you a shrink?" the boy said. "Sent to talk me out of jumping?"

"No. I'm a Jeep tour guide. I take tourists around in a Jeep and tell them about the mountains."

"What are you doing out here?"

"I collect stories."

"You what?"

"I collect stories. I want to know yours."

"I don't even know you. Why should I tell you anything?"

"Fair enough. Maybe I'll tell you my story."

"What's your story?"

"I was a dorky kid. Now I'm a dorky grown-up who makes a living driving people around the mountains in a Jeep."

Silence. Clearly, he was doing a bang-up job so far. He waited, searching for something else to say. How long could he stand here, doing nothing, before the boy got bored and went ahead and jumped?

"Do you like the job?" the kid asked.

"I do. I like people."

"I don't like people. Maybe because they don't like me."

"There are people I don't like," he said. "Everybody is different. That's a good thing, though. I'd be bored if everybody were alike."

"My parents don't even like me. They kicked me out."

"That's rough. You seem like an okay guy to me. What's your name?"

"Craig. My parents said I was messy and I broke curfew too many times. And the teachers are always after me when I don't do my homework. Some of it's so stupid."

Carter remained silent while the boy reviewed a long list of hurts and slights. He reminded himself he wasn't here to judge, only to listen. And he wasn't so far from his own teen years that he couldn't sympathize. Sometimes at that age he had felt that the world was against him, too. And he had a loving family and every advantage this boy didn't have.

"The worst thing is, I don't have any friends," Craig said and fell silent.

"That's hard, too," Carter said. "People are so involved in themselves sometimes it's hard to connect with others. We don't really see the other people around us. It's hard enough to even get a clear picture of ourselves. I'm not sure we ever do."

"When I look at myself I see a loser." Shuffling sounds on metal. Was Craig moving closer to the edge?

Carter leaned farther over the railing, trying to keep the boy in his sights. "You need a new mirror," he said. "Have you done much climbing?"

"Not really."

"Yet with no experience, you climbed down there?"

"It wasn't hard."

"Maybe not for you. We could use someone with your talent in search and rescue."

"Don't you have to be eighteen?"

"Yeah, but you can start training now. By the time you're eighteen you'll be a veteran."

"It sounds hard."

"You've already done hard things."

"I don't know. You have to help strangers. People who have done things to get themselves in trouble."

"That's every one of us. We all make the wrong choices sometimes. Doesn't mean we aren't still good people."

"It's easy for you to talk. You're an adult with a job and friends and a good life."

"Looks that way to you. To other people it looks like I'm a guy who didn't go to college, who's working for my parents and living with my brother. I don't have it all together. Most people don't."

"You're not making me feel good about everything I have

to look forward to." Was that amusement Carter heard behind those words?

"I'm not saying I'm a shining example or anything," Carter said. "But there's all kinds of ways to be a success. On the surface, my life doesn't look like much, but mostly, I'm happy."

"I can't remember what it's like to be happy."

"There are people who can help with that. Medications. Therapy. Depression is a real thing. Nothing to be ashamed of."

"Nobody wants to help me."

"There's a whole crowd of people here tonight who say different."

"You're here because it's your job."

"We're here because we care. We care about you. I care. You've been dealt a really rough hand but you're still here. Tackling some big obstacles. That takes guts."

Silence. Carter held his breath. Had he said the wrong thing? He looked toward the end of the bridge, where Danny and Declan stood watching.

"If I wanted to get down from here, I'm gonna need some help," Craig said.

Carter's legs almost gave out. He put one hand on the concrete railing beside him, steadying himself, then switched on the radio. "We can help," he said. "Look up and to your right."

A light shone on the bridge, where the climbers were staged. "When you're ready, they'll come down and help you out," Carter said.

"I'm not going to be arrested, am I?" Craig asked.

The radio crackled. "No arrest," Declan said.

"You heard the man," Carter said. "And we won't just leave you on the street, either. We're going to do what we can to make things better." His mother would take the boy in, if no one else would.

"All right," Craig said. "They can come down. It's getting cold down here."

Carter moved aside as Ryan and the rest of the team on the bridge went to work. They reached Craig quickly and helped him into a safety harness and helmet, then guided him as he climbed up onto the bridge, offering plenty of praise and encouragement. One of them gave the boy his jacket and someone else handed him a cup of hot chocolate from someone's thermos.

Carter walked up and embraced the boy. Craig looked as if he was trying not to cry, and Carter's own eyes burned.

A motherly-looking woman with short brown hair and kind eyes approached. "I'm Jess Babcock," she said. "I'm going to take you to a place you can stay for a while. We'll talk about what you want to do next."

Danny and Declan joined the small group, and Carter asked Ms. Babcock, "What will happen to him now?"

"We'll contact his parents and assess the situation there. But if it's true they kicked him out, we have a couple of foster parents who are willing to take him in. We'll also get him with some mental health professionals. There's a couple of outdoor programs he could be eligible for this summer, if he's interested."

"We talked about climbing," Carter said. "And search and rescue work. He seemed interested."

She nodded and led the boy away.

"I'd like to stay in touch with him," Carter told Danny when Jess and Craig were gone. "Or is that not a good idea?"

"I think it would be a good idea," Danny said.

"I'll give you Jess's card," Declan said. "You can talk to her about it."

The three of them walked down the length of the bridge, where a small crowd had gathered. Mira broke off from a group of women she had been talking to and hurried to embrace Carter. "What are you doing here?" he asked, one arm around her.

"Craig is one of my students. A colleague sent a text alerting me and some of us decided to come down here to the bridge, in case we could help." She rested her palm on his chest. "What did you say to him?"

"I mostly listened. He said his parents kicked him out and he didn't have any friends. That's a tough position to be in and I wanted to let him know there were people who cared, even if he didn't know us."

"You saved his life," she said.

Was it too much to think that Craig had changed Carter's life, too? "He really made me appreciate all the good things in my own life," he said. He pulled her closer. "Like you."

"Let's go home," she said.

Did she mean his place or hers? Or his parents' house? All those were home in one way or another—places where he was welcome and even loved. He ought never to complain about his life again. Though he knew he would. It was human nature to never be satisfied. But he would be more careful before he dismissed what he had as not enough.

DALTON FOUND CARTER the next morning, as he was preparing for his first tour of the day. "I wanted to let you know what I found out about George Suarez," he said.

"Oh?" Carter closed the lid of the cooler he had been loading with water bottles. "Do you know where he's living now?"

"I wasn't able to come up with that. But I found out a little more about his time in Santa Fe. Apparently, he was living there the same time a kid named David Ketchum was kidnapped and killed. After his conviction as a pedophile, local police questioned him about the murder, but he had an alibi. He served eighteen months in state prison, then was paroled. He was supposed to report to a parole officer, but after a few months he skipped town and apparently hasn't been seen since."

Carter's stomach knotted, remembering what Mira had told him about David Ketchum. "So he could be here in Eagle Mountain."

"If he is, you'd think Mira would have spotted him," Dalton said. "It's harder to hide in a small town."

Maybe more difficult, but not impossible. "Maybe he changed his appearance, or has been careful to avoid letting Mira see him."

"Maybe. Anyway, sorry I wasn't able to come up with something more definite," Dalton said. "But I did come across something else that was kind of interesting."

"What's that?"

"I decided to see what I could dig up about Mitch Anders. Did you know he was born in Santa Fe?"

"The sheriff told Mira about that. That means he would know all about the David Ketchum case."

"Did Mira know Mitch in Santa Fe?" Dalton asked.

"No. She didn't meet him until she started work at the school."

"He and his mom moved away when Mitch was two," Dalton said. "But maybe Mitch went back there to visit relatives."

"His dad—Ed. Did he live in Santa Fe?" Carter asked.

"I could check, see what I can find out."

"Thanks."

He went back to work on the Jeep, but his mind was still

on their conversation. What if Mitch was the one who had sent those letters to Mira? The person who had attacked her on the trail? Carter fought the instinct to find Mitch and confront him. First of all, he might be wrong. Second, even if he was right, the man was built like a tank. Carter had never been a fighter. He hadn't had to be. He'd been able to talk his way out of every tight situation. Once, in a bar back in Vermont, a drunk man had been enraged when he caught Carter flirting with his girlfriend. Carter had ended up talking the guy into buying *him* a drink and the two had ended up playing darts so long the girlfriend had given up and left.

It wouldn't do to act rashly. But he had no words left for anyone who would hurt Mira.

Chapter Eighteen

"I've been thinking about Mitch Anders," Carter said, shortly after he arrived at Mira's apartment Friday evening.

"What about him?" She settled back on the sofa and regarded him warily. She hated to have outside problems intrude on their time together, but it was unrealistic to try to have a relationship in a bubble. And now that he had brought up the subject, part of her was curious to hear what he had to say.

He sat down beside her, the sofa cushion sinking under his weight. "If he's from Santa Fe, wouldn't you think he would have mentioned it to you?" he asked.

"We never really talked that much," she said. "And I gather he moved away when he was pretty young."

"Still, he could have heard about David Ketchum's murder. And how could he live in the same house with his dad and not know Ed was writing those letters to people in town? I have to wonder if Ed didn't say something about David, and maybe even about you."

"It doesn't make sense to me," she said. "It's so convoluted and, frankly, pointless. There's not one shred of proof to link me to David's death. Why would Ed—much less Mitch—want to hurt me? They don't even know me."

She hugged her arms across her chest. "I'm really struggling to accept that Mitch had anything to do with the child abductions here. I mean, I know better than anyone that people can fool us. I just can't believe I've misjudged someone so badly twice."

"I didn't mean to upset you." Carter rubbed his hand up and down her leg. "Maybe Mitch has nothing to do with any of this. I just thought it was interesting."

"There haven't been any more attempts to kidnap children," she said. "And I haven't received any more letters. Maybe whoever was responsible got scared or left town—or both."

"I hate to think they got away with their crimes," he said.

"Maybe the sheriff's department knows something we don't." She patted his knee. "Can we talk about something else? Have you heard anything about Craig?"

"I called his social worker and she said he's settling into a new home. After he's been there a month or two, maybe I can see him."

"That would be great."

He squeezed her hand. "Want to come with me on one of my Jeep tours Saturday? You can be my guest and ride in the front passenger seat. You'll get to hear the spiel I give the tourists."

"I'd love that," she said. "If it's okay with your folks."

"They're fine with it. And they'd love to meet you."

"I'd like to meet them, too." Though the prospect made her nervous.

"Great. The first tour leaves at nine, so be there about fifteen minutes early. Bring a jacket—it can get cool in the mountains."

"I'll look forward to it."

He picked up the television remote. "What movie do you want to watch?" he asked.

"Does it matter?" She slid closer to him. "We never make it to the end."

He smoothed his hand up her thigh. "Can I help it if you distract me?"

She kissed his neck. "Did I say I was complaining?"

He tossed the remote aside. "Maybe we should skip the movie tonight."

"You have such good ideas."

"That reminds me of something I thought we could try."

"Mmm. Why don't you show me?" She smothered his reply with a kiss.

SATURDAY MORNING, MIRA STOPPED for gas on her way to meet Carter at Alpine Jeep Rentals. A white SUV pulled up on the other side of the gas pump and Mitch Anders stepped out. "Hello, Mira," he said.

"Uh, hi, Mitch." She tried to hide her surprise at seeing him, but obviously failed.

"I've been released on bail," he said.

"Oh. Well, that's good." She wasn't afraid of him, just wary of her own judgment. He was so much like George— someone who appeared good and gentle on the outside. But George had harbored an ugly compulsion. Mitch was entitled to be presumed innocent until he was proven guilty, but even his arrest demonstrated how wrong she could be about people's true motives. She looked past him, to the passenger seat where Shayla sat, only the back of her head visible. "How are you doing?" Mira asked, turning her attention back to Mitch.

He shrugged. "It's been a little rough, but I'm hoping everything will die down soon."

Mira glanced back to the SUV. "How is Shayla?"

"Shayla's upset." He began filling the SUV with fuel.

"She told me you and Carter Ames are friends. I heard about how he helped Craig Phillips. That was really something."

"Yes, it was." She was still staring at the back of Shayla's head. Was she not even going to look at Mira?

"I had Craig in one of my classes," he said. "I'm glad he's getting some help."

The fuel to Mira's rental shut off and she turned to remove the nozzle from the car. She needed to get going or she was going to be late. "It was good to see you," she said. "Tell Shayla I said hello." *And that I miss her. And I never meant to upset her.*

"I will. See you around."

Carter was waiting for her in front of the Jeep rental office. "We're almost ready to go," he said. "You just need to sign the waiver."

"The waiver?"

"Basically, it says you're engaging in a risky endeavor and if you get hurt, it's not our fault."

"Are you that reckless a driver?" she teased.

"I'm a very careful driver," he said. "It's the other people out there you have to worry about." He escorted her inside. A middle-aged blonde looked up from behind the desk. "Mom, this is Mira," Carter said. "Mira, this is my mom."

"It's nice to meet you, Mrs. Ames." Mira smiled and hoped she didn't appear as nervous as she felt.

Mrs. Ames stood and offered her hand. "It's so nice to meet you, too, Mira. Carter can't stop talking about you."

Mira didn't think of herself as someone who blushed easily, but her face grew hot. Carter put a hand on her shoulder. "Mira needs to fill out the paperwork, Mom, or we're going to be late."

"Of course." His mom handed over a clipboard. "Even

though you're Carter's guest, we have to have everything in order for our insurance."

She scanned the paperwork, signed her name in two places and returned the clipboard.

"Great." Carter steered her toward the door. "See you later, Mom."

The Jeep was open-topped, with three rows of seats already filled with a family of four and a retired couple. "This is Mira, everyone," Carter said as he opened the passenger door for her. "You can all introduce yourselves later. Is everyone ready to go?"

Everyone was ready, so they set off, headed out of town and up to Raptor Ridge, a popular spot known for its spectacular view. They soon turned off the paved road, onto a narrow four-wheel-drive route, which took them past old mine ruins, splashing waterfalls and expanses of brilliantly colored wildflowers.

Mira enjoyed the view, but perhaps even more, she enjoyed watching Carter. He had probably told the stories he related about local geography and history a hundred times, but there was no sense that he was bored. He told jokes—some at his own expense—and paid special attention to the two children present. At one rest stop, he showed them fossils embedded in the rocks, and stopped in the middle of the road to point out a doe and fawn making their way through the trees. Seeing him kneeling beside the boy and girl, showing them a fossil in a rock wall, made her go all soft inside. He was going to be a great dad someday. How had she ever thought him self-centered and superficial?

Maybe that was the problem with her relationship with George. She had never gotten past first impressions to see the troubled man beneath the facade.

CARTER PULLED OUT all his best stories, hoping to impress Mira. Not that he didn't always try to give the tourists a good time, but he especially wanted her to enjoy herself.

It seemed to be working. She had smiled pretty much nonstop all day, and a couple of times they locked eyes and he felt that special zing of connection.

"I had a wonderful time," she said when they returned to the tour office. "Thank you so much for inviting me."

"It made the trip even more fun for me," he said.

"You're really good at what you do," she said.

This praise from her made him feel ten feet tall. "You'll have to come on a different tour," he said. "We have a mine ruins history tour, and one up to Admiral Mountain."

"I'd love that."

He glanced around to make sure none of the guests—or his parents—were watching, then pulled her close for a kiss. "Dinner later?" he asked.

"I'd love that."

"I'm off tomorrow, so I can stay all night."

"Even better."

WHEN CARTER SHOWED up at her apartment that evening, they decided on pizza for dinner, so they headed to Mo's. "I didn't think about how packed this place would be on a Saturday night," Mira said as they entered. The room buzzed with conversation, punctuated by the clink of glasses and burst of laughter.

"It'll be fine," Carter said. "There are always tables in the back."

They squeezed past a group who were headed out, then threaded their way alongside the bar, where most of the patrons were watching the baseball game on television. Mira stopped so suddenly Carter bumped into her. She grabbed his arm. "Isn't that Ed Anders?" she whispered, and nodded toward the end of the bar.

Ed was indeed seated on the barstool, a bottle of beer and a plate of food in front of him. He ate a French fry as Carter stared. At least he appeared more sober than he had the night Carter had driven him home. As if feeling their gaze on him, he looked their way and glared.

"Go on." Carter nudged Mira. "It'll be okay."

Ed continued to glare at them as they moved closer. Carter nodded. "Hello, Ed," he said. "How are you tonight?"

"What's it to you?" Ed asked. He fixed his gaze on Mira. "What are you looking at?"

"N...nothing!" she stammered. Carter felt her stiffen beneath his hand on her back.

"You'd better watch your step," Ed said.

"Hey, calm down," Carter said. "We're just here to have dinner. We'll leave you alone now." He hurried Mira past the older man, to a booth at the very back of the dining room. He slid in next to her.

"What is his problem?" she asked, irritation sharpening her words.

"I think he's a very unhappy person," Carter said. "After all, he admitted to writing all those notes to people about the things he thought they were doing wrong. Only someone who didn't have enough to occupy themselves would do something like that."

"Shayla said Mitch took him in because he had nowhere else to go," Mira said. "That would be a hard situation to be in."

"Let's forget about him and enjoy the rest of our evening," he said.

They ordered pizza and soft drinks, then fell into a conversation about the morning's tour. Ed was nowhere in sight by the time they left. Carter was relieved. He didn't want anything to upset Mira. They had had a good day and he was looking forward to a good night.

Back at her apartment, she wrapped her arms around him. "I think you need to practice your Spanish," she said.

"You want me to ask you where it hurts in Spanish?" he teased.

"Not exactly." She kissed his neck, her tongue gliding lightly over his skin. "I thought I'd teach you some new vocabulary."

"I'm always interested in expanding my knowledge." Being with her made him feel reckless, ready to follow wherever she led.

"*Bésame*," she said.

"*Bésame?*"

She laughed. "Kiss me."

He did so. "*Bésame otra vez*," she said. "Kiss me again."

A deeper kiss. "*Querido*," she whispered, her lips pressed against the pulse of his throat. "Dear one."

"*Querido*," he repeated.

"Except I'm female, so it's *querida*," she said.

"*Querida*." He began unbuttoning her blouse. "Teach me more."

"*Ven conmigo*." She took his hand and led him to the bedroom. "Make love to me."

She pulled him down beside her on the bed, and whispered the words for everything they did together that evening. He didn't know how much he would remember in the morning, but at that moment, he paid close attention, the conversation focusing him more acutely than ever, her voice a soft, sexy accompaniment to every move.

Afterward, when they lay together in each other's arms, he turned to her. "*Te amo*," he said.

Her eyes widened. "Where did you learn that?"

"I didn't say it wrong, did I? I looked it up online. It means I love you, doesn't it?"

"It does," she said.

"*Te amo*," he repeated.

"Oh, Carter," she said. "I think... I think I love you, too."

"Don't sound so sad about it." He forced a cheerfulness he didn't feel into his voice. Had he rushed her, confessing his feelings so quickly?

"I'm not sad," she said. "Not sad at all. It's just...a big step."

"We don't have to rush." He smoothed her hair away from her face, enjoying its silken slide through his fingers. "I just want to make sure you to know how I'm feeling."

She smiled, and some of the tension went out of him. "*Te amo*," she said, and lay her head on his shoulder.

They fell asleep in each other's arms, covers pulled around their shoulders, his dreams a mix of English and Spanish, scenes from the day and the night jumbled along with the words in his head.

The crash of breaking glass seemed at first a part of the dream, then Mira was shaking him. "Carter!" she whispered. "Carter, I think someone broke in."

She rolled away from him, and groped on the nightstand for her phone. The overhead light came on, momentarily blinding him. A slight figure clad all in black stood in the doorway of the bedroom, holding a large, black pistol. "Don't make another move," the figure commanded. "If you do, I'll kill you. I don't have anything to lose."

Chapter Nineteen

Saturday night, Dalton hunched over the computer, staring at the document he had found, one foot tapping idly as he read it again. Digging around in the archives of the *Santa Fe New Mexican*, he had uncovered an article about a group of men charged with possession of child pornography. Three men were arrested, but a fourth—Ned Solomon—fled and, according to the article, remained at large. Dalton had almost skipped past the brief story, but had stopped cold when he saw the picture of the wanted man. Ned Solomon could have been Ed Anders's twin.

Ned—hadn't he heard somewhere that that was sometimes short for Edward? Anders was Mitch's last name, but Dalton was sure Carter had told him Mitch's parents were never married. Maybe Anders was Mitch's mother's name. Edward Solomon might have started using Mitch's last name as a way to distance himself from his past charges.

Dalton read more. Ned Solomon was the fourth man known to be part of a ring of men who traded in child pornography. The other three were Frank Bartholomew, Gerald Jimenez, and George Suarez. That must be the George Mira had been involved with.

Dalton took out his phone and called Carter. As the call rang out, he glanced at the clock. It was after eleven. Late, but this was important. He was pretty sure his brother was with Mira. Maybe she could tell him more about George, or even Ned.

The call went to voicemail. "Hey, call me, it's important," Dalton said, then ended the call.

He turned back to the computer and began a search for more information about Ned Solomon. It took a little digging, but twenty minutes later he had information about the man's arrest record. Solomon was younger than Dalton had assumed Ed was—only fifty-two, whereas Ed looked a decade older. But Mitch couldn't be much over thirty, so he could definitely have a fifty-year-old dad. And a hard life could age a person.

Or was that a disguise? Was Ed pretending to be older and more disabled than he really was in order to distance himself from his former life?

Or as a way to hide what he was really up to? Fear gripped Dalton. Maybe he was overreacting, but he couldn't shake the sense of danger.

He grabbed his phone and tried Carter's number again. Still no answer. Maybe Carter had silenced the phone so he and Mira wouldn't be interrupted. Dalton didn't bother leaving a message this time. He thought a moment, then called 911. "What is your emergency?" a brisk female voice asked.

"I don't have an emergency, exactly," he said. "But I need to talk to the sheriff. I have information about a possible crime."

"What is the crime?"

Dalton shifted in his chair. "It's more that I have information about an ongoing investigation. But it's important."

"What is your information?" the operator asked.

"I really need to talk to the sheriff."

He imagined the operator rolling her eyes over wasting

her time with someone who was being so vague. But nothing in her voice gave that away. "What is your name?" she asked.

"Dalton Ames. Can you ask the sheriff to call me? It's really important."

"I'll relay the information to the sheriff."

"Thanks."

He ended the call, without much hope that he would hear from the sheriff before tomorrow, if ever. Maybe he was blowing all of this out of proportion. The sheriff had to know about Ned/Ed's past, right? The paper said he had confessed to writing the letters to people around town, so maybe he had owned up to his arrest record, too.

Had the sheriff questioned him about the attempted child abductions? Mitch had been arrested for those crimes, but what if he wasn't the one responsible, but his father?

He pulled out his phone again. Carter wasn't answering. He didn't know how to reach the sheriff. Who else could he call? He scrolled through his contacts, dismissing each one. He stopped when he came to Jake Gwynn. Jake was a sheriff's deputy and a fellow SAR volunteer. And probably asleep at this time of night.

Dalton made the call anyway. The call went straight to voicemail. "Hey, Jake. I've been looking around online and I found out some stuff about Mitch Anders's father, Ed, that has me pretty alarmed. Maybe it's nothing, but it might be important. If you're still awake, call me."

He ended the call, then went back online to see what he could find out. It wasn't as if he was going to be able to sleep.

MIRA KNEW THAT VOICE, but from where? She stared at the black-clad figure, searching for anything familiar. The man—she was sure it was a man—was slight—maybe five foot seven or eight inches tall, with rounded shoulders.

"Get up," he ordered, and motioned with the gun. "Both of you. Get out of bed."

"Ed Anders? Is that you?" she demanded.

"Ed?" Carter echoed. "What are you doing here?"

In answer, he fired the gun. The bullet hit the wall a few inches past Carter's head, the explosion deafening in the small bedroom. Carter and Mira jumped out of bed. She grabbed her robe and wrapped it around her shoulders, clutching her cast protectively across her stomach. Carter stood on the opposite side of the bed naked, his gaze fixed on the gun.

"Ed, what do you want?" Mira asked. She took a step away from the bed, putting more distance between her and Carter. If she could keep Ed focused on her, maybe Carter could get away.

"I'm going to kill you," he said.

"Why?" Carter asked. "What did either one of us ever do to you?"

"You killed my friend." Ed spoke to Mira, ignoring Carter. "The best friend I ever had."

Mira gasped. Was he talking about David Ketchum? Did he really believe she had been responsible for the boy's murder? "I never killed anyone," she said.

"You signed George's death warrant when you turned him in to the cops," Ed said. "Prison destroyed him. He was never the same after that."

"You knew George?" She thought she had known all of George's friends. Not that he had very many.

"He was my best friend. I stayed in touch with him even after he was sent away. We had the same...interests."

The word made her skin crawl. No wonder she hadn't

known Ed. George had done a very good job of concealing that whole side of himself from her. "I didn't turn George over to the police," she said. "I had no idea he was into child pornography until the police came to our apartment."

"That's not what he told me. He said you had ratted him out."

"I didn't. I promise." She held the robe closed with one hand and tried not to stare at the gun trained on her. The shot had been so loud. Surely one of her neighbors had heard. Had they called the police? If she and Carter could keep Ed talking until help arrived, they could stay alive.

"Did you send Mira those letters?" Carter asked. "The ones about David Ketchum?"

"Yes, I sent them." Ed turned his head to look at Carter, though he kept the gun focused on Mira. "I wanted to ruin her life the way she ruined George's life."

"Why try to connect Mira with David Ketchum's death?" Carter said. "She was never even a suspect."

"The police never knew who did it. I thought if I gave them a suspect they would do the rest of the work to prove she was guilty."

"But why bother?"

He said nothing. The silence stretched and Mira strained her ears, listening for an approaching siren. All she heard was Ed's own ragged breathing. She couldn't keep herself from focusing on the gun now, and gooseflesh rose along her arms as she imagined the bullet tearing into her. It wasn't fair. She had just found Carter. She was in love with him. Not the way she had loved George—because he was easy and falling in love with a man and getting married was what everyone expected her to do—what she expected to do. Her feelings for Carter ran deeper. Being with him wasn't about expectations. It was all about possibility. With him, she didn't see only one path, but many, all of them better because he would be at her side.

"I think you sent those letters because if the police focused on Mira, they would stop looking for the real killer," Carter said. "You were in Santa Fe then. I think you killed David."

The words shook her like a physical punch. She stared at Ed. A slight, unassuming man. But one who had admitted to accusing her of a terrible thing. Was Carter right? "Did you do it?" she asked. "Did you kill David?"

"No! Why would you say such a thing?" His voice sounded strained, like a guitar string pulled too tight.

"Those boys here in town? Were you the one who went after them?" Carter took a step toward the older man.

"How could I?" Ed gestured with the gun, but vaguely, no longer pointing it directly at her. "I can hardly walk."

"You didn't have any trouble breaking in here and crawling through the window," Carter said. "You're walking fine now. Standing up straight."

He was right. This wasn't the stooped man, hunched over a walker, who Mira was used to seeing. "You were pretending to be feeble," she said. "So people wouldn't suspect you."

"Did they suspect you after David disappeared?" Carter asked. He took another step toward Ed, the slightest, gliding movement that Ed didn't appear to notice. The older man's gaze was locked on Carter's face, mesmerized by his words. "You took him, didn't you? Just like you tried to take the boys here in Eagle Mountain. You thought you got away with it once, why not try again. No one would suspect you."

"That's right. And they won't suspect me now. Not when I get rid of you two." He straightened and held the gun steadier.

"What happened to David?" Mira asked. She had to keep

Ed talking. She had to give Carter a chance to get away and go for help. "He was a friendly boy. It probably wasn't hard for you to get him to trust you."

"I didn't do it," Ed said.

"One of the boys here in Eagle Mountain will probably be able to identify you," Carter said. "When the police in Santa Fe hear about those crimes, they'll want to take another look at you."

"It was an accident!" Ed took a step back. "He wasn't supposed to die. I was going to let him go but then he started screaming and I just wanted him to stop making so much noise..." He looked away, silent.

Mira's stomach roiled. The image of David's sweet, smiling face—the photo that had appeared on posters all over town—was burned into her mind. The thought of how afraid he must have been threatened to buckle her knees. But she couldn't afford to think of that. Not now, with his murderer standing right here, threatening to kill her and Carter. She swallowed her disgust and tried to make herself sound sympathetic. "You should tell the sheriff it was an accident," she said. "They can find you some...some help."

"They'll never prove I had anything to do with any of that," he said. "The cops in Santa Fe never even questioned me about it. I got out of that place as soon as I could. Started using my full first name, which I never used before, and Mitch's last name—his mother's name. Guess she was smart not to give him mine. I bummed around for a while, got in a little trouble in St. Louis for messing with an underage girl, but I wasn't inside for long. I ran out of money and decided to look up Mitch. He took me in."

"The sheriff's department thinks your son was responsible," Carter said. "Because you used his car."

"I never wanted to involve Mitch. He's a good kid. Doesn't take after me at all."

He was sounding more confident now. More like a man who would shoot them. Mira searched for some way to distract him again. "Why did you write all those letters to people?" she asked.

"Because it was fun. I got a kick out of hearing how wound up everyone got over those. And it proved my point that every single person fudges the law some way. They're not that much different from me."

Mira could have pointed out that there was a big difference between illegally parking or leaving trash cans out overnight and molesting children or killing them, but decided not to antagonize Ed further.

Carter had moved forward another step. Suddenly, Ed swung the gun in his direction. "What do you think you're doing?" he demanded. "Get back."

But instead of moving back, Carter lunged forward, reaching for the older, smaller man. He grabbed Ed's arm and the gun went off. Then Carter stumbled back and fell against the wall, blood blooming red across his chest.

Chapter Twenty

"Thanks for calling me back, Jake." Dalton paced the floor of his apartment, phone pressed to his ear. "I know it's late."

"I'm still up," Jake said. "What's going on? You sound upset."

"I've been digging around online, trying to find out more about Mitch Anders," Dalton said.

"Why were you doing that?" Jake asked.

"Because I'm curious. Look, it doesn't matter why. I just wanted to tell you what I found out. Not about Mitch, but about his father, Ed. He goes by Ed Anders now, but I'm pretty sure his real name is Ned Solomon. He's from St. Louis, and he was arrested there for possession of child pornography. He was also jailed for a while in St. Louis for interfering with a minor. Does that mean he molested some kid? Am I telling you things you already know?"

"Whoa," Jake said. "Back up a little. Say all that again, and tell me why it's got you so upset."

Dalton repeated the information, and added, "Someone sent Mira Veronica letters accusing her of having something to do with the murder of a little boy, David Ketchum, in Santa Fe. Mira didn't have anything to do with the crime, but I think Ed—or Ned—did. He was living there at the time. He's got a record that links him to crimes against children. And he's living here under another name at the same time someone has been attempting to abduct other kids."

"Ed's a disabled old man," Jake said.

"Is he? If he's the same man I think he is, he's only fifty-two. Maybe he's only pretending to have trouble walking."

"Okay. I agree this is worth looking into. But you still haven't answered my original question. Why are you so upset now that you called me at this time of night?"

Dalton stopped pacing and took a deep breath. "I'm worried about Carter. He's with Mira right now, at her apartment. I've been calling, but he doesn't answer his phone."

"Maybe he doesn't want to be disturbed," Jake said.

"Sure. That's probably all it is. But I can't shake the feeling something isn't right." There. He'd said it. All his life he'd denied he and Carter had any special bond just because they were twins. Yet here he was, feeling the closest thing he had known to terror and he couldn't explain why.

"Hang on a minute, Dalton," Jake said.

Silence. Dalton resumed pacing, one arm hugged across his body, nervous energy vibrating through him. Then Jake was back on the line. "Where does Mira live?" he asked.

Dalton gave him the address. "Could you ask the deputy on duty to drive by and make sure everything looks okay?" he asked. "I'd do it but Carter would kill me if he ever found out."

"I'm headed over there now," Jake said. "Sit tight and don't go anywhere."

Jake's voice had a sharper edge to it that told Dalton this was about more than his story about Ed. "What's going on?" he asked. "Is something wrong?"

"A call just came over the scanner. A man reported gunshots coming from one of the apartments in that complex."

SHERIFF'S DEPUTIES ASSEMBLED in the parking lot next door to Mira's apartment complex. Jake had called the sheriff to report what Dalton had relayed to him. "The neighbor is pretty sure the gunshots came from Mira's apartment," the sheriff told the assembled officers. "We've identified the SUV belonging to Mitch Anders parked in the apartment lot, along with Carter Ames's Jeep and Mira Veronica's rental Chevrolet. Mira and Carter aren't answering their phones. Gage is trying to reach Mitch now."

They turned to look at the sheriff's brother, who had a phone pressed to his ear. "Hello, Mitch? This is Sergeant Gage Walker. I'm going to put you on speaker, okay? We need your help with a situation."

"What kind of situation?" Mitch sounded dazed. Probably awakened from sleep. "What's going on?"

"Where are you right now?" Gage asked.

"I'm at home. I was asleep."

Travis nodded. "His ankle monitor indicates that's right."

"Is your dad there at the house with you?" Gage asked.

"I think so. What time is it...it's after three in the morning. Dad's asleep."

"We need to talk to him. Could you wake him for me, please? It's important."

"Okay. Give me a sec."

They waited, scarcely breathing. Soon, Mitch was back on the line, sounding more alert. "Dad's not here," he said. "His bed hasn't been slept in."

"Check the driveway," Gage said. "Is his Jeep there?"

"What is this about?" Mitch asked.

"Just tell me if his Jeep is there."

"His Jeep is there. But my SUV isn't."

"Is anything else missing, that you're aware of?"

"No. What is going on? Is Dad in some kind of trouble?"

"Check his room again," Gage said. "I need to know what he might have taken with him."

"I can't tell you anything. It's not like he has much... wait a minute."

"What is it?" Jake leaned forward, anticipating the answer.

"His walker is here. He doesn't go anywhere without his walker. He can't."

"Are you sure about that?" Gage asked. "Is it possible your father isn't as debilitated as he wants people to think?"

Silence.

"Mitch? Are you still there?"

"I'm still here. And I guess...yes, it's possible my dad can get around better than he lets on. I've suspected that for a while." He sighed. "I guess I don't really know him that well. He only got back in touch with me a few months ago. I was trying to rebuild a relationship with him, but it hasn't been easy. What's this about, Gage?"

"Your father's name isn't really Ed Anders, is it?" Gage asked.

"No. It's Ned Solomon."

"Why go by Ed Anders?"

"He said he wanted us to have the same name. And he needed to make a fresh start."

"Did you know he had a criminal record for indecency with a minor and possession of child pornography?"

More silence.

"Mitch? Were you aware of your father's criminal history?"

"He told me he was in jail because he had hurt someone in a knife fight. He said it was a misunderstanding."

"Not according to the information we've uncovered."

"What else did he lie to me about?"

"Has your father ever said anything about Mira Veronica?"

"Mira? No. Why?"

"Does your father own a gun?"

"No. At least… I don't think so. I've never seen him with a gun."

"But you don't go through his things."

"No. When he moved in he asked me to respect his privacy. He said he would do the same for me."

"Do you have a gun?"

"No." The answer was firm. "Why all these questions? What has Dad done?"

"A neighbor reported shots fired in the apartment complex where Mira lives. She's not answering her phone. Your SUV is in the parking lot."

"I'm coming down there."

"You need to stay out of this, Mitch."

"Ed is my father. And Mira is my friend. If something is going on, maybe I can help. Maybe I can talk to him or something."

"No. Stay where you are. We'll contact you if we need you." Gage ended the call. "Where is SWAT?" he asked.

"They're on their way," Travis said. He checked his phone. "They should be here in another twenty minutes or so."

Jake looked toward the apartments. Most of them were dark and silent. But light glowed behind the curtains in Mira's front windows. "We don't even know if he's in there," Gage said. "And maybe Mira isn't answering because she turned off her phone."

In response, Travis keyed his microphone. "Ryker, what have you got?" he asked.

"The glass in the back window by the fire escape is busted out," Ryker replied. "I climbed up there and tried to look in, but this side of the apartment is dark."

"Get back on the ground and wait for instructions," Travis said. He looked at Gage. "Sounds like someone climbed the fire escape and broke the window." He frowned up at the apartment. "No bars on these windows."

"Because everyone thinks living in a small town is safe," Gage said. "And usually, they're right." He joined his brother and Jake in studying the apartment. "Maybe we should just go up and knock on the door."

"And whoever fired those shots earlier shoots Mira—or us." Travis shook his head. "We wait for SWAT."

It was the smart thing to do, even if it wasn't what any of them really wanted.

CARTER COULDN'T BELIEVE Ed had shot him. And now that his initial shock was wearing off, he couldn't believe how much he hurt. He kept one hand clamped to the wound on the right side of his chest, sticky blood seeping through his fingers, and told himself he wasn't going to pass out.

"What do you think you're doing! He didn't do anything to you!" Mira shouted at Ed, who turned his attention—and the barrel of the gun—toward her. She started toward him.

"Stop!" Ed ordered. "Don't come any closer or I'll shoot you, too."

"You don't think someone hasn't heard those shots?" she asked. "You don't think one of my neighbors hasn't already called the sheriff? Are you trying to make things worse for yourself?"

"Shut up," Ed said.

"You've done enough," she said. "Leave us alone."

Carter's vision was getting hazy at the edges, but Mira sounded furious. He tried to call out to her, to tell her to calm down and not provoke Ed further. But his words emerged as a groan.

Ed turned toward him again, and lifted the gun. "No!" Mira shouted, and launched herself at the older man.

The gun went off again. Mira screamed. Carter struggled, but wasn't strong enough to overcome the darkness.

RAGE OVERCAME MIRA when she saw Ed prepare to shoot Carter again. How dare this man think he could decide whether they lived or died. She wasn't going to let him get away with it. Even as some small part of her brain shouted that she was being foolish, she lunged for him. She put every bit of her strength behind the action, and shoved Ed to the floor. The gun went off again, the bullet hitting a nearby table, splintering the wood. Mira grappled for the gun, her nails digging into Ed's wrist.

Ed fought back, pulling away from her, but she clawed at his face with her uninjured hand, raking her nails across his skin, grabbing whatever part of him she could. When he tried to club her with the gun, she rolled sideways, trapping his arm beneath her weight. She kicked her feet and pulled at his hair, all the while screaming at him to stop and leave them alone.

The door to the apartment burst open and suddenly the room was filled with people. Someone pulled her off of Ed and wrapped her in a bear hug. She was still screaming and fighting, still enraged.

"Mira, calm down, it's okay." Jake Gwynn spoke in her ear. "You're safe," he said. "You don't have to fight anymore. It's going to be okay."

The fiery rage drained out of her, leaving her weak and weepy. "Carter!" she moaned, and looked around for him.

"The paramedics are taking care of him," Jake said. Still holding her, he wrapped her in a blanket. She realized she had lost her robe in the struggle with Ed. Jake turned her so she could see where Carter lay on the floor, surrounded by uniformed paramedics.

"Ed shot him," she said.

"He's still alive," Jake said. "We're going to take care of him."

The sheriff joined them. "Mira, are you all right?" Travis asked.

She nodded, then shook her head. "I don't know." She couldn't look away from the crowd around Carter's prone body. "Is Carter going to be okay?"

"We're doing everything we can for him," Travis said.

That wasn't the answer she wanted. She wanted someone to tell her he hadn't been hurt badly, but having seen the blood seeping out of his chest, she knew that was a lie.

"What happened here?" Travis asked.

"Ed broke into the apartment. He said he was going to kill us. He shot Carter. He tried to shoot me. I was so angry. He had no right to do that." Mortified, she began to sob.

A woman in a paramedic uniform came over and embraced her. She realized it was Jake's wife, Hannah.

"We're getting ready to load Carter into the ambulance," Hannah said. "Come and talk to him."

Carter lay on the gurney, covered with blankets, an oxygen mask obscuring much of his face. His green eyes were cloudy and unfocused. Mira wrapped her fingers around the only spot on his arm that wasn't obstructed by some piece of medical equipment. "Say something to him," Hannah said. "He can hear you, even if he can't respond."

She was afraid to speak, afraid she would burst into sobs. But what if this was her last chance to talk to him? "I love you," she said, shocked that the words burst forth. But saying them was a relief.

Hannah patted her back, then led her away again as her coworkers rolled the gurney toward the door.

Travis and Gage approached again. "We really need to talk to her," Gage said.

"I think she needs a sedative," Hannah said. "She's been through a lot."

Mira straightened her shoulders. "No, I can talk. I want to tell you."

She settled on the sofa—the sheriff across from her, Gage beside her. She reminded herself she was safe now. People were doing everything they could to help Carter. Her job was to make sure the sheriff had everything he needed to stop Ed Anders from hurting anyone ever again.

She took a deep breath. "Ed Anders killed David Ketchum, in Santa Fe three years ago," she said. "He confessed to me and to Carter. He was never convicted of the crime. I don't know if he was even a suspect. He left town after that. He's only been in Eagle Mountain, living with his son, Mitch Anders, for a few months. Mitch took him in because he thought his dad was helpless and had nowhere else to go. But apparently that was an act to fool people. Ed is in good enough shape to climb my fire escape and break my window, and I'm sure he's the person who attacked me on the hiking trail, too. And he wrote those letters accusing me of having something do to with David's death."

"Did he say why he wrote the letters?" Travis asked.

"He hated me because he thought I was the one who turned George Suarez in to the police in Santa Fe. Ed was George's friend. They were part of a group of people who traded and sold child pornography. George apparently told Ed that I had turned them in to the police. But I had no idea what they were up to. I was beyond shocked to learn the truth." She stared down at her hands, knotted in her lap.

"Did you know Ed in Santa Fe?" Gage asked.

"No. I'm sure I never met him. But he apparently recognized me. Maybe he had seen me with George, or a picture of me. Or maybe he only knew my name and recognized it when he heard about the new teacher at the school."

"Did he say if he was the person who kidnapped Bryce Atkinson and tried to abduct two other boys?" Gage asked.

"Yes. He thought no one would suspect him because they all thought he was a helpless old man. But he's not helpless."

They walked her through everything that had happened that evening. By the time they were done, daylight streamed through the front windows and her whole body ached. "That's all for now," Travis said, and stood. "Try to get some rest."

"I need to see Carter." She stood also.

"Where's Mira? Is she all right?"

She turned and saw Dalton pushing his way past the law enforcement personnel who were still examining the scene. Bethany was right behind him. "Hey, Mira." Dalton stopped a few feet in front of her.

Bethany came right up to her. "Are you okay?" she asked, and touched Mira's arm lightly.

"I'm okay. But Carter…" Her voice broke.

"We just talked to the hospital," Dalton said. "He's in surgery right now, but they think he's going to be okay."

"We're on our way to see him right now," Bethany said. "We thought you might like to come, too."

"Yes. Yes, I'd like that. Thank you." She looked down at the blanket she clutched to her. "I need to get dressed."

"I'll help." Bethany put her arm around Mira. "It must have been awful for you."

She could only nod, and let Carter's sister lead her to the bedroom, where she dressed in the same clothes she had worn the day before.

"Mom and Dad are driving separately but we insisted on stopping here first," Dalton said as he led the way across the parking lot.

"We've got coffee and pastry in the car," Bethany said. "That should help."

The coffee and sugar helped, but an even bigger lift came from Dalton and Bethany's assumption that she was one of them now—another member of the family. They didn't ask for details, but she told them anyway—how Carter had goaded Ed into confessing everything.

"I think both of us still thought of Ed as a feeble old man," she said. "We never thought he would really shoot. When he did, I was terrified—and then I was furious at him for hurting Carter."

At the hospital, she followed Bethany and Dalton into the cubicle in the ICU where Carter had been moved after surgery. The three of them crowded around the hospital bed and stared at Carter—the shadow of his beard dark against his pale, pale face.

Mira took one hand and Bethany the other. His shoulder and much of his chest was bandaged, and an oxygen cannula was in his nose. His hand was cold and still. Mira swallowed hard. She wasn't going to cry.

Then his eyes were open, looking into hers. "Hey," he said, his voice a harsh rasp.

"Hey." She leaned forward and kissed his cheek. "How are you feeling?"

"I'm not feeling anything." He squeezed her hand. "How are you?"

"You scared me."

"Yeah, I've gotten in trouble for running my mouth before, but no one ever shot me." His expression sobered. "What happened to Ed?"

"Ed's in jail," Dalton said. "I doubt he's ever coming out."

There was more movement at the door and Mr. and Mrs. Ames peered in. A nurse hovered behind him. "He's not supposed to have more than one visitor at a time," she said.

Dalton put his hand on Bethany's shoulder. "Come on, sis," he said.

At the door, he blocked his parents. "Give Mira a minute," he said, and urged them back into the hallway.

When they were alone, Carter smiled up at her. "You look great," he said.

She put a hand to her head. Her hair was uncombed, her makeup smeared. "I look terrible," she said.

"No. You look wonderful." He squeezed her hand again. "Did I dream it, or did you say something to me when the paramedics were there?"

"Say something?" So he really had heard.

"I swear you told me you love me."

Her eyes stung and her throat tightened. She was not going to cry! She nodded. "I do," she whispered.

"That's all I needed to know." He closed his eyes, and his breathing grew heavy and even. She touched his cheek, and thought of how close she had come to losing this chance at happiness. Carter wasn't perfect, but neither was she. Together, they would find a way to trust each other. To let love lead the way.

Epilogue

"Mama, I'd like you to meet Carter Ames. Carter, this is my mother, Valeria Veronica." Mira shifted her attention from her mother to Carter and back again as she introduced the two at the café where she had arranged for them to have lunch. Carter had "just happened" to drop by as they were finishing up their meal—Mira's plan to make the meeting between two of the most important people in her life less stressful.

Mama took Carter's hand. "So you are the young man my daughter can't stop talking about," she said.

"I hope only good things." Carter's tone was teasing, his smile the flirtatious one she had first experienced on the night they met.

Mama returned the smile. "Oh yes, only good things. You are a superhero, saving lives, exploring the mountains. And you are studying to be a teacher, no?"

"Classes start next month," he said.

"Carter is going to be a wonderful teacher," Mira said. "He really has a way of communicating with people."

"That's a very nice way of saying I talk too much," Carter said.

"A useful talent for someone who gives tours for a living," Mama said. "Do I remember that correctly?"

"Yes. It's a family business." He glanced at Mira, then back at her mother. "While you're in town, I want to take you and Mira on a tour," he said. "It's the best way to see the mountains."

"That sounds like it would be fun," Mama said. "And it will give us a chance to get to know each other better."

Carter paled only slightly at this. Mira resisted the urge to praise him further. She could have told her mother about how he had taken the teenager he had rescued, Craig, under his wing. The two met up regularly now to hike or climb. And he was part of a group of search and rescue volunteers who were working with a financial adviser to strengthen the group's financial picture.

Mama's expression sobered. "Mira tells me you were badly hurt when that awful man attacked the two of you," she said. "How are you doing?"

"I'm pretty much healed." He rolled his right shoulder to demonstrate.

Mira knew the injury still hurt him sometimes, but he had worked hard to get back into shape. In fact, they went to the gym together, since she needed to regain strength in her arm once it was finally out of its cast.

"It's good that the man who shot you is in jail," Mama said. "He will be there for a long time?"

"He's still awaiting trial," Carter said. "But I think we won't have to worry about him anymore."

Mama turned to Mira. "And the man's son is still here? The teacher you told me about?"

"Yes. He had no idea what his dad was doing behind his back. He recently got engaged." Shayla still hadn't forgiven Mira, but Mitch was friendly, so Mira hoped his influence would eventually soften Shayla's heart.

"Carter?"

He glanced over his shoulder to the server, who held a large take-out bag. "I have to go now," he said. He slipped his hand from Mama's grasp. "It was nice to meet you. I'll see you again soon."

"Yes, soon." They watched as Carter accepted his food and left. Then Mama turned to Mira. "I see now why you are not interested in moving back home. He's very good-looking, for a gringo."

"Mama!"

She giggled. "The look on your face, *hija*! I am only teasing."

Mira relaxed. "Carter is very good-looking. But he's also smart and kind, and he treats me well."

"And you love him. I see it in your eyes. And in his eyes." She reached across the table and patted Mira's hand. "So what are you going to do about it? Are you going to get married?"

"We're taking things slow, Mama. We've both been through a lot."

Mama nodded. "Slow can be good. But don't make me wait forever."

"When we've decided, you'll be one of the first to know."

"It's good to see you so happy, *hija*."

"I am happy, Mama." With Carter, and with herself. She had stopped blaming herself for not seeing George's true nature, and learning to trust her judgment again. Yes, she and Carter had been through tough times, but she saw only good things ahead of them. Together.

* * * * *

TWIN THREATS
IN AUSTIN

BARB HAN

All my love to Brandon, Jacob and Tori,
my three greatest loves.

To Babe, my hero, for being my best friend,
greatest love and my place to call home.
I love you with everything that I am.

And to all the readers who are on this journey with me.
You are a blessing beyond measure!

Prologue

Justina Worth could have sworn the cute stranger who had been eyeing her from across the room had walked out of the nightclub fifteen minutes ago. Yet, there he was, staring at her from the other side of the room. Maybe he'd stepped outside to breathe fresh air. *Or to see if you would follow.*

Had she missed an opportunity? Justina smoothed down her hair and reached inside her handbag for lip gloss. She'd read somewhere that men were attracted to thick, shiny lips. There wasn't much she could do about her thin mouth, but she could make those lips slick.

A thrill of anticipation struck. She'd been lonely since her father had died last month. He might have been one mean son of a bitch, but he'd been her papa, and she'd loved him despite his faults and the way he'd treated her.

The Inner Haven Disco Club was wall-to-wall people tonight. Justina hadn't been on the dance floor one time without being elbowed in the back, the ribs, and, once, the boob. The place was hopping.

The stranger's gaze was fixed on her. Something seemed different about him. *What was it?* She couldn't quite put her finger on it. Glancing down at her beer, she wondered if she'd had one too many tonight.

"No such thing," Papa would've said. This was her third.

Papa would've laughed at her and called her a lightweight if he'd still been here. *No, Papa wouldn't have let you drink at all,* a voice in the back of her mind reminded. *He would've said beer was wasted on you and told you to drink water instead.*

The stranger started toward her, looking right at her. Maybe she would get lucky enough to meet a nice guy tonight, after all.

Life had been lonely since losing Papa. Justina had no one to talk to once she arrived home from a long day at work. Papa had drilled it in her head that she might not look like much, but she was a good cook, and she'd always had a smile for him. He'd liked having her around even though he'd lost his temper at her more times than she could count.

Papa hadn't known about Justina's wishes—wishes that sometimes made her feel bad—for him to die. He'd made her steal pills at her job to give to him, so he hadn't had to pay for prescriptions. The residents of Memory Care Assisted Living didn't remember how many pills they were supposed to take, anyway. The ones who did and reported Justina could easily be gaslighted. Who would you believe—a resident with Alzheimer's, or the company's star-of-the-month employee four months running?

Changing all those bedpans and turning residents from side to side each day had prepared her to take the best care of Papa at his end. She made enough to keep the lights on and food on the table, despite them being scraps by the end of every month.

Tonight's miniskirt and tight blouse had come courtesy of the Goodwill down the street. If Papa had seen her, he would've told her to wash that god-awful makeup off her face and put on some clothes. She couldn't help but laugh. Justina liked the way men were looking at her tonight.

They noticed her. Finally.

Cute Stranger stopped in front of her. This close, she could see the whites of his otherwise brown eyes. A baseball cap covered most of his dark hair. At six feet, he was tall and built like a brick house.

"Hey," he said, his voice gruff.

The way he looked at her would've made Papa turn in his grave.

"Hey yourself," she replied, feeling—dared she say—sexy.

Justina stood a little straighter because it made her boobs look bigger. She tucked a lock of hair behind her ear.

"Want to get out of here?" Cute Stranger asked. "Go somewhere I can hear myself think?"

Papa wouldn't have approved.

"Okay," she said, grabbing her beer to give herself some liquid courage on her way toward the door. "But we ain't going to my place."

"Not a problem," Cute Stranger responded, reaching for, and then holding, her hand.

She had to work to keep her body from tensing. Her hand hadn't been held since grade school.

Papa would've told her not to go home with a stranger.

"Take this," Cute Stranger said, pressing a pill into her palm.

"What is it?" Justina asked. She ignored the voice in her head belonging to Papa, warning her to *stop right now, young lady.*

"Something to help you loosen up," Cute Stranger said. A man this good-looking could have any woman in the room.

And he wants you!

Another thrill of excitement rocketed through her body, causing electricity to pulse through her. If she'd known that going against Papa's rules could be this thrilling, she would've done it long ago.

Justina popped the pill and chased it down with the rest of her beer. "Where are you taking me?"

She blinked up at the man who was almost a foot taller than her five foot, two inches.

"Home," was all he said as he smiled down at her. There was something about the way he looked at her. She couldn't put her finger on it, but it caused her to shiver.

Is this what a man looks like right before he makes love to a woman?

At thirty-two, Justina wasn't a virgin, but it had been a long time since she'd been with a man, and she'd sure as heck never done it with a stranger.

After downing the last drop of beer, she set the bottle on the table near the exit. Papa drank beer out of a can. Bottles were classy.

Cute Stranger's big hand covered hers as they exited the club.

At his pickup, he even opened the door for her. Justina smiled at him. She'd found herself a real gentleman this time. If only Papa was alive to watch how this man treated her.

The investment in the miniskirt and makeup was paying off. *See, Papa? Men do like me.*

After climbing into the cab of the pickup with the help of Cute Stranger, Justina felt loopy and a little bit drowsy. Those ten-hour shifts spent lifting overweight old folks were catching up to her. She worked at an old folks' home, except she'd been warned not to call it that anymore. It was still true. At twenty-six dollars an hour, she didn't care what they wanted her to call the place.

Cute Stranger took the driver's seat as her body numbed.

A beer too many? What did it matter? Justina was beginning to relax. She felt loose, like not much mattered, and life was playing out in front of her, no longer happening to her.

"Put this on," Cute Stranger said before handing over a black silk sack big enough to put over her head.

"What for?" she asked, figuring she had a right to know even though she had no power to resist.

"Because I said so," Cute Stranger stated.

Justina didn't like how much Cute Stranger had just sounded like Papa. Though, it was like she was out of her body, watching, so she put the bag over her head anyway.

"Now, you're mine," the man said in a low growl.

Chapter One

Tall, dark, and handsome. Those words fell terribly short of describing the US Marshal standing next to Rochelle Paddock's service vehicle. The man had been patiently waiting.

"Sorry," she offered, still distracted as she sat in her SUV, reading the new missing-person report. "Be with you in one second, sir."

"Everything alright?" the marshal asked as he quirked an eyebrow. She'd been asked to assist him in serving a federal warrant since the perp had been turned in by a relative who'd been pressured to take him in. Austin was the PD's jurisdiction. They were always willing to cooperate with other government agencies.

Rochelle shook her head. "This is the third missing person in a couple of weeks. I'm afraid we have a serial criminal on the loose, and I need to have a conversation with a guy we have a picture of, but not a positive ID."

The marshal frowned. "My name is Camden Remington, and I'd like to offer my services since we'll be working together anyway to serve a warrant once we finalize the felon's location."

"Rochelle Paddock," she said, skipping the labels like *detective* and *Austin PD* since the marshal—*Camden*—already knew that about her. "Never hurts to have a fresh set of eyes on a case." She glanced at him. "Take a look at this."

The missing-person report wasn't the reason they were joining forces today, but a fresh perspective from someone else in a different branch of law enforcement never hurt.

Camden leaned in. His spicy scent filled her as she replayed the footage from the bar where the victim had last been seen.

"Wait a minute," he said. "Do you mind playing that again?"

Rochelle zipped to the part where a ball-cap-wearing male walked out of the nightclub, holding hands with the victim. He'd been smart enough to keep his head down so the camera above the exit couldn't get a good read.

"I know that guy," Camden said.

"How?" she asked.

"I'm the one who arrested him two years ago," Camden explained. "He just got out for good behavior, and I was planning to swing by his apartment while I'm in Austin to check up on him. I don't have to remind him how fast he can end up back in jail if he breaks the rules of his parole."

This might be Thanksgiving week, but it was beginning to feel like Christmas morning. "What charges did you arrest him on?"

"Mail fraud and identity theft," he said. "If you want to talk to my guy before we serve my warrant, I'm coming with you. I know where he lives."

"Which is?" she asked.

"East Martin Luther King Jr. Boulevard and Springdale area," he said. "Sentinel Apartments. Number three."

Rochelle looked into the most mesmerizing pair of clear, Caribbean-blue eyes framed by a set of the thickest, blackest lashes that would make most women envious. It would be impossible to turn down those baby blues.

Camden Remington was seriously hot—so much so that he made everyday things like coming up with a well-thought-out response to the simplest question feel next to impossible. He caused her throat to dry up and her cheeks to flush the second their gazes touched. What the hell? Was she suddenly fifteen and talking to the high-school quarterback again?

The marshal was around six-three with a frame filled out with just the right amount of long, lean muscle. Camo pants hung on hips attached to a torso that formed an improbable *V.* Feeling an attraction wouldn't be unprofessional. Acting on one, on the other hand, would.

Rochelle gave a mental headshake and refocused. "Let's go for a ride then since you know where we're going."

Camden circled the vehicle and then climbed into the passenger seat of her SUV.

"Does this perp have a name?" she asked.

"Kage Durham," he supplied.

CAMDEN MIGHT NOT believe in luck, but he believed in good timing. Approaching the detective's service vehicle as she'd waited for him in the parking lot of the Austin PD substation had been just the right moment. He'd been meaning to check up on Kage while in town. This gave him a good reason to show up unexpectedly and question the man Camden was certain had been involved in more serious crimes.

Still, mail fraud and identity theft were a far cry from kidnapping charges. The man in the grainy video resembled Kage, *and* the man lived nearby. That didn't make the ex-con guilty, but the surveillance footage painted a picture. Kage was most likely the last person who'd seen Justina before her abduction.

"How do you know the suspect?" Rochelle, a stunning redhead if ever there was one, asked. The detective had all the features he loved—doe eyes, pink, heart-shaped and extremely kissable mouth, and long red hair tied back in a ponytail. There was an intensity about her that made him want to get to know her and dive into what brought out that serious line that was etched into her forehead—a line that shouldn't be sexy but was.

Camden guessed the detective was in her early thirties, very early. Which meant she was also very focused on her career to have made detective so soon.

"Durham swore he was innocent."

"Don't they all?" she quipped.

"That's the truth," he muttered with a nod.

"You have a perp who was recently released and now we have three missing persons in a matter of weeks," she said with a sharp sigh. "Which means he got busy immediately after his release—if this is our guy."

"Maybe he was making up for lost time," Camden reflected.

"Maybe," she echoed.

"Let me see if I understand the current situation correctly," he began after reviewing the report a second time. This round, he looked for any additional clues Kage could be the perp.

Rochelle nodded as she turned onto East Martin Luther King Jr. Boulevard.

"The victim was last seen walking out of a nightclub with a man who resembles my felon, but all we have to prove it so far is grainy surveillance video." It wasn't much to go on and wasn't nearly enough to even think about getting a warrant to search Kage's apartment. Plus, Kage was smart and cunning enough not to bring a kidnapping victim to his apartment.

The man had struck Camden as maybe a little too smart for his own good. Smart criminals got away with murder. Smart criminals repeated their behavior. Smart criminals were the serial killers who evaded suspicion for too many years.

Something about Kage had gnawed away at the back of Camden's mind for years.

"That's correct, sir," Rochelle said.

"Camden," he reminded her.

"Then call me Rochelle," she offered. "Please."

"Will do, Rochelle," he said before refocusing on the grainy image that could be Kage. The guy in the photo was a decent size, roughly six feet tall and built. He appeared more muscular than Camden remembered Kage being, but jail time in a federal prison could do that to a person. With nothing else to do, inmates worked out in the yard, bulking up. Plus, pictures could be deceiving, distorting a person, object, or thing based on perspective.

Camden wanted to get eyes on Kage.

Rochelle pulled into a parking spot in the one-story, run-down apartment complex. *Apartment home*, Camden corrected. He'd been schooled on the new terminology while talking to a leasing agent a couple of weeks ago. The new term didn't quite fit with what looked like a roach-infested dwelling.

Whatever. He would try to remember the next time he spoke to a leasing agent, whose job was to "sell" a tenant on a lease with fluffy language.

There wasn't anything homey about the long brick building that resembled a pay-by-the-hour motel.

"Do you want to take the lead since you have a relationship with this person?" Rochelle asked.

"He won't be happy to see me, considering the last time we came in contact was when I arrested him," Camden pointed out. "And I don't want to overstep my bounds since this is your department's case."

"Alright then," Rochelle said.

In truth, Camden hoped the beautiful female detective might catch Kage off guard and maybe trip him up.

They exited the SUV and walked side by side to apartment number three. Out of the vehicle, Camden noted the detective wore a pair of black slacks that did little to hide long, slender legs. She was tall, maybe five-eight, with legs for days. It wouldn't surprise him to learn she'd played volleyball at some point in her past, though she had more of a runner's build.

Even a buttoned-up blouse couldn't hide her figure. A hint of pink silk could be seen over full breasts—breasts that he forced his gaze away from before his physical assessment crossed a line. Whether folks wanted to admit it or not, they were always sizing others up, males and females. The brain took inventory as part of an age-old survival mechanism. It noted if someone was thin or thick, muscled or scraggly, tall or short, along with many other details in the event a fight broke out. In his line of work, he noticed temperament too. Working with a hothead or an officer with a huge ego generally meant tensions soared faster in tenuous circumstances. It could mean the difference between needing to draw his weapon and/or defend himself against a perp.

Camden fell on the calm side of temperament. He was a better negotiator, a peacekeeper. He always looked for nonviolent solutions and ways to bring calm to a situation.

Rochelle's stunning looks most likely caused perps to confuse her for being softer. It could mean she had to defend herself more often than other cops if she was viewed as being weaker.

In his case, all he had to deal with was an inconvenient

temptation. Being attracted to the leggy redhead didn't mean he had to act on his physical reaction to her. His brain was also taking notes with regard to her ability to back him up should a deadly situation arise. Survival at its most basic, given Camden's chosen profession. Noticing she was the most intensely beautiful woman he'd ever encountered was a byproduct and not his original intent.

Whoa, there, Camden. You just came up with a whole defense about why you noticed the woman was beautiful.

You're in deep.

Camden would never let his relationship with Rochelle enter unprofessional territory. He couldn't go there. In fact, this was a good time to file away the description *beautiful detective* and actively ignore the strong pull toward the person he'd just met.

Three rapid knocks on the door were followed by Rochelle identifying herself as law enforcement.

A figure passed behind the peephole, and then the door immediately swung open.

"I haven't done anything wrong," Kage immediately said, blocking their entry with his frame. He leaned against the doorjamb and folded his arms across a broad chest.

Rochelle introduced herself as Kage studied Camden.

"No need to say your name, Marshal," Kage said, his gaze steady on Camden. The chip on Kage's shoulder had grown into a boulder.

"Mind if we come inside?" Camden asked, figuring there was no need to tap dance around their desire to check his apartment.

"As a matter of fact, I do," Kage countered, not budging. A quick appraisal said he'd been working out while in prison. He hooked his chin toward Camden before shifting his gaze to Rochelle. "What's he doing here?"

"Marshal Remington is accompanying me on an investigation," Rochelle explained.

Kage rolled his eyes like he couldn't believe this was happening. "Am I a suspect or a witness?"

"That's what we're here to determine," Rochelle said, palming her cell phone. She'd removed her hand from resting on the butt of her Glock to retrieve the phone. After validating her facial ID, she pulled up the picture from the department's missing-persons report. "Do you know this woman?"

Realization as to why they were at Kage's doorstep dawned. He started shaking his head almost immediately. "No, I don't," he said without hesitation, which was generally a sign of someone telling the truth. *Or a practiced liar.* Psychopaths and narcissists had their own set of rules. But Kage was neither, as far as Camden could determine.

The man was, however, a criminal. That fact couldn't be denied. The extent of which was in question. Camden intended to find the answer.

"Why would I do anything to jeopardize my parole when I've barely been out more than a month?" Kage said with a burning fire behind his eyes. Daggers were being shot at Camden too. Hot, burning daggers from eyes that would probably like nothing more than for Camden to toss aside his weapons and go toe-to-toe with the former inmate.

"No one said you did," Rochelle said, drawing attention back to her and away from Camden.

Normally, Camden was the one to defuse tense situations. Kage had a serious bone to pick with him for doing his job.

Or was there more to it?

Chapter Two

Whatever was going on between Camden Remington and Kage Durham needed to stop so Rochelle could assess the situation. Bringing the man who'd arrested Kage didn't seem like the brightest idea, considering the sheer amount of rage coming off Kage in waves.

"Would you mind taking another look at the photo?" Rochelle asked. At this point, the assumption was that Justina was still alive. Rochelle would like to keep it that way. Could they get to the victim before it was too late?

"What does this have to do with me?" Kage asked, not hiding the contempt in his voice. The man was well-spoken, tall, and most would consider him attractive.

Rochelle needed to come at this from a different angle. "Does the name *Justina Worth* mean anything to you?"

"Should it, Detective?" Kage continued the game of answering questions with another question.

"That's what we're here to find out, Mr. Durham," she stated in as calm a voice as she could.

Kage offered a cursory glance at the photo. "Like I said, I've never seen this woman before in my life, but you can tell whoever's in charge to cut it out with the shadow on me. I can't turn around without someone following."

"What does that mean?" Rochelle asked, cocking her

head to one side, and raising an eyebrow. Was the man delusional? Or did he have a mental condition she wasn't aware of? Paranoia?

"Ever since my release, someone has been following me," Kage said with a frustrated sigh. "At first, I thought it was you." He flicked his gaze at Camden. "But I'm sure the federal government wouldn't waste valuable resources on a small-time criminal like me."

"Justina Worth is missing," Rochelle stated as plainly as she could to bring the gravity of the current situation front and center. Kage was too busy licking his wounds from his arrest and incarceration, and clearly blamed Camden for it, which was misguided at best. "This is serious. We're trying to locate her and thought you—"

Kage leaned in, cutting her off with his glare. "Like I already said. Never heard that name in my life." He bared his teeth like an agitated dog warning its adversary to back off.

"Where were you last Saturday night?" Rochelle asked, needing to redirect.

"I went out for a drink at a nearby nightclub," Kage stated. "Is that against the law now?"

"Depends on what you did while you were there and after you left," Rochelle returned.

"I didn't do anything except have a nonalcoholic beer, realized the place was way too crowded, and then I left," he said, his voice taut.

"What time did you exit the nightclub?" Rochelle asked.

Kage shrugged. "I'm not exactly certain."

"You must have a rough idea," Camden declared, his voice a study in calm.

"Before midnight," Kage said with another exasperated sigh.

"I could call your parole officer," Camden said. "See how she feels about you going to a place where alcohol is served."

"What are you accusing me of this time?" Kage asked, impatience edged in his tone. "Because my parole officer isn't going to care about me stepping out when I didn't drink alcohol or cause a problem."

"Are you denying your conviction, Kage?" Camden continued. "Or the fact that you need to watch your p's and q's or risk going back to prison?"

"No one said I was," Kage countered. "But I deserve to know why you showed up here, asking my whereabouts while simultaneously asking if I know of a Justina What's-her-name. Are you asking if I had anything to do with this woman's disappearance? Because that's outta line. I messed up before and paid my dues." He swept his hand across his body like he was showing the newest model of an expensive automobile. "As you can see, I'm living the high life here. I lost all my business because of that jail sentence."

Nice that he wasn't taking responsibility for the fact that *he* was the one who'd committed the crimes that had cost his livelihood, she thought sarcastically. No, it was law enforcement's fault for busting him. What about the lives he'd destroyed by stealing folks' identities?

It was just like a perp to blame others for their fate because they got caught.

"We're trying to find a missing person," Rochelle said, attempting to bring the conversation back to the point of their visit. A muscle in Camden's jaw ticked as tensions increased. "And we'll be speaking to anyone and everyone who might be connected to the case so we can find this person alive."

Kage shook his head. Those bared teeth came out again. "Once a criminal, always a criminal. Is that it?"

"I'd personally appreciate it if you wouldn't waste our time," Rochelle said out of frustration. Trying to keep Kage on topic was proving impossible when he had nothing but venom for law-enforcement officers.

Camden took a step toward Kage. "The next time we come here, it'll be with your parole officer, and we won't be asking your permission to enter your apartment."

"I'd invite you inside, but I'm fresh out of meat for my charcuterie board," Kage quipped, more daggers shooting from his eyes. One thing was clear—he wasn't going to help them voluntarily. It would take a warrant to cross the threshold the man was protecting like his life depended on it.

Rochelle had been listening for any sounds coming from the apartment that would indicate someone was trapped inside. The low hum of a TV in the background provided enough noise to mask a quiet plea for help. Based on what Rochelle could make out, the show was one of the many sequels to *Rocky*. How many *Creed* movies were they up to now?

Rochelle didn't know. Camden might. The irony of a former convict watching a movie about an underdog wasn't lost on her.

She reached into her pocket and retrieved a business card. "These are rarely used anymore, but if you can think of anything that might help us with the case, I'd appreciate a call."

Kage stared at the small three-and-a-half-by-two-inch card like it was a bomb about to detonate.

Rather than stand there with her hand stuck out in between them, she flicked the card in the open space between the door and above his shoulder.

"Keep it," she said to him before turning to her partner for this visit. "Ready?"

Camden stood there for a long moment, not breaking eye contact with Kage. The timeline worked for the case. A man had been seen leaving with the victim. All signs pointed to Kage being guilty. However, the grainy surveillance video wouldn't be enough to convict. Not to mention, Justina might have run away from her life on purpose. The pain of losing her father might have been too great, so she'd needed to get lost for a while.

"You a Texas Rangers fan?" Camden asked.

"Why would I be?" Kage asked, disgusted.

"Just asking," Camden stated.

What was that all about?

CAMDEN KNEW SOMETHING was fishy with Kage. But what?

"Look, I told you before, and I'll tell you again," Kage said in a tone that was one-hundred-percent believable, "I didn't have anything to do with the disappearance of this lady." He paused as a muscle in his jaw pulsed. "I'm not that unlucky with the opposite sex that I would need to force anyone to be in my company."

The man was built. He had sandy blond hair and brown eyes. He resembled a stockier version of the dude from the popular movies involving shades of gray, chin stubble included.

"Thank you for your time, Mr. Durham," Rochelle said, stopping Camden from commenting on the fact men who hurt women weren't always considered ugly or undatable.

"I'd say it was a pleasure, but I gave up lying for Lent," Kage quipped.

"We'd like to get through Thanksgiving this week before we worry about what comes before Easter," Rochelle murmured, then rolled her eyes and turned toward the SUV.

"A comedian," Kage called after her. "Do me a favor and take your show on the road. You won't find what you're looking for here anyway, and I'm a little tired of being harassed."

Harassment was a serious offense and not an accusation Camden took lightly. Kage was trying to push Camden's buttons with the comment. Camden refused to be baited into an argument by the ex-convict.

Instead, he thanked Kage for his time and then followed Rochelle to the SUV before climbing into the passenger seat.

"Good idea to let the lady drive," Kage shouted as Camden reached for the door handle to close the door. "Can't have a hothead, rogue cop behind the wheel."

Camden closed the door and buckled in. From the corner of his eye, he saw Kage laughing. *Think you got the last word? Think again.*

"That was pleasant," Rochelle said as she started the engine and then backed out of the parking spot.

"He's just trying to rile me up," Camden explained. "He always swears he has some kind of doppelganger out there making his life miserable."

"Why would he think that?" Rochelle asked as she navigated onto the residential road with a speed limit of thirty. Too bad other vehicles on the road didn't seem to notice the sign as one whizzed past.

"Take the surveillance video for example," Camden began. "Kage says he left about fifteen to twenty minutes before the camera caught him walking out with Justina."

"He estimated the time," she said, shrugging.

"His name has come up in other crimes in locations he supposedly left just before the crime occurred," he said. "Coincidence?"

She raised her eyebrows. "If so, the man has the worst luck in history."

"Or he's smarter than we realize and committing crimes without getting caught," he said.

"The male in the surveillance video resembles his build,

but the perp is a master at hiding his face from the camera," she said as she cut a left-hand turn.

"As though he knew he was doing something wrong and didn't want to get caught rather than leaving a nightclub after having a drink," Camden pointed out.

"Do you believe that he didn't have alcohol?" she asked.

"We could always check more of the footage," he replied. "The ball cap bothers me."

"What about it?" Rochelle asked.

"The guy caught on camera had on a Texas Rangers baseball cap," Camden said.

"Yeah?"

"Do you like sports?" he asked her.

"Not really," she answered with a glance in his direction. "I know the irony of living in Texas and having no real fondness for football."

"Some people might consider that a sacrilege," he pointed out with a smirk.

"Don't tell me you bought in to the whole *Friday Night Lights* bit," she said, sounding surprised.

"I played," he said. "I'm from a small town in Texas." He laughed. "If you don't play sports, there isn't a whole helluva lot else to do."

"You got me there," she said. "I was born here in Austin."

"Are you on the keep-Austin-weird committee?" he asked, relaxing a little bit after the tense exchange with Kage. The problem with talking to Kage Durham was that a piece of Camden actually believed the guy, which went against all logic and all of Camden's experience in law enforcement.

But, hey, anomalies were rare. If they were common, they'd be called ordinary. Camden almost laughed at his own wittiness.

"When he was alive, my dad was a huge hockey fan," Rochelle said. "He made a big production of game days. My mom would make cookies in the shape of hockey pucks, complete with icing. She really went all out."

"What was his favorite team?"

"Easy," she said. "Pittsburgh Penguins. His family was from Pittsburgh, and there's a long line of Penguin fans on the Paddock side of the family." She added, "My parents moved to Austin after they got married for my dad's work and then earned their hats and boots years later, after falling in love with Texas."

"Would your dad ever wear a Philadelphia Flyers jersey?" he asked.

"My dad wouldn't be caught dead in one of those," she quipped. "Are you kidding me? That's a sacrilege even to suggest it."

"Exactly," Camden pointed out.

"Kage is a self-proclaimed Houston Astros fan," Camden said. "He wore their ball cap the day I arrested him. I commented about it on the ride to the station and he was clear about his allegiance to the team. Why would he be wearing a Texas Rangers hat?"

"I'm guessing those teams are big rivals if you're comparing them to the Penguins and Flyers…?"

He confirmed with a nod.

"Kage, of all people, would know about the rivalry," Rochelle offered.

Camden nodded again. But Kage might wear a rival's ball cap to throw others off his trail.

"It's also possible that he stopped off at a convenience store at some point and bought the first ball cap he could find," she offered.

"I thought of that too," Camden said. "And, yes, it makes

logical sense that Kage could try to throw law enforcement off by wearing a rival team's ball cap. However, something in me doubts he would go to that much trouble. Wouldn't he just grab a cap that he already owns?"

Even people willing to break the law had a code. That had been niggling at the back of Camden's mind.

A loyal fan wouldn't willingly wear apparel from a rival team.

Kage's TV room in the rental home he'd lived in when he'd been arrested had an entire wall of Houston Astros memorabilia—all bought with money gained illegally. All sold at auction.

Kage wouldn't wear a Texas Rangers ball cap. He just wouldn't.

Chapter Three

"Are you hungry?" Rochelle asked her passenger. Her stomach reminded her that she'd choked down half a dry bagel for breakfast along with a large black coffee too many hours ago.

"I could eat," Camden said in a distracted tone. He knew Kage better than she did, and his wheels must have been turning after this last interaction.

"Mind if we go through a drive-through while we talk through what just happened with Kage?" she asked, motioning toward the famous burger fast-food chain up ahead and on the right.

"Sounds good to me," Camden responded.

Rochelle made the turn and then got in line behind four other vehicles. "Figure we can review the surveillance tape together while we eat. See what else we can find on there."

"Maybe we can catch Kage drinking alcohol," Camden said. "Catch him in one lie, and we'll have a better edge next time we talk to him."

"At least we know where to find him," Rochelle said before inching up one car length. "He's not going anywhere while on parole without alerting his parole officer."

"True," he stated.

"The fan-loyalty issue is something to consider," Rochelle said, moving up another car length. Soon, they'd be at the squawk box, where she could half scream her order into what felt like the void.

"I can't get past that one—the wrong ball cap," he said. "Which might just be bias on my part."

"Makes sense though," she said. "Especially when I apply the logic to my father."

"*Fan* is short for *fanatic*," he pointed out.

"What's your favorite sports team?" she asked, curious about what he liked.

"Used to be the Miami Heat during the Holy Trinity era," he said without hesitation.

"Holy Trinity?"

"LeBron James, Chris Bosh, and Dwyane Wade," he responded like it was common knowledge. "I've heard them called the Big Three."

In Texas, sports held a similar status to religion. The mantra she'd heard repeated over and over again when she'd been anywhere near the high-school-football coach was: family, God, football.

Growing up here, she figured the order was wrong. Football would never have come last to most of the kids she'd gone to high school with. At least Austin had its own funky, artistic vibe, even if it had become corporate before her eyes. The city's flawed thinking had been that no one would move there and overrun the city if they didn't build roads.

The city hadn't built roads, but people had moved there in hordes anyway. Now, the traffic was a nightmare despite the loop that had been built too late. At least some drivers were able to escape the nightmare that was downtown traffic. Not that it bothered her enough to want to move. This was the only home she'd ever known.

Back to sports, she would file the ball-cap information for future use, then see if anything else similar popped up.

"What do you want?" she asked her distracted partner as she pulled up to the squawk box.

"Whatever you're having," he said as he studied his cell.

Rochelle ordered two hamburger meals with Cokes before pulling around to the pay window. Before she could reach for her wallet, Camden handed her a couple of twenties from his pocket.

"This one's on me," he offered.

She thanked him, paid, and then pulled up to the food window. After taking the bags and handing over the drinks, she found a parking spot toward the back of the small lot. No other vehicles were parked there beyond the spaces marked for employees.

Camden set up the food using the console as a makeshift table while she pulled up the surveillance footage and wound it back to half past eleven.

"I figure starting here should give us a sense of what the night was like at the bar," she said, sitting back to watch and take down her burger and fries.

Camden studied the screen with the same wrinkle in his forehead that he'd had a minute ago while he'd focused on his cell phone.

"Did you get anything from your phone worth sharing?" she asked, motioning toward the phone he'd set next to his leg like he might be waiting for a call or text.

"No," he admitted. "It's personal." His tone said it was heavy.

"Everything okay?" she asked.

Camden chewed on a bite of burger before swallowing and then washing it down with a sip of Coke. "Do you want to hear about my family?"

"Sure," she said, realizing he most likely had a wife and possibly kids. A quick glance at his ring finger revealed no tan line. She'd noticed there was no gold band a few seconds after they'd first met. It was habit and had nothing to do with the little frisson of awareness she'd experienced when she first set eyes on him.

A little voice in the back of her mind decided to point out the fact she was attracted to him and there was more to it, but she refused to entertain the idea. Besides, it wouldn't be productive to go down that path at work.

Camden exhaled a slow sigh. "My grandparents were in a crash several months ago that put them both in comas. My grandfather recently woke up and is alert with perfect cognitive function, but he's been with my grandmother since high school, so we're obviously concerned about keeping his spirits up until something happens with her one way or the other."

"That's so sad," she immediately said. "I'm so sorry that happened. Sounds like your family is close."

"You could say that," he said after thanking her for her sympathy. "They raised me, my sister, Julie, and my brother, Dalton, from when we were little kids. They took on our cousins too, so they basically raised six kids while running a small paint horse operation."

"They sound like saints," she murmured.

"They were…*are*," he corrected, his voice revealing a measured calm, as though he couldn't allow himself to get emotional about them, or the landslide would turn into an avalanche. Her heart went out to him. "It's been a roller coaster of emotions since the crash."

"I can only imagine how helpless you must feel watching the ones you love fight for their lives," she soothed. "It has to be the worst."

"It's not easy," he admitted, turning to catch her gaze. A mix of emotions played behind his eyes, making her want to reach over the console and find a way to ease his pain.

At a loss for words, all she could do was listen as he continued.

"Each of us is taking a turn watching over them so they're not alone," he said. "I'm next, and then I guess we'll start over from the beginning again if nothing changes with Grandma Lacey."

"Sounds like they're being surrounded by love," she said, wondering what that would be like. As an only child, she had no idea what growing up with siblings and cousins was like. After relocating to Austin from Amarillo, they'd had no extra money for vacations back to Amarillo, so Rochelle had never developed a relationship with extended family. They'd preferred driving to nearby Galveston to go to the beach or Padre Island when it wasn't spring break and overrun with drunk college kids.

"I haven't thought about it in those terms," he said, "but you're right. I've been focused on feeling like the worst human for being unable to drop everything and be with them after they took me in and raised me like their own."

"We might have only just met, but I generally get a good read on people within a few minutes of being in their presence—call it a job skill or hazard, depending on your point of view." She cracked a small smile, hoping it would be contagious. "It causes problems with dating sometimes."

Camden's face broke into a smile, revealing straight, white teeth. Another quality that made him almost irresistible. "Would it surprise you to know that seems to be a universal problem with law-enforcement officers?"

"Too easy to spot a liar, right?" she said, forcing her gaze away from eyes that reminded her of the sky on a spring morning after it rained.

If only she'd met Camden socially instead of at work...

THIS WAS THE first time Camden had spoken to someone outside of the family or medical team about his grandparents since this whole ordeal had started. Rochelle was easy to talk to. Someone he could see himself trusting. He ignored the voice that tried to convince him a greater magnetism was at work, a pull that shouldn't be disregarded.

"Your grandparents are fortunate to have so much love in their lives," Rochelle said after a thoughtful pause, keeping her gaze trained on the screen as the surveillance footage rolled.

Camden thought he was the lucky one. "My mother took off when I was seven and a half years old. By age ten, my father had died—some say of a broken heart after the woman who birthed me took off, but it was probably heatstroke. I'm the oldest of three."

"You have an oldest-sibling vibe," she said.

"Controlling, high achieving, and entitled?" he quipped.

"I was thinking more along the lines of conscientious, determined, and hardworking," she corrected with a small smile that caused his chest to squeeze. "But you know yourself better than I do."

The mischievous lilt in her voice cracked through some of the shame he felt whenever he was shrouded in guilt about not being bedside, holding vigil for his grandparents.

"Oh, no," he countered. "I like your adjectives way better than mine."

She laughed, and it filled the cab of the SUV with something that felt a lot like hope.

"Then, we go with mine," she said, then added, "I lost

both of my parents a year apart to lung cancer. Dad was a lifetime smoker. For Mom, it was all secondhand smoke that caused hers." She shook her head. "My dad loved her beyond anything I've ever seen or will probably ever experience in my lifetime, so it would've killed him to know he was the reason she followed him in death a year after he left us."

After mumbling a few words that fell short of providing the comfort he wished he could give her, he asked, "How long ago did you lose your mom?"

"Seven months ago," she said, her voice filled with a surprising vulnerability.

Here, he'd been rambling on about his own family situation when her hurt was still so recent and so close to the surface. "I should've asked about you before I went on about my own problems. I hope you'll accept my apology."

"There's nothing to apologize for, Camden," she said. He liked the way his name rolled off her tongue. "My parents had a great love story. I wholeheartedly believe my mom didn't want to be in this world without my dad. Or, maybe that's what I choose to believe because that makes her somehow in control instead of a helpless victim. Does that sound weird?"

"Makes sense to me," he said softly. "I never bought in to the idea we have no control over what happens to us. I mean, sure, the details aren't always ours to decide, but what would be the point if our lives were predetermined, and we had no say? What would be the point of having a brain that allows us to think if we weren't meant to use it?"

"I couldn't agree more," she said. "I never understood or accepted the idea of a scenario that gave us no control over our decisions or responsibility for our mistakes."

Camden liked Rochelle. She was intelligent and fierce when she needed to be.

"I miss them," she said. "I'm thirty-three years old and still wish I could call my mom when something really great happens. Honestly, she's the first person I think about when I have good news and bad news. There are times when I've already picked up my cell before I remember she's not an option to call anymore."

Camden reached across the console, took Rochelle's hand in his, and then gave a gentle squeeze for reassurance and comfort. Lightning struck at the point where their skin touched. The jolt of surprise in her hazel eyes said she'd felt the same thing.

If it had been winter, he'd blame static electricity. But that electricity would've had to be on steroids for the effect it had on him.

Once the initial shock was over, Camden was flooded with warmth the equivalent of a dozen campfires on a cold night.

He stared down at his hand like it didn't belong to his body anymore, like it had taken on a life of its own. *Whoa!*

An awkward moment passed between them as they both seemed to catch on to the rarity of an occurrence like this one, like trying to explain how the engineering marvel that was the Taj Mahal had been built back in the mid-1600s.

Out of the corner of his eye, Camden saw the red ball cap on the screen. He pulled his hand back and refocused. "Can we rewind?"

It took a second for Rochelle to act, but then she nodded and reversed the footage.

"There," Camden stated. "He's walking outside."

Being distracted had caused them to miss the ball cap walking inside. *Dammit.* Camden was a professional. This wasn't acceptable.

Rochelle cleared her throat, then took a sip of Coke. After

rewinding, she pointed at the screen. "The place is practically wall-to-wall people. But, from what I can tell, he walks inside an hour earlier. See?"

Sure enough, the red ball cap entered the nightclub. In the mass of people, it was impossible to see much beyond the back of the ball cap.

"The place is hopping," he said.

"Good place to blend into the crowd and go unnoticed," Rochelle pointed out.

"True," he agreed as she fast-forwarded the footage.

"Here he is again, walking out with someone who could be Justina," she said as she slowed the footage.

Too bad it was grainy, and the place was shoulder-to-shoulder people, making it nearly impossible to make out anything except blobs.

"Justina is tiny by comparison," he stated. "A good defense lawyer might be able to argue it isn't even her with the guy in the red ball cap."

And then something happened. Justina looked up almost directly at the camera, a smile on her face.

She'd had no idea she was about to disappear.

Chapter Four

"This footage is definitely not going to be admissible in court, let alone be enough for a conviction," Rochelle mused, keeping her thoughts focused on the case and away from her traitorous body's reaction to Camden's touch.

"We can't even get a warrant with this," Camden said out loud, explaining what they both knew. "But damned if that doesn't resemble Kage Durham."

"Wish we had more to go on," Rochelle stated, hoping for a miracle at this point. "I guess the only bright spot out of this scenario is that we have a name and, at least, circumstantial evidence. We can watch Kage, and I'll see if my supervisor will place a request for information from anyone visiting the club on the night in question onto our department's social-media page."

"What's the success rate of those types of posts in the past?" he asked.

"We get mixed results, honestly," she said, sighing and holding back about the second text she'd sent while he was distracted by food. "Given this is a nightclub environment with young women present, we might get a hit. Women tend to pay more attention to warnings in order to stay safe than our male citizens."

"Always worth a try," he said. "If a post takes two minutes to put up and solves one case, then it has the ability to save lives."

Especially in this case, she wanted to say. She sent a message to her supervisor while they were stationary in the SUV.

"We should make a list of anyone who might have had contact with Red Ball Cap that night," she said after hitting Send.

"Bouncers can be good resources in cases like these," Camden said after a thoughtful pause. "Owners, not so much. Kage hasn't been out long enough to qualify as a regular, and he doesn't have enough cash that we know of for bottle service and VIP tables."

"The bartender on duty that night would be a good person to speak to," Rochelle added. Her cell buzzed. After checking the screen, she said, "My supervisor is arranging for a message to be put up on the department's social-media page requesting information about a missing person last seen at the nightclub in question."

"Here's hoping for a lead," he said, crossing his fingers. For good measure?

"Are you done?" she asked, motioning toward the fast-food wrappers.

"Yes," he said.

She gathered her empties. "I can't stand the smell of fast food in my vehicle. Sticks around for days."

"I'll throw all of it away," he offered. "Toss it in the bag." He held up the greasy-smelling fast-food bag.

Rochelle dumped her wrappers inside before he exited the vehicle.

He returned and then clicked on his seat belt. "We can swing by the nightclub and talk to the owners and then I'll check on the warrant I'm here to serve."

After pulling up the address, Rochelle took note of the owners' names. "Think we should call first?"

"Nah," he said. "You never know with these owner types. I've witnessed and heard all kinds of things they'll do to cover up a crime they don't want associated with their business. In my experience, it's best not to give them advanced notice before stopping by. Plus, I can tell a lot about a person from their initial reactions when I show up and ask questions."

"Guess protecting their business goes with the territory sometimes," she decided. She'd seen the same with entrepreneurs, too, especially bar owners. Some were on the up and up and were proud of the business they'd created. To others, it was a money machine, and they didn't care what went on as long as the cash kept flowing. Underage drinkers in the VIP lounge? Not a problem for some places, whereas others checked every ID if you looked younger than thirty-five years old. At thirty-two, she'd been carded while meeting up with coworkers for a drink. She'd felt flattered until she'd been told the establishment ID'd anyone under the age of thirty-five. There were places that encouraged law enforcement to stop by after shift by offering a discount on food. Those places liked having officers around for extra security. Patrons hesitated before stepping out of line in a bar where every other barstool was occupied by someone wearing a badge. Other establishments weren't so welcoming. They couldn't refuse an off-duty officer from entering their doors, but they didn't make the place cozy either.

Rochelle started the engine, put the gearshift into Reverse, and backed out of the parking spot. GPS led her straight to the front door of the nightclub in a matter of minutes.

Knowing a kidnapping had occurred on or near this spot

sent an icy chill racing up her spine. Always. There was a dark side to a crime scene that she felt on a deep, unexplainable level.

She parked and exited the SUV. Camden met her around the front before leaning against the bumper. The lot was small and dingy. A couple of forty-ounce bottles in paper bags littered the cracked pavement of the sidewalk.

In the light of day, the nightclub showed its age. An outside wall had a long, crooked line from the corner of the building that slithered down the side like a snake, a product of being built on ever-shifting clay soil—soil that was not meant to hold up any type of building, not even homes. The turquoise paint probably looked amazing when all the manufactured lighting hit it. The sun made the color look cheap and showed all the dirt.

A couple of rent-by-the-minute electric scooters had been abandoned around the area, a common theme for club hoppers. Uber pricing had gone through the roof. After drinking, there was always a group of young people who thought it would be fun to get on a scooter and hit the next bar. Thankfully, incidents and deaths were still low in Austin, but she always feared that number was like a simmering pot of water about to boil.

"No one appears to be here," Rochelle said to Camden, who straightened and started walking the perimeter of the empty lot.

"It's early," he said. "I figured as much."

"Should we walk to Kage's house from here to record the time it takes?" she asked, pulling up the map feature on her phone and checking the distance. "The map thinks it would take us thirty minutes to make the trek. I must be a fast walker because it usually takes me half that amount of time."

He nodded, agreeing. "Too bad we can't tell if Justina

had too much to drink on the night in question. A fifteen-minute walk with someone who was drunk should've drawn attention."

Rochelle agreed. "She might not have been able to walk straight and could have needed help. Then, there's the possibility of ketamine being involved. She might have had little to drink but was drugged instead."

A muscle in Camden's jaw clenched. "Ketamine in unattended drinks accounts for far too many rape cases."

"We should add Justina's coworkers to the list of people to talk to so we can get a sense of her personality," Rochelle added. "Find out how she spent her free time and who she hung out with on weekends."

An eyebrow shot up. "Is this officially your case?"

"I asked my supervisor to reassign me from the case you're on so I can take this one," she admitted. It had been her second text message after asking for the social-media call for information.

Camden walked away as he pulled out his cell. He turned the corner, out of earshot. Was he doing the same? Asking to be moved to this case rather than the one that would have him serving a warrant to pick up a federal criminal?

The temptation to follow him close enough to hear whom he had called and why had to be tamped down. For more reasons than professional ones, she wanted to keep working with Camden. The flicker of betrayal that had crossed his features a moment ago when she'd confessed to her second text caused a vise to tighten around her chest. Would he resent her for making the move?

Camden came walking around the corner, his expression unreadable.

Her heart skipped a couple of beats. She was about to find out.

CAMDEN HAD JUST as much right to be assigned to this case as Rochelle. More so, when he considered Kage Durham had been his responsibility to begin with. She wouldn't even be going down this trail if Camden hadn't walked up when he had, considering he was the one who had identified Kage.

Camden brought up his gaze, locking in on hers. "Looks like you're stuck with me if your supervisor gives final approval." He shot her a look as he stopped and then folded his arms across his chest in a dare. "If you want me off the case, you should probably send another one of those texts." Then he prepared to fire the dagger, turning his back to her. "This will make it easier to go behind my back again."

"I didn't mean to off—"

He turned and stared her down. "What? Upset me?" He took a step toward her. "Offend me?" Another step. They were five feet away from each other now. "You sure about that? Because I was sitting right next to you when you sent the text, so you could've given me a heads-up."

She put her hands up, palms out, surrendering. "I wasn't trying to step on your toes. This is my jurisdiction."

"Kage is my responsibility," he countered.

Rochelle tilted her head to the right side as she studied him. "You did your job when you picked him up and arrested him. What makes you think he's still your responsibility when he lives in my jurisdiction?"

"I take my job personally," he said, gaze narrowed. "And there was always something fishy about his case that I couldn't put my finger on. I can't help but think I dropped the ball somewhere along the line. So, no, my job is not finished."

"You're not the only one who lives for the job," she countered with the stubbornness of a bull facing down a red cape. "And I'd planned on telling you once I received approval because I actually thought we might make a good team."

Oh. Hell.

Had he jumped to a conclusion?

Yes.

Did he feel like a jerk?

Yes.

Could he repair the damage?

Only time will tell.

"I didn't mean to jump the gun," he started, searching for the right words to apologize.

"Forget about it," she said in a tone that said he was dismissed.

"Seriously," he continued, unfazed by the snub. He had it coming, and he could take it on the chin. "My bad."

"You won't get any disagreement there from me," she said a little too fast for his comfort. Rochelle was sharp. She had a sharp mind and a sharp tongue…

Camden didn't need to be thinking about anything in her mouth region because his gaze had dipped down to kissable lips—lips that made him even more frustrated. Kissing Rochelle was an idea that came out of the blue. The last thing he needed was more drama in his life right now, considering everything going on in Mesa Point.

He stopped right there.

His heightened emotions made sense when he thought about the accident that had happened weeks ago and the fact that his grandmother wasn't improving. When he and his siblings and cousins had set up the rotation system to ensure someone was at the hospital 24/7, no one had thought it would drag on this long or make it to his turn. They, him included, had optimistically believed Duke's rotation would be first and last.

How naive had they been?

He shook his head. "I underestimated how much not having the family together for Thanksgiving this year would affect me. I'm taking it out on you, and that's not okay." He issued a sharp sigh as he dropped his hands to his sides. "If you can accept my apology, I'll stay on the case. If not, it'll be better for everyone involved if we go our separate ways. A distraction is the last thing anyone needs while working on this case. I can circle back to my superior and rescind my request."

"We're good," Rochelle immediately responded. "Hey, I get it. What you said about your grandparents earlier…well, I should have connected the dots because I don't get the impression you normally jump to conclusions about other people. So, yeah, I'm good if you are."

Relief flooded Camden. The barrage caught him off guard because it had less to do with the case and more to do with what Rochelle thought about him. If he wasn't careful, he might care a little too much about Rochelle's opinion of him. "Let's head over to Justina's workplace while our superiors discuss us working together. Shall we?"

Chapter Five

After deciding not to walk to Kage's apartment from the nightclub just yet, Rochelle drove them to Justina's workplace. Care to Remember wasn't exactly a veiled name for a memory-care facility that specialized in dementia "residents," as the website had called them.

The outside of the building had been made to look homey, with a wraparound porch and rocking chairs that had been painted white. Ferns still hung despite the last couple of cold snaps. There was a small parking lot to the left of the cobalt-blue-sided two-story with white shutters.

Inside, the aesthetic was colder. White tile floors could best be described as hospital-ready. White walls were a stark contrast to the warmth of the exterior. A bar-height counter greeted them a few steps inside, creating a barrier. A line of fold-up wooden chairs against the wall beside the door made for an uncomfortable waiting area, lending a dentist-office look to the place. This seemed like where Rochelle would go to get a filling rather than a home where she would want to visit a loved one who may or may not remember her on a given day.

Looks can be deceiving.

"How can I help you today?" asked a young brunette

from behind the counter. She was barely tall enough to see from the other side.

Camden stepped forward first and produced a badge. "My name is Camden Remington, and I'm with the US Marshals Service. My colleague here is Detective Rochelle Paddock with Austin PD."

The brunette's smile faded. On closer inspection, the lines bracketing her mouth made her look like she was in her late twenties or early thirties. Bags were underneath her eyes, making it appear as though she hadn't slept well in recent nights. Her name badge read Ally.

Ally leaned forward with a concerned look on her face. "Is this about Justina?"

"Yes, ma'am," Camden said as Ally's gaze looked them over, likely assessing whether they could be trusted. Her suspicion might also have to do with her wondering if she was a suspect. Had she done something wrong? Because a flash of guilt crossed her features.

"Have they…? Have you…? Is she…?"

"No, ma'am," Camden answered. "That's why we're here today. We'd like to talk to you about Ms. Worth."

Ally's gaze widened. "I'm not sure I can help, but I'll do my best."

"How would you describe your relationship with Ms. Worth?" Camden began with the standard line of questioning.

"I knew her from this place," Ally responded.

"Did the two of you ever talk on a personal level?" he continued.

"Not really," Ally said. "I mean, no one really ever talked to Justina. She kept to herself mostly."

"No lunchroom discussions?" he asked.

"I know she cared for her elderly father, who passed away

recently," Ally informed them. "Justina brought her lunch from home. Usually, it was a sandwich and chips. She sat alone in the lunchroom where the staff eats and didn't talk much."

"Would you consider her to be unfriendly?" Camden asked as Rochelle studied Ally, searching for signs of deception. It was a job requirement and a hazard at the same time. It made trusting people difficult when you were always waiting, watching for the lie out of habit.

"Not really," Ally said after careful consideration. Her gaze drifted up and to the right, which was common when someone tried to recall information. She twisted her fingers together and shifted her weight, which was most likely a sign of nerves. People often became nervous when being interviewed by the law, but that didn't mean they were lying. "I'd say she was just the quiet type. You know? Someone who didn't fit in with most of the others."

"How so?" Camden cocked his head to one side. His calm, engaging expression was disarming. He would have made a great detective with the way he made others relax when speaking to them.

"Well, the way she dressed, for one," Ally explained. "Her clothes were old-fashioned, homemade looking, and like she was a pilgrim on her way to church." Ally fidgeted a little more. Was she embarrassed at the description, or that she was one of the people who'd judged Justina harshly for her clothing? Maybe even made fun of her behind her back?

"Is it safe to assume no one attempted to be friends with Ms. Worth at work?" Camden asked.

"She was..." Ally made eyes at Camden. "You know... stiff."

If Justina had been the quiet type who hadn't gotten out

much or had below-average social skills, she might have been an easier target for the perp.

"Justina was a Goody Two-shoes," Ally added as though that explained everything and gave those around her a free pass to dismiss her. She put her hands flat on the counter now. "Surprised the heck out of me and everyone else to find out she went to a bar." She snorted. "Can you even imagine someone like her just walking up to the bar?" The smile wiped from her face when she got a good look at Camden's response—stoic, a hint of disdain flashing across his features.

Rochelle wanted to correct the woman and say that, technically, it was a nightclub. However, the point being made was that going out to a place where alcohol was served hadn't been Justina's normal behavior. The way Ally talked about Justina reminded Rochelle of being back in high school and being told not to sit at the cheerleaders table on her first day at a new school. She'd resisted for the first quarter of the year and had been bullied the rest of her freshman year after refusing to move. The strange part had been the cheerleaders weren't the ones who'd done the bullying. They'd snubbed her by refusing to acknowledge her presence. Humiliating? Yes. Other students had decided to bully her for taking a stance, which had made high school even more hellish. As a result, Rochelle couldn't stand snobs or bullies to this day.

At least Ally caught on fast. She stood up straight, smoothed her hands across the countertop as though wiping off dust, and said, "But we're all broken up about the fact she's missing."

Camden gave a slight nod, and his gaze intensified. "Where were you on the night of Justina's disappearance?"

Ally brought a hand up to cover a gasp. "What? Why?"

She wasn't good at lying. Good to know.

"Just answer the question, ma'am," Camden said in a voice that could charm even the most skeptical person. It was almost as though he'd flipped a switch, except he'd done it so expertly, Ally didn't pick up on it. Instead, she smiled and twirled a strand of hair around her index finger.

"I was home with my feet up on the coffee table, watching a show on Netflix," she admitted, blinking her eyes a little more rapidly. Either fear or attraction caused her eyelashes to flutter—most likely a decent amount of both.

"Which one, if you don't mind my asking," he continued, unfazed. The man was good. Rochelle would give him that. He had a way of lowering someone's guard without them being the wiser.

Good to know. She could see herself falling under his spell with the way his deep timbre washed over her, leaving a trail of goose bumps in its wake.

"Which what?" Ally asked, momentarily distracted. Fake? Was she covering for something? Someone?

"The Netflix show," Camden confirmed.

"Do you want to know what I think is possible?" Rochelle asked. She'd been quiet up to this point, but it was time to play a little game of good cop, bad cop.

Ally blinked at her.

"Maybe you and a few coworkers saw Justina at the club on the night she disappeared," Rochelle began. Ally's hand-wringing picked up pace. "You thought it was so funny that a 'good girl' like her would be out having a drink at a bar, so you or one of your friends approached her. Maybe even asked her to join you." This scenario might be unlikely, but it was possible. "Maybe someone thought it would be cute to slip something inside her drink for 'funzies.'" She made air quotes around the last word. "Then one of the guys decides to walk her out to the parking lot once the drug kicks in."

"Hold on there." Ally was shaking her head, but a flash of guilt crossed her features. "I've always been a good employee here, and I don't hang out with coworkers outside of work."

"She's stumbling at this point, but you guys think it's funny, don't you," Rochelle continued, unfazed by the protest. It was half-hearted at best. Plus, Rochelle noted that Ally didn't deny being at the club.

Ally squinted as though she couldn't stand to see images of what happened next.

"Playing a practical joke on a puritan like Justina Worth for kicks and grins sure would be a lot of fun to some people, wouldn't it?" Rochelle asked.

"I'm a good person," Ally argued.

Again, she didn't deny it. Instead, she was trying to deflect from the subject.

"And then what happened?" Rochelle continued. "Did someone take the joke too far? Give Justina Worth too much? So much so she became sloppy?" Rochelle paused. She remembered Justina looking up at the camera moments before she'd left the club with a smile on her face. A big smile. "And then she became a liability, right? Too many people saw you together inside the club, so you had one of the guys in your group escort her out to the parking lot."

Ally shook her head emphatically. "I would never do anything like that to another human being."

"Like what?" Rochelle persisted.

Ally was beginning to crack.

And then, she said, "I want to speak to a lawyer."

"As LONG AS you didn't do anything wrong, there's no need for legal counsel," Camden soothed, figuring this was a good time for the "good cop," aka him, to show up. He put a hand up to calm Ally before turning to Rochelle, who'd acted brilliantly in her role as "bad cop."

"I, uh, just don't like where any of this is going," Ally managed to say as her gaze darted toward the exit behind them. Looking for an escape? "I'm not a bad person."

"No one said you are," he responded in the calmest voice he could find. At best, Ally had made fun of her coworker behind her back and possibly to her face. At worst, she was involved in the kidnapping of Justina Worth. Neither scenario made her likely to be nominated for sainthood. However, only one scenario made her a criminal. "We're just looking for information so we can find Justina alive."

"Okay, sure," Ally conceded. "I want to cooperate, but I don't know anything."

"Is your boss in today?" Rochelle cut in. Those words sent Ally's blood pressure soaring, judging by the way her pupils dilated and how she started blinking rapidly. Again, her gaze cut to the door behind them.

"Yes," she said, her voice cracking. "If you'll wait here, I'll run back to Mr. Marples's office and ask him to come out."

It was the best way to get permission to speak to the other employees and possibly use an office for privacy.

Ally disappeared.

"What is your impression?" Rochelle whispered.

"A lot of folks are nervous talking to the law," he conceded. "I'd like proof she lied about being home and watching TV. We need to check into her background to see if she has any priors." Some people wore masks. They came across as upstanding citizens at first blush. Then, Camden checked into their background as related to a case and could be knocked on his backside with what he found. It reminded him that lying came easy to some. Not for him.

He could be honest to a fault. It wasn't always a gift. In fact, it had made his life more difficult on more than one occasion, especially when it had come to his love life. He couldn't lie and tell someone he loved them when he didn't. He couldn't lie and tell someone they had a future if they didn't. And he couldn't lie and tell someone he could ever see himself settling down.

He'd been burned early on in a relationship and had no intention of touching that hot stove again. Honesty had kept him single for thirty-five years.

But he'd never met anyone like Rochelle before. She was honest, intelligent, and beautiful from the inside out. She made him want to go out for coffee and ask questions. What was her background? Was she single? What made her tick? Favorite food? Cocktail? Way to spend a quiet afternoon?

Was his opinion changing about long-term relationships? Or was Rochelle special?

Camden feared the latter. Feared it because there was no way either would cross a professional line.

Dating at work wasn't just frowned upon. It could ruin his relationship with Austin PD, a department he'd worked closely with on more than one occasion. He needed to keep allies in all departments, not make enemies. Too many of the women he'd dated in the past had walked away hating him for him to risk it happening with Rochelle.

Could they become friends? Go out for an occasional drink? Catch a movie together?

It never hurt to ask.

"I agree with your assessment," Rochelle said, breaking into his reverie. "She's embarrassed about her actions or hiding something."

"Some people never outgrow a high-school mentality of social cliques and bullying," he conceded.

"Shame," she said.

The real shame was just how much Camden wanted to get to know the detective, and realizing he would never get the chance. He was married to his work. Soon, he would be taking his turn at the hospital and the paint-horse ranch his grandparents had built from the ground up.

Making time for friendships wasn't a priority to him right now.

Then again, maybe this was the exact right time to find someone to lean on. Could it be Rochelle?

Chapter Six

Mr. Marples was a pudgy, ruddy-faced, middle-aged man with a comb-over. He stood roughly five feet, ten inches in height and had a stomach that looked like someone had tucked a basketball underneath his shirt. His rounded shoulders hunched forward slightly as he padded into the waiting area.

After introductions, he asked to see their badges.

"I'm sorry for the request," he said after they produced them.

"Don't apologize for being thorough with your job," Rochelle stated, taking the lead.

"If you'll follow me," he said with a smile of acknowledgment and a hint of pride. Then, he turned and walked them to his office. It was small and had a window that looked out onto the backyard, where various games were set up for residents. "We're short on staff, as you might have already guessed."

"Is this Ms. Worth's usual shift?" Rochelle asked, taking a seat in front of the large oak desk. Camden took the one next to her.

"Yes, ma'am," Mr. Marples said as the executive chair groaned underneath his weight when he sat down. "I have another worker out sick today."

"Can we have a list of employee names, highlighting anyone who routinely worked with Ms. Worth?" Rochelle asked, wishing she could split herself into two people so she could be in two places at once. Three, if she counted Kage's apartment, which she would like to stake out so she could track his movements.

"Yes, ma'am," Mr. Marples said. He banged on the keyboard to bring his monitor to life. Then, he squinted through his glasses at the screen before banging on the keyboard some more. He shook his head as he motioned toward the box that seemed to confound him. "Darned if I'll ever be able to understand these things. One minute, everything is working fine, and the next, I can't get it to do anything." He spoke low and almost under his breath, like he was having the conversation solely with himself and there was no one else in the room.

A couple of framed prints hung on the wall, mostly of turbulent ocean tides with waves crashing against boulders. The kind of art folks chose said a lot about their own lives. Rochelle surmised that life wasn't easy for Mr. Marples. That he saw it as a struggle. Then again, a good part of his job was likely dealing with insurance claims, which had to be a nightmare.

"Here you go," he said after banging the enter button. A printer came to life on his desk, spitting out two pages. He picked them up, squinted at them, and handed them over. "I added phone numbers in case you need to reach anyone."

"Thank you," Rochelle said before taking the offering. She perused the list, looking for any names that stood out that she might know had a criminal history.

"Our hiring process should weed out anyone with an unsavory background," Mr. Marples said. "Of course, we have the occasional hire who slips through the cracks, but most of our personnel issues are with individuals who fudge paperwork or attempt to slip a pill meant for our patients inside a pocket to take home for themselves."

"Does that happen often?" Rochelle asked. "An employee stealing drugs?" It could explain Justina's behavior changes.

"No," he quickly reassured them.

"Can you tell us about Justina Worth?" Rochelle wanted to know if she had ever been suspected of taking anything home.

Mr. Marples shook his head. "Shame. I hope she turns up soon."

"Has she ever missed work without calling in?" Rochelle continued, trying to steer the conversation down the right road.

"No," he stated without hesitation. His gaze moved from Rochelle to Camden and back. "Justina was a model employee. Always on time. Never took too long at lunch. She stayed in the building and ate in the staff lounge." He pursed his lips. "The others weren't the nicest to her. Complained she was too much of a rule follower."

Had she snapped? "She lost her father recently, didn't she?" Rochelle asked.

"That's right," Mr. Marples confirmed. "I didn't know her father had passed until I saw her wearing all black one day and asked her about it. Said she laid her father to rest before coming into work."

"Was she always private about her personal life?" Rochelle asked, figuring she knew the answer, but it never hurt to ask anyway.

"One hundred percent," Mr. Marples responded. "She clocked in on time and did her work without complaining. Most of the residents liked her even though she was quiet."

"Did she ever receive complaints?" Rochelle asked.

"Every person on the floor has had complaints against them," Mr. Marples explained. "The residents here have been diagnosed with some form of dementia. There's not one person on the floor who doesn't have at least one grievance—Justina, too." He paused and issued a defeated-sounding sigh. "We monitor our staff as best as we can. I look at the number of complaints someone gets and their employment history before I start to make a case against any one individual." He flashed tired, sunken eyes at her. "Even I have a list of complaints about me. I can print it out if you want to see it. As for the others, those are matters of privacy, and I'd get into trouble if I took it up on myself to show you those without a reason, as in a warrant." He shook his head. "I hope you can understand."

"Again, we wouldn't want you to say or do anything that would put you in a compromised position," Rochelle stated. Marples appeared beaten down, but he came across as honest and as someone who cared about the job he was doing.

"I appreciate it," he confirmed. "The first thing I look for when hiring someone is compassion for the elderly. In this business, we go through staff because the job is physical and can be an emotional drain. Patients have to be restrained at times. They sometimes strike my staff. They say things they probably shouldn't." Again, he sighed as though the weight of the world rested on his shoulders. And it did. Families made tough decisions to place a loved one with a memory issue into the care of strangers. She could only imagine how difficult it must be for all involved. "Some of my staff come in thinking the job isn't going to be cleaning up residents after accidents or sometimes being spoken to in a derogatory manner. But these residents are special. We take a family's trust to place their loved one here very seriously."

She believed him. Every word. A good detective always followed up, verified everything they were told, and never took anyone at face value. She would continue to investigate Mr. Marples. "Did you ever get a sense of Ms. Worth's home life? What it was like?"

He shook his head. "I don't pry into my staff's personal lives. I don't follow them on social media if they have accounts. What they do on their time is their business. The rule has served me well over the years." It was probably a good practice. Rochelle didn't have time for social media. She had a personal account that she rarely ever used. Since opening it, she'd probably made less than a dozen posts. She didn't stalk exes online either, like some of her coworkers. Why would she torture herself by knowing a guy she'd once liked enough to spend time with had a new girlfriend? A baby?

Rochelle had always been happily single. No entanglements. No one to feel obligated to call after a long day at work when all she really wanted to do was hop into a warm bath and try to forget the day.

On the flip side, there was no one to talk to when she'd had a tough day. A fact she hadn't spent a lot of time noticing until recently. Being around Camden was causing the feeling to intensify.

Pushing away the thought he was special, Rochelle cleared her throat and refocused on Mr. Marples after gaining approval to use this office for the interviews.

"I rounded up half the staff," Ally interrupted after a soft knock at the opened door.

"Are you ready?" Mr. Marples asked.

As much as she'd ever be. "Bring them in one by one." Mr. Marples waved to Ally.

"Sir, we need to speak to your staff alone," Rochelle said.

The supervisor shot her a surprised look, followed by a nervous one, which was understandable given the circumstances. However, his elevated level of stress didn't trigger any warning bells in her. Most people, even those with nothing to hide, got a little nervous in her presence. Add to the fact a US Marshal was sitting next to her, and it made even more sense.

Camden had been quiet. What was he thinking?

CAMDEN STUDIED MR. MARPLES and decided he was telling the truth. One by one, staff walked in, sat down, answered questions, and then walked out. Once they finished the interviews, they thanked Mr. Marples and gave their contact information in case someone remembered anything else.

Outside, Camden waited until they were inside the SUV to speak in case there were cameras with sound-recording devices, like Ring technology, around.

"The consensus on Justina Worth is that she kept to herself, and everyone left her alone," he said to Rochelle.

The beautiful redhead tugged at the rubber band in her hair until it came off. She shook out her long, wavy locks before starting the vehicle. "Ally is still on my radar," Rochelle murmured.

"Same," he agreed. There was something off about her. Unlike her boss, she tipped over into the too-nervous category.

"Should we swing by the nightclub again?" she asked while the engine idled.

"Let's see if we can catch someone there," he said.

After a nod, she navigated onto the road, backtracking to the nightclub. This time of year, it got dark early. The sun was beginning its descent, and intermittent clouds dotted an otherwise blue sky.

"I keep thinking about the life Justina Worth lived," Rochelle said after a few moments of quiet. "How small her life turned out to be. From what we know so far, she had no friends. She didn't do anything after work with coworkers. She basically punched in and out. That was it."

"A couple of the employees said they thought she might have taken care of her elderly father," Camden said. Caring for an ill family member hit him where it hurt since he was in Austin while his grandparents were in the hospital.

"No one knew for certain," she said. "And I get needing to keep work separate from your private life."

Camden nodded. "It's a little too easy to live your life for law enforcement."

"I don't have one single friend who doesn't wear a badge," she said. "But then, how well do I really know them? We are coworkers. We go to the gym together. Grab an occasional beer after work. Complain about aspects of the job we don't like. It's like an extended family, but you don't want too much of your business being talked about by people you work with, so you keep a lot to yourself."

Camden nodded. Her reflection struck a chord in him. "I have family that I'm close to, and yet we all have jobs that make us work different hours. I do the same with coworkers. Keep them at a distance. Like you, I don't like my personal life ending up as the butt of jokes." One way to relieve the stress of the job was to tease each other. Most law enforcement Camden knew released tension by poking fun at each other. It also created a bond as long as it didn't go too far. "What do you think about the suggestion that Justina probably disappeared on purpose to get back at everyone for talking behind her back?"

"I don't know," she said. "Seems extreme, don't you think?"

"Someone would have to be desperate to play a prank like that," he agreed. "Plus, we have two other kidnapping cases. What are the chances they were fake, too?" It was a rhetorical question.

"I meant to request the file on Izzy Hopkins and the other victim so we can look for any similarities," she said, "with any connection that could link the cases."

Their cell phones buzzed at the same time. A bad sign?

"I'll check mine first while you drive," Camden offered.

"Sounds good," Rochelle said after a concerned glance.

He fished his phone out of his pocket and then checked the screen. A second later, he muttered a curse. "A body has been found."

"Justina's?" she asked after a gasp.

"No, the first kidnapping victim," he clarified. "Izzy Hopkins's body has been positively ID'd."

Rochelle cursed under her breath as she cut the wheel right. "Change of plans. Next stop, the coroner's office."

"I was just thinking the same thing," he admitted. Losing a victim was always a gut punch. This was no different. Except two females were missing under similar circumstances. Were they already dead?

"What do we know so far?" she asked. Her tone revealed she was taking a similar hit.

"Based on the location where her body was found, it's possible the perp could have been taking her across the border into Mexico," he reported as he read the text from his supervisor. "Confirmation was made based on dental records."

"So there's no question it's her?" Rochelle asked.

"Not to the medical examiner."

Rochelle took a deep breath as she parked at the medical examiner's office.

Camden exited first and then circled around the vehicle

to open Rochelle's door for her out of habit. Chivalry had been deeply ingrained in him, but it was always his companion's choice as to whether or not he opened doors. Rochelle didn't seem to mind as she was busy reading the text from her supervisor while he came around the front bumper.

Side by side, they walked into the medical examiner's lobby, then the lab after a quick couple of taps on the door.

Rupert Sanders, aka Sandman, had the whole Einstein look-alike bit down. He had to be approaching seventy by now.

Sandman waved them in and then motioned toward the wall where scrubs and masks hung. He had on full gear and was in the process of conducting an autopsy on a female that Camden assumed to be Izzy. The coroner's glasses sat low on the bridge of his nose, and he looked like he'd just rolled out of bed and showed up at work with his uncombed hair, wrinkled clothes, and unmatched socks.

"Have you determined how long the victim has been dead?" Rochelle asked after perfunctory greetings and confirmation this was, in fact, Izzy Hopkins.

Sandman nodded. "Ms. Hopkins has been deceased for seven days."

"The victim was declared missing two weeks ago," Rochelle reminded them.

The bastard kept his victims alive for a week?

Chapter Seven

It took Rochelle all of two seconds to do the math. At best, they had five and a half more days to find Justina. At worst, she'd tried to escape or fight and was already dead. Somewhere in between now and five and a half days, Justina's life would end.

Were there signs of a struggle?

Sandman frowned, nodded. "There have been. See here. She basically lost all the fingernails on her right hand. There are significant contusions and bruising in various parts of her head and body, which would indicate blunt-force trauma." He pointed to areas on the victim's head and chest as he spoke.

"Fingernails were removed?" Rochelle asked as Camden studied the victim. "Wouldn't that indicate she was tortured?"

"If it happened on both hands I might agree with that assessment." Sandman used his knuckle to push his glasses onto the bridge of his nose. "Considering the fingernails solely on the right hand have been removed, the indication for a right-handed person is that someone meticulously removed them before dumping the body so that no DNA could be extracted." He shot a look of apology as he said the word *dumping*.

Rochelle involuntarily shivered. She'd been a detective for three years now and had been in law enforcement many more years than that. However, the brutalization in cases like these haunted her. The fact that another victim was out there, with time running out, haunted her. And a third victim was just beginning to live in a deranged person's twisted fantasy.

Was it too late to save the second kidnapping victim?

The clock on the wall ticked louder than usual as Rochelle studied the victim's body. Then, she realized it wasn't the clock at all. Her toe tapped the floor as she hugged her elbows into her chest. This part of her job, the part where she studied a corpse, turned her stomach. Showing her pictures made it easier to detach her emotions from the reality of what she was looking at. Being in the room with a victim was much more difficult. In theory, it shouldn't be.

Try convincing her stomach.

In the next second, Camden was by her side. His strong presence made her want to lean in closer, absorb some of his strength as she listened to Sandman making voice notes on his cell.

"Multiple lacerations behind the left ear," he continued as bile climbed the back of Rochelle's throat. There were other words spoken that she filed away as Sandman recorded the details in a long list.

When he was done recording, she asked for a copy of the file, so she didn't forget any of the details. A small detail could break a case wide open. Plus, they'd been standing there long enough. Time was wasting and they needed to get back into the field and start canvassing.

Camden gently touched her elbow. The move caused warmth to flood her as electricity sparked at the point of contact. It would be a mistake to look into his eyes right now, so she didn't. Instead, she said goodbye to Sandman and walked out to the SUV.

After reclaiming the driver's seat, she checked her phone. "I didn't realize a text came through from my supervisor. It says we should head to the Maple Road substation, where two bouncers and several bartenders and waitstaff are either heading that way, or waiting for us to interview them."

"That was fast," he said as he buckled in.

She studied her screen. "Looks like the social-media call netted a decent number of responses, including the employees."

"Okay, then," he said, impressed. "Let's roll."

The drive to the substation only took eighteen minutes, a miracle in Austin's traffic. A few text messages came through on Camden's phone. He spent the ride engaged in conversation with someone.

She parked in the lot and turned to him. "Everything okay?"

In a rare moment, he smiled. "It looks like my grandfather is holding up. He's cracking jokes as he faithfully sits next to my grandmother's side, keeping everyone entertained despite his own hurt." He paused for a beat. "I think it's his way of trying to make up for everything we've been through." Another pause. "Not that any of us minded. We love him and our grandmother more than words. We would do anything for them. In fact, my brother is retiring from law enforcement to work the ranch."

"Is that something you would ever consider?" Rochelle asked, finding that she wanted to know more about her partner on this case.

"Me? No," he admitted. "I do want to be more involved in the family business, though. I've neglected going home Christmases and Thanksgivings." He shook his head. "I can't remember the last time all eight of us were together for a holiday. Facing this holiday season with the real possibility we might lose one of our grandparents hits the point home for me. I've been missing out." He put out a hand. "Don't get me wrong, work is important."

"Events like these, losing loved ones, reminds us how fast life goes by, doesn't it?" she asked, but the question was rhetorical. She knew firsthand how awful it could be and how easy it was to take advantage of the people you love most, thinking they will always be around.

Rochelle reached for the door handle as Camden tucked away his cell. She glanced at the clock on the dashboard.

"Ready to go inside?" she asked.

Camden nodded. He hopped out of the passenger seat then came around the front of the vehicle to open her door. She appreciated the gesture but they didn't have time to waste, so she exited before he reached her side.

They walked into the substation to a full lobby and checked in with the desk sergeant, who then led them into a small conference room.

"I've been instructed to bring folks in one by one," he said.

"We'd like to see the bouncers first," Rochelle stated.

"Yes, ma'am," the sergeant said before exiting the door. He returned a few minutes later with a tall dark-skinned bald man. "This is Ray Combs." The irony of his last name was not lost on Rochelle.

"Thank you, Sergeant," she said before he nodded and then closed the door.

"Mr. Combs," she began, extending a hand. He shook hers and then Camden's. "Thank you for volunteering to come to the station today."

"My pleasure," Combs said. Based on the look on his

face, she highly doubted the man was getting any pleasure out of being here, but she appreciated his politeness.

"Would you like to sit?" she asked, motioning toward the metal chair across the table.

Combs did. Knees spread, he rested his hands on thick, powerful thighs. Combs had to be a solid six feet tall. And by solid, she meant muscled. Sturdy. A guy who spent more time at the gym than anywhere else and possibly took steroids. Muscles like his didn't seem natural.

"This is my partner, US Marshal Remington," she continued. She pulled up a picture of Justina on her cell, placed it on top of the table, and then used two fingers to push the screen toward Combs. "What can you tell me about this customer?"

"I know our regulars," Combs said after leaning in to get a good look at the photo. The man looked like a fitness trainer who happened to be the size and weight of a linebacker. "She's not one of them."

"So you don't remember her visiting your establishment at all?" she asked for confirmation.

His nose wrinkled. His eyes squinted. His lips clamed shut. "I couldn't say with one-hundred-percent certainty, but she looks vaguely familiar. I'd say she was in recently."

"Do you remember anything special about her visit?" Camden asked.

"Not really," Combs said. "Just that she seems a little familiar, like I already said." He leaned back. "Wish I could be of more help."

Justina was average in pretty much every way. Height. Weight. Looks. There was nothing about the woman that especially stood out, so it didn't surprise Rochelle that the bouncer didn't remember a one-time visitor like Justina.

"So do we," Rochelle agreed with a small smile. "We appreciate the effort, though." She reached for her phone and then slid it toward her. After tapping the screen and offering facial recognition to unlock the phone, she flipped to a picture of Kage Durham. "What about this guy? Have you witnessed him entering the establishment?"

Combs leaned forward as she pushed the screen toward him a second time. "Yes," he said with certainty and without hesitation. "I've definitely seen him." Kage, on the other hand, was tall, muscular, and would be considered good-looking by most standards. He was the kind of guy who a bouncer would notice and size up just in case an intervention would be needed at some point in the night. She suspected every bouncer kept an eye on those he or she believed could put up a good fight if inebriated and out of order. Combs struck her as street-smart. He was the kind of guy who would notice a physically strong male who could throw a punch and do some damage.

"Is he a regular?" Camden asked, leaning in.

"I wouldn't say that," Combs stated. "The main reason I remember him is that on the nights he does come to the club, he's in and out." That would gain attention as possibly selling drugs on the premises.

"Does he normally come in with anyone?" Camden continued.

Combs studied the screen. "No. He's alone when he comes in."

"What about when he leaves?" Camden asked.

"I've seen him walk out with a female at least once," Combs admitted. "Maybe a couple of times when I really think about it."

"Has this person ever caused a disruption?" Rochelle asked.

"No," Combs said. "Not him. I've never been called in to take care of him."

"What about when he leaves? Is he drunk?" Camden asked.

"Not that I've ever seen," Combs answered.

They needed to speak to the bartender on shift that night next.

"Is there anything else you remember about him?" Rochelle asked, figuring they needed to wrap up this conversation so they could move onto the next.

"No, ma'am," Combs said. He lifted his gaze. "Am I free to go?"

"Yes," Camden said to Combs. "But first, would you give me a call if the male shows up at the nightclub again?"

"You bet," Combs said. "I'm willing to cooperate in any way that I can." He handed over his cell so Camden could put his contact information inside. "It's a shame what happened." He seemed like the kind of person who would take something like this very seriously. A kidnapping happening on his watch wouldn't sit well.

Combs entered his details and then handed the cell back. Camden texted the bouncer to make the connection.

After exchanging courtesies, Combs left the room. A bartender was next. He'd been working that night but had no recollection of the people or events. Three waitresses followed, and none had a distinct memory of Justina or Kage.

Hours passed with interview after interview. Tacos were ordered and then eaten at some point. As Camden was about to suggest they call it a day, the sergeant poked his head in the door.

"I have one more for you," he said. "Amy Adamson was tending bar on the night in question." He stepped aside to reveal a thin woman in her early thirties with a head full of long wiry hair that was barely contained in a rubber band.

"I'm Amy," she said.

Introductions followed as did the same routine of initial questions.

"I do remember the male from that night," Amy admitted. "He was gorgeous. Quiet. Sat at the bar and ordered ginger ale. Who does that?" Amy gestured with her hands that she had no clue. "But when he came in the second time, he seemed different."

"How?" Rochelle asked.

"I don't know," Amy said. "More outgoing, I guess. He circled the dance floor instead of sitting at the bar. He didn't come back to me, which maybe isn't all that odd except that he was the kind of person who would do something familiar. I'm probably not explaining this the right way, but you size up a person when they sit at your bar for a while. You can almost guess their order before they take a seat. Jeans and a T-shirt are gonna order a beer. If the person works out, it's probably going to be a light beer. Guys who dress to impress are always going to go for a mixed drink." She flashed eyes at them. "You do this job long enough and you can guess. I make a game of it to see how many times I'm right in a night."

"What's your percentage?" Camden asked, figuring an attractive bartender would most likely be propositioned many times over the course of an evening, whether they're male or female.

"I'm good," she said. "I usually rock it in the high nineties." She shrugged. "Then again, I've been on the job for a long time. You tend to get better with age, right?"

"I believe that's true," Rochelle agreed.

Camden trusted Amy's memory if she liked to play memory games while on shift. It meant she paid attention to details.

"So, yeah, it surprised me when I saw my customer circling the dance floor with a beer in his hand," she said. "There was something else different about him that I couldn't quite put my finger on." She pursed her lips. "Maybe it'll come to me later."

"Is there anything else you remember about that night?" Rochelle asked as Camden contemplated the fact the bartender had just described a predator circling its prey when she explained what she saw that night. If this was true, Kage was a bold-faced liar. Or just an intelligent criminal.

"No," Amy said after a thoughtful pause. "That's about all."

"I'd like to give you my contact information in case you suddenly remember anything new," Rochelle stated.

They exchanged information. In the past hour, Rochelle had bit back three yawns, a sure sign she needed to wrap up this investigation up for the day.

After the bartender left, Camden urged Rochelle to wrap things up. She started to protest but then seemed to decide against it.

"You're right," she finally said. "My brain is starting to hurt. Plus, ever notice how answers show up when you step away from overthinking?"

He smiled as he thanked the desk sergeant and then began heading out to her SUV. "As a matter of fact, I have." Not that he wanted to have any more in common with the beautiful detective than he already did. Or any more chemistry for that matter. Certain things were outside of his control. Whether he acted on the attraction was up to him. Not only would it be unprofessional to hit on Rochelle, but he also had no idea if she felt the same.

"You can drop me at my truck," he said as they reclaimed their seats.

"Okay."

The drive didn't take more than twenty minutes. Twenty silent minutes. Twenty minutes that he surprisingly didn't want to end.

Rochelle pulled up next to his truck and then idled the SUV's engine. She glanced at the clock. It read 11:48 p.m. "Shall we pick up around six o'clock in the morning?"

"Sounds good." He didn't need much in the way of sleep. A few hours of shut-eye, and he'd be good to go. Camden had developed the habit of rising early and going to bed late while growing up on a horse ranch. Ranchers' days were long, filled with back-breaking work. Not that he'd ever minded.

Why was saying good-night so hard?

Chapter Eight

Rochelle turned up the A/C in the SUV to help stay awake on the thirty-minute drive home. As it was, her eyes were trying to close. Working to the point of exhaustion was a bad habit. Except, how could she do anything else when time could mean the difference between saving someone's life or them becoming a murder victim? Kidnapping cases were the hardest to work on.

She lived on a tree-lined street in a cul-de-sac where bicycles littered lawns on school breaks. With this being Thanksgiving week, the kids would be out in full force.

As she pulled up to her two-bedroom bungalow, she cut off her headlights. The way houses were arranged in the cul-de-sac meant her headlights shot straight into the bay window of her next-door neighbor.

Exiting the vehicle, a cold chill caused her to clutch her shirt, tuck her chin to her chest, and hurry around the SUV. Movement to the left caught her attention. Squirrel?

Not at this time of night.

Rochelle was already halfway across her yard when she saw the boot. Someone was standing behind the tree in her neighbor's yard. Her pulse skyrocketed as she reached for her service weapon in her shoulder holster.

Instinct had her wanting to bolt toward the door. Training had her moving toward the nearest tree for cover.

The crack of a bullet split the air. Rochelle ducked. Wood splintered.

Now, her pulse raced so loud she could hear thumping in her ears. Her heart battered the inside of her rib cage as she took cover behind the tree. The distance to her front door measured roughly fifteen feet.

Nothing would stand in the way of the shooter if she made a move for the door. Plus, she would have to manage unlocking the door, making herself an easy target in the process. Nope.

Rochelle identified herself as law enforcement and directed the shooter to toss their weapon, then come out with their hands where she could see them.

With the tree putting mass between her and the shooter, she risked a glance when no response came. A shot rang out.

Lights came on inside several of her neighbors' houses. A few images flashed in her mind. One had the shooter taking her neighbor or their kids hostage. Let him get inside the house and then there'd be a hostage situation that could end with multiple fatalities. Another had her neighbor taking matters into his own hands with a shotgun, and ending up shot in the process.

Dogs barked as panic seized her. *Stay calm.*

The shooter picked that moment to flee. He wasn't much more than a shadow moving in the night.

"Halt, or I'll shoot," she demanded. But he was too far away and there were trees preventing her from getting off a dependable shot. There was no way she would risk a stray bullet.

So she gave chase.

Shadowman was a lot faster than her. Plus, he had a head

start and longer legs. He must be a good jumper too because he hopped fences like they were nothing. Then again, he came prepared. It was easy to research a neighborhood with all the maps on phones and computers doing all the hard work. As far as Rochelle's needs were concerned, she knew the streets and that was about it. She never ventured into her neighbors' yards. Garages weren't as common in this area of Austin, so most folks parked out front.

After running for several minutes, she cut her losses. Shadowman was gone.

After holstering her weapon, Rochelle leaned against a tree to catch her breath and palmed her cell phone. Her first call was to her supervisor. The next, to Camden. He answered on the third ring with the sound of running water in the background. Shower?

Rochelle didn't need the naked image of Camden stamping her thoughts right now. "Someone was waiting at my home."

"What the hell?" The water turned off as a frustrated exhale came through the line. "Send me your address. I'm coming over."

"That's not nec—"

"Would you make the same offer if the shoe was on the other foot?" he asked.

"Yes," she admitted.

"Text me your address, okay?"

"I will," she said. Having company would be better than going home alone. After ending the call, she immediately sent a message with her address. And then, she made the slow walk back to her bungalow.

Neighbors were standing around in a loose circle, still in their pajamas, talking and processing. Several had rifles or shotguns. This area had a lot of hunters, so it wasn't surprising they'd raided their gun cases to come out with a weapon to defend themselves.

"It's okay to go inside now," Rochelle said to the small group. "Whoever it was ran away."

"Was someone trying to rob you?" Bobby Joseph asked. The perp had been hiding in his front yard.

"The person was armed," she said. "A tall man. So if you see anyone suspicious hanging around, call nine-one-one immediately. Okay?"

"Will do," Bobby said, still looking stunned and a little confused about what had just gone down. *Join the club.*

Not once in all her years of law enforcement had a perp ever tracked her to her home. Having someone shoot at you in your front yard was unnerving.

"And lock up tonight," she urged as she stood in her yard, waiting for every last one of them to go inside and close their doors behind them.

When the lawns were cleared of all people, she scanned the area once more before heading to unlock her front door. Nerves stopped her from going inside until she made certain no one was in there waiting. Habit had her locking every door and window, so she tested the front to make sure it was still locked before moving to the back to do the same. After walking a circle around her home and confirming no windows were broken, she slid the key into the lock and then opened the door.

One last glance to make sure no one had turned up in the last few minutes later, and she stepped inside, closed and locked the door behind her, and then leaned against the door. Back against it, she slid down until she sat on the wood floor.

CAMDEN COULDN'T GET to Rochelle's home fast enough. After safely navigating through late-night traffic, he arrived at the bungalow in her cul-de-sac. He cut the engine off and made a beeline to her front door, hitting the lock button halfway across the lawn.

Lifting a hand to knock, the door swung open.

"Hey," a wide-eyed Rochelle said as she ushered him inside. "Don't stand out there too long in case he's watching."

"Did you call it in?"

"Immediately," she said. "I called my supervisor before I reached out to you." Long lashes hooded the most incredible pair of eyes.

"Tell me everything that happened," he said as she motioned toward the kitchen table. He glanced around, looking for any signs of a male presence. There were none. Her place had white couches with big throw pillows and glass tables with no prints. There were no obvious signs, like hunting or fishing magazines piled on top of the tables. There were no "couple" pictures that some folks liked to place around the room. Camden wouldn't be caught dead with those around his place. He could remember what his significant other looked like without constant reminders everywhere. He definitely didn't need pictures of himself around. No one needed to walk into his place and see mug shots of him everywhere. Or anywhere.

He listened as Rochelle broke down the events for him.

"What's your initial thoughts on whether or not this is tied to our current case?" he asked when she was finished.

"That would be fast," she said. "And why come after me?"

"To keep you from investigating," he offered.

"Is that logical?"

He shook his head. "No. Not really. Someone might stop you from investigating but that leaves me to keep going with the work."

"Do you think those shots were warnings?" she asked.

"I'm not sure," he said, realizing they'd gotten as far as they were going to tonight. "Would you like to try to get some sleep?"

"I highly doubt I could," she said.

"Even with me here?" he asked. "I'd stay awake."

"A shot of adrenaline is still working through my system." She exhaled a slow breath. "And my mind is spinning. There's no way I could fall asleep without images of—of that perp crashing into my thoughts." It would be unnerving to be targeted outside your house. The perp was clear with his intentions. He was targeting Rochelle.

Her cell buzzed. She located it and then studied the screen. A few seconds later, she mouthed a swear word.

"What is it?"

"My supervisor just told me to take a couple of days off," she said, disbelief written all over her features. "Are you kidding me?" She immediately fired off a response. And then her phone buzzed again. "He's not taking no for an answer. But I can't back off this case. Especially after what just happened."

"It takes someone with a lot of bravado to come after a law-enforcement officer at home," Camden pointed out.

"I was just thinking the same thing," she said before smacking her flat palm on the glass table. It left a mark. "Which is exactly the reason I have to stay on this case. Plus, we don't know for certain tonight's incident is related."

Camden cocked his head to one side. She put her hand up, palm out, in defense.

"Okay, maybe that's a stretch," she said. "However, I won't be backed into a corner by anyone."

"What did your supervisor say?" he asked.

"That I've been under strain lately and he thought it best if I take a short leave of absence," she stated. "The underlying message here is that I lost my mother seven months ago and he doesn't think I've given myself enough time to grieve."

"Taking care of your mental health is especially important on this job," he said. "Is there any merit to what your supervisor says?"

Rochelle didn't immediately answer. Instead, she breathed in a slow breath like she wanted to take her time to think it over. "I don't believe so, or I would have pulled myself off the job already. Does that mean I'm not shaken up by what happened tonight? No. But I would have been anyway."

"The question is whether or not you think this will affect your job performance tomorrow," he said.

"What do you think?"

"That you're professional and capable," he said without hesitation. "I think you're one helluva detective and I'd work with you any day of the week."

"Thank you," she said. Her cheeks flushed at the compliments, which only proved to make her even more attractive. How it was possible to make the detective even more beautiful was beyond him.

"I mean it," he continued. "I've worked with the best and I would trust you to have my back any day."

"Same to you," she countered. Then came a sharp sigh. "If you see anything that raises a red flag about my performance on this case, I'd be disappointed if you didn't speak up."

"Got it," he said.

"And you're good to continue working with me. Is that right?"

"Yes, I am."

Rochelle picked up her cell and sent off another text. "I've just told my supervisor that I'm fine and don't need time off. I said you would vouch for me if it came down to it but that I have a good handle on where I'm at emotionally. If it gets to be too much, I'll take a back seat."

"I'm here," Camden reassured. "I'd like to stay together twenty-four-seven while we work the case. We'll waste less time if we're already together and it'll be easier to talk through the investigation."

"Done," she said. "I have a second bedroom that I turned into an office when I bought the place. The sofa folds out into a bed if that's okay with you."

"Believe me, I've slept in worse places."

Based on her expression, he should probably have explained that he meant he'd slept on the hard ground in not much more than a one-person tent. From the looks of it, she assumed he meant that he'd slept in shady beds.

"I didn't mean—"

"You don't owe me an explanation," she said, cutting him off.

"I just thought…never mind." He was probably reading too much into the situation. Even if he wasn't, she was right to shut him down. They were coworkers on this investigation. A romantic involvement would be unprofessional.

"It's fine," she said. "I'll just grab an extra pillow and some blankets for you. It's supposed to get cold tonight." She started to walk away and then turned back toward him. "Thanksgiving is later this week. Are you sure you want to be here instead of Mesa Point with your family?"

The right answer would be wishing he was in Mesa Point. But who did Rochelle have?

Chapter Nine

"I'm good here," Camden said, much to Rochelle's surprise. If she had family alive, her answer would be different. That was the not-so-funny part about life. You didn't realize what you had until you lost it. Seven months ago, Rochelle had a mother. Two years ago, she had both parents. Now?

Orphan. Even as an adult who was more than capable of providing for herself and living her own life, the word stung.

The fact Camden wanted to be here meant more to her than she could afford to let on.

"Okay, then I'll grab those blankets."

Without waiting for a response, she headed toward her linen closet, where she kept spares. After retrieving them, she handed them over. Camden had already figured out the foldout part of the bed. She hoped it wouldn't be too uncomfortable. He was probably being nice earlier when he said he could sleep on pretty much anything. The thought of him in bed with another woman shouldn't be a sucker punch. The two of them weren't in a relationship.

The events of the night had shaken her up. No one had ever come to her home to stake it out until she arrived. No one had ever fired at her in her own front yard. And no one had ever wanted her dead so badly.

An involuntary shiver rocked her body. She would attempt sleep after a shower. Given how much her mind was spinning right now, she highly doubted her racing thoughts would calm down enough for her to get any real rest. She'd give it the ole college try and see what happened.

"Coffee maker is in the kitchen," she explained. "It takes pods. Everything you'll need is within arm's reach of the machine."

"Got it," he said as he took the blankets. Their fingers grazed, shooting an electric current through her hand and up her arm straight to her heart.

Nope. She couldn't afford to give in to an attraction to this man even if he was game, which she highly doubted. They were both professionals. They cared about their careers. They cared about their reputations. If news of a fling got around, her credibility on the job would be compromised.

Rochelle couldn't risk it no matter how much her traitorous heart argued otherwise. "I'll leave my door open. Holler if you need me." The open door was more for her benefit than his.

"Will I disturb you if I'm up and around?" he asked.

"Normally, I can sleep through a tornado."

Camden nodded and smiled. "I promise to make less noise than that."

Rochelle hesitated for a long moment before tucking her chin to her chest and then heading down the short hallway to her bedroom. After a quick shower, she slipped into an oversize Led Zeppelin concert T-shirt and pulled the covers up to her neck.

Sounds from the other room reassured her that someone was awake and alert. Having Camden here calmed her racing mind. Before she realized, she'd dozed off.

Ringtones jarred her from a deep sleep. Rochelle bolted

upright. Feet on the floor, she threw covers off and tried to get her bearings as panic took hold.

The phone. It was only her cell.

She blindly reached for the noisemaker on the nightstand. Her hand swept over the alarm, knocking it off. *Cool. Smooth move.*

In the next second, a tall male figure blanketed the doorway. Camden.

The light flipped on a moment later.

"Everything alright in here?" he asked, a concerned look darkening his features as he drew his eyebrows together.

"Phone," she said, able to see clearly as she snatched it. The call rolled into voice mail before she could answer. Time read: 6:12 a.m. She muttered a curse. "It's my supervisor."

Camden took the couple of steps to close the distance between them. The mattress dipped underneath his weight as he sat next to her on the bed. Rochelle's pulse raced as she breathed in his warm, spicy masculine scent. Heat pooled low in her belly as the insides of her thighs flamed.

Rochelle glanced down, realized her T-shirt had come up on her thighs, revealing her purple silk panties. With her free hand, she pulled her shirt down her legs to cover.

Once the voice mail was finished, she tapped the screen, held up her phone for facial identity software to confirm her, and then tapped again until she could read the voice mail. If her supervisor was in a mood and yelled at her, she preferred to read the message rather than hear a voice.

Victim number two has been identified and located. Same MO. I'm sending over details. However, the body is being transported back to Austin as I leave this message.

Camden's muscled arm touched hers as he leaned in to get a better look at the screen. "Damn."

"I know," she said as her heart went out to the victim and her family. More lives were going to be ruined. Molly Rancor had been a missing person. Now, she would be identified forever as a murder victim.

Rochelle couldn't help but think about the brutality Izzy had suffered at the hands of this killer—a killer that was coming for her.

She mentally shook off the thought and called her supervisor. "What time with the victim's body be returned to Austin?"

"The estimate is noon," her supervisor said. Barron Vandergrift sounded more like a prep-school name than someone who dedicated their life to law enforcement. But the name was where the prep-school fantasy ended. Barron was as tough as they came. Middle-aged with a ruddy complexion, he'd joked more than once about letting down his parents with his chosen career field. Rochelle picked up right away on the hint of shame he carried by not being what his parents expected. If he was going to uphold the law, they'd nudged him toward CIA. Barron laughed when he told Rochelle the story that came up any time she faced disappointed parents in her line of work. He'd been quick to point out that he had a beautiful wife and three amazing kids. The tradeoff, he'd said, had been worth it. Rochelle had never fantasized about having a family of her own and she refused to accept any societal expectations that said otherwise. She was a fully functioning capable woman who'd chosen a career as a detective. "Could be sooner." Barron's words cut through her reverie.

"Okay," Rochelle said, the back of her mind devising a schedule for the day with this new information.

"I like this situation even less after what happened last night," Barron said.

"Agreed." What else could she say?

"Are you certain that you don't need time?" he continued. "Seven months isn't long in the grand scheme of life." He paused. "What do you think about revisiting the idea of you seeing Dr.—"

"I'm good," she said, interrupting. "We've already covered this ground. The best thing anyone can do for me is allow me to do my job. Last I checked, I was still good at it."

"You're one of my best detectives." The compliment from Barron meant the world to her. He wasn't one to hand them out freely. In fact, he wasn't one to hand them out at all.

"Thank you, sir," she said.

"Which is precisely the reason I don't want to lose you," he added.

"If I think I'm in trouble, I'll reach out," she promised.

Her answer seemed to satisfy Barron. He grunted and then mumbled a goodbye. The man had a reputation for getting straight to the point. No argument there.

"Not to jump on a bandwagon, but I don't like the fact a perp went to the trouble of waiting for you at your home," Camden said after a long pause.

"If you're about to tell me to seek counseling, then—"

"No," he said, shaking his head. "I was about to ask you if you wanted to move in with me until we finish the investigation."

Rochelle didn't see that question coming. Her heart fluttered like a schoolgirl with a crush.

Fool heart. Would it get her into trouble with this man?

CAMDEN WAITED FOR Rochelle's response. He didn't realize he was holding his breath until she answered.

"Yes, that's probably a good idea," she said. "I just hate the thought of anyone running me out of my own home."

He understood. "It's temporary. Just until we put this bastard behind bars."

"Are you convinced the person from last night is tied to this case?"

"We won't know for sure until he's locked up, will we?" he asked.

She heaved a sigh. "I guess not."

"I'd rather not risk it," he said. "Next time, he will be more prepared."

Rochelle got quiet. It meant she was thinking. "You're right. I shouldn't risk my life over pride."

"Pack a bag and we'll head to my place," he said. "We have time for you to unpack."

"Think we can stop by Kage's place on the way?"

Camden nodded. "I was thinking the same thing."

"We can talk on the way over." With that, she stood up and retrieved a suitcase from the closet. Camden forced his gaze away from the silky skin of her thighs—thighs that were almost entirely exposed. His brain was still trying to force thoughts of how amazing those purple panties of hers would feel in his hands as he removed them from her body.

Camden swallowed to ease the sudden dryness in his throat.

The best way to distract himself from thinking about how incredible having sex with Rochelle would be was to refocus on the case or check on his grandparents. Speaking of whom, he needed to check on one of his buddies. Ace Kendric had saved Camden's life by jumping in front of a moving vehicle to knock Camden out of the way. The move had cost Ace his career by shattering his ankle.

His friend had gone through surgery like a champ and he

had moved to Mesa Point permanently after falling in love with someone who inherited a building from her aunt. Kayleigh Price had been the perfect person to see Ace through his recovery.

Camden fired off a text to check on his buddy and the business he'd started with his new wife. *Wife.* Camden never thought he'd be thinking that word when it came to Ace. People changed. Hell, everything changed. Change was the only constant. It still caught you by surprise with certain folks. Ace was one of them.

A response came quickly.

When are you coming home?

Camden studied the screen. He sent a message back. Still not sure. Soon.

Okay then. We'll grab a beer.

Camden couldn't remember the last time he'd gone out for a beer after work with a coworker. Too long. Ever?

I'm gonna hold you to it.

Ace responded: Good. 'Bout time.

Rather than dig into what that was supposed to mean, Camden caught up on the updates on his grandparents in the family's group chat. Grandpa Lorenzo, affectionately known as Grandpa Lor, was as spry as ever. Mentally fine but physically weak. There'd been no change with Grandma Lacey. *Damn.* His grandfather was in physical therapy twice a day. Called them two-a-days, like in football. Seemed like his sense of humor was intact. Then again, he'd always been as stubborn as he was strong. He would think he needed to come across as able to handle anything. Like, the accident was just a blip. No one should worry about him or Grandma Lacey.

Camden wondered if he'd ever seen his grandfather let down his guard. Could the man keep up the facade if he lost his wife?

While Rochelle finished packing, Camden figured he could drum up some food and get to-go coffee cups going. After mentioning he'd be in the kitchen, Rochelle bit down on her bottom lip.

"Would you mind staying in here?" she asked. "My mind is spinning and having another person in the room has a calming effect."

Camden agreed, not mentioning how being in the same room with her had the opposite effect on him. It stirred up more than his body.

Refocusing on his cell, he sent an update to his SO and then responded to the messages in the family group chat.

"I'll be ready as soon as I change clothes," Rochelle said after a few minutes passed. She held up an outfit and then ducked inside the en-suite bathroom. A few minutes later, she emerged wearing jeans, a blouse, and her shoulder holster. She slipped her feet into a pair of boots before rolling her suitcase into the living room as he followed. "I packed enough for a couple of days, just in case."

"We can always come back for more if needed," he reassured her. "Plus, I have a washer and dryer in my town house."

"Good," she said. "My favorite coffee place is a few blocks away. They have killer breakfast tacos." She seemed to regret her word choice immediately after she said the word *killer*.

"Breakfast tacos sound good," he said. "Do you want me to drive this time?"

"Since someone might be watching me, that's probably a good idea," she said. "Might be a good way to throw them off track if they come back and see my vehicle here."

He'd take anything that could buy more time. "Then, it's a plan."

Camden took her suitcase after throwing on a shirt and toeing on his boots. He walked out to the truck first, started the engine, and then waved for her to join him. There was no sense testing their luck or giving the bastard a shot if he'd returned. Though, Camden doubted the shooter would come back this fast. He would have to realize her place would be watched. It took a helluva brazen person to go after someone in law enforcement. So Camden wouldn't take anything for granted.

When their cells buzzed at almost the same time, he realized bad news was coming. Since he didn't want to sit in front of her house, he pulled away. "What does yours say?"

Rochelle's gaze swept the area before she turned her full attention to the screen. "There's been another missing-person report. Shiloh Johnson was last heard from while at a Laundromat." Rochelle issued a frustrated sigh. "Hold on. Let me check the map." She released a string of curses. "The victim was last seen near Kage's apartment."

Coincidence?

"We're definitely stopping by," Camden said. "What's the name of the Laundromat?"

"Spin Cycle," she replied as she read more of the message.

Breakfast tacos would have to wait.

Chapter Ten

After a quick stop for convenience-store coffee and a bland bagel, Rochelle hopped into the passenger seat.

"I can't stop thinking about how busy Kage would have to be if he was responsible for these kidnappings and still had time to stalk your home last night," Camden said after gobbling down the awful bagel and washing it down with burnt coffee. He made a face but didn't complain. They'd both done this dance before. The old routine of "get something—*anything*—in your stomach while on the road."

"The kidnapping happened days ago," she pointed out.

"Which would make Justina the fourth victim," he said.

"That's right."

"And, somehow, he still had time to swing by the bar?" he asked. "I don't know. Nothing makes sense to me at this point."

It wasn't unusual for the puzzle pieces of a case to seem unrelated until she found the one bit that connected all the dots. The mental challenge was a big part of the reason she'd become a detective in the first place. The other more important one had to do with putting the bad guys behind bars so they couldn't hurt anyone else ever again. "I know what you mean. It'll click." It had to. There was no way in hell she intended to allow these cases to run cold. The percentage of cold cases that were eventually solved was heart-wrenchingly low.

Families deserved to know what happened to their loved ones.

"Everyone in law enforcement has a story," Camden said. "What's yours?"

"I already told you that I'm an only child," she said. "What I didn't say was that my best friend from age eight to twelve was also an only child. We were thick as thieves, the two of us." She took a second before saying her friend's name. After all these years, it was still a gut punch. "Victoria McGowen was her name." Rochelle breathed in a slow breath as the song "Butterfly Kisses" came to mind. Victoria had been obsessed with them. All things butterflies, actually. "For four years, she was all I had. But her parents started fighting when we were around ten years old. They were probably hiding their disagreements before then. The fights escalated so Victoria stayed at our house most of the time. Then, her father demanded she come home. Back then, I had no idea a person could hurt their own child. Victoria always made excuses for turning up with bruises. It wasn't until years later that I put it all together."

"What happened?"

"He flipped out one day while cleaning his gun," she said. "It discharged by accident. The bullet went through Victoria's bedroom wall to strike her." She stopped to gather her thoughts and stop the moisture gathering in her eyes. She never talked about what happened. She never allowed herself to think about what had gone down. And yet, she realized the irony because that day changed everything for Rochelle. "She didn't survive."

"I'm so sorry," Camden said, his voice a balm to a broken heart.

"Her mother lost it," she continued. "Wrestled the dad for the gun, ended up getting shot in the process."

"That's awful, Rochelle. I couldn't be sorrier for a tragedy like that to have happened, let alone to people you obviously cared about."

"The dad was consumed with guilt after calming down and realizing what he'd done." She paused to take another breath. Being with Camden made her able to talk about a past she'd buried so deep that she was only beginning to realize how deeply the wounds had affected her. "He took his own life."

Camden's hand closed over hers. His was huge by comparison, and rough. Another time, another place, she would allow herself to imagine those hands roaming over her body.

"It's an unimaginable horror," he soothed with compassion that wrapped her in warmth.

"An entire family was gone." She snapped the fingers of her free hand. "Just like that."

"You lost your best friend," he said, his deep timbre offering more reassurance than she should probably allow. It would be a little too easy to lean into his strength. And then what? Have nothing again when this case was closed? Rochelle had learned the hard way that it was so much harder to have a confidant and lose them than not to have one at all. The pain of losing a best friend was almost too much. With Camden, it would be ten times worse because the current running between them was loaded with promise.

"I did," she said quietly. "And every milestone birthday makes me wonder what Victoria would have been like at that age. Would we still be best friends? Would we have gone to college together? Would we have been roommates like we'd planned?"

"It must have been lonely," he said, using his thumb to draw circles around her palm. "Growing up without her."

"You have no idea," she said.

"You've lost so much," he continued.

She should probably end this conversation before she went down the rabbit hole of letting him be her comfort. Because his words soothed her far better than anything she'd ever known.

With a deep breath, she released his hand and sat up straighter in her seat. "We should probably get going."

Camden sat there for a long moment before finally turning on the engine and driving out of the parking lot.

The drive to Kage's place was spent in comfortable silence. Too comfortable. Rochelle was letting down her guard with Camden, bit by bit, despite knowing better.

They were partners while working this investigation. It was only logical to have a desire to get to know each other better. She'd opened up more to him than any of the guys she'd dated. At some point in every relationship, her romantic partner expected her to open up. She'd never once been able or inspired to. One by one, she'd watched each one walk out the door, head down, taking the loss rather than sticking it out in a no-win situation. *She* was the no-win situation they walked away from.

Opening up to Camden had felt like the most right thing in the world. He'd comforted her. His words would stay with her, easing some of the pain she'd tucked away so deep she'd almost forgotten it existed. *Almost.*

"Do you want to take the lead with Kage?" Camden asked.

"Sure," she said absently. Someone had tried to kill her. That someone might be Kage. Rochelle gave herself a mental shake so she could refocus on the case, on the lives that were in mortal danger. There were two murder victims. There were two kidnapping victims. The perp would strike again soon.

Could Rochelle get there in time?

Panic caused her shirt to feel two sizes too small. *Breathe.*

She willed Justina to live. She would be next to die based on the perp's pattern so far.

Rochelle had to stop the bastard before he got the chance.

CAMDEN PARKED THE truck on the street near Kage's apartment. He immediately hopped out and then came around the front of the vehicle to open Rochelle's door. She took his hand as she climbed down, and he realized hers was trembling.

Pausing, Camden pulled Rochelle into an embrace. "Hey. I'm here anytime you want to talk about the past. I'll do anything in my power to comfort you."

"Thank you for that," Rochelle said, pulling away. The moment she'd leaned in, though, the world had finally righted itself. "I'm good now." Chin up, he could see how strong she was trying to be. So he stepped back and gave her space. When she was ready to talk, he would be here. That was all she needed to know. It would be up to her if she took him up on the offer.

Camden resisted the urge to reach out to grab her hand and link their fingers. Instead, they walked side by side to Kage's apartment.

After three bold knocks, there was not even a hint anyone was home. Which meant Kage was home and not answering, or out. Brutalizing his latest victim?

There wasn't enough evidence to haul him in for questioning. Camden hoped that would change very soon. Though, if Kage was responsible, the man was savvy. He'd become a better criminal since his mail-fraud and identity theft schemes. From mail fraud to murder?

The leap didn't sit well. The logic was flawed no matter how circumstantial the evidence might be. Not to mention the evidence against him was weak at best. Camden issued a sharp sigh.

"Guess we should come back," Rochelle said after another round of police-raid-style knocking.

The door suddenly swung open.

"What the hell is going on out here?" Kage said, shirt off. He was wearing jeans and no shoes or socks. "I have neighbors to think about." He stepped outside and closed the door behind him. The chill in the air didn't seem to bother the man.

"We have questions," Rochelle stated.

"Fine," Kage said, crossing his arms over his chest. "Where's your vehicle?"

"I parked on the street," Camden said, motioning toward his truck. Was it a good idea? Now, Kage would know which vehicle belonged to Camden. If he was the shooter from last night, he could follow them.

"Then, let's go talk inside your truck," Kage stated, glancing around. Was there a reason beyond embarrassment that Kage might want to walk them away from his place?

"What about going inside?" Rochelle asked.

"I'd rather sit in your truck," Kage stated. "At least that way, I won't have law enforcement hanging around my front door."

"Fine," Rochelle replied, leading the way to the dual cab pickup. "I'll take the back seat." She walked the trio to the truck and then climbed inside. Kage took the passenger seat while Camden sat in the driver's seat once again.

"Do you seriously believe I'm capable of what you're

accusing me of?" Kage asked, raking his fingers through his hair.

Camden reached for a spare T-shirt. "Here, put this on."

Kage did, looking like he just realized he didn't have on a shirt. "You didn't answer my question."

"Where were you last night?" Rochelle asked.

"Home," he said, "Why?"

"Can you prove your whereabouts from eleven p.m. to one o'clock in the morning?" she asked.

"No," he admitted on a frustrated sigh. "Why?"

Camden would want to know why someone was asking this line of questioning if he was in the hot seat. He didn't normally have compassion for folks who broke the law. The more this case dragged on, the less his instincts said Kage could be responsible. Instincts and a nickel were worth about five cents. Even those that had been honed by years of experience still had to be proved. The best course of action was to follow the evidence.

"For now, it's our turn to ask questions," he said to Kage.

"Does that mean I'll get a turn?"

"I won't promise to answer, but you'll get a chance," Camden said. The answer seemed to satisfy Kage.

"Can I say something?" Kage asked a beat later. His wide eyes and dilated pupils marked fear, which was a shift from anger.

"Go ahead," Rochelle said.

"After your last visit, I did a little digging around," Kage admitted. "I'm not guilty of kidnapping those women."

"We'd like to believe you, but you're going to have to cooperate," Rochelle stated.

"I won't go to prison for something I didn't do," he continued, as if she hadn't just spoken. The guy had every reason to be worried. Kidnapping and murder charges followed by a conviction would lead to a maximum-security prison. Kage had done time in a federal penitentiary for a federal crime. Maximum security housed hardcore criminals—criminals that would eat Kage's lunch if he didn't watch his back at every turn.

Camden couldn't shake the instinct that Kage was telling the truth about his innocence. But the video from the nightclub said otherwise. And now, a kidnapping from a Laundromat near his home.

"Where do you do your wash?" Rochelle asked, barreling ahead with her questions.

"What?"

"You heard me," she said.

"Right, but what does that have to do with anything?" he asked. And then it seemed to dawn on him there must be another victim. He released a string of swear words underneath his breath. "We have a laundry room here on property, but the machines are always busted. I got to a place nearby."

"What's the name of the Laundromat?" Rochelle asked. She would have made a great poker player. Her expression gave away nothing. No matter how upset or fearful Kage became, her face was unreadable.

"The place is called Spin Cycle," he said after a moment of silent recall.

"Do you mind if we head there now?" Rochelle asked in an unscripted move.

"I'm not wearing shoes," Kage said.

"We'll wait here while you go get a pair," Rochelle responded.

With another frustrated sigh, Kage said, "Okay. I'll be right back."

They could keep watch as he walked back to his apartment, so Camden didn't worry about losing Kage between here and the front door.

Kage shrugged out of Camden's T-shirt before tossing it onto the front seat. "I'll get my own shirt too."

Camden nodded, then Kage made the trek back to his place. Every few steps, he hopped on one foot, no doubt stepping on a rock or a stick along the way.

"You think he's innocent," Rochelle stated.

"The evidence will give us the answer to that question," he said.

"That's not what I said," she pointed out.

"I know."

"Why?" she asked.

"Gut instinct," he admitted with a shrug. "But the evidence strongly suggests that I'm wrong on this one."

"What if I think the same thing?"

Camden let the question hang in the air, unsure what to make of it as he watched Kage disappear into the apartment.

Chapter Eleven

Rochelle didn't realize she was tapping her foot impatiently until Camden glanced in the back seat. "Sorry."

"You don't have to apologize," he said. "I do the same thing when I'm deep in thought." He paused a beat. "You were saying you agreed with me about Kage, right?"

"Something is way off in this investigation," she said. "It's the reason for the foot tapping." She'd switched to tapping her thumb on the armrest. Realizing the shift, she clasped her hands in her lap.

"I know," he agreed.

"But what?"

"That's the sixty-four-thousand-dollar question," he said with a small laugh. Something needed to break the tension.

"We can't ignore the fact Kage was photographed leaving the nightclub with Justina on the night she disappeared," she finally said.

"We'll take him with us to the Laundromat and see if the owner caught the victim talking to or leaving with Kage," he said.

"It's a strange coincidence, isn't it? Kage visiting both places." What other reason could there be except the obvious one. Kage was responsible. "And he seemed different this time."

"The gravity of what he could be charged with hit," Camden said.

"I noticed that too." She realized she'd been clenching her fingers together. *Breathe.*

"Is there any way he could be right about having a doppelgänger?" Camden asked.

"You always hear people saying that everyone has one," Rochelle said, compressing her lips. "Not sure that I believe it one hundred percent but the footage of Kage coming out of the club *is* somewhat grainy."

"The bartender said he acted differently when he came back inside the bar a second time," he pointed out. "Could be something there."

"We can study the footage again once we get home," she said, but then corrected, "Get to *your* place."

"It can't hurt, right?" he asked, but the question was rhetorical.

"You're still bothered by the baseball caps, aren't you?"

"Yes," he admitted.

"You don't think it could be used to throw people like us off the trail?" she asked.

"I don't have proof," he said.

Rochelle studied the path to Kage's apartment. "He should be back by now."

"Or at the very least walking toward us," he said as they both exited the truck in a flurry.

The front door was ajar. Weapons drawn, Camden shouted Kage's name as they stood at the entrance.

"We're coming inside," Camden shouted before entering.

The one-bedroom apartment had old brown carpeting that looked like it belonged in an office in the 1970s. The couch was almost as worn and pitiful-looking. There was a flat-screen TV sitting on wooden crates.

The decor left a lot to be desired. However, nothing was out of place. The kitchen to the right was tidy.

Weapon leading the way, Camden pushed farther inside toward the door leading to what had to be the master bedroom.

The scene inside was similar. Brown carpet. Brown curtains. Brown everything. Nothing out of place.

The window, however, was still open and the curtains were blowing in the wind.

Rochelle bit back the same curse Camden said out loud as they cleared the room before running to the opened window. There was no sign of Kage. After quickly clearing the whole apartment to make one-hundred-percent certain he wasn't hiding or trying to pull one over on them, they exited the window and split up.

There was a neighborhood with chain-link fences backing up to the apartment complex. At the end of the alley Rochelle took, there was a strip shopping center. She remembered there being a clothing recycling store, phone repair, and furniture consignment. Spin Cycle was in the opposite direction, the direction Camden had taken. Would Kage go to the Laundromat? Why?

To destroy evidence if there were cameras. It made logical sense.

The fear in his eyes earlier wasn't as simple. There'd been real fear, like he was suddenly aware of the gravity of the situation and expected to be accused of kidnapping and murder. Now he knew someone had been abducted from the place where he did his laundry.

He'd denied being responsible. Rochelle wanted to believe him. Otherwise, he was one helluva good actor.

She continued jogging, listening for the roar of an engine in case he had a motorcycle stashed somewhere, or the loud barking of dogs that would signal a direction change.

The dogs started barking in both directions, which meant they might not be too far behind Kage.

Running didn't make him look innocent. Dammit. Had her instincts been dead wrong? She'd hoped to be able to bring him into the Laundromat. Rochelle picked up the pace to a light run. She didn't want to go full out until she saw him. Saving some of her energy had paid off when she'd found herself in similar situations in the past.

If they could pin the kidnappings on him, what would happen to the victims while he sat in jail? Would they die of starvation? Were they bound somewhere? Locked in a shelter?

Frustration had her pushing her legs a little harder, a little faster, to the point that her thighs started burning. She couldn't let these women die. Their blood would be on Rochelle's hands. Just like when she wasn't there for Victoria.

Clamping her eyes shut to block out the images of her helpless friend and now, these ladies, Rochelle almost tripped over a large rock in the alley. Dammit.

With a few deep breaths, she managed to push on. Her foot was going to hurt like the dickens, and she would most likely lose a toenail or two. There wasn't time to worry about small injuries even though she had to hop a few times due to the pain. At least she'd been injured on her left foot instead of her dominant side.

There was no sign of Kage in the alley. Had he outsmarted them by hiding in shrubbery near his apartment? He would know the area better than either of them. A skilled criminal would definitely map the area around his or her home for situations like these, looking for an escape route.

Had they been outsmarted by Kage?

Why did her gut say no?

Kage could be running away so he could search for the doppelgänger he swore was at work. This fact was all the more reason she wanted to talk to the man. Did he have any idea who this other person could be?

Rochelle slowed her pace as she approached the strip mall. A blast of cold air made her wish she'd worn a heavier jacket.

A dog barked to her right as something jumped out from behind the building on her left.

She gasped, pivoted, and took aim at the moving object. "Police. Freeze."

LUNGS BURNING, thighs on fire, Camden realized he'd taken off in the wrong direction. After turning around, he sprinted. Could he catch up in time? Had Rochelle already caught Kage?

In Camden's career, he'd faced plenty of felons with nothing to lose. It wasn't good and he sure as hell didn't like Rochelle being in that position if she'd caught up to Kage.

Pushing himself to run faster, he finally caught up to Rochelle, who was in the middle of a serious conversation with a pair of tween-looking boys. As he located them, he realized she was giving them a dressing-down over startling a police officer. He had no idea what had just gone down, but decided the boys weren't likely to make the same mistake in the future after Rochelle finished with them.

Once she excused them, they apologized and took off for what he assumed would be home.

"They could have been shot," she said, turning to Camden with a panicked look on her face. "And they distracted me from continuing, so I lost Kage. Though, to be fair, I'm not sure I really had him in the first place."

"He knows this area better than we do," Camden said, trying to offer some reassurance. He felt her frustration though. "We didn't have a fair chance. Not once he got a head start."

"I was beginning to be convinced of his innocence until he pulled a Houdini."

"Same here," Camden said. "I did wonder if he was convinced that we were about to arrest him, so he took off to find this doppelgänger himself."

"We think too much alike," she said with a small smile.

Camden shouldn't like that as much as he did. "Shall we head back to my truck?"

"We should probably stop by and close Kage's front door before an animal or more tweens get inside," she said.

"Okay."

On the way back, Camden's thoughts kept churning. He glanced at the time. "Victim number two should be with Sandman soon. Are you hungry? We didn't eat much breakfast."

"I could eat but, honestly, I'd rather swing by the Laundromat first," she said. "Give Sandman a little time to do his work before we interrupt."

"Good points," he said.

"Plus, there's no way I could eat and then go directly to the coroner's office."

Camden had an iron stomach. It was easy to forget not everyone did. Plus, he'd become a little too good at compartmentalizing his emotions. Stuffing them into drawers, locking them and tossing the key had been his go-to. Rochelle made him want to slow down and figure life out.

Back at the truck, they took their seats and buckled in after closing Kage's door.

"We were inside his apartment and I didn't see one single sign that he could be the person we're searching for," Rochelle said as he started the engine and then navigated out of the neighborhood.

"We cleared the whole place in the course of trying to

locate him too." He made a right-hand turn. "What sounds good to eat?"

"I should probably say something healthy like a salad or a bowl from one of the many vegetarian places in town, but Torchy's sounds like heaven right now," she said.

"Torchy's it is." Camden pulled over to check for a close location. Once he found it, he was back in the action, dodging vehicles and trying not to hit pedestrians that came out of seemingly nowhere. Austin streets were like an ant farm.

Shouldn't students be home for Thanksgiving yet?

On second thought, they might be in the middle of exams. No wonder many appeared like they were sleepwalking. Some most likely hadn't slept last night. University of Texas at Austin had a reputation for having a rigorous curriculum and being a party school, an odd mix to be sure.

He pulled across the street from Torchy's, giving up on finding parking in the lot.

A quiet meal while sitting outside on the patio gave him the second wind he needed. Outdoors had a way of replenishing his soul. It was one of many reasons he worked in law enforcement and not at a desk somewhere. He understood and respected his friend Ace's decision not to become a desk jockey.

When he glanced up, he realized Rochelle was studying him.

"What you said before was right," she began. "Everyone in law enforcement has a story. What's yours?"

A distraction could keep him from overthinking the case.

"The person I looked up to the most was a US Marshal long before I was a gleam in my father's eye," he said. "On Sunday nights after a barbecue, we'd sit around a fire, and he'd tell us stories about his time in law enforcement."

"Why did he leave the job?"

"He missed his wife," he said.

"That might be the sweetest thing I've ever heard," Rochelle said, dropping her gaze. Those thick, long lashes of hers hooded her hazel eyes.

"They're something when they're together," he said with a smile, unsure he would ever find a love like that in his life. He hadn't in thirty-five years. Was he getting too old for young love? "Grandpa Lor didn't romanticize the job, but I could tell he had a healthy respect for his profession."

"Your grandmother didn't like him working in a dangerous job?" she asked. It could be difficult to find someone who was willing to be in a relationship with a person who didn't make it home for dinner every night. Or, if a case really went south, ever.

"It was more like he wanted to be with her, so they saved enough money to buy land and then started the business together," he explained. "Grandma Lacey did most of the heavy lifting around the place for years before Grandpa Lor was able to leave the job. He had a foreman he trusted, so that helped with the more physical aspects of horse ranching."

"Sounds like they figured it all out," she said.

"All except for their sons," he said. "My father was a good person who died young. My uncle was a jerk who walked out on his kids after his wife died following childbirth."

"What about your mom?" she asked.

"She left before Dad died," he said. He didn't normally talk about the past with anyone. It was a little too easy to talk to Rochelle. That made her more dangerous than felons with guns. His body could take the hits.

Could his heart?

Chapter Twelve

"I'm sorry to hear that, Camden." Rochelle couldn't imagine growing up without her parents. Her time with them had been too short, for sure, but she was grateful for every minute spent together.

"It's fine," he said. "The tricky part is that we recently learned that she's been talking to our grandfather." He made a face.

"Does that blow your mind?"

"Well, yeah, wouldn't it blow yours?" he asked. Before she could answer, he continued, "I haven't heard from her since I was a kid. Too young to have much more than a couple of distant memories. But I grew up wondering what the hell I'd done wrong to make my own mother run off."

Her heart ached for him when he put it like that. "That's awful, Camden. There are no words." She paused long enough to take another bite of food. "So she just left without warning, and you never heard from her again?"

"Yes," he said.

Wow. Rochelle could scarcely fathom a parent abandoning their young child. Or what kind of circumstances would make someone to that to something so defenseless.

"And you have a brother and a sister, right?" she asked.

"That's right," he said, shaking his head.

"Did she ever say why she left?" Rochelle asked.

"Why would I ever speak to the woman?"

Rochelle realized she'd walked into defensive territory with Camden. "Believe me when I say there's no excuse for turning your back on your children. But I think I'd always wonder about it if I didn't give her the chance to explain herself."

"Yeah? That's where the two of us are different," he said with a coldness in his voice she hadn't heard before. He had every right to be upset.

"You aren't the least bit curious about her?" she asked.

"I can't deny that I've had the occasional fleeting question or two while I'm getting a physical and the nurse or doctor asks about family history," he admitted.

"You never asked your grandparents?"

"Nah," he said. "No real reason to and I didn't want them to think they weren't enough."

"What if your mother had been calling to check on her children all these years?" she asked. "Would that change your impression of her?"

His full armor came up. "Why would I care?"

"Point taken," she said. "We don't have to talk about it if you don't want to."

"Are you finished eating?" he asked. Not exactly a subtle hint, considering her food wrappers were empty.

"Sure," she said softly. "We should head to the Laundromat."

With a curt nod, he stood up and then stacked his tray on top of hers before taking both to the garbage. A sign above the trash read: Your Mother Doesn't Live Here. Clean Your Own Table.

She followed after grabbing the empty drinks, and wondered what the tip jar at the cash register had been for.

They'd stood at a cash register to give their order much like every fast-food chain she'd ever patronized. They'd picked up their order when their name had been called. And they'd bussed their own table when they were finished eating. Last she checked, tips were for service. Maybe she should slide herself a couple of bucks instead.

The thought amused her, which was much needed after the serious conversation with Camden and the reality of diving back into the investigation.

Since the Laundromat was close and they would arrive within the office hours listed, she didn't see the need to call ahead. If the owner wasn't there, she could get his number and they could drop by his or her home. Surprise visits often revealed how much someone already knew. When they expected you, they had information. Or were guilty of something. Because most honest people reached out to law enforcement to offer information or help if their establishment was at the center of a criminal case.

The drive was as short as it was quiet.

Camden hopped out of the driver's seat and came around the front of the truck to open her door at the same time she exited the truck. There wasn't time for courtesies, no matter how much she appreciated the attempt at chivalry.

Kage was dangerous. If he was innocent, he could get in the way. If he was guilty, then he'd just evaded arrest.

However, nothing inside his apartment pointed toward guilt. On the surface, at least, he appeared to be walking the line. Jumping from a white-collar crime like mail fraud to kidnapping and murder was a stretch. Plus, the ball-cap issue, a small detail that didn't add up. She would have like to go over the nightclub footage with Kage to get his reaction.

While deep in thought, Rochelle barely noticed they'd

reached the glass doors of the Laundromat. Camden held one open for her. A bell chimed.

The place was kept tidy. Clean, white machines lined the walls. Those were the dryers. Washers were in a row in the middle of the room, splitting it in half. At the end of each row was a table for folding. Metal laundry carts dotted the space. To the right was an office and what looked like a two-way mirror.

Several machines were in various stages of their wash cycles. A set of chairs against the back wall were mostly empty, save for one person who stared at the phone in their hand, not bothering to do much more than glance at them as they entered the space. A sign on the door boasted late-night hours. The place was cleaner than Rochelle expected. She had to give it to the owner. The person ran a tight ship. Was it always this well-kept?

Camden tapped on the door.

A few seconds later, an older Asian female emerged.

"My name is Camden Remington and I'm a US Marshal," he began, offering a handshake.

She nodded before taking the offering. "Millie Wong."

"This is my partner, Detective Rochelle Paddock," he continued.

"How may I help you?" Millie asked. She was five-one with a head of mostly black hair. Gray crept in. She had a round face and a warm smile.

"Are you the owner?" Camden asked.

"Yes," Millie said.

"Are you aware a female was reported missing after visiting your establishment?" he asked.

Millie's gaze widened. "No. Can't say that I am."

"I noticed you have cameras," he said, motioning toward the corner of the room.

Millie nodded and waved them into her office, padding in first. "Yes. Yes. Tell me the day and I will see what I can find."

The small space was every bit as neat as the rest of the Laundromat. Several folding chairs were stacked in one corner. An oak desk was pushed up against the corner.

"Would you like to sit?" Millie asked, motioning toward the stack.

Camden nodded, retrieved two chairs, and then set them up to view the computer screen on Millie's desk.

"I don't have video because it would take too much memory," she explained. "But the cameras take pictures for me every so often." She threw her hands in the air. "I don't know exactly how it works because my son set it up for me."

"Pictures work," Camden said.

"First, could I ask you to take a look at one of my pictures?" Rochelle asked, retrieving her cell from her handbag. Someone who ran a tight operation like this one might keep a good eye on her clientele. If Kage was a regular, she might recognize him.

"Yes, of course," Millie said. The woman had an almost regal bearing.

After positively identifying herself to her phone, she thumbed through pictures until she found a good one of Kage's face. She held out the screen. "Do you recognize this man?"

"Oh, yes," Millie said as her face lit up. "He is a regular customer of mine."

"Do you know his name?" Rochelle asked.

"No," Millie admitted. "It never came up. He says hello and I respond. I ask how his day is going, and he tells me. We never got to a first-name basis." Her expression dropped. "Is he alright? Did something happen?" And then it dawned on her when realization played out across her features. "Oh. Really? You think he might be connected to the lady who went missing?"

"That surprises you?" Camden asked.

"Yes," Millie admitted. "It does. Very much. He is always so polite." She shrugged after a thoughtful pause. "But I guess you don't really know a person, do you?"

"I'm rarely surprised anymore," Camden said. "Job hazard."

Millie offered a thoughtful smile. Then, she turned to the keyboard. A moment later, the screen came to life. "When did this happen?"

They gave the date and then Millie's fingers went to work.

"Let's see," she said as images clicked across the screen. She leaned back and folded her arms across her chest, studying the time-stamped pictures. "Hold on. He usually comes in later."

Day turned to evening as she fast-clicked. And then she stopped. Several photos ticked by. Then, bam.

"Here he is," Millie said.

Kage was at the Laundromat on the night in question.

Chapter Thirteen

Camden resisted the urge to curse as Millie froze the screenshot on a picture of Kage facing the window as he pulled clothes from the dryer. The camera over the glass doors snapped a photo of him. Once again, he was at the scene of a crime, caught on camera.

"You said you don't know how often the camera takes pictures, right?" Rochelle asked.

Kage running away from them today wasn't helping his case for innocence.

And then something caught Camden's eye on the grainy photo. "Can you zoom in?"

"Sure," Millie said. "Where?"

Camden pointed to a spot on the window.

"His reflection," Millie said.

"Is it?" Camden wasn't certain. "Could we have our experts take a look at the image?"

"Anything you need," Millie said.

"Would you mind emailing it?" Camden asked before rattling off his email address.

"Mine too," Rochelle said, doing the same.

"Okay," Millie said. She minimized the screen after taking a note of the numbered picture. A few seconds later, the email showed up in his inbox. Using his cell, he forwarded it to his supervisor, and Rochelle did the same to her boss. "Two heads are better than one."

Getting as many experts on the case as possible would only help them. With any luck, they'd find Kage before someone else in law enforcement did. Which reminded him, they should consider updating his parole officer. Would that make matters worse?

Hope that Kage would lead them to the pair of kidnapping victims died the moment he'd taken off. And yet, a growing part of Camden believed the man was innocent. How messed up was that?

Despite the evidence, Camden couldn't wrap his thoughts around Kage being so careless as to abduct women near his own home. The old saying "dogs don't go to the bathroom where they eat" applied. A good litigator would point out the fact Kage was merely an opportunist, taking women near where he lived. They might conclude no one else but Kage could be responsible for the kidnappings and subsequent murders because of the pictures and video footage. The evidence might be circumstantial, but it was damning.

And yet, it didn't fit. The escalation of crimes didn't make sense. And the baseball caps kept haunting him.

Hopefully, this image would provide clues. Because Camden's reasons for defending Kage wouldn't hold up in court.

"How often would you say this customer used the Laundromat?" Camden asked.

"Every Tuesday evening after dinner at seven thirty," Millie responded. "I could set my watch to it."

The killer was meticulous. He was thorough, not leaving behind any DNA.

"Is there anything else you remember about your customer?" Rochelle asked.

"Just what I already said," Millie said. "I never had a

problem with him. Not even when a machine acted up. Some people get upset. This one never did. He was always polite."

He'd done his time. Paid his debt to society for his crime.

"Did he ever come here with anyone?" Rochelle continued.

"No," Millie answered. "He kept to himself except when I came out and said hello." She shrugged. "He's the last person I would suspect to commit such an awful crime. Or any crime." Her gaze shifted from Rochelle to Camden and back. "What do I know?"

"Thank you for your time," Camden said, hoping the tech guy could find something in the picture to send them in a new direction. More and more, he found himself rooting for Kage.

Was it because Camden could see himself taking matters into his own hands if he believed law enforcement was unfairly targeting him in a murder investigation? Camden would likely strike out on his own to find answers too. He'd always had an independent streak a mile long, and his stubbornness was legendary in the family.

All of this had him thinking about second chances. Did Kage deserve his?

What about Camden's mother?

Whoa! Where did that come from?

After thanking Millie a second time, Camden walked out of the Laundromat behind Rochelle. Once inside the truck, he said, "I keep thinking Kage took off because we're missing something."

"I have the same feeling," she said, buckling into the passenger seat.

"Guess we just have to keep pecking away at it until we get a breakthrough," he said.

"You aren't used to that, are you?"

"Investigating?" he asked.

"Yes. I keep forgetting that your primary job is to serve warrants once you get a location on someone," she said.

"I do more stakeouts than interviews," he said.

"We'll figure this out," she reassured.

He didn't feel the need to point out that Kage's life depended on it. They might be the difference between a life behind bars and freedom for a crime Camden was more and more convinced Kage might be innocent of.

Either that, or Kage was one of the best actors of his time. He'd be wasting his talents in Austin if that was the case.

"We could stake out Kage's apartment," she said. "See if he returns to pick anything up."

"Okay," he said for lack of a better idea.

They'd wait and see what turned up.

HOURS PASSED AS Rochelle and Camden sat in the truck nestled in between two vans, waiting for any sign of life coming from Kage's apartment.

The silence was almost deafening after getting to know Camden and all that he'd been through, revealing those fractured parts of himself to her and only her. To have him suddenly close off to her at this point hurt.

Relationships hurt.

Opening her heart to someone hurt.

After losing her mother recently, she didn't have the resolve to allow her heart to be broken again. Whatever was happening between her and Camden needed to stop. Especially because they were coworkers. Starting a relationship while on assignment would be horribly unprofessional.

Rather than sit there and idly stare out the window, she decided Camden could handle watching the apartment while she studied the photograph of Kage at the Laundromat on her phone. The grainy photo made details a little difficult to make out. There were no other photos with that time stamp, so there wasn't anything else to use as a basis for comparison. Maybe she should go back and ask Millie for every Tuesday-night photo for the past few weeks to compare.

Deciding it was an idea worth chasing, she sent the email request and informed Camden of what she was doing.

"Good idea," he said. "I'm not sure why I didn't think of that while we were still with Millie."

"I was distracted too," she said. "There's something about that photo that just keeps eating away at me."

"Same here," he said.

She blew up the photo on the screen. The faces were so similar it was like Kage was looking into a mirror. Therefore, the reflection theory made sense. However, what she hadn't noticed before was that Kage's dark gray T-shirt looked black in his reflection. A trick of the fluorescent lights?

"Hey, did you notice this before?" she asked Camden as she outstretched her hand so he could get a better look at the screen.

"I knew something was bothering me," he said. Then he took the phone and studied it intensely for a few long moments. "The shirts. Aside from the color variance, Kage is wearing a V-neck. The reflection is more of a scoop neck."

Rochelle leaned over the console. This close, Camden's spicy male scent filled her senses. Under any other circumstance, she would find it sexy. But right now, she couldn't allow herself to focus on anything but Kage and that shirt. Camden was right. "I see what you're saying."

"The devil is in the details," he said.

That expression had never applied to any situation more than it did this one in this moment. From the corner of her eye, she saw movement in Kage's apartment complex. "Hey, look there." She pointed toward a woman who walked slowly and seemed to check over her shoulder nervously a little too much for this to be random, unless the woman was selling drugs or something else Rochelle didn't want to think about.

"Who are you?" Camden said out loud, but the question was obviously rhetorical.

Rochelle's muscles tensed as she watched the woman stop in front of Kage's door. The female with shoulder-length black hair glanced around a few more times before knocking. From this distance, it was impossible to tell if she had a secret knock or, honestly, if she even knew him. The man was attractive and would have his fair share of female fans. Most women would agree with that assessment.

The secrecy and carefulness with this woman made all of Rochelle's tingly Spidey senses come to life. The answer was as plain as the nose on Rochelle's face. This woman knew Kage's apartment was being watched.

Black Hair put her hand on the doorknob. Froze. And then she hastily pulled a piece of paper from her pocketbook and slid it into the door, closing it so just an edge of paper was visible.

Did this person have prior knowledge that Kage wasn't home?

Why wouldn't she just go inside to leave the note in a secure place?

Because the answer was simple. Rochelle suspected the black-haired woman knew Kage wasn't going to answer the door because of the cops, or she must have expected the possibility of him not being home. Otherwise, why have a note ready?

"Do you think we should go ask her about her relationship with Kage?" Rochelle asked.

"I have a better idea," Camden said. "Let's follow her."

Rochelle was out of the car in two seconds flat. She met Camden at the front of his truck, where he wrapped an arm around her shoulder, leaned close to her ear, and whispered, "Follow my lead. Okay?"

"Alright," she said, ignoring the way her heart raced the second he touched her.

"Is it okay if I touch you like we're a couple?" he whispered.

"Yes," she answered, hearing the frog in her own throat. Somewhere in the back of her mind, she tried to convince herself the excitement had more to do with finally getting a small break in this case and not with the fact that her attraction to Camden was getting ahead of her. She had the discipline to keep it at bay. She had the professional sense to know what a disaster it would be for her career and therefore her life if she gave in to a momentary distraction like Camden.

The knowledge didn't exactly make the attraction go away, but she could deal with it. All she had to do was remind herself of how easy it was for him to shut down anytime they had a breakthrough or started getting closer to fully opening up to each other. His instincts shut it down before anything could transpire, which was probably for the best even though her heart wanted to argue otherwise.

Black Hair hadn't driven unless she parked her car a block away, which would be smart so anyone watching the apartment wouldn't be able to get her license plate.

If that was the case, this woman was either a criminal herself and knew exactly what she was doing to avoid capture, or an expert at making certain she wasn't tied to a current case. There was another possibility and that was that Kage had told her to stop by and had warned her that someone might be watching his apartment, in which case surely he would have given her a reason. No guy was gorgeous enough to risk a felony just to go see him at his apartment. *Right?*

Then again, having a twisted set of morals was exactly the type of people Rochelle came across on a daily basis in her work.

Black Hair slipped around behind the complex in a surprise move and then cut left, disappearing from view. She must have, in fact, stashed a car behind the building. Was it a getaway car?

"Should we grab the note before we do anything else?" Rochelle asked.

"I had the same thought," Camden admitted. "We can split up. I'll follow her while you go check the note."

"Deal." Rochelle banked a right while Camden disappeared around the side of the apartment complex. The second his arm left her shoulder, she noticed his absence. But she couldn't think about that right now.

Technically, she had no authority to take a note out of Kage's door. However, if the note fell on the ground and onto public property, then she wasn't in any violation. It would be in public domain and, therefore, fair game.

Or she could just stand there until Kage returned and then ask him to show her the note.

Rochelle almost laughed out loud at that one. After everything that had happened today, Kage wasn't going to be inclined to share information with the law. In fact, he would run in the opposite direction if he saw her standing at his front door.

Wind whipped her hair around as she made the walk toward his apartment. Part of her wanted to retreat to the truck and watch to see if Kage returned. However, the contents of the note could be lost forever, and he could deny it was ever there in the first place.

Rochelle's curiosity about the note was getting the better of her. By the time she made it to the door, it took all her willpower not to accidentally elbow the piece of paper to dislodge it from the door.

She'd been around detectives who started cutting corners. It never led to anywhere positive in their career or personal life. So even if it meant taking longer and unfortunately risking lives that were somewhere out there hanging in the balance, she had to play this by the book or risk losing the case in court. As much as letting the perp get away ate at her, she couldn't let herself become sloppy.

The note was flapping in the wind and there wasn't a damn thing she could do to free it from the door. There was at least a small chance it would break free and she could then catch it legally. In the meantime, she pulled out her cell phone and started snapping pictures.

Where are you, Kage?

Cell phone in hand, Rochelle had to resist the urge to call or text Camden to see if he was making better progress than she was.

She didn't realize she was tapping her toe on the concrete sidewalk in front of Kage's apartment until she glanced down.

Shifting her focus to the screen in her hand, she didn't catch the barrel pointed at her from a tree across the street until a shot had been fired.

Too late, she saw the flash and then a second later heard the bullet whiz past her head by inches, lodging into the door and nailing the piece of paper.

What the hell?

Chapter Fourteen

Camden slowed his pace as he neared the alleyway behind the apartment complex. Splitting up from Rochelle sent his pulse through the roof. The effect it had on him had caught him off guard. However, it couldn't be helped. She was a professional who was very good at her job. She knew how to handle herself.

So why the hell was he stressed about leaving her to do it?

The woman with black hair turned around to check behind her twice, but he was relatively certain she hadn't seen him. Her quick glances and his ability to blend into his environment seemed enough to keep him out of her line of sight at critical moments.

There was no car parked in the alleyway. The black-haired lady picked up her pace to a jog the farther she got away from Kage's apartment. Camden noticed that she had on a tight blouse and a short-short miniskirt that could only be called a micro mini. He hoped she didn't overpay for it because she only had on about four dollars' worth of material, his Grandma Lacey would say. He missed her more than words.

Right now, though, he had to maintain focus.

The high-heel boots the black-haired lady was running in had him scratching his head. He would never understand how someone could run with their heels on what looked like the points of needles, let alone do it in an alley filled with potholes.

She half wobbled, half ran toward the strip shopping center that Rochelle had told him was at the end of the alley.

The woman rolled her ankle. She landed on her left thigh before her bottom nailed the gravel. She let out a yelp and a groan as she hit the ground.

The lady couldn't get up and out of there fast enough. Rather than hobbling, she was limping at this point, hopping on her right foot. How she maintained balance was a question he would never be able to answer, but she made it to the strip center before disappearing left. Camden moved down the alley quietly. Dogs barked, still riled up from her.

She made her way to a white, two-door hatchback as he peeked around the corner into the lot.

Camden retrieved his cell phone and took a picture of the license plate. It should be easy enough to find her address from here, so he doubled back toward Rochelle. An uneasy feeling had settled over him and he couldn't get back to her fast enough.

From a place down deep, Camden needed to know Rochelle was okay.

Running as fast as he could toward Kage's apartment, Camden's heart pounded his ribs so hard he feared it might crack one.

As he rounded the corner, he almost ran smack into her. She was frantic, causing his heart to free-fall.

"There's a shooter," she said. "He's here. He followed me here and barely missed."

Camden hauled her against his chest, wrapping her in his arm protectively as he scanned the area.

"Where is he?"

"Gone," she answered. "I think. We should be safe here, but I need to call it in." She took a step away and flattened her back against the wall. Phone in hand, she made the call to her supervisor while Camden risked a glance around the building.

He didn't see anything or anyone. Didn't mean the perp wasn't out there.

"Yes, sir," she said into the phone. "The shooter was in a tree across the street from the Sentinel Apartment Complex." She paused. "We were here to interview a possible witness." Another pause. "The suspect should be considered armed and dangerous." She paused for a few more beats. "Yes, it would make sense that it is the same person from last night. Do we have a ballistics report?" She fell quiet again. "My partner and I will stay on the scene until a uniform arrives." She shook her head. "No, sir, I lost visual on the perp."

Camden could almost feel the frustration rolling off Rochelle in palpable waves. She ended the call to her supervisor and then turned her attention toward him.

"I can't believe I lost that son of a bitch," she said.

"This doesn't exactly clear Kage of suspicion, does it?"

"You deal with people with nothing to lose all the time and yet you haven't been convinced that Kage would pull a stunt like firing at an officer," she said. "He would have had to go pretty far off the rails to do something like this, wouldn't he?"

"Yes," he said. "He would. So someone is either trying to teach us a lesson, scare us away, or kill us."

"*Kill me*, you mean." Rochelle issued a sharp sigh. "So far, this perp followed me to my home and now here. I seem to be the only one who's getting shot at."

He couldn't argue her point there.

"Kage would know that firing at my task-force partner would only make me more determined to find him and lock him behind bars," he said. "It would mean war. And the only reasons I could think of for him to attack my partner and not me is to teach me a lesson." He tensed. "But then that doesn't make any sense either."

"It doesn't?" she asked. "Didn't you take his life away from him when you arrested him?"

"You make a good point there," he said. "I still think he would come after my family instead of my task-force partner."

"Anyone who knows anything about law enforcement realizes when two people work together they become family real fast," she said.

"Again, you make a good point," he admitted. "If he means to make this personal, we can go to war. Either way, I'm going to do my job and right now my job is to protect you."

Sirens blared in the distance. Help was on the way.

"I'm guessing the ballistics report is in based on your conversation with your supervisor," he said.

"You would be correct," she said.

"Good, then we'll have this bullet fragment to match up with the other," he said.

"What are the odds they're not gonna match?" she asked.

"I'd say they're pretty slim," he said. "I didn't hear it."

It was impossible not to feel like he'd failed her a second time.

"THE LADY YOU were following," Rochelle said as she remembered the reason he'd taken off in the other direction. "What happened?"

"Got a license plate." He compressed his lips in a frown.

"Better than nothing," she said.

"What about the note?" he asked.

"I didn't touch it for fear the evidence would be inadmissible in court," she said. "Then, a bullet whizzed past my ear, so I didn't stick around long enough for the perp to hit me with a second shot."

A marked SUV came roaring up, sirens blaring. It was probably safe to come around the corner of the building. Rochelle gave the area a once-over and headed toward the SUV. A female officer emerged from the driver's side.

"Gabby David," the officer said after closing the door behind her. She offered a quick handshake.

"Detective Paddock, but you can call me Rochelle."

"Only if you call me Gabby," the officer said with a small nod as she skimmed the area. Her gaze fixed on Camden. "I take it that's US Marshal Remington."

"Yes, it is," Rochelle confirmed before giving a quick rundown of the situation.

Gabby looked to be in her early thirties. She had brown hair that was tied back in a ponytail and a CrossFit-honed physique.

"There's a note," Rochelle informed her, motioning toward Kage's door.

The pair joined Camden after Gabby grabbed tongs and a paper evidence bag from her vehicle.

With the tongs, Gabby removed the note. It was folded in two, making it easy to open without destroying or adding fingerprints. It read: *Not cool how you left me. I thought we had something special.*

"Kage was having a relationship with the black-haired woman?" Rochelle asked. The same question was most likely on everyone else's mind.

"Interesting," Camden said before giving Gabby a summary of Kage's background and history with law enforcement.

"Did he have any priors before the mail fraud?" Gabby asked.

"No," Camden responded.

"I'm no detective," Gabby started, "but isn't it a stretch to go from mail fraud to murder?"

"And kidnapping," Rochelle added before outlining the torture victims endured.

Gabby shook her head.

"You reported not being able to see who was in the trees," Gabby continued.

"That's correct."

"Or being able to make out who came to your home last night," Gabby added.

"Correct again."

Gabby turned to Camden. "Can you think of any reason someone would want to set Kage up?"

"Maybe our black-haired witness can shed some light into Kage's personality," Camden said.

Rochelle thought about Millie. The Laundromat owner did nothing but sing Kage's praises. The photo sent a cold chill up her spine. The doppelgänger theory was too out there to mention to Gabby. And yet, it would explain a lot.

Still, why would a doppelgänger haunt the same places as Kage? Why make it seem like he was guilty?

To throw law enforcement off the real trail?

A doppelgänger was also a convenient excuse. *No, Detective, it wasn't me. It was my evil twin.* How many times had she heard that excuse thrown out during an investigation?

More times than she cared to count.

"Did you send in the plate?" she asked Camden.

"Yes," he said. "My supervisor should have a res—"

His cell dinged, stopping him in midsentence. He checked the screen already in his palm. "Detective, we have an address."

Rochelle shifted her gaze to Gabby. "Are you fine here

if we head out?" As she spoke, a second SUV pulled up and parked.

"I'm good," Gabby said.

After exchanging courtesies and contact information, Rochelle and Camden headed back to his truck.

On arrival, they discovered four flat tires and an obscene word written on the front windshield of the passenger side.

"What the hell?"

The anger in Camden's voice said this was war. Again, Rochelle noticed the attack had targeted her.

Was someone taunting Camden?

"Now, we have to wait for roadside assistance," Camden said after assessing the damage.

Was someone trying to slow them down?

"The shooter?" she asked.

"That's my guess too." Camden didn't look up from his cell, obviously busy making arrangements.

"It takes a lot of guts to vandalize the vehicle of someone in law enforcement while they're investigating you," she pointed out. Kage?

He gave the impression he couldn't get far enough away from them. Would he circle back?

A few minutes later, Camden said, "My supervisor is sending a new vehicle and a tow truck." He shook his head as his lips formed a thin line. "This is getting more and more personal."

Which meant they were getting close.

"A good sign, don't you think?"

Camden stared at her like she had two foreheads.

"This person is telling us to back off," she said.

"Or the perp is trying to show us who is really in charge," he said.

"Because they don't believe we're smart enough to catch them," she added.

Camden bit down on his bottom lip. "Which could mean the person is hiding behind something."

"Or someone."

"Kage," he said. "But how?"

A tow truck pulled up with a Ford Bronco a car length behind. The driver introduced himself and reassured Camden that his truck would be up and running in a matter of hours.

After they were inside the Bronco, Rochelle decided to ask the question that had been on her mind ever since hearing they would get a replacement vehicle.

"Why didn't the tow-truck driver just change your tires?" she asked.

"Precaution," he said.

The implication smacked her like a ton of bricks as the tow-truck driver swept his hand along the outline of the truck. Whoever tried to shoot her could have dropped a tracking device or bug on the truck. They might have done other things she didn't want to think about.

As she watched the men sweep the truck in the sideview mirror, horror struck as they slowly backed away from the truck.

Bomb?

Chapter Fifteen

The white sedan was parked in front of a small brown brick duplex. The concrete parking lot had buckled from last year's drought. The Bronco's suspension was more than adequate to handle the potholes and ridges created by the combination of too much heat and not enough rain.

Cooler weather had finally arrived. Winds had kicked up and the temperature had dropped ten degrees in the last half hour alone. He was still waiting for the full report as to what had been done to his truck. No surprise there since the black-haired female's home wasn't far from Kage's apartment.

Sabrina Sanchos came up as the car's registered owner.

The ride over had been quiet. Rochelle had been lost in thought, so he hadn't wanted to disturb her. She'd been right about the perp targeting her.

"We should probably come up with a plan as to who leads this conversation," she said to Camden after he found a visitor spot and parked. Rather than look at him, she stared out the front windshield. "Unless you want to play it by ear."

"Why don't you take the lead?" he suggested, figuring a woman might open up to another woman about being jilted easier than she would to a man.

"Okay," she said, absently.

He exited the driver's side and then rounded the front of the Bronco before opening her door.

Taking his hand, she climbed out of the vehicle. "It's not him," she finally said. "There's no way he would shoot at me in front of his door. Kage ran away from us. He wouldn't risk getting close again."

"Let's go see if we can figure out who is impersonating him," Camden said.

"What do we know about his birth certificate?" she asked.

"Those are public record," he said. "I'll see what we can discover." He fired off a text with the request for research.

He followed her to 316A, hanging back. From here, the TV volume sounded through thin walls.

Rochelle knocked at the door. Nothing.

As she lifted her knuckle to go for round two, the door opened. "Hello. My name is Detective Rochelle Paddock with Austin police. I have a few questions about Kage Durham."

"Who?"

"Detective—"

"Not you," the black-haired woman said. "I don't know who you're asking about."

"Kage Durham," Rochelle said. "I'm sorry, you are Sabrina Sanchos, correct?"

"Yes, I am." Ms. Sanchos tensed. She looked to be in her midthirties and had spent a little too much time out in the sun. Her skin had that leathery look. She was five feet three inches max and had curvy hips and implants that gave her body an out-of-proportion look. Bright orange lip gloss and heavy eye makeup gave her a raccoon appearance up close. She still had on the micro miniskirt, but the boots were gone and she had an ice pack around her ankle. Toenail polish matched her lips. A large green-dragonfly tattoo covered her left arm, covering a decent amount of space from her shoulder to her elbow.

"You just left Kage Durham's apartment, correct?" Rochelle asked, leaning against the doorjamb.

"I'm not sure who you're talking about," Sabrina said, eyebrows furrowed. She genuinely appeared to be stumped. Would Kage give her a fake name?

"Do you mind telling my partner and I where you were an hour ago?" Rochelle asked.

"I dropped off a note at a...*friend's* house," Sabrina reported.

"And that friend's name is...?"

"Asher Foley," Sabrina supplied.

"Do you mind if I ask you the nature of your relationship with Asher Foley?" Rochelle asked without skipping a beat. Meanwhile, the wheels were turning in Camden's mind. Had Kage given the woman a fake name?

"We spent time together," she said after a pause, as if she was searching for the right words.

"Were the two of you in a relationship?" Rochelle asked.

"Can I ask what this is about?" Sabrina asked rather than answer Rochelle's question.

"Mr. Foley is wanted for questioning in connection with a murder case," Rochelle stated.

Sabrina's eyes widened. She exhaled a sharp breath. "He wouldn't do..." She flashed eyes at Rochelle. "You aren't suggesting he could have..."

"We can't comment on specifics of an ongoing investigation," Rochelle said, leaving the questions unanswered. Rochelle was a good investigator.

"Well, then, let's see," Sabrina said, keeping most of her weight on her good ankle. "We were in a relationship, or so I thought." Her eyes widened again. "But we always had to come to my place." Shock was followed by fear in her eyes. "The first sign someone is married is that you can never go to their house. I confronted Asher but he swore up and down that he was free as a bird."

Asher Foley. Camden hadn't heard the name before. It was too soon to send a text asking for research into Asher Foley's background. He couldn't do that while he was still in Sabrina's presence.

Was this a made-up name? Had Kage lied so Sabrina wouldn't be tied back to him?

"How did you find out where he lived if he never took you there?" Rochelle asked.

"I saw him yesterday at the grocery store and followed him home," Sabrina said. "I'm not proud of the fact. I don't normally have to chase men, and I've certainly never stalked one. But Asher stopped calling and coming around. He must have blocked my calls because I couldn't get through to him either. He ended it without a word. So when I saw him, curiosity got the best of me. I sat across the street from his apartment for hours waiting to see if his wife came out but there was no sign of one." She shrugged. "I caught one of his neighbors and asked if they'd ever seen a woman in the apartment and the man said he hadn't." Her gaze shifted from Rochelle to Camden as she then studied him. "Men can be unpredictable, but I thought Asher and I had something special."

"One minute, you're lying in their arms as they promise the world," Rochelle agreed. "The next, they turn the other way when they see you out in public."

"I know, right," Sabrina responded. Suddenly, a solidarity between wronged women emerged. It was an effective tactic and yet it still caused Camden to be embarrassed on behalf of jerks who deceived their partners. He was always honest about the fact he wasn't looking for a relationship. If two consenting adults wanted to spend time together with no strings attached and have sex, the rules had to be clear up front. Honest communication was critical. Attachment wasn't something Camden could do. Not with anyone. Then again, he'd never found anyone like Rochelle before.

Camden quashed the thought. He might have had amazing grandparents, but his mother's abandonment had taught him early on not to count on anyone but himself. Getting attached was lethal to the heart.

But Rochelle was nothing like his mother.

"Men can be such jerks," Sabrina said, shooting Camden a disgusted look.

"That's my cue to leave," he said, taking a step back. "I'll leave you two to speak in private."

Sabrina practically glared at him as he stepped away. He was grateful to leave a conversation that had turned into male-bashing. On Rochelle's part, it was an act. But not Sabrina's. She'd been burned and the last thing she wanted was a man around to hear about her rejection.

Plus, it had turned out to be the perfect moment to disappear so he could have Asher Foley researched.

Back in the Bronco, he sent off a text with the request as he checked on the group chat to see if any progress had been made with Grandma Lacey. There was no update. But there was a text from his younger brother, Dalton. Call me ASAP.

Camden's heart sank. He immediately pulled up his brother's contact information and tapped the screen to initiate the call.

"Hey," Dalton said, sounding like he hadn't slept in days.

"Everything okay?" Camden asked.

"Yes, sorry," Dalton said. "Didn't mean to scare you with the text. I probably should have told you the reason for the request, but I thought it would come across better if you hear it straight from me."

"Ok-a-a-y," Camden said, drawing out the word. His stress levels jumped at the sound of Dalton's voice. "What's going on?"

"Are you sitting down?" Dalton asked.

"I'm in a Bronco," Camden answered.

"Are you driving, because—"

"No, I'm sitting in a parking lot," Camden said. "My partner is interviewing a witness and needed a minute alone. So I came out to the parking lot to wait. What is it, dude? You're starting to freak me out."

"She wants to meet," Dalton said. "Our mother has been in contact with Grandpa Lor and has requested to meet with us."

"What the hell could she possibly want after all these years?" Camden asked.

"I guess there's only one way to find out," Dalton said.

"You want this?" Camden couldn't believe his brother had done an about-face when it came to their mother. Then again, neither had brought up the subject in longer than Camden could remember.

"I'm asking what you think," Dalton said.

"What does Jules think?" Camden's answer was "not no, but hell no" when it came to a meetup, but he wondered what his siblings thought.

"That it might be a good idea to clear the air," Dalton said.

"After all these years?"

"That's what she said," Dalton reported.

"And just like that we're supposed to agree to this? To think it's suddenly a good idea after she abandoned us all those years ago?"

Dalton got quiet.

"Sorry," Camden said. "I didn't mean to go on a rant."

"I have no memories of her," Dalton admitted. "None. It would be like meeting a stranger. And yet…"

"You're curious?"

"I didn't think I was when I first heard the idea," Dalton said.

"Whose idea is it?"

"Grandpa Lor mentioned it." Dalton issued a sharp sigh. "At first, I thought no way, but I guess now that Blakely and I are starting our life together I'm curious about where I came from. Does that make any sense?"

Camden listened, trying not to judge his brother's reasons. "We all think differently about the situation." Camden never allowed himself to think about their mother. He'd closed that door years ago and never looked back. "And, yes, it makes sense. For you."

"If Jules and I arrange a meeting, are you saying you don't want to know about it?" Dalton asked.

"That's exactly what I'm saying," Camden confirmed. He repeated the words to make sure Dalton heard correctly.

"Okay, then," Dalton said. "We'll respect your decision."

"I appreciate it."

"Is there anything you'd like us to say on your behalf if she asks?" Dalton continued.

"Not a thing," Camden said. "Let her wonder about me like I did about her in those early years after she took off." A surprising cramp in the center of his chest made breathing difficult. Feelings that took him back to his seven-year-old self surfaced. Feelings that brought on stabbing pain with every intake of air. "My partner should be coming any second now and I have to send a text to my supervisor," he finally said, hearing the strain in his own voice. "I have to go."

"Take care of yourself, Camden."

"You know I will," he assured his brother.

"See you soon."

With that, Camden ended the call. His cell buzzed while it was still in his hand. A text from his supervisor came through: check your email.

Camden tapped the screen to open his account and then his inbox filled the screen. At the top was a note forwarded from his supervisor from Research. He opened the email to find a rap sheet on Asher Foley involving sexual harassment and multiple cases pending that demonstrated a history of violence against women.

He scrolled down to the mug-shot attachment from the man's last arrest.

Oh, hell.

"You'll let me know if Asher shows up, right?" Rochelle asked as she was beginning to make her exit plan from this conversation. It was possible Kage had created a second identity so no one could track him.

It would be a lot of trouble to go through and didn't make sense considering he had a white-collar-crime conviction. Did he really think it would hurt his dating life?

"I'll sure do that," Sabrina promised.

Rochelle gave over her number and then headed back toward the Bronco. Camden's serious expression told her something was up.

She climbed in the passenger seat. "What did you find out?"

"You're not going to believe this," he said before handing over his cell.

What the actual hell?

Chapter Sixteen

Rochelle's eyes widened as she studied the screen on Camden's phone. "The picture at the Laundromat," she said.

"Asher Foley was born a twin," Camden said, still trying to digest the news.

"His rap sheet is long," she said.

"And he has a violent history," Camden pointed out.

"Kage doesn't have a doppelgänger," she said as her jaw dropped.

"He has a twin," Camden said, finishing for her.

"What are the odds?" she managed to ask.

"I didn't believe him," Camden said. "All this time, he knew something was off and I dismissed him as dodging justice for his crimes."

"The mail fraud?"

"That was him," Camden reassured. "But the violence against women, the torture, the murders—those fit with Asher's background. He haunts Austin but his home address is a trailer park outside the city."

"I wish there was a way to get a message to Kage that we believe he's innocent." She blinked a couple of times. "He doesn't know about the twin."

"The baseball caps make more sense to me now, as well." Something had always been off. The niggling feeling that had been bothering Camden could finally be explained. Kage was innocent. No one believed him. "He must have seen the writing on the wall and decided to figure out what was going on for himself."

"We missed the boat completely," she said.

"It was impossible to predict a twin considering there's no evidence of one on Kage's side," Camden reflected. Coming up with an explanation did little to ease his guilt for not giving Kage the benefit of the doubt.

"So much about this case makes sense now," Rochelle said as she handed his cell back. "Like the bartender who said she felt like the person who came in for a second time was nothing like Kage. How he circled the dance floor like a predator."

Camden nodded his agreement. Many puzzle pieces clicked together with this news. They needed to follow the evidence with this new information and see how much everything changed. "I think we already have the answer as to whether or not Asher knows about Kage's existence."

"I don't have the impression the opposite is true."

"Same here," Camden said. "Now, we need to figure out where to find Kage."

"Do you think stalking his apartment would work?"

Camden glanced at the clock. It was long after dark and Rochelle's stomach just growled. "We'll think better on a full stomach."

"Okay," she said. "Where to?"

"My house to cook?" he asked. "This seems like a good time to pause to let the new information percolate."

"Sounds like a plan to me," she said. "I got an agreement from Sabrina to reach out to me if Asher shows up or contacts her."

"My supervisor has an address on him," Camden said. "It's out of the way from my place but we could make a detour."

"What are the chances he'll be home?" she asked.

"If it was truly him taking shots at you, then I suspect he has a better hiding spot than his trailer," he said as he navigated out of the parking lot. "But you never know about people, and we would be remiss to overestimate or under-estimate any individual."

A question struck him. Why would someone hold a grudge against a twin they'd never met? Was this a convenient way to blame someone else for their crimes? Or could that person want revenge for a perceived slight?

Twisted minds worked in ways Camden might never understand. But they had a name now. Asher fit the profile of the kind of person who would kidnap, torture, and murder women. They needed to find the abducted women while they were still alive.

Rochelle mentioned becoming a target because they were getting closer to the killer. Would that drive him to do away with his victims?

"Change of topic?" Rochelle asked, cutting into thoughts that were already turning into a hamster wheel.

"Yes, please," he said. Overthinking never provided the answer he was looking for. Distraction had a way of clearing the way.

"Fair warning, this is personal," she said.

"Oh?"

"I accidentally saw a phone call had come through on your phone from your brother," Rochelle said. "Is that one of the texts you excused yourself to send before?"

"No, I wanted to check up on Asher Foley," he said. "My brother asked me to call because he's considering a meeting with our mother and wanted to know how I felt about joining."

"What did you say?" Rochelle asked without hesitation.

He liked that she felt comfortable enough with him to ask personal questions and get him talking about subjects that were normally off-limits.

"That I'm not interested."

"You aren't?"

"Should I be?" he asked.

"It's probably just me, but I would be so curious about her," she admitted. "You reach a point in life when you want to know more about what made you who you are. Plus, I can't imagine not knowing my parents."

"Because they didn't abandon you at the ripe old age of seven," he stated.

"True," she said, biting down on her bottom lip as he pulled into his town-house complex. "Still. I think I'd have even more questions if I didn't know them."

"Even if it was her choice to leave?"

"Especially if that were the case," she said. "Aren't you curious as to why she did what she did?"

"A little," he said. "Not enough to want a face-to-face."

"What's the worst that could happen?" She leaned her elbow on the console as he pulled into his garage.

"I hadn't really thought about it in those terms," he admitted as he cut off the engine and closed the garage door behind them.

"She's the one who wants the meeting, right?"

"I assume so," he said. "It sure as hell isn't me."

"Which means you can set the terms," she said. "If you don't like what you're hearing in the first few minutes of the conversation, you can get up and walk out."

Why did the thought of seeing his mother reduce him to that kid who'd cried himself to sleep every night after she disappeared?

"What if she's a disappointment?" he asked.

"At least you'd know," she reasoned. "This way, you must have lingering questions about her even if you are able to shove them aside most of the time."

He could admit that was true as he exited his side and then rounded the front to open her door for her. She thanked him and then followed him into his town house. His cell buzzed again. He checked the screen. His truck would be dropped off out front in visitor parking in a matter of minutes. Good timing.

"Everything okay?" she asked as she followed him into the kitchen.

Having Rochelle in his home almost convinced him everything would be.

"Yeah," he said without making eye contact for fear she would be able to read him.

ROCHELLE SET HER handbag down and slipped out of her shoulder holster, then fixed it on the back of a chair for easy access. The weight of it normally comforted her but she'd been wearing it for long hours during this case.

Her neck hurt. Her back hurt. Her head hurt.

Being shot at multiple times in a matter of days had a way of jacking up stress levels. Body aches were never far off.

"Can I help with dinner?" she asked.

Camden moved to the fridge, opened it, and stood there for a long moment. "On second thought, there are menus in the drawer." He motioned toward the top drawer nearest the window.

"Ordering in sounds like a plan," she said, moving to the drawer and grabbing the ones on top. "What sounds better? Bowls or pizza?"

"Normally, I'd go for something healthier, but pizza sounds damn good to me right now," he said.

"Excellent choice," she said. "I hope you like the works."

"Run it through the garden and then add the meats as far as I'm concerned," he said.

"This place actually has a meat-and-garden-lovers delight," she said.

"My favorite."

"Done," she said, then grabbed her cell and made the call. He tried to give her a credit card, but she refused to allow him to pay. When it came time to give an address, however, she handed over the phone and let him take the lead. Then she added a salad so they could pretend they were eating healthy.

"Nice touch," he said with a smile while listening to the salad order.

She winked. Being here with Camden felt like the most natural thing. Rochelle needed to shove the thought down deep. Another time. Another place. Camden was exactly the kind of person she could see herself dating.

Whoa! Dating. This was the first time she'd had a thought about picking up her life and moving on to consider her future since losing her mother.

"What's next after dinner?" she asked, rubbing her temples.

"We should probably swing by Asher's trailer to see if he's home and will answer the door for us," Camden said.

"I'm tempted to send a uniformed officer instead," she said, reasoning he might be more inclined to open the door if only to lie. If she was the one standing on the opposite side of the door, he might answer with a shotgun blast before disappearing permanently.

"Understandable, considering the man might be the person who has fired at you twice now," he admitted.

"True, but my bigger concern is how much time it will

take to drive to Asher's place and back," she reasoned. "I hate to be away from Austin and from Kage's house very long. Plus, what if Sabrina calls? What if Asher shows up at her house? We'll be too far away to make a difference."

A loud engine pulled up in front of the town house. Rochelle tensed.

"That will be my truck," Camden said with a smile and a wink.

She exhaled. Since when did every noise make her chest tighten?

Of course, staring at Camden while he winked would send anyone's pulse racing, but this wasn't the same thing. This was fear and she had no time for a reaction like that if she wanted to stay in this line of work.

Some fear was good. Fear kept her alive, told her when to panic and when to run. The kind of fear that gripped someone and didn't let go was the kind that caused mistakes—mistakes that couldn't happen in a job like hers.

Camden's town house was unfinished. There were no pictures hanging on the walls. There were no plants. In fact, there was just enough furniture to survive. The open-concept floorplan had the kitchen flowing into the dining area into the living room. There was a stairwell to the right that led to a second story, which would have the bedrooms. The floor-to-ceiling windows in the living room would let in a lot of light being south facing, except that miniblinds were closed. The kitchen had a granite island with bar chairs on one side. There was a rectangle-shaped dining table made of glass with black chairs. In the living room was a black leather sofa, love seat, and console with a flat-screen TV on top. A pair of running shoes were parked next to the front door. The living room had a rug underneath a glass coffee table.

She half expected unpacked boxes to line the walls. It would explain the lack of decorations. A stack of mail sat on one end of the table, and that was about it. The granite island had a laptop in front of one of the bar chairs.

There were enough supplies in the kitchen to make coffee and cook a simple meal based on what she'd seen so far.

"Do you want me to put on a pot of coffee?" she asked. He was old school with an actual Mr. Coffee machine instead of one of the fancier pod-type jobs. She'd been inside some homes that could run a small coffee shop out of the kitchen for how deluxe their machines were. Or should she say how extravagant their espresso bars were?

"Would you mind?" he asked as he rounded the white granite island.

"Not at all," she said, taking the opposite way toward the machine. Being close to Camden in his home felt surprisingly intimate. As much as she might be able to get used to the feeling under different circumstances, these weren't different circumstances.

Coworker. She chanted the word in her mind as she assembled everything needed to brew a pot of coffee. Turned out, Mr. Coffee machines were a lot like riding a bike.

Camden disappeared out the front door, closing it behind him.

The move shouldn't cause her stress levels to skyrocket again.

Then again, being shot at not once but twice had a way of getting under your skin. Would it interfere with her ability to conduct the investigation?

Chapter Seventeen

The truck was as good as new. Camden stepped out to speak directly with the tow-truck driver about what had happened that caused him and the Bronco driver to back away from the vehicle.

"What's the rundown?" he asked, purposely taking this one on his own. Rochelle looked like she might jump out of her skin at an unexpected noise. Okay, that analysis was probably an overkill, but he wanted to give her time to hit the reset button. He had no doubt she was a professional who could handle herself under any circumstances. He also trusted her to pull herself off the investigation if she couldn't.

In fact, he might talk to her about whether or not it was a good idea for her to take a step back, like her supervisor had suggested. This might be a good time to take a couple days of vacation to let the clock unwind.

"We found a device," the tow-truck driver began. "Needless to say, we took all precautions after to ensure everyone's safety."

"And?"

"Turns out the device was one of those trackers you can buy at a spy store," he supplied. "An amateur job but, hey, they work nonetheless."

"Which means someone decided to keep tabs on myself and the detective," Camden said.

"Looks like it," the driver agreed as he unhitched the truck. "Okay if I put it down here?"

"Yeah," Camden said but his mind was already spinning. Was a tracking device being used on Rochelle's service vehicle? Was that the reason the perp found out her home address?

A determined criminal could find out almost anything they wanted these days with all the information gathered, stored, and available on the internet. There was no accountability on how that information could be used either. Personal data was there for the taking.

"Just one device?" he asked.

"Yes, sir," the driver said as he finished and then unhooked the truck from the winch.

Good to know.

"Thank you for bringing my truck to my doorstep," Camden said.

"No problem," the driver said before offering a handshake. "I'll leave you to it, but rest assured the vehicle has been swept and is all clear."

For now.

"Much appreciated," Camden stated before locking up and heading back inside to find Rochelle sitting at the granite island. Her back was to him, but he could tell she had her cell phone out and was studying the screen. He closed and locked the front door, a habit he'd picked up since moving away from Mesa Point.

Before he got far, the doorbell buzzed. Camden circled back and checked before opening. Pizza had arrived.

He opened the door, took the box with a bag on top, and thanked the driver. The bill had already been paid, tip included, so he toed the door closed and brought dinner to the table.

"The plates are there," he said, motioning with a nod. After setting down the food, he locked the door once more and then joined Rochelle at the table. She was already putting out plates.

Rochelle retrieved coffee cups and grabbed a couple of bottled waters from the fridge, then joined him. "This pizza smells like heaven."

He liked making her smile.

"Coffee's cold," he said. "Do you want a fresh cup?"

"I'll drink it this way once I'm finished eating." She pulled another slice out of the box. He noted neither raced toward filling their plate the rest of the way with salad. "Cold coffee never bothered me."

"Same here," he said.

"What about the truck?" she asked, so he filled her in while they finished eating and then ate a few obligatory bites of salad. Then, it was back to the case. "I wish there was a way to notify Kage about his twin."

"He wasn't lying all this time about the doppelgänger," Camden said, his thoughts cycling back to the unexpected twist. "What did we decide about going to Asher's?"

Rochelle glanced toward the window. "It's dark outside. I could put on a baseball cap and keep my head down, so he won't immediately recognize me. It's probably a good time to make the drive."

"Okay then," he said. "Let's roll."

The trailer was situated on a couple acres outside the tiny little town of Buda, Texas, about twenty minutes north of Austin. Twenty minutes with no traffic. However, day or night, there was always traffic in Austin. Vehicles filled the roads.

Gravel crunched underneath tires on the dirt road leading toward the single-wide trailer, which had been blocked on the map feature of the internet.

Camden had slipped his shoulder holster back on before leaving his town house, same as Rochelle had done. He'd given her a baseball cap with the words *Gone Fishing* embossed on it, a leftover from ages ago on some fishing trip he'd taken. He couldn't remember if it belonged to his brother or his cousin, but the black cap with white lettering did little to hide Rochelle's beauty. Her long fire-red hair was pulled back in a ponytail, off her face and mostly out of sight. They might get away with the disguise if she kept her chin to her chest.

Halfway down the lane, Camden had flipped on his parking lights and cut down his headlights.

It was black as pitch outside.

Rochelle had been quiet on the ride over. Without a word, she exited the passenger side half a second after he cut off the engine, parking where the trees opened into a yard and the small trailer sat.

Camden wasn't sure what he expected to find when he got out of the Bronco. The stench of a dead body? A shed next to the trailer with female voices begging for help? But it occurred to him this was exactly the kind of place a serial killer might bring someone they'd kidnapped.

The thought was not lost on Rochelle based on the look she just gave him. Despite the fact they'd only known each other for a few days, he felt like she'd been his best friend for most of his life. As much as he didn't worry about whether or not he'd lived a past life or if he had more cycles of birth and death to endure in the future, his soul had recognized hers from some place deep. Some place that knew more about the world than him. Some place that knew more about love that him.

And some place that drew him toward her on a cellular level.

Camden shook off the thought, refocused on the task at hand.

Rochelle was a damn fine detective. But she didn't need to be one to figure out what he'd just thought about this hellhole.

Making almost no sound, Rochelle eased her service weapon out of her shoulder holster as he did the same. There was no helping the echo of the Bronco doors closing in the night, no matter how quiet they wanted them to be. Other than a cacophony of insect sounds, they were the only ones making noise. This place was out in the boonies. No cars. No highway. No strip shopping centers. If Asher had taken dating Sabrina seriously, he had to realize they wouldn't be together long if he brought her to a place like this—a place that gave off serial-killer vibes.

Camden and Rochelle walked almost side by side as they moved toward the trailer.

Neither spoke.

Camden's eyes had not quite adjusted to the blackness. There hadn't been enough time yet. He could make out general shapes once his parking lights turned off and not much else. Anyone who knew the terrain would have an upper hand. *Asher.*

As they approached the trailer, he noted the windows were blacked out. Getting close, he could see the details a little more clearly.

Before knocking on the door, they needed to clear the perimeter and investigate to see if there was an outdoor building in case his suspicions turned out to be true.

ROCHELLE STEPPED ON something that made her withdraw her foot in a heartbeat. Something—a snake?—slithered away, completely freaking her out.

She suppressed a gasp by clamping her lips shut. There was literally no time to panic right now. She couldn't afford to make a noise no matter how much she wanted to scream.

Rochelle hated snakes.

She hated pretty much every other creepy-crawly thing that went slithering around in the dark. But if she thought too much about it, she would freak herself right out. Taking a deep breath, she exhaled slowly and regained her composure.

After circling the building, she took note of the fact there was no shed or outbuilding or anything else that might be used to store equipment anywhere in the yard area on the property. Then again, that didn't mean there wasn't some type of building stashed out there in the woods.

Her body involuntarily shivered as icy fingers gripped her spine at the thought Justina Worth might have been brought here, might *still* be trapped here somewhere.

Without a warrant, Rochelle had no right to search the property. She didn't have probable cause to trespass.

In all truth, Kage could have known that he had a twin out there. The man could be toying with them, pulling an innocent act. He could be using the Asher Foley identity with women he dated. He could have a dual identity.

Anything was possible at this point. However, those assumptions were a stretch. Intuition honed by years of experience told her that Kage had been telling the truth and had disappeared in order to figure out why he was being framed for kidnapping and murder.

Justina Worth. Rochelle repeated the name several times in her head. It was moments like these when focusing on the victim gave Rochelle an extra push to keep going, keep thinking.

Justina Worth. Based on the other victims, she was being tortured at this very moment.

Justina Worth. Based on the kidnapper's pattern so far, she would be next on the chopping block.

Not on my watch. This woman deserved a fair chance to live and justice if she didn't.

Rochelle took the lead, circling the small trailer once again as she listened for any signs of someone inside.

Technically, she wasn't trespassing. She had reason to ask Asher Foley questions, giving them the right to be on his property. Dotting every *i* and crossing every *t* during an investigation ensured the best chance at a conviction. Jeopardizing the case wasn't an option.

At this point, she could see a bit more clearly as her eyes had adjusted to the darkness. She glanced toward the tree line, searching for anything that might be lurking in the shadows. Honestly, it was too far to get a good look. There was enough of a breeze to cause the branches to sway.

If not in the trailer, Asher Foley could be anywhere, and they might not see him until he got off a shot. The thought sat hard in Rochelle's thoughts as she stepped back, allowing Camden to take the lead as they approached the door. She tucked her chin to her chest to hide her face in case Asher looked out the window. There was no car parked anywhere near the trailer, so it seemed unlikely that Asher Foley was home. Except that he could have stashed his vehicle away from the trailer and then hoofed it on foot. This was his territory, and he would know the land like the back of his hand.

Camden stepped up onto concrete blocks positioned as a makeshift staircase leading to the door, and then knocked on it three times with bare knuckles. He said, "Open up.

US Marshal Camden Remington here. I need you to open the door."

Identifying themselves immediately held no room for confusion as to who was banging on the door past midnight. It was no secret guns were plentiful. A shotgun blast through the door could be sold as self-defense with a good attorney.

No answer.

Camden banged on the door once again. "Open up. Police."

Still nothing. No sign of life. Not a sound came from inside the trailer.

They waited. Minutes passed. Camden tried a third time, shouting louder this time. So much so, his voice echoed.

When it was obvious no one was going to answer the door and no screams for help came from inside, they retreated to the Bronco.

Camden turned it around, keeping the headlights off. It wasn't until they made it safely down the lane with trees blocking the view to—and from—the trailer that he turned on the Bronco's parking lights. It enabled the two of them to see around the vehicle and as much as four feet ahead.

"What do you think?" Camden asked.

"He's not here," she said. "The victims aren't being kept at the trailer, but they could be on property."

He tightened his grip on the steering wheel and cut the headlights off as they emerged onto a dirt road and out of the lane. "We don't have enough for a search warrant."

"I know," she agreed. "It's a shame because I feel like we might find answers if we could get inside that trailer." She shook her head in frustration. "Then again, he might not link his home with his crimes."

"True," he said. "I just wish I'd been smarter about how I treated Kage. He could have been useful."

"We can stake out his apartment," she offered. "Asher might have returned if he was the shooter from earlier."

Camden nodded. He didn't state the obvious. They could go to her home or put her anywhere in the open near Kage's apartment to draw Asher out. She would volunteer if she thought the idea had a snowball's chance in hell of being accepted. There was no way Camden would use her as bait.

Just then, out of the corner of her eye, she saw something. "Did you see that?"

The question might as well have been rhetorical because Camden was already pulling over to the side of the road.

Chapter Eighteen

Camden pocketed the key fob as he bolted through the trees a few steps ahead of Rochelle. Hat gone, her red hair flowed behind her as she ducked through the low-hanging tree branches.

Limbs slapped him in the face and chest as he tore through the woods in the direction of whatever had moved.

After several fruitless minutes of running, he stopped to catch his breath.

"We lost him," she said through heaves after catching up to him. "Or it. Whatever we were chasing."

"Might have been a deer for all we know." Deer weren't uncommon in these parts.

"Dammit. Dammit. Dammit. What if we were close?" she asked. And then she tensed as though she realized Asher could be hunting them. His rifle could be searching through the trees for a good shot.

Camden moved next to her to block a shot as she leaned against a tree trunk. There were too many holes in this plan to consider Rochelle to be safe right now. He couldn't block her from every angle. "This is dangerous. Let's head back to the Bronco."

"Did you remember to bring the key?" she asked.

"It's in my pocket," he said.

"Good." She held up a hand, a silent request for a few more seconds. When she could somewhat breathe normally again, she nodded. "I'm good now."

Finding the way back was going to be trickier than he realized. How long had they been running? He vaguely remembered a zigzag pattern but had no idea how much they'd zigged versus zagged.

He checked the GPS on his smart watch. *Hell. No signal.*

They could head in the opposite direction and keep moving until they found the road. The very real possibility they were walking prey right now sent his blood pressure up. He kept his gun out, ready to go in case they ran into Asher. But it was likely the movement they'd been tracking was a deer. Or another large animal. Black bears were common in these parts.

"Stay close to me, okay?" he asked despite the fact Rochelle was capable of taking care of herself. She brought out a protective instinct inside him that had been dormant far too long.

Carefully, quietly, and methodically, he moved through the woods in search of the road. He must have checked his cell phone a half dozen times for bars in twenty minutes. Nothing. To Rochelle's credit, she wasn't distressed.

"Let's try this way," she said, taking the lead. If Asher came up from behind them, she'd be safe. But, damn, she was exposed out here no matter what Camden did.

Thankfully, they both had on protective gear. Still, there were armor-piercing bullets and plenty of real estate the gear couldn't cover. Getting off a deadly shot wouldn't be as hard as Camden needed it to be under these conditions.

Much to his surprise, Rochelle found the road in a matter of minutes. The Bronco was half a football field down the road. He kept toward the tree line as they walked toward it.

Asher could be hiding on the other side of the Bronco, so he moved next to Rochelle and walked beside her. From this vantage point, he could nudge her into the trees if a shot rang out.

By the time they reached the Bronco, his stress levels were through the roof. There was no sign of Asher, so he reached for the key and clicked the button to unlock the doors. Rochelle climbed in the front seat and then he came around to the driver's side.

After taking the seat and starting the engine, it occurred to him that he hadn't remembered to lock the doors.

Turning to face Rochelle, he mouthed the words *get out* as he checked the back seat through the rearview mirror. There was no one hiding on the floorboard behind his seat, but that didn't mean they weren't led on a wild-goose chase so someone could hitch a ride without their knowledge or find the right moment to kill them both.

Rochelle did as requested, stepping away from the Bronco after abandoning her seat.

Camden came around to the back, and then tapped the button. The door slowly raised up. Keeping a safe distance, Camden led with his service weapon.

A swift kick knocked the gun out of his hands, causing it to go flying into the middle of the road. In the next second, a male figure dove at Camden as Rochelle seemed to catch on to what was happening. She came around the side of the vehicle a second too late.

Camden was on the road, wrestling for control. A large male had exploded from the back of the Bronco, diving at Camden. The two landed hard on the pavement. Was this Asher?

A blow to the ribs caused air to whoosh out of Camden's lungs, but he was able to quickly counter with a knee to the man's groin.

"Stop," Rochelle demanded. "Police."

Those words had little impact as Camden began to get the upper hand.

"Asher Foley, I'm telling you to stop right now," Rochelle commanded.

Asher's muscles tensed and then his body went limp like an exhale. "You know about him, so why are you still coming after me?"

"Kage?" Camden asked as he took advantage of the moment and seized control of the fight. He rolled on top of Kage and then pinned the man's arms together with his thighs.

"I need to see some ID," Rochelle demanded. "Tell me where I can find your wallet."

Kage was on the concrete, face down. He cursed. "I have nothing on me to prove who I am."

"I'm going to check your pockets anyway," Rochelle said as she moved closer.

Camden waved her off, then patted down Kage. "He's not lying."

"Then, how can we prove he is who he says he is?" Rochelle asked. She made a point. He had an identical twin who clearly knew Kage.

"Tell me something only Kage would know," Camden said. "Like how you feel about being a Texas Rangers fan."

"Why would I be?" Kage asked.

"Okay, then," Camden said. The response was the same one he got when he first asked Kage, word for word.

"Why are you here?" Rochelle asked, her expression still tense.

"Because I found out about my brother," he explained, sounding more than a little put off they were questioning him.

"Identical brother," Camden pointed out. Could they risk trusting a felon? Take him on his word?

"I had no idea he existed, but recent events make so much sense now," Kage stated as Rochelle retrieved and then tossed zip cuffs toward them.

Camden placed the zip cuffs on Kage's wrists and then rolled off the man. Chest still heaving as he tried to catch his breath, Camden sat on the concrete. He'd taken a fist to the ribs that made breathing hurt. He was going to have a nasty bruise. But a physical wound would heal. He couldn't say the same for the emotional scars left behind, for example, when a parent abandoned you. "You have a hell of a lot of explaining to do, Kage Durham. If that proves to be your name."

"Give me a chance," Kage said.

Camden shifted his gaze to Rochelle. She gave a slight nod in response.

Then again, what were their options? They were going to the same place whether they believed him or not. They were taking Kage back to Austin and the nearest substation off the highway, so he could be locked up while they fingerprinted him and checked the database. Even identical twins had slightly different fingerprints.

"Here's an idea," Kage began. "Let me go."

Camden almost laughed out loud. Then, he issued a grunt. "No chance in hell."

"I didn't do it," Kage responded with a mix of anger tinged with bitterness in his voice.

"A jury can decide once they're presented with the evidence," Camden stated.

Rochelle read Kage his Miranda warning from memory.

Though Kage was familiar with his rights, it still had to be done.

"Give me one good reason we should honor your request," Rochelle said in a surprising twist. Had she read his warning as a way to remind him of the stakes here? Of what he faced?

"Because we both ended up here, for one. We'll get a whole lot more done if we're both coming from different angles. And I deserve a chance to prove my innocence considering you're about to lock me up for the rest of my life."

"That's more than one reason," Rochelle said.

"I could keep going," Kage responded.

"There's no need," Rochelle said through gritted teeth. She'd been keeping a safe distance while intensely studying Kage. "And I don't take arresting someone lightly, just so you're aware."

Kage studied her. "He came after you. Didn't he?"

She blinked a couple of times, rapidly. Had she been thrown off balance by the question?

ROCHELLE TOOK A step back as though someone had thrown a physical punch. The question was simple enough. It shouldn't have thrown her off like it did.

Kage was well spoken. Astute. *A convict*, she felt the need to remind herself.

And yet for reasons she couldn't immediately identify, she wanted to trust him. Or was she just becoming that desperate to catch the bastard who'd shot at her, taken away her sense of safety, attacked her at her home?

Either way, they needed to find a reason to keep Kage with them and in cuffs without violating the man's rights. She needed to talk to Camden in private. "Can I have a word?" She nodded toward the front of the Bronco.

Camden pushed up to standing with some effort, and then followed her out of earshot from Kage.

"We can use him," she said to Camden.

"Not without his permission," Camden pointed out.

"I realize that," she said. "However, if he agrees to be a witness and cooperate, we could surprise Asher with his brother. Maybe give us some sort of advantage for the first time."

"That assumes Kage, if he is who he says he is, will be willing to cooperate with us," Camden said. "I'm not exactly his favorite person."

"Anyone in law enforcement is his enemy right now," she said. "We have mutual interest here and both parties stand to benefit. We all want Asher behind bars."

"Again, you're assuming that this isn't Asher," Camden said. He was right. She could have put on her rose-colored glasses out of desperation to save Justina in a way she hadn't been able to save her best friend years ago. Right a wrong that Rochelle had buried so deep she never thought about it again.

"What's your honest opinion? Is he telling the truth? Because a growing part of me believes he is, and if it's true then we can use him to our advantage and possibly find Victoria before it's too late." The words came rushing out.

"Victoria?"

Rochelle's hand came up to cover her gasp. "Did I say Victoria? Because I mean Justina."

Whoa!

Camden closed the distance between them and captured her hand in his. His warmth, his touch, calmed her in places she'd buried so deep she was surprised they'd ever see the light of day again. "I just don't want us to get blindsided here. I don't want him to use our desperation against us. Plus, even if he is Kage and not Asher, what are the odds that he's going to ditch us and run the second he sees an opportunity?"

Dammit, Camden was making logical sense. Was she losing perspective?

"That's why I'm asking you," she said. "I want you to be the one who makes the call because I'm afraid my objectivity has been compromised considering I've become a target and with everything going on in my personal life."

"Anyone's objectivity would be affected," he said with compassion in his beautiful eyes. "Don't be hard on yourself."

Rochelle wasn't being hard enough on herself. She was bringing personal feelings into an investigation.

"It's late," he soothed. "Let's get back to Austin and grab a few hours of sleep. Okay?"

"We can't, Camden. The clock is ticking for Justina. I can't let her down." She left out the rest of the sentence... *like I did my best friend.*

With Camden's gaze locked on to hers, the world righted itself for a moment. It was a flash, nothing more. And yet, it gave her the strength to keep going.

Rochelle had never needed anyone. This feeling should scare her instead of comfort her. Because from somewhere deep inside, she sensed that he needed her too. That rather than draining from each other, their connection was a power source that strengthened them both.

Was something special happening between them?

Because her heart said *yes* as she stared into his eyes.

"What should we do?" she asked, hearing the raspiness in her own voice.

Camden blinked a couple of times before clearing his throat. "If you want to trust him, then I say we take a risk and go for it. We won't know what we're dealing with until we do."

They would find out fast if this was the real Kage. Though, even he might jump ship at his first opportunity.

"We should ask him if he'll help us before we make any plans," she said.

Camden nodded before letting go of her hand.

The second they rounded the side of the Bronco, she froze.

Empty zip cuffs sat on the concrete. Kage was gone.

Chapter Nineteen

"He can't be far," Camden said even though Kage, or Asher, could have disappeared into the woods.

"It makes the most logical sense that he would go this way." She pointed toward the section of the woods blocked from view by the Bronco from where they'd been standing. "Or this way." She motioned down the stretch of road behind them. "We could split up to cover more ground."

Camden was already shaking his head before she finished her sentence. "I'm not losing you again." This wasn't the time to examine all the aspects in which he meant the statement. Right now, they had to focus on finding the man who'd escaped their custody. As far as Camden knew, he'd never met Asher. Kage had no reason to trust Camden or put his life in Camden's hands.

"I read his rights," Rochelle said. "How do we classify this?"

"If we call it in, Kage will be in trouble for evading arrest," Camden said.

"Meanwhile, he could be innocent." She studied the woods. The look on her face said she didn't want to go back in there under any circumstances. Plus, Asher might come home or be home, in which case they were at a disadvantage since he would know the area.

"He sure did disappear on a dime," Rochelle said.

"Only someone who knew these parts would be able to pull off a feat like that," he concluded. Then, bit out a few choice words. Wouldn't Kage have had a wallet with him? Some ID? "Not having a way to identify himself sure was convenient."

"I was just thinking the same thing," she admitted.

"We could go back to the trailer and knock on the door again."

"To what end?" she asked. "He won't answer and we might have just scared him away from the property anyway."

"Asher would have some type of vehicle stashed out here, wouldn't he?"

Rochelle issued a sharp sigh. "Makes sense to me that he would."

"Which means he'll be long gone soon," he said.

"Yes," she agreed as she bit back a yawn. "There's no reason for him to stick around. Plus, he might be headed to the location where he keeps them."

More good points.

"Let's get out of here," he said. "We could both use some sleep. We'll get back at it tomorrow once we have fresh eyes."

Camden half expected Rochelle to put up an argument against rest. However, she simply nodded and then walked toward the passenger door.

Midstride, she stopped. "Asher would have stashed a weapon nearby. He would have already shot at me."

"Let's get inside the vehicle just in case," he said, moving to her side to put his body in between her and the tree line.

He opened her door while scanning the area. It was the middle of the night at this point. And whoever had been in custody was long gone.

"I'm sorry," Rochelle said the minute he took the driver's seat and started the engine.

"For what?"

"It's my fault he got away," she said with anguish in her voice. She glanced down at hands that were folded in her lap.

"We'll get to him before…"

She sat there, quiet.

"And even if we don't, you're doing everything humanly possible to find Justina before anything else happens to her," he said. "Asher Foley is responsible for Justina. If she dies, it'll be at his hands, not yours."

"Why does it feel the opposite way?"

"You're an amazing person and a skilled detective," he said as he navigated them onto the highway. "I'd work with you any day of the week."

Still quiet.

"None of us make the right calls all the time," he continued. "At best, we hope to make the right call eighty percent of the time. A great detective probably hits around the sixty-to-seventy-percent mark."

"I appreciate what you're trying to do here, but I'm the one who asked for the conversation a little while ago," she said. Another trait of a great law-enforcement officer was taking every case personally. Except it was also the downfall, and the reason many ended up burned out and walking away from the badge at some point.

"Do you think I was irresponsible for agreeing to step away?"

"No," she said without hesitation. "Of course not."

"Then, you don't get to blame yourself either," he said.

She sat there for a few minutes contemplating those words. "It's hard not to take it personally. Every misstep. Every wrong decision."

"I know," he said.

"How do you do it?" she asked.

"What?"

She studied the patch of road in front of them. "Detach?"

"I'm probably a little too good at compartmentalizing my emotions," he admitted, realizing for the first time that he'd become a master.

"I guess it can be a hard balance to get right," she said. "We have to pull back because emotions, too often, blur logic."

"Especially when it comes to family." Camden had mastered detachment in too many areas of his life, including allowing himself to get close to anyone else. Being with Rochelle was different. She made him want to open up and spill his secrets. "I've been thinking about what you said about meeting with my mother."

"And?" She didn't seem caught off guard by the pivot.

They had a little more time to kill on the road and there wasn't anything else they could do with the investigation, so he figured he could bounce his decision off Rochelle. "I'm going to tell my brother and sister to include me."

"That's amazing, Camden." She reached over and touched his arm. Contact sent fire bolts of electricity rocketing through him even through his clothing.

"You think so?"

"I do," she said without hesitating. "If it goes badly, you'll know. You'll be able to put the past behind you and move on."

"I've been fine," he said.

"Are you sure about that?"

Rochelle had a way of cutting right to the truth. The ability caught him off guard. She was also one of the most honest people he'd ever met.

"I'm doing alright," he countered, hearing the defensiveness in his own tone.

"Okay," she said, putting up her hands, palms out, in the surrender position. "You don't have to convince me."

Camden exhaled a slow breath. "How is that we barely know each other and yet you have an ability to see right through me? You call me out on my—"

"I don't know," she said. "There's something about you. Something different. Something familiar." She shrugged. "I'm doing a terrible job of explaining it."

"Some things don't have the right words." He felt the same way. She was different than anyone he'd ever met before but familiar to him. "But I think you did a better job than you realize."

"No," she said. "I believe you just get me."

Those words hit him in the center of his chest, causing a knot to form. Because he wanted to know her beyond this case.

Would she let him in?

Could she?

ROCHELLE NORMALLY HAD a difficult time finding the right words. And yet, Camden seemed to understand her perfectly.

"Home sweet home," he said as he pulled into his garage, parked, and then cut off the engine. A second later, he was at her door, opening it for her. She loved his chivalry.

Loved?

Hold on there. She was getting ahead of herself.

Rochelle didn't do love. So she hopped out of the Bronco and headed into the town house. "All I need is a shower, a toothbrush, and a bed."

"Take the main bedroom," he said. "It's more comfortable."

"I'll do okay in the guest room," she countered.

"Trust me, you don't want to sleep on a foldout," he said. "Whereas I'm good anywhere. I'll just grab my clothes and toothbrush and be out of your hair."

The image of the two of them curled up in a king-size bed, naked and entwined, stamped her thoughts. She gave herself a mental headshake and then made a beeline for the staircase, picking up her overnight bag along the way.

Upstairs, Camden moved to the dresser before pulling out clean clothes.

"Why don't you stay and take a shower in your own bathroom?" she asked. The image of his broad naked chest assaulted her. She cleared her throat to ease the sudden dryness.

"The other one is fine," he said.

A growing part of her wanted to admit to the attraction simmering between them. Did he feel it too? The way he looked at her sometimes convinced her that he did. Would he allow himself to admit it even if it was true?

The man was the picture of professionalism. As he walked by her to leave the room, the back of his hand brushed up against her. Rochelle had never felt such an intimate moment with another person while having so many clothes on. Need welled up inside her, sending her pulse racing and warmth to settle in between her thighs.

Way to keep it professional, Paddock.

"Excuse me," she whispered, unable to find her voice.

"My fault," he responded. His gravelly voice traveled over her and through her. "I'll be across the hall if you need me."

Rochelle wasn't about to touch that statement. The best she could do under the circumstances was muster a weak smile as she made a beeline for the master bath.

Camden's hesitation didn't help matters. Need rolled off

him in palpable waves. Waves that called her toward him. She took a step backward until they were almost back-to-back. From here, she breathed in his spicy scent. It was earthy and warm.

Temptation drew her another step backward. Now, their backs touched. The man was tall, gorgeous, and pure sex.

Rochelle stood there for a long moment, allowing her senses to take him in.

She curled her free hand into a fist to stop it from reaching for him.

With a guttural groan, he summoned the strength to be the first one to walk away. Rochelle stood there, alone, listening to the sound of her frantic heartbeat as it rushed in her ears. For the first time ever, she'd been overcome with need, a need so strong it had taken over her body and soul. She should probably be very afraid of its power and yet she was drawn to it instead. She *wanted* to be as close to Camden as she physically could.

The fact both surprised her and reassured her because she didn't believe anyone could make her feel that way.

Had she been protecting her heart? Refusing to let anyone in? Reminding herself on an almost constant basis that she didn't need anyone else?

Rochelle had no intention of standing there allowing those questions to dominate her thoughts. She was tired. She needed a shower. She needed to go to bed. If only to wake up with a fresh start, find Asher Foley, and then put this case behind her.

Could she do the same with Camden?

Chapter Twenty

Camden didn't sleep a wink. He'd tried. Thoughts of Rochelle invaded his thoughts all night, causing him to toss and turn until he threw off the covers and put on a pot of coffee. Focusing on the case should have been the distraction he needed.

Rochelle was different. She made him feel different. More alive than he'd ever been. She made him want to rethink his position on being single in favor of putting down roots and starting a family.

How wild was that for a person who didn't do long-term?

He shook off his reverie as Rochelle bounded down the stairs. She wore an old AC/DC concert T-shirt that fell midthigh, revealing the silky skin of her thighs.

"Coffee?" he asked with half a smile, amused at himself. Self-discipline and focus had never been problems for him. Until her.

"Please," she said.

"What do you like to eat for breakfast?"

"I'm good with pretty much anything," she said. "But I'd do anything for a bagel right now."

Camden cleared his throat.

He poured a fresh cup of coffee and then handed it over before popping bagels in the toaster. "I have cream cheese and…"

"Jelly?"

"As a matter of fact, I do," he said. After pulling together the ingredients, he set everything on the granite island along with a butter knife.

Another ten minutes passed, and plates were rinsed and in the dishwasher.

"Where do we go today?" she asked.

"Good question," Camden said, biting back a yawn.

"Did you sleep?"

"Not much," he admitted. Between thinking about Rochelle, lack of progress on his grandmother's condition, and the case, he doubted he'd get quality sleep anytime soon.

"Any update on your grandmother?" she asked.

"No improvement," he said, which was a bad sign. "My brother, sister, and I decided to meet my mother at the hospital as soon as this case is over. They're setting it up."

"That's good," she said, hopeful. "If you need moral support, you can always call me. I'd like to stay in touch after the case is over."

"Okay then," he said. Friendship was better than nothing. Besides, what else did he have to offer? Nothing she would be willing to take. She deserved better than *let's hang out and see what happens.*

Camden shook off the thoughts and refocused.

"Oh. I almost forgot to mention the ballistics report came back. The bullets match. The same person who shot at me at my house tried again at Kage's apartment."

"I was just about to suggest we go back to Kage's place," he said. "Maybe that's not such a good idea after all."

"What other choice do we have?" she asked, a hint of desperation in her voice.

"It might be best to work the case from here," he said. "Have the higher-ups send someone else to stake out Kage's apartment while we go over the details of the case. We have to be missing something else."

"Kage is in danger as long as Asher is out there running free," she pointed out.

"I know," he agreed. "We could go back to the trailer. See if we can get a warrant to search the place."

"My supervisor would insist we bring uniformed officers with us," she said.

"I can tap into county resources since the trailer isn't in Austin," he offered. "See if my boss can put together a quick task force."

"Sounds like a plan," she said.

Considering the fact she'd been shot at twice, they should be able to get a search warrant now that they could connect Asher Foley to the cases.

Could they get there in time to find Justina alive?

Both busied themselves on the phone and updating reports on computers. An hour passed, and then two before they agreed to get dressed and meet down in the kitchen in half an hour.

True to her word, Rochelle came downstairs at a half hour on the dot. Camden was already downstairs, waiting, drinking a second cup of coffee. After sliding into their shoulder holsters, they were out in the Bronco in a matter of minutes.

Even with her fiery locks pulled into a ponytail off her face, she was gorgeous. There was no hiding a beauty like hers, the kind that came from the inside out.

"We'll meet the team on the drive, parking in a line," he said. "The sheriff is sending two deputies."

"My supervisor is sending a pair of uniformed officers, which should be a big help," she said. "One will be carrying a search warrant."

All in all, they would have a team of six. Not bad. That

should give them good coverage around the trailer while others could watch the property. Depending on what they found inside, they could fan out and search the property. Drones were a huge help in cases like these. They could help cover more ground literally from the air, allowing them to scan greater distances in search of outbuildings or sheds on expanses of land.

Rochelle was a capable detective. More than capable. She was a damn fine law-enforcement officer. And yet, he wished there was a way to convince her to step aside on this one. She'd become a target. If anything happened to her on his watch...

He couldn't let himself go there. Not even hypothetically.

By the time he pulled onto the gravel lane, two SUVs were already parked in front of him. One belonged to a deputy. The other to someone from Austin PD.

"They sent Benny," she said as Camden parked. "Officer Collin Bennett as he's known to everyone."

He cut off the engine.

"I'll introduce the two of you," she offered with a little more pep in her voice than he liked. The way she smiled when she waved at Benny sat like a hot poker in his stomach. *Jealous much, Remington?*

"In a minute," he said before exiting the vehicle. Before he could get around to open her door, Benny was there. *Cool.*

Camden nodded and then kept walking to meet up with the deputy who'd parked and was in his vehicle. A quick glance back at Benny's ring finger didn't reveal a gold band. Camden needed to check his attraction to Rochelle. She might already be spoken for.

Why did that gut him?

ROCHELLE WATCHED CAMDEN a few seconds too long as he walked away based on the way Benny stared at her.

"Earth to Rochelle," he said as he snapped a finger in the air.

"Hey, sorry," she said before giving Benny a quick hug. "Don't mind me. I didn't get much sleep last night and it's been hell on wheels lately."

"I heard a rumor someone is using you as target practice," Benny said. He was six feet tall with a runner's build. Most would consider the sandy-blond-haired officer good-looking. He had a personality to boot. But Camden was more Rochelle's type.

"Yeah, it's not fun."

"Do you want to crash at my place?" he asked.

"I have it under control," she said, not wanting to admit that she stayed with Camden last night and wanted to do the same tonight if the offer stood.

"You call me if anything changes," Benny said.

"You'd be the first on my list," she said with a smile. He'd always been a good friend. Ever since going through the academy together.

"I read the report about what we're about to walk into," Benny said, the jovial quality gone as he shifted gears into law-enforcement mode. "Or should I say possibly about to walk into?"

"This is the home of Asher Foley," she said. "But I doubt he keeps the victims here if he's our guy."

"Is there any doubt about him being the perp?" Benny asked.

"Not in my mind," she said. "The evidence is too strong against him."

"Except that he has a twin brother," Benny said. "I did some digging and found out the mother dropped the other twin off at a fire station." He shook his head. "Pretty cold-hearted if you ask me."

"I don't know how you would pick which twin to keep," Rochelle said. Motherhood had never been something she'd craved. Except an image of Camden holding their infant had crept into her thoughts. It was projection, she decided. Nothing more. "Maybe there'll be something inside that can tell us more about what makes Asher tick."

"I hope so," Benny said. "Losing you isn't an option." As he said those last words, Camden came walking up. He introduced himself. His tense expression reminded her of the danger they were in just by standing out in the open.

After Camden and Benny shook hands, Camden said, "The others are almost here. We can wait or we can deliver this warrant and let them catch up."

"There's four of us here," she said. "That should be enough to knock on a door."

The probability that Asher would answer was low. He most likely wasn't home. He could be anywhere.

"Oh, one more thing," Benny said. "Foley's mother died of cirrhosis of the liver five years ago."

"Alcoholic?" Rochelle asked, since it was the most common reason for the disease.

"Sissy Foley was in and out of jail for prostitution and drug possession," Benny said.

"Doesn't sound like someone who paid attention to her child," Rochelle stated. "Let's go see what kind of mess she left behind."

The morning sun beat down on Rochelle's face despite the cool breeze. The sun in Texas was as relentless as the heat that accompanied it. Nerves on edge, she headed toward the door. Camden walked in front of her while Benny came up from behind. The fact she was being sandwiched by two tall, broad people wasn't lost on her. They were forming a protective barrier in case the shooter took aim.

As much as she could hold her own, arguing with these two stubborn people would only waste precious time. Since they'd been here for more than fifteen minutes already, any residents of the trailer would be alerted to their presence.

Camden knocked on the door. No answer. He demanded anyone inside should open the door and then identified himself.

The second round of knocks came with the warning they were about to enter the residence with or without permission.

One last look at everyone gathered around the door was all Camden needed before trying the door handle. Locked. He stepped aside as an officer brought forth a battering ram. With one thrust, the door split open.

The next couple of seconds happened in a flurry of coordinated activity. All four law-enforcement officers rushed in as a pair joined them from behind. Everyone fanned out, weapons drawn.

Stench from stacked pizza boxes and dirty dishes in the sink hit full force as Rochelle stepped inside the dwelling. The brown carpet was a relic from the seventies. There was an equally old brown-and-yellow checkered sofa sitting four feet from a flat-screen TV on a console. A TV tray was positioned as a makeshift coffee table.

In the kitchen, there was a broken-down oak table and pair of chairs in equally bad shape. Not that it was used for eating. Stacks of pizza boxes with flies buzzing around them filled the round table.

After scanning the living room and kitchen, Camden signaled for a set of officers to take the hallway to the right, where typically there would be two small bedrooms and a bath. He led Rochelle and a uniform across the kitchen into the adjoining master suite.

Flies buzzed around, scattering as the trio blazed through the kitchen.

"What the hell?" Camden muttered as he entered the bedroom. He immediately headed toward the closet and then the bathroom as Rochelle cleared the bedroom. Instead of a bed, there was a twin-size mattress on the floor pushed up against one wall. On the other side of the room was an old desk that was propped up on one of the legs with old magazines. A ragged baby doll was on the floor. A blown-up picture of a woman that had been used as target practice with darts was taped to one wall. Darts littered the nasty, beer-stained carpet.

The wall above the desk was covered with taped photographs of…

Rochelle moved closer to get a better look. Kage?

Had to be.

"Is that what I think it is?" Camden asked as he cut across the room to join her.

"Kage walking into the Laundromat," Rochelle said. "Kage walking into the nightclub."

"Asher has been stalking his twin," Camden said. "Why?"

"They were separated at birth and the mother kept Asher," Rochelle said. "Benny said Kage was dropped off at a fire station."

Camden studied the battered picture of the woman on the wall next to them. "I'm guessing this is Sissy."

"Hey," an officer from the opposite side of the trailer called out. "You gotta see this."

There was more? Rochelle took a deep breath—a mistake, given the stench—and turned toward the kitchen.

What else waited for them?

Chapter Twenty-One

As Rochelle crossed the kitchen, she saw movement out of the corner of her eye in the backyard along a patch of trees. A flash of red caught her attention. She froze as she realized what was happening. "Camden."

He doubled back, walking toward her in a couple of quick strides. "What is it?"

As he looked out the window, the first flame was lit.

"Everyone out!" he shouted. But the flame spread in a matter of seconds.

"Gasoline," she said as she searched for a fire extinguisher or anything they could use to break through the fire circling the trailer.

"Shirts up over your nose," Camden said as everyone gathered.

"The twisted bastard has a mannequin with a blond wig that he's been pounding with a hammer," one of the officers said.

"He wants the evidence to go up in flames," Rochelle stated as she bolted toward the front door. "We have to make a run for it."

Before she could say another word, Camden and Benny were to either side of her. A bonus for this perp would be to kill her in the process of wiping out evidence.

Then what?

Didn't Asher Foley realize he would be on the most-wanted list for the rest of his life after killing six law-enforcement officers from multiple agencies? Then again, maybe he didn't care.

As the trio emerged, a shot rang out.

Camden pulled her back inside. They ran to the back door instead, and then bolted outside. "Stay close to me."

The rest scattered.

One of the officers jumped the fire and then rolled onto the scrub brush to put out the flames. Others followed suit after finding a spot. One by one, they went for it. As someone made it across, they rolled to put out any flames and then pulled their weapons so they would be ready in case shot at or attacked.

Smoke filled the air, whipping around in the wind. Rochelle lost sight of Camden in the flurry of activity. Rather than wait, she saw an opportunity and then went for it.

The jump took all of two seconds as flames licked at her. She immediately dropped and rolled just to be safe. A fireproof vest covered her chest, but the rest of her body was exposed. In the melee, she lost a shoe but that wasn't important right now.

Where was Camden?

She had to know he'd made it across safely. She scanned the area, still sitting on her bottom after making sure all the flames were out. Shock kept her left hand from hurting despite the burn marks. In the jump, she'd rolled her ankle, but she was otherwise okay.

"Rochelle," Camden called out.

Rather than give away her location, she moved toward the sound of his voice. Hopping on a shoeless foot, she landed on a thorny stick, lost her balance, and smacked the hard dirt once again.

"Hey," a familiar voice whispered from behind her. She immediately shifted her attention toward Kage. "Let me help you get out of here."

"Camden," she said through a wince as she tried to stand up, keeping her weapon aimed at Kage.

His hands came up, palms out. "Don't shoot. I'm here to help."

"You disappeared on us," she stated.

"Because you tried to arrest me," he said with disdain. "Remember?"

She nodded.

"Don't let my brother kill you," Kage pleaded. "He's done enough damage already."

Reluctantly, Rochelle waved him over to help her, lowering her weapon but keeping it at the ready.

"I'll come back for Camden," he promised. "Just come with me before you end up shot."

Could she trust this person?

Did she have a choice? She could shout for Camden and give away her location to Asher, or she could go with Kage and let him bring Camden to her.

On a sharp sigh, she took the hand being offered.

"Lean against me," Kage said. Up close, she studied his features. How would she know if this was Asher?

Rochelle leaned against the man she believed to be Kage. There was something in his eyes that made her trust him. A raw honesty that she'd noted from the first time they'd knocked on his door in what felt like ages ago. Funny how time had a way of speeding up or slowing down based on perception.

Kage—at least she hoped so—led her deeper into the woods, where he'd set up a makeshift shelter that blended into the woods. "You should be safe here while I go get your partner."

She climbed into the shelter and turned around, gun at the ready and pointed just to Kage's left. A moment of hesitation could mean the difference between life and death. Kage had helped her to safety. Would Asher do that? To what end?

The answer came quickly. To taunt Camden and torture her.

"I'll whistle so you know it's me," Kage said, drawing her attention back to him. He demonstrated a tune.

"Got it," she said, wincing as the pain in her foot hit full force. She leaned forward and picked a tiny stick out of the tender part of her arch. As she withdrew her hand, she saw blood. "I'm not exactly going anywhere. Find Camden and bring him to me."

Kage—at least she believed it was him—nodded before disappearing.

The makeshift shelter would keep animals from reaching her. The other predator wouldn't be so easily detoured. Asher was out there, searching. Was it too late for Justina?

Should Rochelle move to a different location in case this was Asher and not Kage?

Logic kicked in. Wouldn't Asher have attempted to kidnap her by now? Why would he leave? He had her in his grasp. She was in a vulnerable position, injured. He could have made a move on her already.

What if Asher got to Kage? The innocent man could be injured or dead at this point. The secret whistle had been a good idea because she wouldn't know which one of them turned up based on looks. Kage had on a blue flannel shirt and jeans. He also wore brown boots. She repeated the description a couple of times in her mind to ensure it stuck. Memory was a tricky thing during stressful times.

It dawned on her that she hadn't checked her cell. She fished it out of her pocket and checked to see if she had bars. There was no service out here, as she'd feared. The remote location was likely the reason she hadn't thought to check before. Somewhere in the back of her mind, she remembered how difficult it had been to get bars the last night.

The sound of sirens echoed into the woods. Fire trucks? More law enforcement?

It was possible Asher had already been apprehended. Kage too. He would be detained for questioning if not arrested in his brother's place. Without ID, there was no way to prove his identity.

Should she sit tight? Or head back toward the trailer?

On balance, sitting here and doing nothing proved more stressful. Rochelle decided to make the walk back. She might be slow considering all she had to work with was a rolled ankle and a shoeless foot to stand on.

She could take her time, and check for cell coverage along the way. In her experience, even remote locations had spots of connectivity. Camden would be worried sick by now if Kage hadn't delivered the message she was okay and hidden in the woods.

The blaze could be seen from this distance. The air filled with the smell of burning rubber, which meant the fire had reached the trailer. The taste of steam and sulfur sat on her tongue as she lifted her shirt over her mouth and nose to filter the smoke.

At her present location, she was downwind, so she headed east in a zigzag pattern toward the activity.

By the time she limped back to the scene, a flurry of activity was going on between attempting to put out the fire, to law enforcement either being attended to by EMTs or searching the area. She scanned the faces, needing to find Camden.

The burn on the back of her left hand hurt. As she made it to the yard, an EMT immediately looked up and then stopped what he was doing to run toward her. Based on his reaction, she must look like hell.

None of that mattered. Because she was desperate to see Camden's face again and know that he was okay.

"Where is Marshal Remington?" she asked as the EMT with a name badge that read JT stopped her.

"I'm more concerned about you right now," JT said as she kept limping past him. "Ma'am. I need to examine you. Okay?"

Rochelle didn't realize how much of her strength had been drained just walking back to the site. Her gaze locked on to Benny. The second he saw her, she waved him over.

Benny came running as the EMT helped her sit down and lean against a tree trunk.

"Where's Camden?" she immediately asked her friend.

Benny blanked. "I don't know. I thought he was with you."

"No," she said, reaching for JT's arm so she could pull herself up to standing. Her burned hand gave out and she landed on her backside. Hard. "Find him. Please."

"Stay here," Benny said, holding his hands out to stop her from getting up. "I'll see what I can do."

"I have something for that burn," JT said before reaching into his bag. He pulled out a jar of white cream and then slathered it on the burn.

"That's better," she said, surprised by the miracle in the jar.

"Let me wrap it so the salve stays," JT urged as she scanned the area. At least she was out of the smoke.

She gave a slight nod for JT to keep going.

"What happened to your shoe?" he asked after finishing up with the burn.

"Lost it during the jump," she said.

"You're cut up pretty decently," JT said, examining the bottom of her foot next.

"Do you have a boot in that bag?" she asked.

His eyebrows furrowed in confusion.

"I rolled my other ankle," she said.

"As a matter of fact." JT held up a finger to indicate he'd be right back. He ran to the ambulance and was back in a flash. He held up a boot. "This should stabilize that ankle and make getting around easier. For the swelling, you'll have to elevate it above your heart."

"Okay," she said to appease JT. The minute he cleared her, she intended to find Camden. With every passing minute Benny was gone, her stress levels heightened.

Where are you, Camden?

CAMDEN CAUGHT SIGHT of a male in a black hoodie and matching joggers running into the woods. Asher?

He didn't have time to hesitate if he was going to keep Hoodie in sight and he couldn't risk losing the man if this was Asher. At this point, it could be Kage, for all Camden knew. He'd been in the area last night, in this exact location. Was he still here? Hiding? Trying to find answers for himself? Or evidence to prove he wasn't the one responsible for the kidnappings and murders?

Guilt for being wrong about Kage struck like a physical blow. Guilt for letting Rochelle down nailed him. And guilt for being terrible to the folks who'd been kind enough to bring him up slammed into him.

Hoodie was nothing more than a dot weaving through

the trees at this point. He was too far away to catch. Camden's lungs burned from inhaling smoke. He couldn't get a deep enough breath to fuel him. His thighs screamed for relief as he continued to push.

This had to be Asher unless Kage had memorized the terrain.

The dot suddenly disappeared. Was there a ravine up ahead? A splash echoed.

Camden cursed, pushing a little harder. Pumping his arms like a track star, he managed to increase his speed.

By the time he reached the bank, Hoodie was nowhere to be found. The deep creek snaked through trees that blocked his view downstream.

Chasing Hoodie turned out to be a lost cause. At least Rochelle was safe back at the trailer. It dawned on him that he hadn't actually seen her again after she'd jumped across the flames. His opportunity to do the same came seconds too late to make eye contact with her on the other side.

She was safe. Right?

Dammit. Camden doubled back. He'd been running for a long time and could no longer see any signs of the fire through the canopy. By this point, he hoped the blaze had been put out and emergency crews had arrived.

A quick check on his cell revealed no coverage out here. He'd expected no less but it was always good to be certain. His GPS wouldn't work either. He couldn't be one-hundred-percent certain this was the same trail he'd taken a few moments ago. Was he going in the right direction? Was he lost?

A twig snapped. Camden whirled around. A thought struck.

Was he lost or being hunted?

Chapter Twenty-Two

An hour passed without any sign of Camden. The fire had long since been put out. Yellow crime-scene tape cordoned off the trailer. Benny had found and returned Rochelle's shoe. Her foot was tender to walk on, but JT had done an amazing job with the bandages. Now that she had a boot on her left ankle, she could put weight on that foot again.

"He had to be in the woods somewhere," she said to Benny. "I'm going in."

Benny's face morphed into concern. "Absolutely not. I won't allow it."

"Seriously?" she asked. "You know how well I operate when I'm told I can't do something." She hadn't moved up the ranks and made detective before age thirty because it had been easy. In fact, everyone told her to slow down. She had time. Rochelle realized early on after losing her best friend that time was guaranteed to no one. She was also beginning to realize just how much that loss had impacted her from an early age. Kept her from opening up to anyone. Kept her from letting herself fall in love.

Now?

Her strong feelings for Camden both scared and reassured her. At the very least, she was learning that she was, in fact, capable of falling in love.

"I do know how you are," Benny said. And then he looked at her with the most lost look she'd ever seen. "Why couldn't it have been me?"

"What?" She was genuinely confused by the statement from her best work bud.

"The way you look at him," Benny said before stopping himself. "Never mind. We're friends, right? It's best that way."

She caught his gaze and studied him for a long moment. "I used to have feelings for you." Not like the way she felt with Camden but it was the closest she'd ever come.

"When?" He seemed genuinely shocked by the admission.

"We were in the academy," she said.

"I was living with Lori back then," he said. Realization dawned. His eyes widened.

"Being best buds kept us close," she admitted. "Eventually, those feelings went away and turned into a brother-sister kind of love. But I do love you."

He wrapped an arm around her and offered a wistful smile. "The ship sailed, and I didn't even know it was in the harbor."

"Something like that," she said, giving him a jovial elbow jab. "This way, we stay in each other's lives forever. It seemed like a good compromise."

"I can't imagine a life without you in it," he said. "Let's go find him."

"You'd come with me?" she asked.

"It's what best buds do for each other, right?"

Rochelle smiled back. "I think so."

"Then let's go." With that, Benny started toward the tree line.

"While we have cell coverage, we should let our supervisor know what we're going to do," she said, pulling hers out and then firing off a text.

"I can do better than that," Benny said. He rallied three other officers who were either fresh on the scene or not badly injured. After a quick update, they all spread out with one task: find their own.

"Thank you," Rochelle said to Benny as they entered the woods. "Kage was here. He took me to safety. It's possible he found Camden too."

"Can you find the spot again?" Benny asked.

She hoped like hell she could. Camden's life might depend on it. "This way."

Rochelle led Benny around in circles for a solid hour. There was no communication possible between them and the others. Camden might already be back at the trailer, safe. Meanwhile, she'd gotten lost in the woods. Hunger pangs nailed her but she doubted she could eat a bite even if she stood in front of a buffet of her favorite foods. Acid churned in her stomach as her chest squeezed.

Not only did she have to find Camden, but she also needed to locate Asher if they were going to have a prayer of finding Justina and the latest missing person. Rochelle bit back the urge to scream when she recognized a tree they'd pass four times already.

"We're going in circles," she said along with a few choice words.

"I noticed," Benny responded, calm as usual.

"We'll never find Camden at this rate," she said.

"Maybe he'll find us." Benny was always reasonable.

Emotions didn't normally get the best of Rochelle, so it caught her off guard that hers were the equivalent of a runaway train.

At least they had plenty of daylight to work with. This time of year, the sun would set early, but they should have a lot of day left. *This time of year. Hell's bells.* "What day is it?"

"Thursday," Benny answered.

"Thanksgiving?" she asked but the question didn't need answering.

"I believe you are correct," Benny said. It was easy to lose track of upcoming holidays now that both her parents were gone. Her mother would have been sending texts all week, asking what Rochelle liked better this year, pecan or apple pie. Their holidays had been small with the three of them, and then down to two, but their traditions meant everything to Rochelle. An ache formed in her stomach.

"This is your first year without your mother," Benny said, catching on.

"It's fine," she said, trying to shake off the onslaught of emotions. Tears welled in her eyes, blurring her vision. One broke free and spilled down her cheek. She turned her face away and sniffled. No way was she letting Benny see her weak side.

And then she saw it.

"This way," she said, making a beeline in the woods toward the stack of limbs that had been made into a makeshift shelter. And then she realized someone might be waiting inside. She froze, putting an arm out to stop Benny from going past her. From this vantage point, it was impossible to see inside.

Had she been too noisy? Spoken too loudly?

If someone was hiding inside, they would have been alerted to Rochelle and Benny's presence. The mistake could cost them dearly.

"Hold on," she whispered. "My mistake. We have to go back." She said those last words out loud and then tromped on the ground, marching in place. She locked gazes with Benny to make certain he realized what she was doing.

Benny gave a slight nod. He didn't move. She didn't move. They waited for what felt like an eternity but was probably less than five minutes. And then, Rochelle tiptoed best as she could with the boot on toward the back of the shelter. Light peeked inside through the cracks.

If someone heard them, they could be watching as they neared the makeshift structure. Could she risk Benny's life if this went south?

Asking him to step back or stay away wasn't an option. Benny would laugh at her and keep moving. She would do the exact same.

A twig broke from somewhere behind them.

"Gotcha!" the familiar voice said. *Asher.*

CAMDEN SAT TIGHT as his muscles pulled taut. He'd been circling around the woods, lost, for hours at this point. Before he knew it, night would fall. It got dark in these parts early this time of year. Tree coverage would shield evening sun, which meant he only had a few hours left to figure out how to get the hell out of here.

He'd given up on finding Asher despite the feeling of eyes on him for longer than he cared to admit. The feeling of being watched had subsided roughly thirty minutes ago. Had the predator gone on to find new prey? Realized Rochelle wasn't with Camden or that he couldn't lead Asher to her?

From a distance, he heard the crunch of footsteps on the branches that littered the ground. Camden crouched down low, making himself as small as possible as he tried to pinpoint the exact direction the noise came from.

At his height, blending into his natural surroundings might be a stretch, so he moved to the largest tree trunk he could find. Then, he listened.

More footsteps, and they were coming closer.

Camden didn't so much as breathe as the sound neared. There were deer in this part of the county, so he might be panicked for nothing. Weapon out, he waited until the noise-maker was roughly fifteen feet away before coming around the tree with his weapon aimed directly at the sound.

The second he moved around enough to see, he lowered his weapon and identified himself.

"You're the person I'm out here searching for," the deputy said after identifying himself as Deputy Lee. The tall Asian deputy took in a deep breath. "A law-enforcement officer on site formed a search party for you."

"What was her name?" Camden asked.

Deputy Lee shot a confused look as he joined Camden and checked his phone. "No service, which means I can't let the others know that I've located you."

"The officer?" Camden asked, circling back to his question.

"Officer Bennett," the deputy replied without looking up.

"There was a female detective on the scene," Camden persisted.

"That's right," Deputy Lee said as he lifted his gaze from the screen. "Detective Paddock. She's with Bennett."

"She's safe?" Camden asked.

"I saw an EMT attending to her on scene, but she refused to go to the hospital," Deputy Lee stated.

"Where is she now?" Camden asked.

Deputy Lee waved a hand. "Out here somewhere searching for you."

Camden couldn't be angry at Rochelle, considering she was attempting to save his life. She was the type of person who rolled up her sleeves and went to work when she thought someone needed her, ignoring her own pain and risking her own life in the process.

"I haven't had any cell service," Camden said. "What about you?"

Deputy Lee checked his cell. "Same here." He glanced around. "Should we head back—"

Camden was shaking his head before the deputy finished his sentence. "I'm not leaving these woods without her."

"What if she's waiting for you at the crime scene?" Lee asked.

"She won't go back without me," he said.

Deputy Lee stood there for a moment.

"It's not in her nature to leave a job unfinished." Camden felt the need to clarify their relationship.

"She would make a good marine," Lee said with a nod. His tight-clipped haircut had tipped off Camden to the fact Lee might have served in the military. He thanked the deputy for his service.

"You're welcome," Lee said with a proud smile.

"You can head back and tell the others you found me," he said, realizing the deputy might not want to keep going in the woods. "Stay at the crime scene."

"Can't do that," Lee said.

From somewhere to their left, the crack of a bullet sounded.

In the next second, Camden was on the ground. His head was two inches from a tree trunk. He'd dove on top of Lee, who grunted as he hit the hard earth. Lee cursed.

Camden rolled off him, staying on the ground. He glanced down at the red dot on his shirt. Blood.

A moment of panic seized him as he checked his body for bullet fragments, but found none. And then it dawned on him as he glanced over at Lee. His gaze was fixed on the side of his hip just above the waistband of his pants. He pulled out a tucked shirt to reveal he'd been hit just below his body armor.

Weapon drawn, Camden moved to block the shooter from taking another shot. Crouched on his heels, he asked, "What does it look like?"

"I'm losing blood," Lee said, shock in his voice.

Camden tore off a piece of his undershirt. "Use this to put pressure on the wound until help arrives."

"Out here?" Lee said, taking the offering as Camden resumed a defensive position.

"We aren't alone," Camden pointed out. "Someone will have heard the shot. You said there's a search team."

"I did," Lee said as he grunted again.

"Everyone will descend on this area," Camden said. "It won't be long before the cavalry arrives. Hang tight, okay?"

"No choice."

"You're going to be fine," Camden said with authority.

"No choice there either. Got a wife and six-year-old kid depending on me to walk through the door every night," Lee said matter-of-factly.

"And that's exactly what you're going to do," Camden reassured him. The bleeding was manageable if Lee kept pressure on the wound. The problem wasn't the bullet fragment.

Asher had fired at two law-enforcement officers—three, counting Rochelle.

The dart-filled picture of his mother that was hanging on the bedroom wall spoke volumes about his mental condition. He'd snapped in the past few weeks. And now, Camden needed to figure out a way out of the woods while keeping a wounded man from bleeding out. Help might be on the way.

Camden had learned never to count on someone else showing up to save the day. He'd been lucky once when Ace jumped in front of a moving vehicle to knock Camden out of the way.

Had his luck run out?

Chapter Twenty-Three

"We're losing track of the area where the shot was fired," Rochelle said to Benny.

"At least we stopped moving in circles," he said. "I haven't seen anything familiar in the last five minutes since we started heading this way."

They'd began moving in the direction of the gun blast seconds after hearing it. Rochelle couldn't go in her mind to a situation where Camden was lying in a ravine somewhere. She couldn't let herself believe he was gone before she got a chance to tell him how she really felt. It would be a shame to have to hold that in for the rest of her life.

The thought of losing another person she loved pierced her in the center of her chest.

Those thoughts, looping around in her head, fueled her to keep moving despite the pain in the bottom of her right foot. At least the boot gave her more mobility. Either way, she was making a beeline toward the sound.

She was keenly aware of the fact she had to be careful not to make too much noise as they neared the area where Asher Foley had to be. It had to be him. They were close. Lives beyond Camden's were still on the line. At least she prayed Justina was still alive.

Deep breaths.

Moving swiftly through the woods as branches slapped at her face, she realized the sun was beginning its descent. Night would fall soon, making finding anyone or a way out even more difficult.

Dammit.

Not to mention, they'd been in the woods for what felt like hours without running into anyone else.

Rochelle stopped. "Are we even on the right track anymore?"

Benny shook his head. "I have no idea."

And then she heard a noise. An animal?

"Did you hear that?" she asked, but Benny had already turned toward the sound. The trees were thick in this area, but light peeked in ten yards away. "Over there." She turned toward the light and aimed her weapon as she methodically stepped toward the noise. If it was, in fact, a wounded animal, she would do the right thing and put it out of its misery if there was no way to save it.

If this was some kind of trick to catch her off guard, she would deal with that too. Heart pounding, she made it to the small clearing.

The noises intensified. But this time, she recognized them as human.

"Cover me," she said to Benny as she focused on finding the source. Walking straight into the light, she stepped on a wood plank.

Rochelle looked down. "I found something."

Benny kept his gaze focused on skimming the area for any signs of movement while she checked for a trap. She found a trapdoor instead with a small gym lock on it.

"Hello?" she said into the slats. "Is there anyone down there?" She identified herself as law enforcement as muffled wails came from the other side of that door.

She crouched down beside the door and checked the lock. "I need something to break this open."

Benny bent down while keeping focus on the woods, ran his hand along the ground until he found a rock and tossed it over. "It isn't much."

"Might work, though," she said, using the rock to slam into the cheap device. The sounds from below intensified. "I'm not here to hurt you," she reassured. "We're here to get you out."

There was more than one person down here. The thought she might have just found Justina gave her even more resolve to break this lock and get the people below to safety. She had no idea what condition either person would be in, so she steeled herself as she smashed the rock a third time. Turned out, three was her lucky number.

Immediately, she pulled the metal hood off the door lock. And then, she opened the door. The stench of urine and sweat slammed into her full force as she lifted the wooden barrier. Light filled the eight-foot-deep concrete hole.

Two women.

"Justina, I'm going to get you out of here and to safety, okay," she reassured the women, who clung to each other as though for dear life. Dirty, tear-soaked faces stared up at her, drawing back from the light as though their eyes couldn't take it.

Arms and legs bound, mouths gagged, they couldn't make the climb as they sat huddled together. They looked weak, pitiful, but they were alive. They were safe.

Lifting them wasn't an option for Rochelle. "Let's trade places, Benny. You're going to have to pull them out. I can't."

Rochelle stood up in time to see a figure dart behind a tree. She bit back a curse. Asher? He was the only one who would hide.

"Did you see that?" she asked Benny.

"I sure did," he stated, moving to a nearby tree trunk to put some mass in between him and person hiding.

"It's Kage," the person shouted.

What the hell?

"Step out from behind the tree and let me see you, hands up," Rochelle demanded, moving to a tree on the opposite side of the door. She and Benny exchanged a look that said they weren't moving. These ladies deserved protection, and Rochelle would have to be forcibly removed from this sight before she would willingly abandon them. "Hang in there," she said to them, hoping it was enough reassurance to tide them over.

"Don't shoot," he said.

From this distance, it looked like Kage. Sounded like Kage. But he had an identical twin.

"How do I know it's you?" she asked out of desperation.

"We've been down this road before," he said, and then whistled the tune.

He was wearing a blue flannel shirt and jeans earlier. This was Kage.

"Come toward us but keep your hands where we can see them," she said. At this point, she had to risk trusting him. She turned toward Benny while keeping her gaze fixed on the man walking toward them. "Help the ladies, please."

"Okay," Benny said as he went to work.

She had no idea how the ladies would react to seeing a man. "My partner is going to help you out of here. I trust him and you can too."

Kage approached as Benny struggled.

"Let me help," Kage said.

"No," Rochelle stated. "I need you to keep watch for your brother while I do it."

He shot her a look.

"A man who looks just like you kidnapped these ladies," she said to Kage. "I have no idea how they'll react to seeing your face."

His lips formed a thin, angry line but he nodded. It must be hell to be in his position. The man deserved sympathy.

Right now, though, she needed to focus on saving the ladies.

The minute her face came into view, both ladies relaxed a little bit.

"I'm going to have to jump in with you in order to hoist you up to my partner, okay?" Benny asked.

Two pairs of frightened eyes shifted to Rochelle.

"It's okay," Rochelle reassured. "He'll help you."

When they gave the okay, Benny jumped down and quickly removed their mouth coverings. He then freed them from the tape binding their arms and legs before hoisting them up, one by one.

Justina came out first, rolling onto her side. Her gaze landed hard on Kage.

"It's a twin," Rochelle immediately said. But Justina scooted as far away from Kage as possible, much like a wounded animal escaping a predator.

In her condition, she couldn't get far. Plus, there was one more lady to bring out. Once the second was free, she had the same reaction.

Benny came out next. "We have to figure a way to get everyone out of here before *he* finds us."

Traveling with two seriously wounded women was going to be a challenge. Not to mention Rochelle wasn't up to her usual strength. It had taken everything just to lift them to safety.

But they weren't out of the woods yet.

Deputy Lee lost more blood than he wanted to let on. A puddle had formed on the ground next to him before he successfully stopped the bleeding. His face paled and his lips tinted blue. Not good signs.

Camden was caught between a rock and a hard place. He had to be vigilant against the shooter in case he returned, *and* Lee needed medical attention. Considering Camden had no idea where they were, he could end up walking around for hours and still not make it out of the woods. Then, there was the fact he refused to leave here without finding Rochelle first.

The buzz of a drone overhead gave him the first sign of hope.

Wary of the shooter being nearby, biding his time for another opportunity to shoot, Camden had to risk it to get the drone operator's attention. With a sharp sigh, he quickly maneuvered toward the noise.

Every step meant exposing himself to Asher.

The drone neared. Camden bolted toward it faster than a deer in a hunter's sights seeking safety.

Finding a small clearing, he made himself visible from the canopy and then waved his arms wildly.

The device stopped overhead. Camden turned his face toward it as he heard sounds coming from his right. He scrambled away from the area before he ended up shot. He needed to get back to Lee in case Asher returned and got to the deputy first. Since Camden had lost visual of Lee, he had no idea what might be going on.

The second break came when he found Lee right where he left him. Lee had enough energy to sit up against a tree trunk. That was another good sign. He hoped to keep them rolling as he realized help might be too late.

The drone didn't follow. Instead, it resumed activity in the area not far away. Could it find Asher?

And then what?

"He's still here," Camden said to Lee. "Can you keep pressure on the wound with your left hand?"

A twig snapped nearby. Camden turned to the noise, leading with his weapon. He waited, finger hovering over the trigger mechanism.

The face he most wanted to see emerged.

"Rochelle," he said. "Look out. Asher might still be around here."

She came bolting toward him as he met her halfway. After a quick embrace, she said, "I headed this way after hearing a shot but we got lost until I saw the drone hovering. I hoped it was you, but I couldn't be sure."

"You found me," he said as a tsunami of relief washed over him. "Deputy Lee has been shot."

She took in a deep breath and then moved toward the deputy. "Help is here."

"Good timing," he said. "My family will be expecting me to come home."

"And you will," she said before turning to Camden with a look that sent a wave of panic rushing through him. She moved a few steps away and then lowered her voice. "We found the victims."

"And?"

"They're alive but weak," she said. "Benny and Kage—"

"Did you just say—"

"That's right," she said. "He found us and is helping carry one of the victims because they're too weak to walk."

Camden nodded. "I can carry Lee if you want to guide us to safety."

"I'm turned around," she admitted. "And I need to run

back to tell the others that I found you. They're slowly making their way but we're an easy target."

"A caravan moving through the woods will be hard to miss," he agreed.

"What about the drone? Did it see you?"

"I think so," he said.

"What if we stay here until help arrives?" she asked. "Do you think Lee will make it?"

"He lost a lot of blood, so I'm not sure," he whispered. "We could be here overnight if we wait for a search-and-rescue team."

"True," she said.

"Plus, Asher is still out there," he added.

"And we took what he believes to be his," she said. "The concrete cellar he kept them in isn't far."

"Then we should get on the move," Camden said.

"Can we risk it?"

"Do we have a choice?" he asked.

Rochelle bit down on her bottom lip. "I guess not."

Camden's gaze shot down to her boot. "How badly are you injured?"

"Me? I'll live."

"What about your mobility?" he asked.

"I'll do whatever I have to," she said. "We have to get these people to safety, Camden. I can't let them die. Not after everything they've been through."

"I know," he said.

"We might not make it out of here, but I have to keep fighting," she said. "I can't let this bastard win by giving up."

"Then, let's not waste any more time," he said. They were losing sunlight. This place might be confusing during the day, but it would only get worse at night.

"Hey, guys," Lee said. They turned to catch him staring at his phone. "I have half a bar."

"Can you send out an SOS?" Rochelle asked.

Lee cursed. "Just lost it."

"Try anyway," Camden said. "Let the sheriff know that we just saw a drone, have the victims and multiple injuries. Tell him that we're heading back to the crime scene."

The message may or may not go through, but Rochelle was right. They had to try.

Chapter Twenty-Four

"When we get out of here, we need to have a conversation," Camden said to Rochelle. Her heart skipped a couple of beats at the intensity in his beautiful eyes as he said those words.

He was right. They needed to talk.

"I was thinking the same thing," she admitted.

"Okay, then," he said.

"Can you lift the deputy?" she asked.

"Cover me," he said to her before bringing a hand up to touch her face. His touch was so tender, it caused goose bumps to run up and down her arms. With a look of resolve, he turned toward Lee, walked over, and then picked the deputy up fireman-style.

Lee grunted in pain.

They needed to hurry.

"How did you know it was Kage?" he whispered.

"Blue flannel," she said.

"Asher is wearing the dark hoodie," he said.

She nodded as the caravan of seven moved toward eventual freedom. If they could make it back in time.

A buzz overhead revealed a drone that skipped right on by without pausing. Rochelle didn't want to take it as a bad sign. It was almost dark, and she couldn't be certain they were going in the right direction toward the trailer.

"I've spent the past twenty-four hours out here," Kage finally spoke up. "We should be on the right path."

"Do you know how long before we make it back?" she asked, lowering her voice.

"Another thirty to forty-five minutes, if I had to guess."

The timeline wasn't reassuring. Deputy Lee might bleed out before then. The strain on Benny's face said there was no way he could carry Justina much longer, not to mention Kage and Camden. Should they stop and take a break? Or keep marching ahead?

Commotion ahead caught her attention. She put up a hand. Everyone stilled. Were they sitting ducks?

Rochelle drew her weapon and motioned for everyone to wait. She headed to the left to make a circle around whatever made the noise.

Several quiet steps away from the caravan, she froze.

"The drone must be mistaken," a male voice said.

"They might have drifted to the left or right, but they should be in this area," a second voice said, this one female.

The cavalry?

Rather than startle either one of them, Rochell identified herself.

"We've been searching for you," the female said. "I'm Lieutenant Andrea Warner and we've been sent to find you."

Rochelle emerged from behind a tree to find a swarm of helpers. "We need you. We found them. And a deputy has been shot." She immediately turned. "Follow me."

Boot on. Injured foot. Neither of those things mattered right now. All she cared about was getting help to those who desperately needed it.

Lee sat propped up against a tree trunk. The victims sat

on the ground, huddled together, looking pitiful. But thankfully, they were alive. Rochelle studied them as law enforcement and EMTs flooded the scene. It was a shame her work stopped here because she wanted—no, needed—to make sure they would get the help they needed.

Maybe she'd seen too much but needed to switch gears and be on the other side. On the side of helping victims rebuild their lives.

The revelation caught her off guard. And yet, it was undeniable how right it felt. Her supervisor was right. She needed to take some time off. Figure out her next steps. Because it was time to make a change.

"You found him." A male wearing a hoodie stepped out of the woods.

Rochelle immediately drew her weapon and pointed the barrel at Asher Foley.

His hands flew up, palms out in the surrender position.

"Asher Foley, you are under arrest," she began before Kage jumped in between them.

"You," he said to his twin.

"I'm Kage Durham," Hoodie said. "This man is Asher Foley."

Their faces were identical. Their voices the same. It was impossible to tell them apart. Except that Kage had been wearing blue flannel. Asher had on the hoodie. She was certain. The person who'd helped her to safety wore the blue flannel. There was no way Kage would willingly change clothes with a twin who was trying to frame him.

"Why would you do this to me?" Kage said before bumrushing his twin—a twin who was trying to flip the script. It would be the perfect crime. Kidnap and murder, then let your twin take the blame allowing you to get off scot-free while he spent the rest of his life behind bars.

Hoodie's expression morphed as an officer stepped in between the two men, keeping them from a fistfight.

"You didn't grow up with our mother," Hoodie said through clenched teeth. "You didn't spend your life being told what a mistake it was to keep you. She said I was the bad twin, and she hated me. But *you*. You were the perfect twin in her mind." Asher bared his teeth at Kage like a wild animal. His eyes were wild too. "She punished me for not being you. And then she died. Do you know how many times I wished I'd killed her a long time ago and ended the pain? But I was too weak." He puffed his chest out. "Not anymore. Now, I'm the strong one. And look at you. You broke the law too. You're no better than I am."

Kage stood there, fists clenched, ready to pounce on the brother he never knew existed until recently. "Oh, we're different. I made a mistake and then paid my dues. I changed. You, on the other hand, are pure evil."

With that, he turned his back on Asher. The twin lunged toward him but was immediately wrestled to the ground and placed into cuffs.

"It ends here," Kage said, walking over to console his brother's victims. "I'm sorry he did this to you. And I plan to help make it right in any way I can, if you'll allow me to."

Justina blinked at him like he was a mirage. And then, she nodded. Slowly. Purposefully.

That was the difference between the twins. Kage wasn't a bad person. He'd gotten off on the wrong track, made mistakes, and then decided to make a change for the better.

Rochelle would find a way to help him too and she would start with writing a glowing report to his parole officer.

The lieutenant walked over to Camden. She must have delivered a powerful message because his expression morphed. The lieutenant pointed him in a direction. For a split second, Rochelle thought he was going to leave without saying goodbye.

Then, his gaze searched for her. The second their eyes met, he made a beeline toward her. This was it. This was going to be the end of the case. And the end of her time with Camden.

"My grandmother is awake," he said. "I have to go."

"I understand," she said, turning away before the tears welling in her eyes escaped. She tucked her chin to her chest so he wouldn't see her cry.

Camden cupped her chin and lifted her face until their gazes met. "I want you to come with me."

A tear escaped. He thumbed it away.

"Okay…" It was all she could manage to say.

He reached for her hand and then linked their fingers, as they headed out of the woods and toward the Bronco.

Chapter Twenty-Five

The drive to the hospital went by in a flash as Camden received an escort for most of the trip. He took calls from his siblings and cousins along the way, receiving updates as each one made their way to the hospital. He would be the last to arrive.

His cell buzzed four miles out from the hospital. It was Dalton.

"Hey," he said after answering. "Everything okay?" Their grandmother's condition was fragile. She hadn't spoken yet but her eyes were open and she squeezed Grandpa Lor's hand when he asked her questions.

"Yes, sorry, didn't mean to make you stress," Dalton said.

"How's Grandma Lacey?" Camden asked.

"Still touch-and-go," Dalton replied. "The doctor tried to kick Grandpa Lor out of the room." Dalton chuckled. "He quickly realized it would be over Grandpa Lor's dead body, so he let him stay. Grandma Lacey does better with him in the room anyway."

"Have you seen her?" Camden asked.

"I got to peek my head in the door," his brother responded. "Her coloring is improving, according to the nurses. They also warn these things can be up and down."

"We already experienced that with Grandpa Lor," Camden pointed out.

"How far out are you?" Dalton asked.

"I'm close. Not more than a couple more minutes until I'm in the parking lot. Why?"

Dalton was silent for a moment. His voice changed to all business when he said, "She's here and I didn't want you to be caught off guard."

"Our mother?"

"That's right," Dalton confirmed as Rochelle reached across the console to make contact with his arm. Her touch sent a wave of warmth rippling through him. With her by his side, he could face anything.

"Thanks for the heads-up." Camden wasn't sure how he felt about the woman who'd abandoned him, except to say he was ready to hear her out. Rochelle had made good points before and questions he'd never allowed himself to ask had been swirling in the back of his mind ever since. Questions he was ready to have answers to thanks to Rochelle. "Have any of you guys spoken to her yet?"

"No," Dalton said. "We all thought it best to wait until we're all together."

"Alright then," Camden said. "I'm about to pull into the parking lot so you won't have to wait much longer."

"See you in a minute, bro."

Camden exchanged goodbyes before finding a spot and parking. He turned to Rochelle. "I would still very much like to have a conversation with you."

"Same," she said. "But first, I'd like to meet your family."

Camden smiled before exiting the driver's side and then rounding the front of the vehicle to open the door for Rochelle. He could get used to being with her and hoped like hell she felt the same way about him.

Hand in hand, they walked into the hospital. The elevator bank was to the right.

Within minutes, they were on Grandma Lacey's floor. Almost the second the elevator doors opened, Dalton greeted them.

First, he brought Camden into a bear hug.

"This is Rochelle Paddock," Camden said, introducing her.

Dalton's grin went from ear-to-ear when he introduced himself. He stuck out a hand. "What am I doing?" Last minute, he pulled his hand back and brought Rochelle into a hug. "Looks like you are family now."

Camden left that statement alone.

Rochelle smiled.

"Everyone is gathered in the waiting room," Dalton said. All his family in one place for the first time in years sounded pretty damn good to Camden.

"Let's go," Camden said, holding tight to Rochelle's hand. She gave a slight squeeze, which offered more reassurance than words could.

"By the way, her last name is Arnoult now," Dalton revealed.

The trio walked into the waiting room, Dalton leading the way. Camden wasn't sure what he expected to find or how he expected to feel. Warmth spread through him at seeing his entire family together in one place. The only people missing were his grandparents, but knowing they were together down the hall was enough.

After a round of introductions with all the new faces in the family, Camden's gaze landed hard on the woman who'd been sitting quietly in the corner. She was a shadow of the person he remembered. The years had not been kind to her.

She stood up when all eyes ended up on her. "First of all,

thank you all for allowing me to be here with you." Her chin quivered. "I've imagined this day for more than twenty-five years." She sniffled. "I'd like to say you've all grown up to be people your father would have been so proud of." A few tears rolled down her cheeks. Dalton couldn't help but notice the rock on her ring finger. "I'd like to explain what happened all those years ago if you'll allow me to."

"Go ahead," Jules said. "Some of us have been waiting a long time to hear what happened."

Camden didn't realize, until now, how important this moment might be for his brother and sister. Even his cousins were rapt with attention. Did they have questions too? Camden's father was their uncle, after all. They were all connected by marriage and blood.

"Okay," Sandra Arnoult said after taking a sip of coffee from the Styrofoam cup. "After I had Dalton, I suffered from postpartum depression. Of course, no one called it that at the time. Or knew much about how it impacted a woman. Your father did his best to help me, but I was in too deep." She glanced around the room. "Have any of you suffered from depression?"

Heads shook.

"It's hard to explain unless you've felt it," Sandra continued. "But I fell into a dark hole." She set down the coffee and then crossed her arms over her chest like a barricade. "So much so, that I began to believe I might harm one of you. The thought scared me to the point of not allowing myself to hold Dalton or be in the same room alone with either of you." Her gaze shifted from Camden to Jules. "I convinced myself that you'd be safer if I left."

A man entered the room. Before anyone could tell him this was a family meeting, he walked over to Sandra and put an arm around her shoulder.

"This is my husband," she said. "We met at the hospital where I eventually sought treatment. By then, too many years had passed. I learned your father died. I reached out to your grandfather, who thought reintroducing me back into your lives might cause more confusion than anything else. I respected his wishes."

Jules gasped. "Grandpa Lor asked you to stay away from us?"

"He was only looking out for your best interest," she said. "And I learned a long time ago that no one is perfect."

"You two met at a hospital?" Jules asked.

"I'm the attending physician at Dallas General, where your mother was in group therapy," Dr. Arnoult said. "I'm on the third floor. She was on seven."

Sandra looked up at her husband with adoration. "We passed each other in the hallway one day because I got off on the wrong floor."

"Bumped into each other is more like it," Dr. Arnoult said with a warm smile.

"And then the next day in the elevator," she said.

"That might have been planned on my part," he said.

Sandra looked around the room. "I know it's too much to ask for your forgiveness. I just thought it might help for all of you to know that I didn't take leaving this family lightly. In fact, it broke me, but I believed in my heart that I was doing the right thing for you. That I was keeping you safe. So I suffered without realizing how much more I might be hurting the ones I loved by walking away."

She broke down in tears.

Jules was the first to walk over and bring their mother into a hug. At this point, there wasn't a dry eye in the room. So many missed opportunities. So many years had gone by. And for what?

Grandpa Lor had done his best to protect those he loved. Camden couldn't be upset about what was already done. But they had today. And they had tomorrow. And the next day.

It was time to let go of the past and charge toward a bright, new future. A future he hoped to spend with Rochelle.

When chatter had quieted and hugs died down, Camden brought Rochelle to the center of the room.

He took her hand, and got down on one knee. "Rochelle Paddock, I could live a thousand lifetimes without ever finding anyone like you. It's the only certainty in life. Of that, I'm sure. So here I am in front of my family, asking if you think you could possibly ever feel the same way about me. I'm head over heels in love with you and I want to ask you to marry me in front of my family and my mom." He took a deep breath as he gazed up at her. "Will you do me the incredible honor of marrying me?"

Rochelle glanced around the room before locking on to him. His heart skipped a few beats as a knot tightened in his chest. The thought of losing her would gut him. Had he asked for too much, too fast? Because he was willing to wait until she was ready if she'd give him the chance.

"Camden Remington, I think I fell in love with you the second I laid eyes on you," Rochelle began. Her racing pulse was visible at the base of her neck. "I've never in my life met someone who so perfectly understood me without words, or so perfectly fit. I couldn't say anything about what I felt during the case but that's over now. I'm ready to start a new life. *With you.* I would be honored to marry you and start a life together."

She tugged at his hand. He stood up.

"I have no idea how I got so lucky to be partnered with you on the case," he began, "but loving you is all I need for life. Because I've finally found where I belong. I've finally found home."

"Time is precious," she said. "I don't want to waste another second. I'll marry you any day of the week but I don't need a piece of paper to tell me how much I love you or that we belong together."

Camden kissed his future bride, forgetting anyone else was in the room until the whoops and congratulations started, surrounding them with love.

A nurse stuck her head in, interrupting the celebration. "Please follow me."

A hush fell over the room.

The nurse waved for them to hurry.

They did. Everyone filed out of the room. Camden's mother, his stepfather, his siblings, and his cousins. Plus all the new additions to the family. They were quite a sight following the nurse to Grandma Lacey's room.

Grandpa Lor sat there, holding his bride's hand as she sat up, bright-eyed and bushy-tailed. "Your grandmother heard your voices and said she's missed out on enough already."

"She's going to be alright," the nurse reassured them.

Grandpa Lor brought their clasped hands to his lips, kissed hers. "She came back to me."

Camden coughed to clear the frog in his throat. He could scarcely believe they'd gotten their second miracle. He had no plans to take it for granted either. "Who is coming home for Christmas?"

"We should start a group chat," Jules practically chirped. Everyone jumped into the conversation with ideas about food and who would put up the tree.

They were coming home and Camden, for one, planned never to take anyone for granted again. His future bride tugged him out into the hallway.

"I thought you should be the first to know that I decided to take time off work," she said. "I'd like to be on the other side with victims. Help them rebuild their lives. What do you think?"

"If that's what you want, I'm all for it." Camden stared into eyes that sparkled like jewels. "What do you think about moving to the ranch while we figure out our next steps?"

"You love your job," she said. "Would you consider leaving it?"

"I did love it," Camden admitted. "But I love the ranch too. I think it's time for a change. I miss the open skies and being on the land. Getting my hands dirty. How does that sound to you?"

Rochelle pushed up to her tiptoes and pressed her lips to his. Camden kissed his future bride. The slow, tender kiss gave way to passion and a fire he'd never known.

By the time they pulled back, both had to catch their breath.

"I like the part where you get dirty," she whispered with a twinkle in her eyes.

"We have time to catch up with everyone later," he said. "What do you think about getting out of here and getting some privacy?"

"I can't think of a better idea, Mr. Remington."

"Good," he said. "Let's go home."

Side by side, they walked out of the hospital and into their future.

* * * * *

COMING SOON!

We really hope you enjoyed reading this book.
If you're looking for more romance
be sure to head to the shops when
new books are available on

Thursday 18th December

To see which titles are coming soon, please visit
millsandboon.co.uk/nextmonth

MILLS & BOON